King of Ashes

King of Ashes

Firemane: Book One

Raymond E. Feist

An Imprint of HarperCollinsPublishers

HarperCollins books may be purchased for educational, business, or sales promotional use. For information please e-mail the Special Markets Department at SPsales@harpercollins.com.

FIRST HARPERLUXE EDITION

ISBN: 978-0-06-286388-1

HarperLuxe™ is a trademark of HarperCollins Publishers.

Library of Congress Cataloging-in-Publication Data is available upon request.

18 19 20 21 22   ID/LSC   10 9 8 7 6 5 4 3 2 1

This book is dedicated to the memory of
Jonathan Matson.
He was perhaps the finest man I've ever known. His
generosity, support, and affection went so far beyond
any business relationship, he held me together more
than once. He never judged; that was the heart of his
wisdom, and the wisdom of his heart. His memory will
endure and he is missed every day.

Contents

Acknowledgments

This book would not have been possible without the wisdom, kindness, editorial ability, and hand-holding of three terrific ladies.

Thank you to Jane Johnson, Jennifer Brehl, and Emma Coode.

I have been blessed far beyond good business relationships; I have been blessed with friends.

Prologue:
A Murder of Crows
and a King

Angry dark clouds hurried across the sky, foretelling more rain. A fair match for today's mood, conceded Daylon Dumarch. The battle had ended swiftly as the betrayal had gone according to plan. The five great kingdoms of Garn would never be the same; now the *four* great kingdoms, Daylon amended silently.

He looked around and saw carrion eaters on the wing: the vultures, kites, and sea eagles were circling and settling in for the feast. To the north, a massive murder of crows had descended on the field of corpses. Rising flocks of angry birds measured the slow progress of the baggage boys loading the dead. The carrion eaters were efficient, conceded Daylon; few bodies would go to the grave without missing eyes, lips, or other soft features.

He turned to gaze at the sea. No matter what the weather, it drew Daylon; he felt dwarfed by its eternal nature, its indifference to the tasks of men. The thought soothed him and gave him much-needed perspective after the battle. Daylon indulged in a barely audible sigh, then considered the beach below.

The rocks beneath the bluffs of the Answearie Hills had provided as rich a meal for the crabs and seabirds as the banquet for the crows and kites on the hills above them. Hundreds of men had met their death on those rocks, pushed over the edge of the cliff by the unexpected attack on their flank by men they had counted as allies but moments before.

Daylon Dumarch felt old. The Baron of Marquensas was still at the height of his power, not yet forty years from his nativity day, but he was ancient in bitterness and regret.

Thousands of men had died needlessly so that two madmen could betray a good king. While others stood by and did nothing, a balance that had existed for nearly two hundred years had been overturned. Art, music, poetry, dance, and theater would soon follow the army of Ithrace into oblivion.

Daylon did not know exactly what plans the four

surviving monarchs of the great kingdoms had for the lofty towers and flower-bedecked open plazas of the city of Ithra, but he feared for the most civilized city in the world, the capital of the Kingdom of Flames. Of the five great kingdoms of Garn, Ithrace had always produced the most artistic genius. Authors of Ithrace had penned half of the books in Daylon's library, and Ithra was a well-known spawning ground for talented young painters, musicians, playwrights, poets, and actors, despite also providing refuge for thieves, mountebanks, whores, and every other form of unsavory humanity imaginable.

There had always been five great kingdoms, and now that Flame was ash only four remained—Sandura, Metros, Zindaros, and Ilcomen—and no man could anticipate how history would judge what had occurred this day. Daylon realized his mind was racing; he was barely able to focus on the moment, let alone the long-term political consequences of the horror surrounding him. It was as his father had said to him years ago; there are times when all one can do is stand still and breathe.

Daylon resisted letting out a long sigh of regret. Somewhere up the hill from where he stood, Steveren Langene, King of Ithrace, known to all as Firemane, lifelong friend to any man of good heart, ally of Daylon and a host of others, was being bound in iron shackles and cuffs by men he'd once called comrades, to be marched up onto the makeshift platform his brother kings had ordered constructed for this farce.

Daylon turned his mind from the coming horrors and his revulsion at his own part in today's treachery and searched for somewhere to wash the battle from his face. He found a supply wagon overturned, its horses dead in their traces, but somehow a water barrel had conspired to remain mostly upright. Using his belt knife he cut away the waxed canvas cover and stuck his head into the cool, clean water. He drank, and came up sputtering, wiping the day's blood and dirt from his face. He stood staring at the water as it rippled and calmed. It was the only thing Daylon could see that wasn't covered in death; all around him, the mud of the battlefield was awash in piss, shit, and blood, pieces of what had once been brave men, and the muck covered banners of fools.

His life had been scarred by battle and death. Married twice before he was thirty-five, Daylon had deeply loved his first wife, but childbirth had taken her in their third year of marriage. He didn't care much for his current wife, but she had brought a strong alliance and a fair dowry, and despite being vapid and silly, she had a strong young body he enjoyed and she was already expecting his first child. The promise of an heir was the one bright hope in his life at present.

He forced his attention from dark thoughts and saw a familiar figure approaching. "My lord," said Rodrigo Bavangine, Baron of the Copper Hills, "you have survived."

"The day is young," replied Daylon, "and there's still treachery in abundance. Keep hope. You may yet be able to pay court to my young widow."

"A black jest," said Rodrigo. "Too many good companions lie befouled in their own entrails, while men I would not piss on were they afire celebrate this day."

"'Tis ever thus, Rodrigo." Daylon studied his old friend. The Baron of the Copper Hills was a dark-haired man with startling blue eyes. At court he wore his hair long, oiled and curled, but now had it gathered up in a bright red head cloth designed to keep it under his helm in battle. He was pale of complexion, like most people from the foggy and cloud-shrouded land he ruled. Daylon had always found it odd that they had become close, as Daylon was a man of deep consideration and Rodrigo seemed to barely consider the consequences of his impulses, but he knew Rodrigo's moods as well as he knew his own. He saw the man's face and knew without words they were of like mind. Both men wondered if the battle would have swung the other way had they stood with Steveren rather than opposed him.

Rodrigo narrowed his pale eyes and moved closer to speak quietly, though there was no living man within a dozen paces. "I can tell you this one thing, Daylon: from this day forward I shall never take to my bed without the benefit of a strong drink or a young ass, most likely both, and sleep a night without haunting. This business will bring more destruction, not less as was promised."

Daylon leaned against the frame of the wagon watching the carpenters finishing up the executioner's platform and turned to look at his old friend.

Rodrigo recognized his expression and manner. "You are a man of ideals, Daylon, so you need justification. Therein lies the cause of your distress."

"I am a far simpler man, Rodrigo. I merely picked the side I knew would win."

"And I followed you."

"As did others," said Daylon, "but I ordered no oathman, nor asked friend nor ally, to serve at my whim. Any could have said no."

Rodrigo smiled, and it was a bitter look he gave to his friend. "Aye, Daylon, and that's the evil genius of it. It's a gift you have. No man in your orbit would oppose your counsel. You are too versed in the games of power for me not to heed your wisdom, even to serve foul cause."

"You could have opposed me and served Steveren."

"And find myself with them?" he said, indicating the rotting dead in the mud.

"There is always a choice."

"A fool's choice," Rodrigo said softly, "or a dreamer's." Pointing to the workers at the top of the hill, finishing up the platform, he changed the subject. "What is going on up there?"

"Our victorious monarchs require some theater," said Daylon sourly.

"I thought Lodavico closed all the theaters in Sandura?"

"He did. After complaining that the plays were all making a jest of him. Which was occasionally true, but he lacks perspective, and a sense of humor." Daylon added, "And he's completely incapable of seeing the bitter irony in this."

"This theater is entirely too macabre for my taste." Rodrigo passed his hand in an arc around the battlefield littered with dead. "Killing men in the heat of battle is one thing. Hanging criminals or beheading them is another. I can even watch heretics burn without blinking much, but this killing of women and children . . ."

"Lodavico Sentarzi fears retribution. No Langene left alive means the King of Sandura can sleep at night." Daylon shrugged. "Or so he supposes." He kept his eyes fixed on the makeshift stage at the top of the hill. The workers had finished their hasty construction of the broad stage: two steps above the mud, elevated just enough for those on the hillside to be able to see, sturdy enough to support the weight of several men. Two burly servants wrestled a chopping block up the steps while a few of Lodavico's personal guards moved between the makeshift construction and the slowly gathering crowd.

"This business of bashing babies against walls, ugly that . . . and killing those pretty young daughters and nieces . . . that wasn't merely a waste, it was an iniquity," complained Rodrigo. "Those Firemane girls were breathtaking, with those long necks and slender bodies, and all that red hair—"

"You think too much with your cock, Rodrigo." Daylon tried to sound light-hearted. "You've had more women and boys than any ten men I know, and yet you hunger for more."

"To each man his own appetites," conceded Rodrigo. "Mine easily turn to a pretty mouth and rounded ass." He sighed. "It's no worse than King Hector's love of wine or Baron Haythan's lust for gambling." He studied his friend for a moment. "What whets your appetite, Daylon? I've never understood."

"I seek only not to despise the man I see in the mirror," said the Baron of Marquensas.

"That's far too abstract for my understanding. What really fires you?"

"Little, it seems," Daylon replied. "As a young man I thought of our higher purpose, for didn't the priests of the One God tell our fathers that the Faith brings peace to all men?"

Rodrigo looked at the nearby battlefield littered with the dead and said, "In a sense, life eventually brings peace."

"That may be the most philosophical thing I've ever heard you say." Daylon's gaze followed Rodrigo's and he muttered, "The One God's priests promised many things."

Rodrigo let out a long, almost theatrical sigh, save Daylon knew his friend was not the sort to indulge in false play; the man was tired to his bones. "When four of the five great kings declare a faith the one true faith, and all others heresy, I expect you can promise most anything."

Daylon's brow furrowed a little. "Are you suggesting the church had a hand in this?"

Rodrigo said, "I suggest nothing, old friend. To do so

would be to invite ruin." His expression held a warning. "In our grandfather's time, the One God's church was but one among many. In our father's time, it became a force. Now . . ." He shook his head slightly. "By the time of our children, the other gods will have withered to a faint memory." He glanced around as if ensuring they were not overheard. "Or, if their priests are clever enough, they might contort their doctrine to become heralds of the One God and survive as shadows of their former selves. Some are saying thus now." He paused for a moment, then said, "Truly, Daylon. What moves you in this? You could have stayed home."

Daylon nodded. "And had my name put on a list with those who openly supported Steveren." He paused, then said, "Truth?"

"Always," replied his friend.

"My grandfather and my father built a rich barony, and I have taken what they've left me and made it even more successful. I wish to leave my children with all of it, but also have them secure in their holdings."

"You are close to a king yourself, aren't you?"

Daylon shared a rueful smile with his friend. "I'd rather have wealth and security for my children than any title."

Satisfied no one was within earshot, he let his hand come to rest on Daylon's shoulder a moment. "Come.

We should attend. This is not a good time to be counted among the missing, unless you happen to be dead already, which their majesties and Mazika might count a reasonable excuse. Anything else, not."

Daylon inclined his head slightly in agreement and the two noblemen trudged the short walk up the muddy hillside as the rain resumed. "Next time you call me to battle, Daylon," said Rodrigo, "have the decency to do so on a dry morning, preferably in late spring or early summer so it's not too hot. I have mud in my boots, rain down my tunic, rust on my armor, and my balls are growing moss. I haven't seen a dry tunic in a week."

Daylon made no comment as they reached the top of the hill where the execution was to be held. Common soldiers glanced over their shoulders and, seeing two nobles, gave way to let them pass until Rodrigo and Daylon stood in the forefront of the gathering men. The platform was finished and the prisoners were being marched out of the makeshift pens where they'd been kept overnight.

Steveren Langene, king of Ithrace, had been fed false reports and lies for a year, until he thought he was joining with allies to meet aggression from King Lodavico. Daylon was one of the last barons to be told of the plan, which had given him little time to consider his options. He and Rodrigo had less than a month to ready their forces and march to the appointed meeting place; most importantly, they were given no opportunity to warn Steveren and aid him effectively. Distance and travel time prevented Daylon or others sympathetic to the King of Ithrace from organizing on Steveren's behalf. Even a message warning him might be discovered by Lodavico and earn Daylon a place on the executioner's stage next to Steveren.

This morning, they had arisen to fix their order of battle, trumpets blowing and drums pounding, Steveren's forces holding the leftmost position, awaiting Lodavico's attack. The battle order had been given and suddenly King Steveren's allies had turned on him. It had still been a bitter struggle and most of the day was gone, but in the end, betrayal had triumphed.

Daylon could see the prisoners being forced out of the tents on the other side of the platform. While Steveren's army had been in the field, slogging through the mud of an unseasonably heavy summer storm, raiders had seized the entire royal family of Ithrace from their summer villa on the coast less than half a day's ride away.

Cousins of blood and kin by marriage had already been put to the sword, or thrown off the cliffs onto the rocks below the villa—by all counts more than forty men, women, and children. Even the babies were not spared. But the king's immediate family had been granted an extra day's existence to suffer this public humiliation. Kings Lodavico and Mazika were determined to show the world the end of the Firemane line.

Now that royalty was being marched at spear-point to their deaths.

The children came first, terror and bewilderment rendering them silent. They shuffled along with eyes wide, lips blue from the cold and limbs trembling, their red hair rendered a dull dark copper by the rain. Daylon counted the little ones, two boys and a girl. Their older siblings came after, followed by Queen Agana. Last was King Steveren. Whatever finery they had worn had been torn off, and they were all dressed in the poorest of robes, their exposed limbs and faces showing the bruises of the beatings they had endured.

King Steveren wore a yoke of hardwood, with iron cuffs at each end confining his wrists, and his legs were shackled so he shambled rather than walked. He was prodded up the steps to the platform while the army gathered. From the swelling bruises on his face and around his eyes, it was miraculous that he could walk without aid. Daylon saw the dried blood on his mouth and chin, and winced as he realized the king's tongue had been cut so he could not speak to those gathered to watch him die.

A few soldiers shouted half-hearted jeers, but every man standing was tired, some wounded, and all wished for this to be over quickly so they might eat and rest. For most, the approaching sack of Ithra was why they had served today, and that would not begin until this matter was put paid to, so all wished for a hastened ending.

Daylon glanced at Rodrigo, who shook his head ever so slightly in resignation. There was no precedent for this butchery, and no one could reconcile what they were about to see with what they understood of the traditional order of things. History taught that a king did not kill a king, save on the field of battle; even barons were rarely executed, but usually ransomed for profit and turned to vassals.

For as long as living memory on the world of Garn, five great kingdoms had dominated the twin continents of North and South Tembria. Scattered among them were independent states ruled by the most powerful barons, men like Daylon and Rodrigo, free nobles allied with, but not subject to, those kings. Other, lesser nobility held grants of land and titles from the five great kingdoms.

Daylon locked eyes with Rodrigo, and in that instant knew that his friend understood as well as he that an era was ending. What had been a long period of prosperity and relative peace was over.

For two centuries, the five great kingdoms of North and South Tembria had been bound by the Covenant: the solution to centuries of warfare over control of the Narrows, the sea passage between the two continents. It was the choke-point at which two outcrops of land had created a passage so constricted that no more than half a dozen ships—three eastbound and three westbound—could navigate and pass safely at the same time. The need to reduce speed here and the overlooking rocks had made this the most prized location on Garn, for whoever controlled the straits controlled all east-west shipping across two continents; the alternative sea routes around the north or south of the twin continents were so difficult and time-consuming that they were considered to be close to impossible. Alternative land transport would take triple the time, and twice the cost.

The Covenant guaranteed right of passage for all. A circular boundary of Covenant lands had been drawn around the Narrows on both continents. No city could be built there, only small towns and villages were permitted to flourish, and all rulers guaranteed its neutrality. This mutual ceding of land by the five great kingdoms had created peace and fostered trade, the arts, and prosperity.

Until today, thought Daylon bitterly. The survivors of this madness might continue the fiction that the

Covenant still existed, but Daylon knew it was over. The pact might appear to die slowly, but in reality it was already dead.

He studied the faces of the Ithraci royal family, the terror in the eyes of the children, the resignation and hopelessness in the faces of the women, and the defiance of their king. Two soldiers gripped the ends of Steveren's restraining yoke, holding him upright on his knees as he began to collapse.

Daylon wished he could be at home with his wife, dry and clean, fed and abed with her. The future security of his barony and his heirs had been his price, he bitterly conceded. The kings of Sandura and Zindaros had agreed to ratify his chosen heir without question should he perish without blood issue on the field or in the future. He had agreed, forestalling any claim on the freehold barony of Marquensas; he owed his people the hope of peace. Even with Steveren alive, without that assurance, the other four kings would each push forth their own claimant, for Marquensas was the most powerful and wealthy freehold barony on Garn. Without a clear line of succession, war and destruction would be his dying legacy. So he had betrayed a man he loved like a brother to spare his people future ravages. As the priests of the One God would say, Daylon had made his pact with the Dark One; he had sold his soul.

It proved to be a black irony: upon the morning of his departure, his wife had informed him that she was with child. Too committed to withdraw from this butchery, Daylon had been sick in his soul from that moment.

Last to step upon the platform were Lodavico of Sandura and Mazika of Zindaros, their tabards and armor noticeably free of gore and mud. "I see two kings are missing," muttered Rodrigo.

Daylon nodded and as the gathering crowd of soldiers was unusually quiet for a public display such as this, he whispered, "Bucohan and Hector both claim fatigue and minor wounds keep them abed. They may be complicit in this, but they're content to stay in their tents and let Lodavico and Mazika take all the credit for this charade. And it is in Lodavico's nature to claim as much credit as possible; he confuses it with glory."

"No charade," whispered Rodrigo, "when the blood is real."

As Daylon expected, it was Lodavico who stepped forward to speak. The king of Sandura was easily the most loathed noble in the five kingdoms, for his rule was harsh and arbitrary. He despised anything that he saw as being a threat to his dignity, not realizing that he had none by nature or act. Daylon had called him a doleful monarch of a melancholy nature after their first meeting more than twenty years ago and nothing he had seen of the man since had altered that opinion. His red-trimmed black garb did little to lessen that perception, as well.

"We are here to restore order, to deliver an oath breaker to his fate, and to end a threat to the sovereignty of our brother kingdoms." For a man who hated theaters, thought Daylon, Lodavico had a penchant for theatrics. His posturing and accent were overly broad, to the point of self-mockery, though the king of Sandura could never see it, and no one would dare apprise him of the fact. So men stood by and endured the histrionics, only to deride him privately later over drinks. At this moment, however, Daylon found little humor in Lodavico's bad acting.

Since the plot to kill Steveren had been hatched, rumors that the king of Ithrace coveted the crowns of other nations had spread. There was no foundation for it; the most trivial of acts were characterized as evidence of his ambitions, and men anxious to plunder the riches of a great kingdom needed little excuse for feigned belief and mock outrage. The sack of Ithrace could provide a noble or fighter with more wealth than a lifetime of skirmishes on the borders of the Wild Lands, the Burning Lands, or the Mountain Barriers.

A rebellion by malcontents within the Covenant lands

had been staged. *Another charade with real blood,* thought Daylon. Word was then passed to Steveren that Lodavico was behind the incursion: the only truth in the string of lies. Steveren had answered duty's call, as Lodavico and his allies knew he would, leading the core of his army into as vicious a betrayal as could be imagined. Nothing in Garn's recorded history matched the scale of this treachery.

"The poison tree bears poison fruit," continued Lodavico, pointing at the children. His face contorted in a mask of theatrical rage, eyes wide, brows arched, his head tilted as if listening for menace: the behavior expected of a madman trying to convince his audience that such innocents were a threat to their existence. "All of this line must perish," finished Lodavico, slamming his right fist into his left palm for emphasis. A soldier stepped up behind the smallest child on the platform. Daylon tried to remember the boy's name and failed before the soldier grabbed a handful of the child's fire-red hair and yanked back his small head. A quick slice of a sharp dagger and the boy's eyes rolled back up into his skull as blood gushed from his neck.

A weak cheer rose from the soldiers, and Daylon knew they just wanted this grisly spectacle to be over so they could rest, eat, then set about organizing for the march south to Ithra. He had no doubt several free companies had already departed, eager to be first to choose spoils; mercenary companies were free of political considerations and would race to be first to claim spoils. If there was any justice, Steveren had left behind a big enough garrison to inflict real pain on those adventurers. Let the early companies pay the price for their greed, and perhaps give some of the populace the opportunity to flee before the bulk of Lodavico's forces descended on them. The only nations with fleets big enough to blockade a sea escape were Meteros and Zindaros. Zindaros's navy had transported their army here, and Meteros had chosen to stay aloof from today's butchery. Their navy was big enough that they could ignore Lodavico's demands. The day might come they'd regret their choice, but Daylon welcomed their decision. If some of Ithra's citizens could find boats and reach the open sea, perhaps one day they might rebuild their nation . . .

Daylon shook off a rush of guilt and shame, to face the last blood that would be spilled today. What was done was done, and regret served no good purpose.

With swift precision, the executioner moved down the line, pulling back the heads of the children and then the women. Rodrigo asked, "Who's missing?"

"The two eldest sons," said Daylon. "Both fell in battle."

Steveren Langene, the last king of Ithrace, watched in silent rage and torment as his family was slaughtered before his eyes. Daylon almost physically winced at the sight of a man he loved like a brother losing his ability to stand unaided. Two soldiers gripped the ends of Steveren's restraining yoke, holding him up as his legs began to give out. The last to die was his wife of over thirty years, his queen, and the mother of his children. She fought when her hair was grabbed, not to avoid death but so that she could see her husband's face as her life fled.

"There's no glory here," muttered Rodrigo.

"Our four remaining kings wish to ensure there is no doubt that the line of the Firemanes is done."

As soldiers dragged the dead off the platform, Lodavico felt the need to reiterate all the fabricated sins of the Firemanes, embellishing the lies with innuendo that even more perfidy and treachery might yet be uncovered. "Will this ever end?" whispered Rodrigo.

Finally, they came to the king. Lodavico finished his speech and stepped aside as a soldier moved forward, a large two-hand sword in his grip. As others held Steveren's yoke firmly, lowering it until he was on his knees, the soldier measured the distance from the wooden collar to the base of the king's skull, then with a single circular swing he brought round the blade and cleanly sliced head from shoulders.

The crowd cheered, again with no real conviction. As if disappointed by the lack of enthusiasm, Lodavico motioned for the headsman to pick up the dead king's head by its flame-red hair and then he shouted, "Behold the fate of a betrayer!"

Again came a weak response.

Lodavico looked at the hundreds of soldiers before him, as if trying to memorize their faces for a future accounting. His forehead creased as he scowled, his lower jaw protruding as if ready to challenge the entire army to a fight. The awkward moment was broken when Mazika Koralos, king of Zindaros, shouted, "Finish tending the dead and wounded, eat, and rest, for at dawn we march to Ithra!" This brought a more enthusiastic cheer and the men began to leave.

Daylon turned away and saw an unspoken question in Rodrigo's expression. Softly, almost through clenched teeth, Daylon said, "A king executing a king? On the field of battle is one thing, but this murder?" He locked eyes with Rodrigo. "It is not done."

"You killed Genddor of Balgannon, after you took his castle." There was a hint of challenge in that statement.

"He was no king," answered Daylon. "He was a usurper and pretender. And I killed him as he stood at bay in his great hall. Besides, Balgannon was no kingdom."

"No more," agreed Rodrigo, "since Ilcomen annexed it." He sighed. "It was hardly a real barony. Genddor's father was nothing but a puffed-up warlord. You should have kept it for yourself." He looked around and saw the men moving away from the platform, so he nodded to Daylon that they too should depart.

Walking down the hillside, Daylon said, "Now comes the reward."

Rodrigo said, "So, the riches of Ithrace are ours for the taking?"

Daylon put his hand on his old friend's shoulder for a moment. "You can have my share, I will march my men home. I am tired of this."

Daylon had been one of the few free barons who were truly independent and unallied. The rulers of Marquensas and Copper Hills had sworn to no king, but most of the remaining thirty barons had social or monetary obligations that effectively bound them to one of the great monarchs, at least until debts were repaid or obligations discharged.

"Your oathmen won't object?" asked Rodrigo.

"My oathmen are free to travel with Their Majesties,"

Daylon replied dryly. "I have no plans to campaign again soon, so should they wish to wager blood against gold, so be it. My castellans will come with me without complaint. I provide for them well enough."

"You may feel free to choose, my friend," said Rodrigo, "but from Lodavico's mood, your departure may be seen as an insult. He might not care that mercenaries and other lowborn left without his leave . . . you are hardly anonymous."

"He's going to be too busy fighting over Ithrace to notice I'm not there." He shrugged as if it was of no concern. "And if he does notice, he will not dare make an open issue of it, lest he offend the other free barons."

Rodrigo forced a smile. "You are so well loved, then, my friend?"

Daylon returned his faint smile. "No, but should my freehold and lands be taken by Lodavico, what is your first thought, Rodrigo?"

"Who's next?" he conceded. Rodrigo paused, stopping where he would leave Daylon to make his way back to his own encampment. "You've thought this through."

"I have. All that I have done I did to ensure my family and people's survival. Lodavico is covetous, and more than a little mad, but he's not stupid." Daylon gestured toward the carnage around them. "A stupid man cannot scheme to end a rival kingdom in a single day. Lodavico planned this for a long time and in great detail, and he paid no small sum of gold to make it happen.

"So, would he turn on me out of spite?" Daylon shrugged and let out a small sigh of fatigue. "He knows that every free baron, and their oathmen, would think as we do; and while alone none of us are a threat, united we could end his rule."

Rodrigo nodded in agreement. "More than a few of Lodavico's oathmen would seize the opportunity to change their allegiance if all the free barons rose at once: he does not treat them gently. Release from his yoke would be worth the risk."

"The day will almost certainly come, my friend, when Lodavico has earned enough ire to force an alliance of enemies, but that day is still years away. Too many rivalries have been exploited, too much distrust seeded among those who need to unite against Sandura, and too many willing to support him out of fear, or hope of benefit."

Daylon took a deep breath and let it out slowly, then with a wry smile he said, "Yes, that day will come, but not today."

Rodrigo was thoughtful for a moment, and then dismissed the notion with a wave of his hand. "Well, return home to that young wife of yours. If I don't go on to Ithra, I'll have rebellion to deal with: my castellans haven't been paid for a while and I need my share of the booty to cover wages and leave us a little besides."

"Scavenge well, my friend," said Daylon with a faint smile. The friends gripped each other by the right hand and touched chests. "But a word of warning," Daylon spoke quietly in Rodrigo's ear. "A wise man prepares for the next war after his last battle, not when it is already sweeping across his land." He locked gazes with his friend. "As I said, that war is coming, not soon, but eventually. The balance of power has shifted." He waved back toward the hill where Lodavico had stood minutes before. "Sandura has the advantage for the moment, but with things now as they are, another may choose to seize it. One day someone will seek to become the new fifth king. Be ready for that day."

"Do I hear ambition?"

"I seek no enlargement of my own holdings, but I'd topple another ruler rather than lose what's mine. You need to think on this, old friend. Prepare not for the little wars, which will plague us soon, but for another such as this"—Daylon nodded toward the bloody field—"where crowns are the prize." He leaned even closer. "Perhaps it will take five years, or ten, or longer, but certainly there will be that war. Lodavico is mad to be the high king." He lightly poked his finger against Rodrigo's chest. "In your heart you know his ambition as well as I do." Glancing around one more time to ensure they were unheard, he continued. "But Lodavico will eventually overplay his hand, and that's when we need to be prepared."

Rodrigo shook his head. "Bleak advice." Then he sighed and said, "But well considered." With a wave he walked away, and then paused as if a thought had struck him. He turned back to look at Daylon. "Wasn't there a new baby?"

"I don't take your meaning." Daylon's brow furrowed.

Rodrigo looked into Daylon's eyes for a long moment. "I thought I'd heard word that the Firemane queen had delivered a late autumn child."

"The queen had a late child, yes . . . ," said Daylon. He let out a long sigh. "Most likely it died during the taking of the villa. They threw babies from the cliffs to the rocks when the household was slaughtered. Perhaps he was one."

Rodrigo shrugged. "Perhaps." He turned away again and left without further word.

Daylon lingered. "A baby," he muttered, amused for the first time in days. Tales of a surviving Firemane baby would prevent Lodavico from sleeping well for the rest of his days, even if the whispers were false.

He briefly considered tossing coin to a rumormonger to fuel such gossip. Nothing else in this evil business was worthy of mirth. He looked skyward, attempting to ignore the circling flocks of carrion eaters and enjoy what he could of the lowering sun and blue sky on the western horizon. "Well, at least the world didn't end," he muttered to himself.

Of all of the nobles present, Daylon was among the very few who could be considered scholarly. He had studied the legends surrounding the oldest houses and knew of one myth in particular that predicted that a rampant chaos would be unleashed upon the world should the Firemane line end. Having witnessed no thundering hordes of demons racing toward the battle-field, Daylon moved toward his pavilion wondering if Steveren had indeed been the last of his line . . .

He passed by huge mounds of dead bodies awaiting burial. Exhausted soldiers labored over the digging of mass graves, while priests of the One God said their prayers over the corpses. Daylon resisted an urge to curse in the name of the old gods; he had no desire to be denounced and burned at the stake.

Lost in thought, he barely realized he had reached his pavilion when he noticed two men standing quietly before the tent flap. Reinhardt, captain of Daylon's household guard, wore the tabard of House Dumarch:

a tough veteran, he had earned his position through years of loyal service.

The man next to him was also familiar to Daylon. He was a broad-shouldered, thick-bodied man, strong and keen eyed, but one who had also started to show faint signs of aging. His dark eyes were underlined with shadow and they possessed wrinkles at the edges that were evidence of a hard life. His brown hair was turning steel grey and was receding. His walk betrayed a stiffness in one hip, most likely the result of a wound taken in a fight years before. Covered in grime, soot, and dried blood, the man bowed slightly, barely more than a nod, but enough to satisfy Daylon's need for deference.

"Edvalt," said Daylon in greeting.

"It is the day, my lord," said Edvalt.

Daylon released a tired sigh and said, "Must we do this now?"

"It is the day, my lord," Edvalt repeated with emphasis.

"Ten years? Has it really been ten years?"

"At the noonday sun, ten years exactly," said Edvalt.

"It's midway to sundown; you tarried?"

Edvalt found nothing humorous in the remark. "I was busy staying alive at noon, my lord. King Steveren mounted a counterattack on your rear: they overran the luggage and my smithy." He looked the ruler of Marquensas in the eye and asked, "Your pledge, my lord?"

Daylon bristled at the implication that he might not honor his pledge but reined in his urge to strike the man. He was angry and fatigued, and he also knew part of his frustration was caused by losing Edvalt's services.

Captured in a border dispute, Edvalt had been spared the slave collar only because Daylon had noticed the quality of his enemy's weapons. He had quickly identified Edvalt as the weaponsmith and offered him a choice: enslavement for life, or ten years of skillful service in exchange for his freedom. Daylon had gambled that the smith needed the promise of freedom to do his best work for his new master.

Daylon let out a long, measured breath and took control of his temper. "Yes, I remember."

"Ten years of faithful service in exchange for my freedom," said Edvalt, his tone even, his expression revealing a resolution Daylon knew all too well.

Daylon put his hand on Edvalt's shoulder. "I know," he said with a tone of resignation. "It's a bargain I regret," said the Baron of Marquensas. "Had I fully understood your gifts, I would have offered you your freedom that day in exchange for a pledge never to leave my service."

"Hardly freedom," said Edvalt.

Daylon was frustrated. He had hated every moment of this journey, and losing Edvalt to a promise made after another bloody confrontation was almost more than he could bear. "I need you, Edvalt, as certain as the rising sun at dawn. There's more war coming, for Lodavico has turned the world upside down, and you are the finest smith I have ever known. And more, you're a good man. Stay and I'll make you wealthy."

Edvalt paused for a moment, as if taken slightly off guard by Daylon's request. He looked out over the field of carnage around them and said, "I thank you for the compliment, my lord, but my most fervent wish is that I never have to behold a sight such as this again." He looked Baron Dumarch in the eye and said, "It is time."

Fatigue, frustration, and anger threatened to boil inside Daylon. He could simply ignore his pledge and keep Edvalt in service, but he knew that to do so would be to lose his skill forever. He waited a long moment, then finally let his better nature take control.

"As of this moment, you're a free man, Edvalt Tasman." He turned to Reinhardt. "Find a scribe and have him write a free passage for Edvalt—"

"And for Mila," interrupted the smith.

"Who?" asked Daylon.

"My woman, Mila."

Daylon assumed he referred to one of the many camp followers, or a local girl from the city, but saw an opportunity. "Have you wed her without leave?"

Edvalt stiffened. As a bound man he should have sought permission to marry. He hesitated, then said, "Not before a priest. We pledged to each other. We have a daughter."

"Your woman is of no concern to me," said Daylon, "but your daughter is, by law, my property. She was born in bondage."

The slight shift in Edvalt's posture and expression were signs that both Daylon and Reinhardt recognized instantly. They showed that the smith was ready to fight with his bare hands against sword if need be.

Daylon mustered all the wisdom he had left and waved away Edvalt's rising anger. He let out a long sigh and said, "I'll not take your child from you, Edvalt. But in exchange you must give me your pledge."

Edvalt's eyes narrowed as he said, "To what end, my lord?"

"I'll answer that question in a moment, but first where will you go?"

Without a moment's hesitation, Edvalt said, "The Narrows. I'll find a village in need of a smith and begin my new life in the Covenant lands. I can forge plowshares, carve coulters, shoe horses and mules. If I must, I will repair a blade or forge a new one . . ." He shrugged. "But should I never make another weapon, I'll be content."

Daylon weighed his answer. The finest weaponsmith he had ever known would not, at least, seek service with a rival lord. The Narrows was free of armed conflict, for the time being, so Edvalt would find little demand for weapons there.

"Very well," said the Baron of Marquensas, "then we have no issue, but for the pledge: if you find an apprentice who trains to be your equal, you will send him to me."

"I'll not put another in bondage," answered Edvalt.

Annoyed by the answer, Daylon snapped, "I would not take a freeman into service against his will. You were a captive in war, and it was my right to put you to death or sell you as a slave. I did neither." Both men knew his largesse was solely due to Edvalt's talent, and not any generosity of spirit on Daylon's part. "I will ask him to serve freely, and reward him greatly if he agrees."

But the weaponsmith seized the moment. "Should I find such a lad, I will send him to you first," agreed Edvalt. "If he willingly takes your service, that is his choice, but should he wish to make his own way in the world, that is also his right?"

Daylon nodded. "Agreed. Then we are done. Take your woman and child and travel safely." He nodded to Reinhardt. "See that they are given safe conduct." As an afterthought, he said, "Find him a serviceable wagon or cart, as well, so he might carry his tools with him, and give him half a weight of gold."

The captain nodded and said, "As you command, my lord." He signaled to Edvalt to follow him.

Taken aback by Daylon's unexpected generosity, Edvalt muttered, "I thank my lord," and the two men departed.

Daylon stood alone at the entrance of his pavilion watching the finest sword maker he had ever encountered walk away. He knew the day approached when he would need many fine weapons. He was just grateful it was not today. He turned and pulled aside the canvas flap.

Stepping inside his tent, Daylon found the clean clothing set out for him by his body man, Balven. He was constantly amused by the fact that the only person he truly trusted in this life was his bastard half brother. Balven had come to their father's castle as a boy, to be a companion for the young heir. When their father died, Daylon had kept Balven close at hand as his body servant, but in truth he was a more trusted adviser than any of Daylon's official advisers.

Balven waited beside a wooden bucket of fresh water and a heavy towel. A proper bath would have to wait until he reached home, but he could at least remove the worst of the mess from his body.

As Balven began to strip off Daylon's armor, the Baron of Marquensas wondered again about the Firemane baby. What if there *was* a child out there, destined to plague the sleep of the four remaining kings?

Balven was the younger brother by two years, but he had been with Daylon since the age of six and could read his moods well. Daylon's mother had done all she could to put a wedge between the half brothers, but all that she had succeeded in doing was bringing them closer. Daylon had possessed a rebellious nature as a child, and he dared not reveal it to their father, so his poor mother had borne the brunt of it. As a result, the two men were far closer than master and servant.

Balven was an average-looking man of middle height, with close-cropped brown hair and dark eyes; his appearance was unremarkable, but he resembled Daylon in small ways, the set of his jaw, his brow and nose, and how he carried himself. Balven studied his brother's face as he soaped his body. "You are troubled?" he asked softly. He had anticipated his master's changeable mood and had a girl waiting in the corner of the tent rather than in Daylon's bed, as he knew that his brother's disposition could swing in either direction after a battle. The girl's brown eyes were fixed upon the Baron of Marquensas, silently awaiting his order.

Daylon considered her for a moment, then shook his head. He felt tired deep in his bones. Balven dismissed her with a tiny motion of his head. She nodded once and silently left.

Daylon watched her depart with no hint of desire. He wished only for a hot meal and a long sleep after today's bloody work. He endured the cold water and harsh soap; the discomfort was worth the loss of muck and blood. "I miss a hot tub," he said to Balven as he toweled himself dry.

His bastard half brother nodded in agreement. "I miss home."

Daylon grunted assent. He also longed for the warm sun on the shores of Marquensas, where his castle over-looked an orchard that ran across the hills and down to the coast of the Western Sea. He missed the rich orange blossom scent on the spring breeze from the ocean and the sheer beauty of his holdfast. He missed his wife's lithe body and the promise of children. As he donned the robe Balven held for him, Daylon said, "Mostly I miss the peace. The sounds of war still ring in my ears."

"They echo in mine, as well, my lord," agreed Balven.

"But at least our world didn't end this day," he added in a lighter tone.

Daylon laughed. One of the many things he shared with his half brother was a love of their father's library. Balven knew of the legendary Firemane line and the supposed destruction attached to its end. They had almost had an argument before Daylon agreed to participate in Steveren's betrayal; Balven had contested their joining Lodavico and the others. As was his usual tactic, Balven had argued against the course Daylon had almost certainly already chosen, to explore any failings of logic that the baron might have overlooked; neither man placed much faith in auguries, omens, and prophecies, but after ample wine, the discussion had factored them into the decision, or rather ignoring the legend had, as part of Balven's last argument on the matter.

"Food?"

"I'll fetch your meal straightaway, my lord."

Within a few minutes Balven placed a hot plate of beef and vegetables, with some edible bread and a sliver of cheese, next to a full bottle of wine and goblet. He set the small table and departed without instruction. He knew that his half brother's mood called for solitude.

Daylon ate alone, his silence broken only by the faint sounds of knackers, scavengers, and body robbers in the distance. Then he fell heavily into bed.

Daylon had a dagger in his hand before he was fully conscious. He listened. It was quiet, though occasionally he made out the shout of a distant sentry or the faint sound of looters arguing over spoils. He heard a rustle in the corner and sat up, blade ready. Had the camp girl returned without bidding? As the fog of sleep lifted, he decided that a camp girl would not lurk in the corner but would have probably slipped into his bed.

Then Daylon heard a strange sound. He took up his night lamp and opened its shutter to illuminate the tent's interior. In the corner where the girl had waited lay a bundle of cloth, and he could see it moving.

He approached it warily, as he would not be the first noble of Garn to be gifted with a venomous serpent or rabid animal. Then he recognized the noise and knew that the cloth held something far more lethal.

The Baron of Marquensas crouched and pulled aside the covers to see a tiny face looking up at him. He held the light close and saw large blue eyes in a little round face and a forehead crowned with wispy hair, silver-white in the lamplight. In that moment, Daylon was certain that this baby was the last of the Firemanes, as certain as he was of his own name. He guessed that the child's fine silver-white hair would turn a brilliant copper when it was two or three years old, but around the baby's neck a woven copper wire had been placed, and from it hung a gold ring set with a single ruby— the signet ring of Ithrace, the king's ring.

Who had put this child in his tent? How had that person passed his sentries, or stolen past Balven, who slept before his threshold? He gently picked up the child to examine it in the light of his night lamp and saw it was a boy. The child looked into his eyes and Daylon was even more certain that this was the Firemane baby.

Crouching on his heels as the baby watched him silently, Daylon Dumarch, Baron of Marquensas, muttered, "Gods old and new, why me?"

Along the shore, away from the battle site, a man waited by a cluster of rocks. Daylon could see him clearly in the early morning sunlight as they rode slowly toward him.

The man wore a covering over his nose and mouth, leaving only his eyes exposed; the only clue to his identity was the age lines at their corners. Other than that, he appeared to be a common soldier without badge or tabard, but he was a member of the unseen army of Coaltachin, the legendary Invisible Nation.

Coaltachin's rulers had never affixed their names

or their seals to the Covenant, and this exclusion had made them a nation apart, yet they had honored the pact since its inception. Few nobles and fewer commoners understood the genius of Coaltachin's security, and their success was due to their *Quelli Nascosti,* meaning *"The Hidden."* Coaltachin had the finest spies, infiltrators, saboteurs, and assassins in the world. On the street they were known as *sicari,* "the dagger men."

The Invisible Nation was publicly loathed and privately employed by every ruler with the means to pay them. They were also universally feared, for legend claimed they could walk through walls, kill with their breath, and become undetectable at will, or at least that was the myth surrounding them. In reality, they were the most effective assassins, spies, and provocateurs on Garn.

The true strength of Coaltachin lay in the extent of its network. It had placed agents everywhere, from the tables of nobility to the gutter gangs of the most dangerous cities across the world. Few knew exactly where the Invisible Nation lay among the thousands of islands off the eastern shore of South Tembria. Only a few, trusted, eastern traders could navigate the route to Coaltachin. All anyone else knew was that it might lie somewhere between South Tembria and Enast.

Daylon had been certain that the *sicari* would be at

hand during a battle of this scope. A betrayal so majestic was far beyond the skills of men like Lodavico Sentarzi or Mazika Koralos. It had taken Balven a full day and a night to find someone to carry word and relay the message to arrange this meeting at dawn on the second day after the bloodshed, a time during which Daylon had been left to look after the baby. Balven found a goat with a kid among the livestock, made a makeshift nursing rag, and tore up strips of linen to keep the child clean. Daylon, who had never touched a baby in his life, managed to keep the boy hidden from view. He thanked the gods that the child seemed to want to sleep most of the time.

He did not know exactly what to expect from this meeting and spared a little time to wonder who this man might be. Before the battle he might have served in Daylon's army or even Steveren's, as a porter, baggage cart driver, cook, or vendor among the camp followers, faceless in a sea of faces. Daylon was certain that this man, or others of his order, had infiltrated the Ithraci army, to shout contradictory or confusing orders to paralyze Steveren Langene's forces as he tried to organize a defense against the sudden betrayal.

Daylon smiled ruefully. Perhaps he also overestimated his own power and security, particularly now as he stood next to his brother and faced a deadly killer.

The bulk of Daylon's army was already on the road home; only his castellans remained to protect their master, laid low by a stomach ague that kept him abed. It was unlikely that anyone would call at his pavilion since most of the combined armies had already departed for Ithra, but the excuse kept the baby from prying eyes while they waited for a reply from the man who now awaited them. Word had come after sunset and Daylon had spent a restless night in anticipation of the dawn.

Daylon rode carefully through the rocks along the shore, the ever-present roar of the breakers masking the clatter of his horse's hooves as he made his way to the meeting point. Behind him came Balven, carrying the Firemane baby.

When they reached the man, Daylon held up his hand and asked, "Do you know me?"

"I do," said the false soldier.

"I have a charge for you. Will you accept my gold?"

"Name your charge," replied the man.

"This baby must travel with you to your homeland. He is to be cared for as if he were a child of your master's household and be given a name, though I do not wish to know it. Only send word should the child perish; a message must reach me saying, *The colt went lame and had to be put down*. If nothing unfortunate occurs, there will be no reason for words between us ever again.

"For this charge I will pay you five weights of gold each year until the boy becomes a man." That day was seventeen years away.

Daylon gestured toward his half-brother. "This is my man, Balven. He can be known by the mark near his heart, earned in a hunting accident." Balven moved the tiny baby to his right arm and with his left hand pulled aside the collar of his tunic to show the man his scar. "He is the only man on Garn I trust completely. Seventeen years from this day, he will be at the main gates of Marquenet. The child must be brought to the city and given over to him at dawn.

"Should Balven meet an untimely end, I will choose another to take up his charge and send word to you. I will name his replacement using these words: *The caretaker has passed, his heir is . . .*

"Your master may treat the child as he pleases but the boy is not to be harmed or abused. He must be educated, as he is of noble birth, and trained to protect himself. The gold shall cease to be paid after his manhood day, and it is then you will bring him to the city gates to meet with Balven."

The assassin considered the deal and finally said, "Ten weights a year."

Daylon looked at the dark eyes above the black mask, then finally said, "Seven and we are done."

"Seven," agreed the assassin.

"Can you reach your homeland without the baby being seen?"

"I will require eight weights for the journey, if we must remain undetected."

"Done," said Daylon. He reached into a small bag hanging from his horse's saddle and counted out small bars of gold, each as long as an average man's hand and as wide and deep as a man's thumb. Each one could feed a village for a year. "Here are eight, and this year's seven: fifteen in all. Seven more will be sent each year, on this day. Send word where to deliver the gold to my barony."

The agent of the Quelli Nascosti took the gold, then went to Balven's side and took the baby. Balven gave his master one long look, then handed the child over.

Daylon watched the man ride away until all he could see was the rising sun burning off the morning's fog, and all he could hear was the sound of gulls on the wing and the crashing of waves on the rocks. Turning his horse around, he motioned for Balven to walk beside him.

The body man looked up at his half brother and said,

"Am I incorrect in assuming that might have been the most impulsive thing you've ever done?"

Daylon shrugged. Then he chuckled. "Probably."

"If Lodavico catches any hint of your business this morning, he'll turn his army around and march straight on to Marquenet to hang you from the first tree he finds."

"He might try that anyway. I will have to answer for my decision to forgo the plundering of Ithra, as the king of Sandura may well infer my disapproval." Daylon chuckled as they traveled back toward the path leading to the top of the plateau. "Even Lodavico isn't quite that impulsive. No, he'll harbor his grudge over my going home today. I'm free to despise the king of Sandura, just so long as I do so in private."

Wondering at his recent impulsiveness, Daylon cursed himself for not keeping his army at home, leaving the fate of Ithrace to fall on other shoulders, and the blood of a friend from his hands.

Balven saw the expression on Daylon's face and knew what he was thinking, but it was Daylon who put the thought into words. "Perhaps I should have killed the child."

Balven said, "While that might have been the most expedient solution, you could never bring yourself to kill a helpless baby. Killing the Firemane child was never a choice, my lord."

Daylon knew his bastard brother was right. He would never have been able to see or hear his own child and not think of the one dead at his hand, especially that of a friend betrayed. Daylon nodded. "You are correct, as you often are."

Balven chuckled. "Had our father left me to die . . ."

"I'd never have found anyone to trust in my household," finished the Baron of Marquensas. "You might be a bastard, but we share blood."

"How many brothers and sisters do you think we are still ignorant of?" asked Balven.

Daylon gave a cynical laugh. "The only man I've met who rivals Father's appetite for pretty young women is Rodrigo."

"And Father had no taste for pretty boys."

Daylon nodded. "He had a few, I suspect." He stared off into the distance, toward the sea, as they started upon the path to the battlefield above.

Balven said, "What troubles you, my lord?"

Daylon took a deep breath and let it out slowly as he urged his horse upward. "It might be years yet, but this matter is far from over."

Balven nodded and said, "This day may prove useful. Many do not suspect the Firemane baby may be out there in the world. A few do, but we *know* he is. Entrusting his care to the Lords of the Unseen was an . . . unexpected move, but it may prove to be a great advantage."

Daylon lost some of the tension in his features. "You always anticipate the advantage in any situation."

"Worry not, my lord. Turn your mind to more pleasant prospects and let me worry for you."

Daylon said, "That's one of the reasons I keep you around, brother." The notion that this baby would someday prove useful comforted him, but the idea of another baby, soon to be in his home, made him smile widely.

1
Passages and Departures

His name was Hatushaly, though the other boys and girls called him "Hatu."

He was by nature a youngster prone to anger, often barely able to control it and quick to erupt, but at this moment, Hatu was trying very hard not to laugh.

His two closest friends flanked him as they lay on a heavy awning of bright green and white striped canvas extending from the rooftop of an open-front shop, hidden from the view of those below. They were trying hard not to be detected.

Hatu's anger was usually forgotten in Hava's or Donte's company. For reasons he would never understand, they had become his friends despite his constant rage and furious outbursts, and both had conspired to make his life even more complicated. When he was alone, Hatu became introspective and angry, but when he was with them, the dark thoughts that threatened to overwhelm him were forgotten.

Donte, Hava, and Hatu had been given a task: to observe the comings and goings in the market. Donte had insisted on adding a ridiculous commentary to the scene that had nothing to do with their lesson but threatened to expose their position to the merchant in the shop below as his companions struggled not to burst into laughter. One of Donte's many talents was a wry wit, but he often lacked any sense of appropriate timing, which earned him his fair share of reprimands, disciplinary duty, and beatings.

Hatushaly tried to ignore his friend's commentary, while Hava simply closed her eyes and lay with her forehead against her left forearm, both trying not to hear Donte. Hatu could do so with more ease than Hava. The market square was busy: fisher folk, farmers, traders, and travelers crowded every corner of the town. Harborside was actually a part of the city of Corbara, the main port on the Island of Coaltachin. The Kingdom of Night centered on the large island but also spread across dozens of smaller isles, home to many fishing villages, farm communities, small fortresses, and the moorings for a huge fleet of trade and war ships.

The three youngsters were taking advantage of the excursion: the instructors rarely sent them away for a day. Hatu, Donte, and Hava were students at one of the many nameless schools in Coaltachin, on Morasel, a little island that was home to a small fishing village on the coast and a farming hamlet inland. All who lived there labored under the firm command of Master Facaria.

Hava was a girl of intense moods, both light and dark, who performed few tasks without thought and determination. Her dark hair usually hung to her shoulders, but today she had bound it in a simple black scarf to keep it out of her face. She wasn't what most men might call pretty, but Hatu liked her appearance. Her face was narrow and she always seemed to be squinting, even when inside, though her vision was superb, as she proved every time she shot a bow. Her mouth was slightly turned down at the edges, but he thought she had a wonderful smile. He'd known her all his life. She was agile and strong, and as Hatu had started to change from boy to man, he had also begun to find her lithe body more attractive and disturbing. He'd seen Hava naked many times, for the students often swam or bathed together in the stream behind the school, but now he sometimes found the sight of her troubling, even more so than that of the other girls. Right now she was struggling not to laugh, which made it difficult for Hatu not to laugh.

Donte seemed always to be smiling or laughing. Like Hava, he had dark hair, but his locks were much darker, bordering on black. He was broad shouldered and stronger than any boy in the school, and faster than all but Hatu and Hava. When Donte decided to become friends with someone, they didn't have much say in the matter. There was a quiet madness in his approach to life, a willingness to put himself in harm's way for the thrill of it. No matter how dark the moment, Donte could always contrive a joke, often a completely inappropriate one, to bring sudden laughter; even if his joke itself wasn't particularly funny. Hatu worried about him, but Donte seemed to move through life without a single care or concern. He was diligent enough in his lessons that his careless manner caused him no serious difficulties. While Hatu considered the future, Donte lived for the moment, seeking only immediate gratification, be it a stiff drink or a pretty girl. Yet Donte was still Hatu's closest friend among the boys at the school.

"Look," said Hava, pulling them out of their joke. She thrust her chin toward the main street from the docks to the market. "Far side, four men."

Hatu spotted the men, sailors by the look of them,

but of a fashion new to him. Coaltachin sailors favored baggy trousers of light weave, their linen shirts worn loosely to protect them against the heat. Coaltachin people tended to tan or have dark skin, with brown and black hair, but these men were fair skinned and burned red-bronze by the sun. Two of them had light brown hair, one was blond, and the last was red haired.

"Kin of yours?" asked Hava.

Hatu sighed. "That joke was old years ago."

Only the students who had been raised alongside Hatu knew what his normal hair color was. He dyed it regularly and had been forced on a few occasions to rub dirt or grease into the roots until he could wash and dye it again. Hatu stood out among the rest of the students. The islands to the east of the twin continents had for centuries been home to a people known as the Igara. They tended to range in height, but most possessed skin easily bronzed by the sun and hair that was typically colored black to medium brown. A few were blond, but Hatu was one of the two people he knew to have red tresses. Hava's dark auburn hair only truly looked red after hours in the hot sun—sun bleaching was common with the fishermen and farmers if they didn't wear hats—but Hatu's was a unique copper red with golden highlights. "Look at that low forehead;

more like your kin," he said weakly, which caused Hava to chuckle slightly, almost a sound of pity, and Donte to shake his head dismissively.

"Ya," said Donte. "It's not bright enough. Hatu's is more like a flaming copper. That man's is . . . dark carrot, if such a color exists."

Hava chuckled again. "Why don't you just shave it off?"

Hatu shook his head. "If you think a flame-haired boy stands out, how about a bald one? If I need to run and blend in with a crowd, dirty brown hair is best."

"So until he can learn to grow a new head of brown hair in under a minute, he'll have to dye it," added Donte. "Besides, what would happen if he's doing a job and gets caught with a razor?"

Hava nodded. "No weapons."

"No weapons," repeated Hatu. As they approached adulthood, the students had been taught that when violence erupted, they stood a better chance with the authorities if they tossed their weapons aside rather than be captured armed. Loose clothing sewn with rags, to rip away splattered blood, and a host of other tricks had been drilled into the future agents of the Invisible Kingdom.

All of their training aimed to make the youngsters as useful as possible to their nation. They pledged not to a king, despite their nation's name, but to a ruling council, a system that had existed for centuries in this region.

While the preceptors bore responsibility for educating the boys and girls, the masters were the final authority in Coaltachin. Each hierarchy within the gang culture of the island had a captain, crews, gangs, and regimes, but the person at the top of the order was simply called "master." Above any single master was the Council, made up of the seven most powerful masters in Coaltachin, and heading the Council was Master Zusara, the single most powerful man in the nation, as close to a king as it was possible to be.

"I'm hungry," muttered Donte.

"You're always hungry," replied Hava and Hatu in unison, which provoked another burst of barely contained laughter as they struggled to remain hidden.

The forays into the various cities, towns, and villages of Coaltachin were part of the students' education, but Donte always treated them as an excuse for a holiday, much to the consternation of both his master and his instructor. He began to construct a miniature lance from a windswept tree branch on top of the awning where they lay, using his dagger to whittle it into something he could use to impale a sausage sizzling on a grill below. Muttering, he said, "Wish I had a proper spear."

Hatu shook his head while Hava grinned and chided their friend. "We're supposed to be observing discreetly. Strutting around the market with a spear is hardly inconspicuous."

The merchant below was busy selling his wares to people hurrying to their own places of work, and to servants from nearby homes seeking the spiced delicacies for their master's breakfast. If any of the customers noticed that three youngsters were causing the brightly colored awning of waxed cloth to sag a little deeper than normal, no one spoke of it.

When his opportunity finally came, and no customer looked on, Donte thrust his lance and successfully impaled a stout link on the grill. He quickly pulled it up while the merchant had his back to the fire.

"You're going to get us all a beating," whispered Hatu.

Donte tried to remove the hot sausage from the makeshift harpoon and burned his fingers in the process, while his companions continued to stifle their laughter.

A small tearing sound caused Hatu to look down in alarm, and he whispered, "The awning!"

The students scrambled back to the tiled roof above the awning as quickly as they could, but as they moved, the tear widened and the cloth began to give. None of them could see through the canopy yet, but an angry shout from below made it clear that the merchant had noticed that his striped awning now sagged heavily with a widening tear at its front.

All three youngsters reached the peak of the roof without pause, then quickly scrambled down to the eaves at the back of the house. Like all of the buildings surrounding the market square, the house was a merchant's dwelling and place of business. There was a good-size yard below them with a wagon in it and a gate opening onto the alley beyond. Donte glanced one way and then the other, and then signed for Hava and Hatu to follow him as he tiptoed along the edge of the roof. When he reached the alley at the side of the house, he knelt and jumped, and was followed by his two companions. Donte looked back toward the busy market before he motioned for them to follow him to the trade alley behind the yard.

They moved swiftly but didn't sprint, as they had been taught that running drew too much attention. Donte turned a corner only to find them confronted by a large, broad-shouldered man with a heavy black beard and blue knit cap. He held a long billy in his right hand and his arms were crossed.

"Been stealing sausages?" he said.

Before any of the students could reply, the man

stopped them with a dark look, and with a nod indicated that they were to follow him back into the market. "Lose the sausage," he instructed Donte, who immediately tossed the warm, savory treat to the ground. They followed the burly man, a gang captain named Hilsbek, who had been put in charge of Facaria's pupils while the island master was in a meeting. This wasn't unusual, as the youngsters spent as much time in the field as in the classroom or training yard.

"The sausage?" repeated Hilsbek.

"I got hungry," said Donte, trying not to smile.

A quick cuff to the ear told Donte that this wasn't amusing to the gang leader. The blow was hard enough to get the student's attention without damaging him. Donte's eyes glistened from the pain, but he didn't let tears come. His face and stance shifted to a position Hatu and Hava knew all too well. Donte would usually have challenged anyone who struck him like that. He'd even risk fighting a crew captain if he thought he could win, but would not defy anyone of a rank higher than that.

Donte was the grandson of Master Kugal, one of the seven masters on the Council, which granted him some additional status, though it was never openly commented upon. The students were supposed to be treated equally, but in practice, their privilege was often dictated by the amount of power held by their close relatives.

Though rank was not official, the pecking order among students had been well established by the time they could leave their mothers. Hava was unusually gifted, among the best archers, runners, and hand-to-hand fighters, both boys and girls, which earned her more respect than was normal for a farmer's child. Hatu was an orphan, an anomaly without connections, but he was treated with greater care than might be expected.

"What was your duty?" asked Hilsbek, his eyes narrowing as he looked from face to guilty face.

Hava and Hatu glanced at each other as Donte, with as impassive a tone as he dared, replied, "To watch the market for anything unusual."

Hilsbek nodded. "You were on that roof for over three hours—"

"And I got hungry," added Donte, which earned him another cuffing, one hard enough to leave a red mark on his cheek and tears in his eyes.

Hilsbek glared at the youngster, as if daring him to utter another word.

Donte fell silent.

Hilsbek remained quiet for a while, then spoke in an even tone, "What did you see?"

Hava said, "A busy market."

Donte hesitated, as if anticipating another slap, then added, "Nothing unusual."

Hilsbek looked at Hatushaly next. After a pause, the youngster said, "There was one group of men trying to appear . . . normal. They came from the docks and moved a little too fast, as if they were in a hurry but trying not to be noticed. They wore simple robes with deep hoods. One wore boots, the rest sandals. They moved to the north and I couldn't see them leave."

Hilsbek looked at Hatu. "Well enough. If you were to see such a group while on duty, what would you do?"

Hatu said, "What I was told to do. If I was told to report at once, then I'd leave and report. If told to wait until relieved, I'd—"

Hilsbek interrupted. "Enough."

Pointing at Hatu, he said to the others, "He knows how to see. You looked, but you didn't see. Learn how to see."

Hilsbek regarded the three youngsters for a moment, then he said, "You are only months away from being placed . . ." He fell silent again and shook his head. "If you left training today, you would find a trade, but soon . . ." A third silence fell.

Finally Hilsbek said, "Find another roof. Watch from

there until sundown. See if you can find more men trying . . . to appear normal. Meet at the safe house after sunset."

As the students started to move away, Hilsbek slapped Donte in the back of his head. "I don't care who your grandfather is, boy. Do something stupid like that when you're working, and at some point you'll get yourself and your companions killed."

Donte grudgingly held his peace as they walked away, but once out of hearing range, he said, "I'll settle with him someday."

Hatu shook his head in silent disbelief, while Hava laughed openly. "Your grandfather will not always be around to get you out of trouble. We all make mistakes, we all get beaten."

Hatu nodded in agreement.

"You make a mistake, you just get sent to your grandfather," Hava continued.

"Ha!" laughed Donte. "The preceptors and the other masters are afraid of my grandfather, so he beats me harder than any of them. My grandfather is afraid of no one." After a moment, he added, "Well, other than my grandmother."

Hava laughed, but Hatu said, "Do you ever take anything seriously? You know what Hilsbek was saying, don't you?"

"What?" asked Donte as they began to look around for a new observation post.

"The day is coming when we'll know too much," whispered Hatu harshly.

"Too much?" asked Hava.

Hatu's expression held exasperation. "To let us live," he whispered. "Once we know all of the secrets . . ."

Hava's eyes widened. Hatu nodded; it was about time she understood. "We need to be more careful," he added in low tones.

"Life's too short to be careful," Donte responded with annoyance as they reached the center of the market. He halted and looked around. "Where?"

After a quiet consideration, Hatu said, "Over there, I think."

He didn't point—another lesson learned early—just raised his chin in the direction of a large building on the far side of the market. It wasn't situated as advantageously as their last post but offered a good view of anyone arriving from the docks.

"How's your ear?" Hatu asked Donte as they moved quickly through the crowd.

"Hurts," was all Donte said.

Hava shook her head and furrowed her brow as she said, "One day you're going to say something that will get you killed."

"Maybe," said Donte as he led his companions into the alley beside their new vantage point. He took a quick look around and with a nod of his head indicated that Hatu should be the first to climb. Donte formed a stirrup with his hands and his friend hopped into it without hesitation. Thrown upward, Hatu caught the eave of the roof and pulled himself on the roof with ease. He turned and lay flat, letting his arms dangle over the edge.

Donte lifted Hava so she could grip Hatu's arms and when she reached the roof, she lay next to him. Donte leapt and caught his companions' hands, and together they pulled him upward.

Settling in, Donte said, "Two hours to sunset."

"Try to stay awake," chided Hatu.

Hava chuckled as they started to scan the crowd below for anything unusual.

The port was the heart of the Coaltachin nation, and yet at the same time it wasn't. To those who lived in the Kingdom of Night, and their trusted associates, it was called Corbara: the capital city of a sprawling set of tiny islands, populated by a people whose main export was assassination, espionage, and crime. Its residents were expert at detecting which newcomer should be respected and which should be misled. By tradition and habit no one used the name of the city in front of strangers in the port. Corbara was only ever called "here," "home," or "this city." Some travelers had passed through the port more than once and still had no idea where they had been. Such was the culture of Coaltachin.

This combination of secrecy and commerce forged as strong a brotherhood as there was among any tribe on Garn. The lowest peasant in Coaltachin felt akin to the highest of the masters, and while few natives acknowledged it, the outsiders who had dealings with the island nation were forced to navigate the insular, chauvinistic nature of its people with sensitivity. Anyone not of Coaltachin was at best a necessary nuisance, and at worst a potential enemy. This attitude toward strangers, even friendly visitors, was so ingrained that it was never spoken of, simply learned from childhood.

The three youngsters watching the market and harbor were already part of the nation's elite. The sons of masters and preceptors, like Donte, were automatically selected for the schools, as were the children with exceptional potential, like Hava. She had been a combative child, and her early willingness to stand against much larger and stronger children had caught the attention of the local master, Facaria. The others knew nothing about Hatu's past, but his admittance to the academy marked him as exceptional, and so the fact he came from outland stock was ignored by those who had been raised alongside him.

The students were training to become soldiers, but soldiers unlike those of any other nation. The forces of Coaltachin included squadrons of ships, often disguised, but ready to repel the rare incursions by seafarers who didn't understand whose waters they entered. Some of the larger islands held defensive garrisons with small units of archers, pikemen, and swordsmen. The true militia of Coaltachin was invisible, a thing of reputation and rumor, myth and lethal ability.

In the old tongue, Quelli Nascosti meant "The Hidden," and it was possible that someday the very best among these students would count themselves among their ranks. As the grandson of a powerful master, Donte would almost certainly advance.

Hava was among the finest students in combat and weapons training, and possessed rare athletic skills.

Hatushaly's advantage was unique. He knew he was receiving special treatment: he had heard of no other outland child at his or any other school. The mystery was one of the sources of his constant smoldering anger, as was the uncertainty over his future.

That evening twenty-three students sat in small groups at the back of a cluttered warehouse. Most of the youngsters were known to the three friends; several were from other villages, here because their masters had been called to an important meeting. As they made their way from the door to the rear of the warehouse, where food waited, Hatu saw a familiar face watching them walk past. Hava saw his expression change and quietly asked, "What?"

Hatushaly lifted his chin toward the youngster who stared in their direction. "Raj," he said in a venomous tone.

Hearing that name, Donte turned. Across the room, near to where the students' travel bags were stored, squatted three young men, eating silently. Raj's lopsided smile was easily recognizable. The boy had a strange face: delicate features and deep brown eyes that were overshadowed by a heavy brow, giving him an unbalanced appearance.

Donte sighed and said, "Do not start anything, do you hear me?" He gripped Hatu's tunic and said, "I know Raj's look; he's ready to start something. He knows he can goad you, so just leave it alone."

Hatu forced himself to look away, and Donte added, "We're already in trouble with Hilsbek, and if you start a fight with Raj . . ." He made no further comment, simply put his hand on Hatu's shoulder and steered him to the waiting food.

After a few steps, Hatu shrugged Donte's hand away and said, "I'm not going to start anything . . ." He glanced back at Raj and saw that the boy was still staring at the three of them.

"What is it between you two, anyway?" Hava asked.

Hatu remained silent as they reached the table where food had been laid out on wooden plates. When they had settled into an unoccupied corner of the room, he said. "I don't know, it started . . ."

"Years ago," supplied Donte. "Do you even remember what that first fight was about?"

"He called me a name," said Hatu, "I think . . ."

Hava's brow furrowed. "You think?"

"It was before you came to school," said Donte. He took a bite from his platter. The food was plain, and as usual cold, but they ate gratefully, for over the years they had trained for periods of privation, and going without food was a normal part of their lives, even if only for short periods of time in training.

It was quiet in the warehouse. Students rarely spoke while eating. From an early age, they had been taught to focus on things most people took for granted, like food, water, and rest, to conserve and build their strength. These drills and lessons had been hard ones: two days without food was not life threatening, but to a child it felt like an eternity of starvation. Many mornings had broken on severe stomach aches as the youngsters learned which foods were safe to eat and when. Water was always close at hand, for while going without food for days was possible, severe dehydration would kill sooner, and incapacitate even faster. Rest was precious, for the rigors of life under their masters would often require long periods of sleepless exertion.

Hatu looked at the small square of wood that served as his plate and ate his food with his fingers: cold lumps of sticky rice in a congealed broth, a slice of a roll, and a small portion of bitter greens. He would finish every bite.

After a moment of silence, Hava asked, "Before I came? How old were you when it happened?"

"Seven, or eight," said Hatu quietly.

Donte shrugged. "I've lost count of the fights they've had."

"Seven," said Hatu, keeping his voice low, though both his friends could sense his rising tension. He glanced at Donte. "Eight?"

"More," said Donte. "I lost count about eight."

Hava shook her head in disbelief. "Ten, eleven? So at least once a year you and Raj just decide to fight?"

"Sometimes you just don't like someone," said Donte. "For no reason. It takes most people a while to dislike Hatu, but Raj hated him from the first moment they met."

"I don't care what his reason is, or even if he has one," said Hatu, clearly on edge. "He's a piece of shit to everyone. I just fight back."

"True," said Donte, turning to Hava. "You and I are the only two people on Garn who truly like Hatu, but nobody likes Raj. He just bullies people into pretending they like him."

"I know that," replied Hava. "I just wanted to know what started the whole thing."

"Can't remember," replied Donte. He smiled, then purloined the greens from Hava's plate, a theft she allowed without protest. She couldn't abide the bitter leaves and would always eat them last, and only then if one of the gang captains or a master was watching. They made her sick but that didn't matter to those supervising the students' meal.

Donte, on the other hand, would eat most anything. He had won many bets for eating all manner of disgusting things, including some large insects that were still alive.

Hatu didn't care much for food one way or another. He enjoyed some tastes, but he didn't seek them out to satisfy a craving. As far as he knew, food was necessary for life and beyond that he took little pleasure in it.

While he ate in silence, Hatu's thoughts turned inward, and his frustration began to grow. He found

Donte's antics amusing at times, especially in Hava's company, but on other occasions the big lad's disregard for authority caused problems.

Raj's presence did not help calm the situation. Hatu could feel the boy's gaze upon him, and it took all of his self-control not to turn and meet it. He felt his anger building as he tried to push his mind away from their previous encounters, and from his annoyance that Donte had pulled him away from this fight; more annoyed that Donte was right to do so rather than anything else.

If Hatu dwelt on this intervention, he could easily start to resent his friend, and knowing this unsettled him, for among the male students, Donte was his closest friend and one of the few for whom he'd risk his life. Hatu hadn't fully accepted the lesson that he might one day have to choose to complete a mission over saving a friend. When asked to envision it, he had little difficulty forsaking most of the other students but he could never reach the place in his imagination that permitted abandoning Hava and Donte to a lonely death. But there were moments where his friend's antics got on Hatu's nerves so much that he felt like killing Donte himself. He knew he was letting his deep seething anger rise up and forced himself to practice a calming exercise silently while he ate.

He finished his food and put down his plate. The orders had been simple: silence until everyone had finished eating and then they were to wait for instructions.

He looked around the room, avoiding Raj, and saw only a few faces he recognized in the scattering of strangers. Hava was now leaning against the back wall with her eyes closed. Hatu admired her profile and felt a stirring. He pushed aside the sudden emotion and felt an unexpected rush of foolishness and then anger at himself. He saw Donte also scanning the room for someone to cajole, bully, or bribe for extra food, so he was oblivious to what Hatu thought must have been an obvious display of his reaction to Hava. Donte could usually read Hatu's moods easily.

Hatu settled back against a crate, finding scant comfort. He tried to calm his mind and failed; instead his impatience grew. The students were often kept waiting; Hatu suspected it was designed to stem their restlessness. When they were little, students would often act up, unable to abide the silence. Hatu quickly realized that repeat perpetrators of such behavior disappeared from the school.

Thinking of the school made Hatu recall his earliest memory. It was a painful one, a sudden startling sting that quickly faded. It was a memory that had been repeated many times since the first birch had struck the back of his hand, a sharp memory of correction rather than punishment.

He remembered his first experience vividly: He had reached for a carp, golden in the afternoon sun, swimming just below the surface of a pond, and had fallen into the pool when one of the matrons had been distracted.

Perhaps the odd combination of sensations, the metallic burn of water in his nose, his sudden blurry vision, and his heavy coughing, was why he remembered that moment so vividly, but he'd only been a toddler and had cried until the sharp sting of the birch wand had shocked him into silence. He recalled every second: standing there dripping wet, shivering with the sudden cold, and struggling to understand what had happened.

Hatu shifted slightly while those around him finished eating. As usual old emotions rose with the memory, a mixture of anger and fear. He could even feel an echo of that first flare of shock and it reverberated within him.

The experience had marked Hatu: from that moment to this, he'd had a deep need to know what was expected of him, to understand all aspects of any situation he faced. He was content to rise or fall on his own ability, but when he failed due to lack of information, Hatu flew into a rage—often at himself for not acquiring the knowledge, or at others for not providing it. Unreliable information was what he hated most.

He was told he had been a difficult baby, prone to tantrums and fits of violence, and even now his constant frustration often put him at odds with the demand of the clan for obedience and silence. Hatu had learned to stay silent when there was need; to keep the building rage inside, away from others. He held his anger deep, rarely allowing it to reach the surface, but for most of the time, he was on edge.

No matter what caused his anger to rise, it always felt the same: a burning, seething tension that formed as a tight knot in the center of his body. Only after many lessons, and many beatings, had he learned to control it. But it was always there, a burning just below the surface of his skin, like a fire that would not be quenched. The thrashings he received for fighting had taught Hatu to keep his retaliation in check, though from time to time the instinct bubbled to the surface. It had been months since his last brawl, sparked by a casual remark from a student at the end of a particularly grueling day of training, when his temper got the better of him.

A sharp poke in the ribs brought Hatu out of his reverie. He glanced at Hava, who had come to sit beside him and now regarded him with a half smile, an expression very familiar to Hatu. He had been so lost in thought he hadn't noticed her come over.

"What?" he snapped, keeping his voice down lest he draw unwanted attention.

"You're doing it again," she whispered.

"What?"

"That thing where you . . . go inside your head and get angry."

"I do not—" he began.

"No!" she cut him off, raising her voice slightly. "You do it. You know you do. I've seen you, many times, go back and remember something and get angry over it, all over again, for nothing! Now, stop it!" she hissed.

Hatu sat back, blinking. He wasn't introspective by nature, despite clinging to certain memories, and a part of him knew she was right, but his anger flared toward Hava, erupting alongside his annoyance with Donte and loathing of Raj. He glared at her with full force.

"Fine," she whispered. "Be annoyed with me if you must be angry with someone, but seething over things that happened so long ago is going to get you killed someday if you don't—"

He grabbed her wrist and hissed, "Stop! Now!"

Her eyes widened, and she yanked her arm away,

standing up. Hatu followed her a second later. As they locked eyes, they both knew Hatu was just moments away from losing control.

Donte finally took note of their confrontation. He hurried back to stand next to them as they faced each other in silence. "What is going on?" he whispered, conscious of other eyes being drawn to the trio.

Hatu could barely speak, he was so close to losing his temper. Finally, he managed to swallow his anger and whisper back, "Nothing."

"It doesn't look like nothing," Donte hissed. "You want to get us all punished?"

Hava held Hatu's gaze, then she turned to Donte to reply. Her words were cut off by a shout. "Attention!" All eyes turned to the gang captain, Hilsbek. Hatu, Donte, and Hava quickly squatted where they stood so as not to be noticed while the others sat. Next to Hilsbek was a man Hatu, Hava, and Donte recognized: Bodai was one of the most important masters, a member of the Council. He looked around the room and spied Hatu in the corner. He pointed and motioned for the boy to stand up. As Hatu did so, Hilsbek shouted, "Go get your bag. Meet us outside!"

Hatu hurried to the pile of ragged bags in the corner of the warehouse and quickly dug out his pack. It looked much like the others and contained a change of clothing, a few coins sewn into a seam, some cleverly disguised tools, and a flat tin can of hair dye. It was an oily dye, and dirt clung to it, but it was a necessity. Unlike the women and men who sought to restore their youth or change their appearance for vanity, Hatu needed only a little to turn his eye-catching red-gold locks to a dingy brown.

He hurried toward the door and suddenly found himself falling forward. He rolled, avoiding injury, though he would sport bruises on his shoulder and hip soon, and came to his feet to see Raj scurrying back, his half-mocking, half-defiant smile daring Hatu to react while those around diverted their attention, not wishing to be even remotely associated with a confrontation.

The anger that had been simmering inside Hatu now boiled over. He took one step toward Raj, then felt arms encircle him from behind as Donte lifted and pulled him back.

At the same moment, Hava stepped past Hatu and with wicked speed spun and delivered a punishing wheel kick to the side of Raj's head before he could react as he tried to stand to face Hatu. Raj flew sideways, slamming against a crate, his eyes rolling up into his head before he slumped to the floor.

Donte held Hatu for a second as Hava turned and

with one step had her nose almost to his. "Are you stupid?" she spoke loudly, not caring who overheard. "You were just summoned by a master and you're trying to fight Raj?"

Donte released Hatu, who had ceased struggling. The sudden intervention of his friends had somehow drained Hatu's rage. Hava leaned over and picked up his bag and handed it to him. "Go!" she commanded, obviously angered by what she saw as her friend's intransigence in letting Raj goad him.

Hatu looked around and saw that every student in the warehouse was watching them. A few were looking around to see if anyone in authority was present, for their schooling had taught them all that, as unfair as it was, entire groups were often punished for the misdeeds of one. The fact that the crew boss was outside with Master Bodai had some of them settling back with expressions of relief.

He stumbled toward the door and realized he had said nothing to his friends. He looked over his shoulder and saw Hava and Donte watching him. Hatu nodded his head in farewell.

This was not the first time a student had been singled out to accompany a master or a preceptor on a mission. Hatu had traveled with both, but it was the first time he had been ordered to accompany one alone.

On such assignments, he usually traveled with a small group of students.

Outside the warehouse, Hilsbek narrowed his gaze at the boy, as if he was about to say something, but before he could speak, Master Bodai turned and said, "I know you, don't I?"

Hatu shrugged. "Yes, master, I have seen you before—"

"Call me 'brother,' for I am a holy man and you are now my beggar boy."

Hatu instantly fell into his role. "I have seen you before, brother, when you came to visit Master Facaria. But we have never spoken—" Bodai held up his hand, indicating Hatu should say nothing more. He nodded at Hilsbek.

Hilsbek wished them a safe journey and then returned to the warehouse. For an instant, Hatu wondered if Raj's condition would be noticed, but immediately returned his attention to Master Bodai.

Bodai nodded. "Then we know each other by reputation." He motioned for Hatu to follow. "We take ship soon, and will have ample time to go over details, but for now, tell me what you have heard."

Hatu was so taken aback by the question he paused for a moment and had to step quickly to catch up. Bodai was old enough to have lost some hair, and had what was known as a "high forehead," but what remained of it was streaked white and grey, and hung to his collar. Hatu guessed he was in his sixties, though he walked with a lively step for a man of his age, and had a sense of strength about his movement that marked him as a dangerous opponent despite his advancing years. Experience and core strength might well overcome a younger, stronger enemy.

Hatu said, "I know only what other students have said, brother." He looked concerned as he struggled to say the right thing. "You explain things. To prepare them for . . . whatever it is they need to do. Some of them like you."

Bodai smiled slightly, his tanned face creased like wrinkled leather around his blue eyes, broken nose, and jutting chin. "Some of them like me?" he asked. "What of the others?"

Hatu hesitated, and Bodai said, "They think I talk too much?"

Hatu nodded once.

Bodai halted and laughed. "Perhaps I do. But I'd rather bore you to death than be killed because of your ignorance."

Hatu was surprised that he found the response both amusing and reassuring. He appreciated the master's mirth, and the man's attitude appealed to Hatu's hunger to understand everything. There was no such thing as too much information; his desire to learn lay at the root of his constant frustration and anger.

Bodai paused, narrowing his gaze. "This amuses you?"

"No, brother, it pleases me."

"Well, then," Bodai responded with a playful slap to the back of Hatu's head, "as it is my mission in life to please you, boy, we have begun well."

"Yes, brother."

"I shall call you . . . Venley. How many languages do you speak, Venley?"

"Eleven," said Hatu, "but only five fluently."

"Name the five."

"Our tongue," he began.

Bodai frowned as he resumed walking. "Of course you do. Don't waste my time with the obvious. So, you speak four tongues that are not native to you. What are they?"

"Westernese—"

"Which dialect?" interrupted Bodai as they turned a corner and moved into a busy boulevard that led to the docks.

"Ilcomen."

"Good. It won't take long for you to master the different patois, if needed. Others?"

They crossed a small street and approached the market where Hatu and his companions had spent the day. Hatu said, "I speak the trading language of Matasan, as if I were a native of the island of Katalawa." Bodai nodded as if this was good. "And I also speak Ithraci."

"Who taught you Ithraci?"

"A language preceptor, brother. It was by Master Facaria's order, he insisted I learn." Hatu shrugged. "It's a dead kingdom, so I never understood the point."

"Not quite dead," muttered Bodai. "And the last?"

"Sandurani, as if I were born there."

"Good, because Sandura is where we need to be."

Hatu thought on that as they crossed the market and headed toward the docks. "So we're a priest and beggar boy of the One?"

"Not quite," said Bodai. "I'm a monk, not a priest. I'll explain the rest of it when we reach the city of Sandura's main harbor."

The expression on Hatu's face revealed his impatience. He wanted to understand now, not later.

"You will be busy until then," said Bodai as they reached the docks and moved toward a ship readying for departure.

Hatu let out a sigh of resignation; he was to be a sailor again. It was his third assignment aboard a ship, and although he didn't hate the work, he could have named a dozen things he'd rather have done with his time. He knew it was likely he'd draw the night watch, for the students were often kept apart from most of the crew.

Seeing that Hatu understood, Bodai smiled. "Come then, let us be off," he said as they reached the gang-plank of the ship. It was a wide-bodied trading vessel, a wallower in rough seas, Hatu guessed. He hoped he didn't have to experience that high in the rigging at night. Resigned to the coming trials, he followed Brother Bodai up the gangplank.

2

A Task Completed

The smithy was windowless. It was entered via a long hall that followed an outside wall and turned a corner before emptying into the forge through a curtain. On the opposite wall, massive doors covered with hardened leather sealed out light; the glow of the furnace was the only illumination.

Horseshoes, bridles, stirrup irons, plow blades: all manner of common tools could be fashioned as the sun streamed through the massive doors, but the forging of swords was always performed in the dark, for the smith had to see the truth hidden within the color of the metal.

Journeyman Declan had been given responsibility for overseeing the forge for the first time, and had been smelting iron into steel for three days. He knelt to examine the slag at the bottom of the furnace before returning to the huge bellows that hung from the ceiling. Declan and Jusan, the apprentice who at present napped in the corner, had been tending the bellows day and night. Declan pumped them slowly, watching the glowing embers rise on hot air into the hood above the fire, then looked back at the slag to study the colors of the flaming metal.

The journeyman smith stared into the furnace, looking for unwelcome changes in the hue. The red, orange, and white flames spoke to Declan, telling him if the iron was becoming the steel he desired. He added layer upon layer of iron sand and charcoal, paying constant attention to the heat, and within the glowing heart of the slag, something miraculous formed: jewel steel.

It was the steel from which the greatest swords were fashioned, and a material that few men could produce.

Intelligent and talented, Declan had a rare skill. He was a handsome youth nearing his twenty-second birthday but had achieved the rank of journeyman at eighteen, five years sooner than most. And he was now attempting his masterpiece a dozen years earlier than was normal for any master smith. It was unheard of for one so young, but Declan's master, Edvalt Tasman, felt he was ready for the challenge.

The young man's lanky frame hid the strength usually apparent in the bull shoulders and barrel chests of most smiths. Declan's exceptional strength showed only in his forearms, wrists, and hands, which were more muscular than his otherwise slender build. He had green eyes and fair eyebrows, and his head was covered with a thick thatch of red-blond hair.

Jusan, a well-built youth of fifteen years, snored loudly in the corner. Declan turned to him and called, "Hey!"

The boy awoke instantly and blinked for a moment before he quickly came to stand behind the journeyman smith. Peering over Declan's shoulder, Jusan said, "Is it time?"

"Just watch and learn," said Declan.

Jusan watched closely as Declan used a long iron hook to pull the clay out of the furnace. Waist high and six feet on each side, the furnace had taken a day and a half to construct, and flaming coals spilled out as Declan pulled the slag out, inspected it, and put it back in the coals. "Just a moment longer . . ." Declan muttered.

Jusan smiled at his teacher and nodded. He had a wide face and large brown eyes, and often reminded Declan of an owl as the smoke made him blink furiously. The boy was also starting to grow out of his gangly stage and his strength was approaching that of a man. He watched with interest as the mass of steel collected at the base of the furnace was revealed. Declan silently studied the pile of cooling steel, then turned to Jusan with a smile. Declan nodded once. "Go fetch Edvalt."

The master smith arrived shortly after and knelt to inspect the smoldering blue-grey mass. He leaned forward until the heat threatened to singe his eyebrows and then sat back on his heels wearing a satisfied expression. A single nod indicated to Declan that he had passed the first stage of his goal: creating the steel.

Declan used large tongs to pull the slag from the bottom of the furnace and hurried to the larger of the two anvils in the smithy. While the steel was cooling, he quickly hammered it into an almost perfect cube, then moved it to the anvil where the work would be finished.

Jusan grabbed a bucket and poured water over it. Steam rolled off the hot metal as Declan retrieved a length of heavy paper and slid it under the metal, quickly wrapping the slag. For a moment the three smiths halted and prayed silently to the ancient god of the forge, Hagama.

When Edvalt's father was a boy, smiths had performed a ritual with the prayer, but the One God's priests had named many smiths heretics and burned them since then, and now the words were never uttered aloud.

Jusan handed Declan a pot of clay, and he applied a thick layer to all sides of the steel cube while Edvalt turned it. When it had cooled enough for the clay to be sticky but not hardened, Jusan passed the young journeyman a large jar of ashes, which Declan layered over the cube as Edvalt continued to rotate it. The ashes, clay, and paper would keep the air from the metal as the next step commenced, for the balance between air, heat, and carbon dust was vital for the final step in fashioning the steel.

Declan nodded to Jusan. "Bellows," he said quietly.

Jusan stepped away while the other two smiths picked up their hammers. Edvalt handed the tongs to Declan while Jusan pumped the bellows to encourage the fire back to its hottest point.

Declan thrust the block into the flames and watched as the paper caught and the clay quickly hardened around the steel. He waited for the perfect moment, then returned the glowing mass to the anvil.

The steel they produced was called "jewel steel," or "precious steel," in the secret language of the smiths. It was a mixture of iron sand and carbon dust that produced a steel of remarkable strength and durability. This part of the process was not a secret—any competent smith could create respectable steel—but the forging of jewel steel required an artistry that few smiths possessed. Edvalt was one of those few, and Declan was determined to become his equal.

"Jusan, tongs," Declan instructed.

Jusan hurried to take the tongs from Declan, who glanced at Edvalt and then brought his hammer down on the cube, causing steel, clay, and paper to erupt in a burst of brilliant sparks. Declan slammed his hammer with the precise tempo of a bass drummer as Jusan deftly turned the long ash-covered metal bar with the tongs. Declan alternated blows in perfect counterpoint: crash, turn, crash, turn; the timing was critical, for this was steel for a sword of rare quality, worth the price of a hundred lesser weapons.

Edvalt watched Declan's every move. This was the sixth time the young journeyman had participated in the creation of such a weapon, but the first time Edvalt had given Declan responsibility for every step. From judging materials to the final polish, Declan alone would determine the success or failure of his first jewel-steel sword. If successful, it would be his masterpiece, and the weapon that would elevate him from the rank of journeyman to the rank of master smith. If he made one mistake, the forging would begin again from the very start.

"Good," muttered Edvalt, the only encouragement he would give Declan in his decision making. Baron Bartholomy, the future owner of this blade, had given Edvalt ample time to fashion the weapon, and if Declan made any misstep, the old smith had enough time to fashion another.

Edvalt and Declan shared a bond closer than that of father and son. Fathers and their sons often disagreed, but masters and journeymen had one purpose: to ensure that the knowledge never died. Declan was the son Edvalt had never had; his daughter was now grown and married, and except for a stillborn son, there had been no other offspring.

They pounded and folded the steel, until Declan indicated with a nod that Jusan needed to insert the lengthened blank into the furnace. With one long stride, the young apprentice thrust the blade deep into the coals and began to turn it.

Declan watched every glimmer and spark on the hot metal, then put his hand on Jusan's shoulder. "Now," he whispered, as if speaking loudly might imperil the process.

The young apprentice returned the blank to the anvil. Again their hammers landed powerful blows, and the heavy lump of red-hot metal slowly lengthened into a long flat blank of steel.

Declan said, "Tongs," and Jusan gave him the long handles.

As Edvalt took a step back to watch, Declan flipped the steel over at an angle and struck hard, then he folded the still-glowing metal over on itself, beating the oblong into a square. Edvalt could fold steel in half the time, but Declan's speed would come with practice. All that mattered now was the quality of the steel.

This was crucial in the creation of the great blades. Declan would double this steel more than a dozen times; hours of deft hammering and heating lay ahead of him, but with each fold the process continued until hundreds of layers of metal would be created. When he was finished, this blade would hold at least five thousand, each strengthening the sword.

When Declan was satisfied with the square, he plunged it back into the forge, and Jusan pulled down the remaining clay walls of the steel furnace. No one outside the smithy would witness the manner of this sword's construction, from how the clay was molded into the furnace, every piece crushed to dust, to preparing the coal bed and stoking the ashes, and how the bellows would be repositioned above the open forge when they were finally finished: the special steel required for the commission was one of the most closely guarded secrets in all of Garn. Even Jusan was allowed only to see part of the process; most of the finishing work had been done by Edvalt alone or with Declan as he mastered the craft.

Jusan would be Edvalt's last apprentice and Declan's first, and one day he too would move on and establish his own forge somewhere. Good smiths were always in demand, and often among the most important commoners in the world, particularly those who forged weapons for the barons. Smiths and millers could also rise in position, accruing wealth enough to challenge the barons. They might never command armies, or live in castles, but they could live a life of decadence only dreamed of by other commoners.

Declan was driven by two desires: to forge his masterpiece and to make no mistake that would reflect badly on his master. He was an orphaned child, the son of a murdered tavern wench and a nameless father, who had been taken in by Edvalt and his wife, Mila. His master was as close to a father as Declan would ever know. The smith was a taciturn man who rarely showed emotion, but he had always tempered his stern nature with kindness, and Declan had a fierce desire to please him.

The young journeyman pulled the blade close to his face for the briefest instant, a habit he had learned from Edvalt as a means of testing the metal's readiness for the next step. Declan judged the combination of colors in the metal and the level of heat rising from the steel. The young smith pushed the blade back into the coals.

Declan nodded, and Edvalt looked at Jusan and said, "You did well, too. Depart. Eat and rest."

The younger apprentice needed no urging as he was hungry and tired, and he exited through the smaller door to the hall outside. Jusan knew that his lesson was over; the secrets now passed between master and journeyman might be his to learn one day, but it was not to be today.

Declan was to be shown the final step for the first time: the secret key to mastering the art of creating the blade.

"Bellows?" asked Declan.

Edvalt nodded agreement and put down his hammer to seize the massive arms of the bellows.

Suspended by thick chains, each wooden arm was the length of a cart trace and as thick as a man's forearm, the large bellows bag fashioned from toughened leather. The old smith threw his considerable strength into pulling the arms apart, and the intake of air was like a giant's gasp; then he pushed hard, sending a fountain of embers upward into the copper and iron hood above the forge that kept them from igniting thatch roofs in the village.

Declan studied the hue of the blank and found the perfect spot within the embers. Then, without a word, Edvalt released the bellows, stooped to pick up a shuttle of coals, and deftly sprinkled them at the edge of the fire. Declan put down the hammer, picked up an iron, and, as Edvalt watched, began placing the new coals into the furnace, selecting spots where the new fuel would not lower the heat under the metal.

Then within seconds Declan moved to the bellows. As he worked, the heat washed over master and journeyman in waves, but they ignored the discomfort, their attention focused completely. "Perfect," Edvalt muttered.

Years of patient training only manifested when the steel reached the proper temperature. Declan suddenly dropped the bellows handles and ducked underneath them. Seizing a pair of heavy tongs, he grabbed the near-flaming metal as Edvalt released the coal shuttle and reached for his heavy hammer. Declan grabbed another hammer and, without any instruction, struck down. As soon as his hammer cleared the steel, Edvalt's smashed into the now-malleable metal.

Perspiration poured from their brows, backs, and arms, yet the men continued to hammer in a rhythmic pattern born only from years of working together; the steel flattened out. "Now we make magic," said Edvalt in the single most poetic statement Declan had ever heard from the smith. He had assisted Edvalt before in making this sort of rare blade, but until now had never been permitted to witness the final step.

Edvalt went to a tool chest and lifted out a modest wooden box. Declan had noticed it on the first day of his apprenticeship and had often wondered about its contents, but he had never voiced that curiosity.

Edvalt opened the box and inside it Declan saw fine grains of something that looked like salt, glowing red-orange in the forge's light.

"Sand from the Burning Lands," said the master smith. "You need to learn to do this alone, so come and stand where I am. This is the last secret of our craft that I can teach you."

Declan moved to the other side of the forge, the tongs and hammer ready. "Flatten," Edvalt commanded, and Declan started to beat the red-hot metal, making it thinner on every blow.

"Be ready," said the old smith as he placed the box next to Declan. "When I say *now*, you must do three things very quickly: First, judge the color of the steel. Then take a handful of sand from this box and sprinkle it down the very center of the blade. When the sand sparkles like stars in the heavens, you must then fold the steel one last time."

Perspiration flowed in sheets down Declan's face

and chest, from both the heat and the concentration. He studied the metal, moving the blade around as he struck, then just as he judged it ready to fold, he heard Edvalt say, "Now!"

Declan put his hammer down and pulled the blade toward him as he grabbed a handful of fine sand; he felt the weight of it, measuring the amount he needed, and sprinkled the sand onto the flaming metal.

Smoke and flame erupted. Sand sparkled and flared into tiny bright pinpoints of white, and some stuck to the surface. "More along the right edge!" instructed Edvalt at exactly the same moment Declan decided he needed more on that side. The young journeyman felt exhilarated: he was creating the soul of the sword.

"Now! Edges only!" said Edvalt, and suddenly Declan understood the secret: the sand hardened the steel with each blow. The slightly softer, more resilient center prevented the sword from shattering, while the extra sand at the edge created a harder steel that could be honed razor sharp.

He knew!

Without hesitation or a second thought, Declan started to beat the steel until it began to look like the weapon the baron had commissioned: a stout sword of moderate length, long enough for reach over a horse's neck, to use against men on foot without being a hindrance in the saddle. When he reached the end of the blade, he took it back to the furnace and inserted the tip into the coals. Declan tried not to show any excitement as he neared the end of his task, but he was almost light-headed with the anticipation of reaching this milestone. He forced himself to calm. When the color deepened in the butt end of the blade, he pulled it from the coals, returned to the anvil, and deftly flipped the blade around so he could shape the blank, where the tongs had gripped, into a proper tang. Quickly he hammered the steel into submission.

Then it was done.

Declan looked at Edvalt. The smith held a bucket of water ready. Most smiths would plunge the rough blade straight into the water, quenching the heat and setting the steel's hardness fast, but Edvalt preferred to hold his blade out as his apprentice poured water from the large wooden bucket across the metal. He claimed it was easier for him to judge the cooling process, to watch the color of the blade change as the steam exploded on contact. Declan didn't care what other smiths did; he knew the quality of his master's work and was determined to be his equal.

This time it was the student who held the blade and the teacher who quenched it. When the blade had cooled enough, Edvalt gave his journeyman a quick nod of approval.

Declan used a heavy cloth and gripped the still-hot blade. He selected a guard and slipped it over the tang, ramming it down hard into a hole at the end of the anvil cut specifically for this purpose. Guards did occasionally break and need to be replaced, but Declan believed his sword would serve years without the slightest problem.

He retrieved a roll of thin bull hide, cut an inch wide, and quickly wrapped the tang to form the grip. When that was finished, he held the blade for a moment, testing its balance. He could hardly believe how perfect it felt. Hefting the sword, he glanced at his master.

Both men felt tears welling at the beauty of what they had created, and words between them were not necessary.

Edvalt moved to the large smithy doors and unlatched them, sliding them aside. Brilliant afternoon sunlight blinded both men for a moment; then a relatively cool wave of air refreshed them. It was a hot late summer day, but the air inside the smithy when forging a sword was hotter still.

Declan asked, "Pommel?"

Edvalt shook his head. "If his lordship wished some

fancy stone or metal, he failed to mention such. I will offer him the choice when he arrives."

Declan tossed the blade hilt first and Edvalt deftly caught it. Declan went to the well and hauled up a bucket, unhooked it, and carried it back. Edvalt tucked the blade under his arm and took the bucket between large muscular hands, lifted it to his lips, and drank heavily, then allowed his student to follow suit.

Edvalt held up the sword and inspected it in the sunlight. He looked down its length and finally tossed it back to Declan.

The young man caught it and wielded it as a swordsman might. The sword was bluish-grey and needed to be ground to an edge with a fine finishing stone, then polished, first with foundation polish, then fine polish, then at last silk cloth. In another few days the blade would be ready and gleam a brilliant silver-grey in the sun. He glanced at his master, who looked on expectantly, and finally Declan handed it back and said, "I find no flaw."

"Because there is none," said Edvalt, and with an unexpected show of affection, he reached out with his free hand to give Declan's shoulder a squeeze. "It is a fitting masterpiece. You did well."

"I was taught well," said Declan, emotions threatening to rise up.

Glancing around against being overheard, even by someone as trusted as his wife or apprentice, Edvalt spoke softly, just above a whisper. "The sand comes from the north side of an island. From the port city of Abala, on the edge of the Burning Lands, you ride a day eastward along the shore until you come to bluffs. Follow the beach until you come to a jutting headland, and look up. You will see above you three massive trees, like dark sisters of cursed legend. Look due south, and if the day is clear, you will see the island. A strong man can swim there in an hour; do not rent a boat lest someone divine your purpose. Gather what you need from the deep sand above the high water line; this box has served me for ten years. You know how much is needed for the blade, and in all your years here I have made but five such. One box should last you a lifetime.

"Once safely hidden from curious eyes, sift the sand, many times, taking out all impurities, then boil it to a slurry and filter that. Cover the sand as you let the slurry dry, protected from impurities—even dust— then sift it again. That sand will be salt white, without blemish, and it is what sets this blade apart from other blades, even those made with jewel steel. This is what gives the blade a sharpness none can match. No other sand will do this. This sand is a perfect mix, put there by the old gods for smiths, for this secret goes back before the coming of the One God." He paused, then concluded: "You now possess the secret of king's steel."

Declan was astonished. Until this moment he had believed king's steel was a legend, spoken of by smiths to amaze their apprentices, for it had been said in ancient times skills in armor and arms surpassed what was known today, that through war and time arts had been lost.

"Five such blades have I made."

"But you never named the steel—" began Declan.

Gripping his former apprentice's shoulder, Edvalt stopped him. "And you must never give its name, until you have an apprentice you prize as highly as I prize you. Then you may share it, but to none other. Few smiths know it is not legend, and fewer still would recognize it." He smiled. "Most would judge it jewel steel, accomplishment enough by their lights, but those few who would see it for what it is . . . they would hold silent with that name as well.

"This is the most valued secret of our craft and only a handful of us know it. Now you are the newest to that secret. Guard it with your life. For it is what will someday earn you a fortune. Teach it to your son, or another you love as a son."

Declan nodded, fearful to speak lest his voice crack. Edvalt had been a father to him, though for his entire life the subject was never openly spoken upon by either man. Moisture gathered in his eyes and he nodded once.

Edvalt retuned the nod, swallowing hard. Then he smiled slightly. "If Baron Bartholomy pays the agreed-upon price, I shall never again worry about the future, even if you do not buy this smithy from me.

"One more caution: should you be approached to make such a weapon, do not even admit you possess the skill until you have a sworn oath that such a thing"—he indicated the sword Declan held—"will never be spoken of to another; you are sharing in this secret with Baron Bartholomy because he is the buyer." Edvalut paused, looking deep into Declan's eyes. "This is your masterpiece. Not even your apprentice must know of the difference between jewel steel and king's steel until you name him master of the craft. You may never have such, so do not let your fear of the secret being lost cause you to give this gift to a lesser smith. There will always be a few." He put his hand on Declan's shoulder, his eyes glistening; softly he added, "I was ready to take this to my grave, save that you appeared." He swallowed hard and returned to his brisk manner. "Aye, and should you have cause to even admit to another master your knowledge, it is done thus.

"Ask or be asked, 'This is a rare blade. It's a jewel of

a thing.' Then if you do not trust to answer or the other smith does not know of such a thing as king's steel, you give thanks for the generous appraisal. But if the man is a master like yourself and you need to speak of this, the answer is, 'Thank you; I think it a jewel fit for a king.' Then you will know you speak to your equal."

Edvalt stopped speaking. After a moment, as if anticipating something remarkable in his life, he looked around slowly. Declan followed the sweep of his vision and saw what Edvalt saw.

The smithy was located at the west end of the village of Oncon. Their location kept them downwind most of the time from the other inhabitants, so the smoke, soot, and noise was less bothersome. That was a happy accident of terrain and weather; the location of the smithy had been chosen because of the ample supply of water from the well and easy access to the road above.

Edvalt continued to look into the distance, and Declan tried to guess what Edvalt was seeing. Declan recalled little of his life before coming here at roughly five years old. Still, he paused and took in what Edvalt was watching, because something about this moment seemed vital to the smith.

The ancient village of Oncon lay on Covenant lands near the kingdom of Ilcomen and was typical of many of the Covenant communities. So close to the border,

it fared poorly in bounty from travelers; most continued on eastward to the village of Bashe, or westward to
Ilagan, the first town of Ilcomen. It was an unfortunate
traveler who timed his journey such that he needed
to spend the night at Oncon's excuse for an inn; there
were no rooms and guests would sleep on the floor,
even under the tables. The town survived on trade
with local farms, mostly sheep destined for Ilagan's
spring fair, and there were enough fish from the sea to
feed everyone. No one was rich in Oncon, but no one
starved.

The local area, called the Narrows, was a bottleneck
between the Western and Eastern Realms, and the fast
route for traveling between North and South Tembria.
It had changed over the years, slowly at first, but lately
things seemed to be getting more dangerous. The Covenant was still being observed for the most part, but
rumors of troubles in the east heading their way had
caused Edvalt to caution the rest of the villagers to keep
alert to strangers and be ready in case of trouble.

Declan occasionally wondered about that larger
world away from his home village. He could see the occasional ship pass by if he was outside the smithy, and
sometimes wondered where it was from.

This village, in the small area known as the Covenant,
bridging North and South Tembria, was Declan's world.

The rest of Garn consisted of five smaller continents. The two closest, Alastor and Enast, were populated by barbarians and warlords, some self-proclaimed kings, gathered in city-states and holdfasts, but they were considered unworthy of mention by civilized men. Only traders and outlaws risked traveling there. Or that was what he had been told as a boy by those who stopped to have horses shod, or their wheel band or yoke repaired, and took a moment to speak to a curious boy. One man had actually claimed to have traveled to Alastor, where he met men who had been to the other side of the world.

All that was known of the other three continents was their names; their locations were often contested by mapmakers, and they were reputed to be home to monsters, malignant spirits, practitioners of the darkest magic, and a multitude of horrors and wonders. Declan had always doubted those claims. He had met enough travelers and overheard enough boasting at the little inn in Oncon to know stories grew with time and ale.

But he only knew Oncon.

Declan thought it wasn't a bad place to live. He enjoyed the weather, for the seasons along the shores of the Narrows were clement: summers warm, winters mild. There was always ample food and ale. The sea breeze picked up, as it did this time of day, and Declan drank in its cool freshness; he realized he was tired to his bones and parched.

Taking a drink from the bucket, Declan looked up to see Edvalt watching him. Just loud enough to be heard, the old smith softly asked, "What do you see, boy?"

Declan smiled. "Home."

Edvalt nodded. "Aye, and not a bad one as such things go." He put his hand on Declan's shoulder. "When you came here, you traveled with a family that wasn't your own. They apprenticed you to me in exchange for fixing their wagon . . ." His voice fell away. "It took only one glance to see their story was true, for you were a large boy, with eager eyes, and their children were all small, frightened things." He chuckled. "Mila was so angry that I'd taken in a lad who would be no help to us for years, for you were so young. Yet from the start you sought to earn your keep, struggling to haul the big coal scuttle, or bravely holding the fractious horses while I shoed them.

"But you won her over, lad." He lowered his voice. "You're the best I've trained, Declan, and if I had a son of my own, I would want him to be like you. Should you wish to start out on your own, I understand, but if you've a mind to agree, I would be pleased for you to take this forge as your own."

"You've a lot of good years left, Edvalt, and I don't

know if . . . I don't know." Declan hesitated. He wasn't entirely sure how Edvalt's offer made him feel. "I've been of a mind to set out and find my own way, settle down with a good woman, start my own family."

"Not a bad choice. Think on it. For today I pronounce you a master smith and my equal."

"Never that, master."

Edvalt's eyes showed his feelings, but being a man of few words, he could only put his hand on the young man's shoulder, squeezing it lightly before he turned and headed into his home.

Declan remained alone for a while, as fatigue and emotion threatened to overwhelm him. Then after a few minutes, he followed Edvalt into the house.

3

Dangerous Discovery

Dockworkers hauled the ship into its berth in the north dock of the city of Sandura. Seven men pulled on a thick hawser, while two youngsters quickly arranged the wooden fenders between its hull and dock, so that the tidal motion of the sea wouldn't damage the ship as it rubbed against the stone. It had arrived in port on the morning tide, but by the time a harbor boat with a hawser had rowed out and tossed lines to the crew in the prow, it was nearing noon.

Hatu finished reefing the sails and slid down a rope to the railing, jumped over it, and made for the sailors' deck, where his go-bag was stored. The deck crew made fast everything that needed to be tied down, while Hatu and the rest of the aloft crew headed belowdecks.

As Hatu wended his way through the clutter of sailors to his hammock, he saw many of the men removing leather neck thongs and untying small objects from their belt loops. He recognized them as various icons of Othan, goddess of the sea and weather, and realized the crew were hiding them in various spots on the sailors' deck. Hatu understood that meant they were now somewhere the Church of the One held sway and to be seen with any item associated with an old god could land a man on top of a heretic's pyre.

On reaching the main deck, Hatu spied Master Bodai. Seeing the boy, he motioned for him to come stand at his side. When the youngster reached the man playing the part of a mendicant friar, Bodai said, "We wait." He leaned on a shoulder-high walking stick, almost a battle staff but not as conspicuous, though Hatu was certain Master Bodai could employ it as such with lethal effect should the occasion warrant.

It took Hatu a moment to realize that the play had begun; as one of the most important masters in Coaltachin, Bodai would usually be first off the ship, but here, as an impoverished monk, he would be among the last passengers to leave.

When the passenger before them had departed, Bodai put his hand on Hatu's shoulder. "Be ready," he instructed.

Hatu nodded. He had questions but knew they would keep until a more private moment; until then, he would simply follow instructions and Brother Bodai's lead. Hatu fell into step behind Bodai, moving last onto the gangplank, keeping his head down, and attempting to look the part of an inconsequential servant.

On the dock, they were just steps away from the gangplank when two men approached, a soldier with the yellow and red badge of Sandura on his tunic, and another wearing a large black badge with a solid white circle at its center: the sign of the One.

It was the servant of the Church of the One who spoke, "Who are you, traveler?"

"Brother Chasper, late of Turana, an island of Lanobly."

"Brother?" he replied. "You wear no vestment or badge."

The newly named Chasper smiled broadly and said, "I am a mendicant friar of the Order of the Harbinger. This is my beggar boy, Venley."

A look of confusion crossed the soldier's face and the officer of the Church looked annoyed. "We expected an episkopos of your order and his retinue . . ." He left the sentence unfinished and made a general circular motion encompassing the itinerant monk.

"The episkopos hasn't arrived?" said Bodai, feigning alarm. "I was supposed to join him, to then carry news . . ." He gave a sigh that Hatu, now named Venley, thought a bit too theatrical.

It worked, however, as the church official waved them toward the city and said, "Go down the main boulevard, across the small plaza, and take the northern street on the other side, two crossings, then west again until you see the burned-out building that was once your order's temple." He almost spat the last word, for all buildings of the One were called churches. The followers of Tathan had been among the first to modify their doctrine to integrate themselves into the Church of the One, claiming the god of purity had been only a prophet, the Harbinger of the One. Many in the church viewed the followers of Tathan as only slightly better than heretics.

Bodai nodded, bowed slightly, and then pushed Hatu's shoulder in the direction the man had indicated.

When they were safely away, Bodai said, "Interesting, don't you think?"

Hatu glanced at his master and waited for a moment to see if the question had been rhetorical or if the old man actually sought his opinion. Finally, he nodded agreement.

"What do you judge from that?" asked Bodai.

Hatu thought about that question for a moment,

then said, "They're looking for someone, or they're worried about strangers, perhaps both. The manner in which they questioned you, brother, makes me think that the Church of the One is concerned about something, and that the king is supporting them." He shrugged.

Bodai nodded once. "Look around, what do you see?"

Hatu did a quick survey of the long street. When they neared the plaza, he said, "It's a beautiful day."

"Yes, it is," agreed Bodai. "The weather here is often overcast and dark, cloudy, or raining, but today, sunshine. What else?"

As they entered the small plaza, Hatushaly looked around, taking a moment to appraise their surroundings, then said, "This is far from a happy place." Rather than busy market stalls, which he would have expected to see in any city he visited, only a few people moved around a small, well-kept, but otherwise unremarkable fountain in the center of the plaza.

"Why do you say that?" asked Bodai as he paused before the water, reached in, and made a show of rubbing his face and neck.

Hatu followed his example and leaned over the water to freshen up before he replied, "No one lingers here. There are no sellers, despite this being a wonderful market, so someone—the king?" he speculated. "Or someone important has decided to keep this plaza free of merchants." Hatu splashed a little water on his own face, glancing around as he wiped it with his hands. "They don't want people gathering here. There are three armed men in identical garb: the city guard? For a place this size, with so few people, there are too many soldiers. They watch. People passing near to them avert their eyes. We saw the same behavior on the streets from the docks."

"Enough," whispered Bodai, shaking his hands as if ridding them of excess water. "Come along."

Hatu followed the counterfeit monk through the streets as instructed by the church official. They found the site of the former Temple of Tathan, now a skeleton of burned timbers and an altar charred black. Rain and wind had scoured the abandoned building of ash and cinders, and they could walk across the stone floor without turning their sandaled feet black.

"Some time ago," said Bodai softly, "the king of this dolorous nation embraced the Church of the One. All other gods and goddesses were pronounced lesser and demonic beings, and in their enthusiasm to rid the city of the evil places of worship, the king's soldiers got a little carried away. They failed to remember that this order had contrived a narrative, a wonderful story that named Tathan the Pure a prophetic being, a heavenly messenger who proclaimed the coming of the One."

The false monk knocked on a still-upright timber with his staff. "Hmmm, with some good craftsmen, this place might be restored sooner than I thought." As if musing to himself, he muttered, "Scrape off this char, see how much good timber is left . . ."

After studying the burned timber, Bodai came out of his reverie. "Now, as I was saying, this king was the first monarch of stature to elevate the Church of the One above all others, and by seizing this opportunity Lodavico Sentarzi, ruler of Sandura"—he lowered his voice—"known widely as 'the King of Sorrows,' not only gained a new title, 'His Most Holy Majesty,' which he seems to find most agreeable, but gave the Church of the One an official base from which to operate, a home, as it were. Word reached us some months ago that the ancient city of Sandura"—he gestured to their surroundings—"was now being called 'the Holy City,' which also seems to please Lodavico.

"You will learn that some places are often very important," Bodai continued. He found a relatively clean piece of masonry, a support for an interior wall now missing, and sat. He motioned for Hatu to sit at his side. "The obvious places are defensible positions along routes others wish to take or occupy, or advantageous sites from which to launch assaults. Being near a good water supply and fertile land, a tidy harbor, or other natural features often persuaded people to choose a place to build a city, or rather they did in ages past; we do not see a lot of cities being built now, do we?"

Hatu could see it was a rhetorical question and so said nothing, merely nodding his understanding and agreement.

"Other important places are symbolic: Sites where great battles were undertaken, so we remember the victors' heroics or lament the loss of the vanquished. Or the holy places." He motioned out of the burned doorway, and Hatu looked up at the high plateau barely visible above the rooftop of the building across the street. "Up there," continued Bodai, "the Church is constructing their most holy place: a cathedral, the grandest of their churches and the seat of an epis-kopos. Only this cathedral will be the home of many episkopos, their entire ruling council." He sighed the-atrically, sounding, in Hatu's opinion, far too amused, and said, "And they're building it right next to His Most Holy Majesty's palace."

Hatu looked confused. "But—"

"That compromises the defensible position of Lo-davico's castle, I know." Bodai waved his hand around, indicating the entire city. "His castle is now a citadel given how much his capital has grown since his fore-fathers built the fortress. Should an army knock at its gates, the addition of the cathedral will hardly matter. He will have already lost the war." He smiled at Hatu. "But it's good to see that you pay attention when your preceptors speak about military history. Unlike that rock-headed friend of yours."

Hatu tried not to smile, for he knew Bodai was speaking of Donte. Being the grandson of one of the seven masters on the Council had often saved Donte from receiving more severe punishments he deserved. Any other student would have been sent away for several of his infractions, and certainly for the number of rules Hatu's friend had broken over the years.

As a boy, Donte had been merely fractious, but as he grew older, his behavior had turned to a near-constant defiance. Hatu judged that within a few years Donte could be a crew captain, or perhaps a gang captain, or even dead, but he doubted his friend would rise to his father's and grandfather's status. He might have a chance if he learned to curb his impulses, but Hatu doubted Donte would ever become a master.

Students who were sent away from the schools when they were little, returned to their parents, were apprenticed to crafts in the town, or sent to work on farms or in fishing villages. But after a certain age, when certain secrets had been learned . . . Hatu didn't care to think about it but had made the assumption that those students were discreetly murdered.

That was the curse of the chosen: to be selected to train as a sicari and potentially become a member of the Quelli Nascosti, the secret army of Coaltachin, meant that after a certain point you would know too much to be allowed to leave. Hatu sensed that he, Hava, and Donte were close to that point. While certain intricacies about the inner workings of the army were still kept from students of their age and experience, Hatu had observed enough to extrapolate how the Coaltachin nation might be organized, and little of what he had been told of late had come as a surprise, which had bolstered his confidence. Remembering the conversation he shared with his friends after being scolded by the gang boss Hilsbek, Hatu realized that they had perhaps already passed that point. Hatu was uncertain, for he had little more than speculation to go on. There was an old saying about what happened within powerful families when someone like a Donte failed to rise: "Those who know don't talk, and those who talk don't know."

For the deepest secret of the Kingdom of Night was that, beyond its islands, it represented the largest, most extensive criminal empire on Garn. Coaltachin was not a kingdom, as there was no king, but it was ruled by a council of seven masters, each of whom controlled a "family." Within these families were the regimes who directed many gangs across many cities.

Council titles usually passed from family member to family member—unless a family was displaced by another, more powerful family, often at the cost of bloodshed and the creation of factions; this organization had been formed to settle such disputes and, most important of all, to protect an ancient way of life. Master Zusara was the final arbiter for issues that the Council was unable to settle, and while masters might contest with one another, all united against outsiders.

Criminal activity provided the island nation with the bulk of its wealth, but the agents sent around the world to work on behalf of distant rulers, or affluent merchants, provided the most vital commodities: they uncovered critical economic and political intelligence before anyone else; they produced significant riches, for the services of the island nation did not come cheaply; but their most important commodity of all was information, and their most potent weapon was fear. Those above who were crew bosses and regime bosses were sicari. Not only the best fighters, they had to be smart enough to command criminals and maintain effective control over their gangs.

Above the sicari were the *nocusara*. The term meant

"invisible," "hidden," or "unseen" and was reserved for only the most skilled sicari, those who achieved the highest level of training and trust. They were the legendary ghost warriors: the assassins, spies, and agents of the Kingdom of Night who could enter any building, no matter how well guarded, and take the life of any ruler. They were the agents who diverted information and gained some nobles power over their rivals. Most of their reputation was due to clever planning, theatrical tricks, and selecting agents who were suited and trained for specific tasks. While not supernatural beings, the nocusara were among the finest-trained assassins and warriors on Garn, the very best of the sicari.

The Kingdom of Night relied on its reputation, well earned by the Quelli Nascosti and their sicari, but for the most part it was a nation of thugs, bandits, confidence tricksters, thieves, and smugglers. Practically none of the significant criminal activity across the eastern half of North Tembria or the northeast quadrant of South Tembria, or even in the Ten Thousand Islands, was undertaken without Coaltachin's notice or participation. And none of it occurred without their tacit approval.

As was his nature, Hatu had countless questions, but painful experience had taught him to keep them to himself unless an opportunity for him to ask without repercussions presented itself. Master Bodai's playful reference to Donte's behavior was not permission to press forward with unwelcome questions, and might even have been a test of some sort; the masters and preceptors often lured students into logic or behavior traps to judge, correct, or punish as the situation warranted.

Bodai said, "We shall wait here, though I think not for too long. A day or two more; perhaps one or two beyond that." He looked around and said, "But tonight we shall act like dutiful members of a questionable sect under the fastest-rising power in this world. And also we need to eat." He looked at Hatu. "Bowl?"

Hatu pulled open his go-bag and withdrew a simple wooden bowl, slightly flatter and wider than a soup bowl. He had used it for his meals, but it now became his beggar's bowl.

"We shall begin the mummery in earnest tomorrow." Bodai threw some small coins into the bowl. "There is a larger square three streets west of here, the second largest in this city, and at the northwest corner you'll find an alehouse. It is not one of ours, but we have agents there. Should anything befall me, that is where you must go and ask for a man called Luke. Do you know what to say to him?"

Hatu nodded once. "I'm traveling from an island to the east."

Bodai smiled. That was the correct code to identify someone from Coaltachin in need of assistance.

"Do not go there for any other reason, unless you are in dire need." Sitting back, ignoring the soot on the wall behind him, Bodai slapped both hands on his knees. "To the south of there, across the mouth of the most northwestern street and three doors down, is a bakery. There, you will haggle for a bit with the owner for a loaf of bread—he makes an excellent one with rosemary and a hint of garlic—and as you return, you'll pass a cheese vendor. Buy something not too far gone, with only a bit of mold, and finally get a skin of wine. Manage that on the coins I gave you."

Hatu glanced at the sky and saw it was barely past noon. "How long should I linger, brother?"

"As long as it takes to overhear gossip, discover interesting rumors, or ascertain anything of value. Now go!"

Hatu gripped his beggar bowl and said, "Yes, brother," and was off.

Hatushaly wandered with purpose, changing his walking pace and never lingering overly long in one spot. The market was a fair size; he could weave his way completely through it in slightly over an hour. He moved neither too fast nor too slowly, careful not to attract attention, and knew better than to approach any merchant's stall too closely. A beggar boy near to their wares would instantly draw scrutiny from any experienced merchant, for the grab-and-dash was a constant threat they endured. The more valuable goods were always placed near the back of the booths; some merchants organized their tables into open squares, so you had to enter the stall to fully inspect the merchandise, while smaller stalls with a single table front challenged a thief to reach to the back of the booth to steal the better-quality goods, an action sure to bring a club or blade crashing down on all but the quickest miscreants before they could escape.

Hatu also made a quick surveillance of the area of the city between the plaza with its market and the main road that ran up the hill to the citadel where the cathedral was under construction. From the northeast corner of the square, the road wended its way upward, doubling back and rising rapidly from the northern edge of the plaza; it was fenced or walled until it reached the edge of the grounds abutting the old castle. The main road was busy, and from what he had learned, the establishments closest to the old castle were likely to be the oldest and most successful, for their proprietors could quickly retreat into the castle if the city were attacked, while those below were more likely to be sacked.

Hatu's first impression of this city was reinforced by the mood and manner of the people in the market. Too many watchmen patrolled the area, and when he passed one of them Hatu did his best to imitate a local going about his business, but if it was safe, he watched the crowd. He looked for vantage points where he could pause for a few minutes and observe. There was no hint of joy in the noise surrounding him. In most open markets you would hear the occasional laugh, or the sound of music if entertainers were earning coins, but here in Sandura the population seemed suspicious, as if constantly under watch, and by now Hatu was of the opinion that they were.

Finishing up his last task, finding an inexpensive but palatable wine, he began his journey back to Bodai, constantly observing as much as possible. For once he was pleased Donte was not with him. Subtlety was not among his friend's good qualities; he seemed to have a need to call attention to himself at the worst possible moments. It was as if Donte couldn't stand quiet. Hatu wondered how he would do once he left the school; he didn't seem to fit the role of sicari. Perhaps Donte would do well in the more traditional, if modest, army of the Coaltachin nation. Or perhaps he would rise to be a regime captain, responsible for running multiple crews in one or more cities.

Hatu would have welcomed Hava's company. She had an almost perfect set of abilities and an even-tempered nature that would serve a mission like this well. Her presence both calmed and excited him, and lately his feelings toward her were becoming more complicated. She had been his friend and confidant for almost a lifetime, but she confused him. He didn't know if she understood him or simply accepted him. In an environment where everyone had tried to either change him or find his flaws, she had taken him just as he was.

He'd been with girls before: the town girls were more than pleased to have sex with the students, for the chance to become the wife of a captain, or even a master, was perhaps their only opportunity to rise in station above their parents. Hatu never heard of it happening, but the daydream lived on. But his feelings for Hava were more complicated than simple desire. He struggled to put a name to them, though familiarity and comfort were there. He felt a growing desire, but students were not permitted to have sex with each other. Such attachments were forbidden, and should a talented girl like Hava become pregnant, the boy involved would be given a death sentence.

Hatu pushed Hava out of his mind as he realized he was becoming distracted. He paused to look around and take stock of what he had missed, then returned to the task at hand. Circling back through the market to where he'd started, having found nothing noteworthy to report, he finally reached the burned-out temple, where he found Brother Chasper dozing. However, as he neared Hatu saw it was a ruse; Master Bodai had been watching the passing traffic closely. Without looking up, he said, "Anything?"

Hatu shook his head. "Nothing unusual: normal market commerce, people arguing, others speaking of family, business, gossip." He shrugged.

"Ah," said the older man, making a show of awakening. "Good, I am hungry."

"Shall I find wood for a fire?" asked Hatu.

Shaking his head, Bodai said, "Cold camp tonight. Besides, nothing we have needs cooking."

Hatu had the merchant wrap the bread, cheese, and wine in stiff paper that rustled loudly as he unfolded it into a makeshift platter. Without a word, Bodai took the small slice of cheese and broke it in half, tore off a large hunk of bread, and began eating.

The meal passed with little conversation, as Bodai was intent on studying those who passed on the road as the late afternoon wore on to evening. Hatu drank sparingly of the wine. He honestly couldn't tell if it was good or not, as drinking wine and other spirits was still new to him, and he had a slight dread of becoming intoxicated. He hated the feeling of being out of control.

As they finished their scant meal, Bodai said, "How do you feel about some after-dark prowling?"

Hatu smiled. The old man wasn't asking if he was willing but informing him of what he would be doing. "That should depend on where you're sending me."

Without a word, Bodai looked above the building across the street and Hatu realized he was about to be sent to investigate the new cathedral next to the palace, and its surroundings, perhaps inside the citadel itself should they find a way in. He took a breath to calm himself and began mentally retracing his steps through the city leading to the road up to the old castle. Now he wished he had paid a little more attention to the route.

Earlier in the day, Hatu had chanced a quick journey up the road leading to the plateau above the city. For this evening's foray, he hurried past a row of businesses preparing to shut down for the night and quickly entered a shop near the top of the winding road leading up to the palace, one that was about to close. He wanted to avoid attracting the attention of the guards at the end of the road, denying them a glimpse of anyone unusually close to their post.

Hatu nodded to the vendor of fine cloth and glanced around for a moment as the merchant narrowed his gaze at the scruffy-looking lad; then, with a smile, Hatu darted back through the door, hugging the wall and insinuating himself between this building and the next. He crouched and glanced around, hoping his movement hadn't been seen in the failing light.

The bored-looking guards showed no sign of having spotted him, as they chatted about something across the distance between them—one stationed on each side of the gate—their subject unintelligible to Hatu. He studied closely what he had only glanced at for a few seconds earlier in the day.

A gate and a cleared area of ground lay before the entrance to the citadel. The ancient stone walls sat a good distance from the edge of the plateau. Hatu had been taught some military history and theory, so he assumed there was a reason for that clearing but had no idea what it was. He imagined that it might be transformed into a road leading to the cathedral, but he knew nothing about engineering, so how that could be achieved was a question he would have to ponder another time, should such curiosity return to visit him.

He had difficulty understanding the differences

between temples, churches, and cathedrals, all of which seemed interchangeable in his mind; they were all places people went to worship. Their size, if anything, seemed to have significance. Hatu had seen a few temples in out-of-the-way places, a couple of which had still been in use, and for the most part they were modest buildings, perhaps as large as a decent inn. A few had even been small enough to be called shrines, with just a roof and a single bench. Churches were not much bigger but tended to be far gaudier, from what he could remember. The cathedral on the plateau, however, seemed to be a massive undertaking.

One point of its construction struck Hatu as odd: a tower had been built that seemed to look down into the old marshaling yard on the east side of the palace. He felt an itch of annoyance that some key information was evading him and pushed it aside to concentrate on the task at hand: to get past the guards at the gate. Slipping past them would be impossible. The gate was closed for the night, and had a door in it that only one person at a time could pass through.

Hatu looked back along the narrow passage between the two buildings and saw a crate nestled against the side of the next building. He could easily use it to jump to the roof.

He had run rooftops before, though he had no love

for it, especially alone and in the dark. The crate seemed providential, as he had no companions to boost or catch him. He wasn't completely certain, but he thought he could clear the gaps between the buildings to reach the last roof before the gate.

The tricky part of roof jumping was the landing. To aim for the peak of the roof was ideal, as it would be braced and solid. Stories were told in school about students crashing through thin thatch with no support, old flimsy tiles, or even thin sheets of wood. But the problem with aiming for the peak was that it was a narrow target, often mere inches wide, and missing it, losing your balance, and rolling off the eaves was as bad an outcome as crashing through the roof.

A successful landing on any roof could be noisy, so it had been drilled into him only to try that if he was running for his life. Some stone tiles were tricky, as well. Nailed shingles were best. He had studied the rooftops earlier in the day as a matter of habit and those along this street seemed to be heavy tiles or wooden shingles, so he thought he had a good chance to reach the cathedral this way.

He hurried to the crate, saw it was sturdy wood, and easily gained the top of the first roof. There were four more houses and he crouched low, timed his first jump, and landed as silently as he could, very close to the peak. While it sounded a little too loud to him, Hatu realized anyone not standing directly below where he'd landed was unlikely to have noticed the noise.

Hatu reached the edge of the penultimate roof and judged the distance to the last. He realized it was only slightly further than takeoff to landing in a yard game he had played when he was younger; he reconsidered his run and jump, took two steps back, and executed a simple hop, squat, and jump, and landed with both feet squarely on the peak of the final roof with barely a sound.

Feeling uncharacteristically smug for a moment, Hatu tiptoed quickly along the peak and reached the end of the roof. In times past, a wall might have existed along the edge of the plateau, long since torn down as the city erected more distant outer walls. Nothing remained but some irregular mounds, probably foundation stones covered by centuries of earth, rising and falling at irregular intervals.

The remaining wall lay across the road, complete with a massive gate and guards. The building Hatu stood upon constituted a barrier blocking access to the citadel.

He judged the width of the wall that almost abutted the building, to see where he might land safely, but those points were too far away to make any reasonable attempt at jumping down.

He reversed his position and lowered himself to hang from the eaves, then dropped, remaining as silent as possible. He bent his knees when he landed and continued into a low crouch, turning to look at the guards by the gate.

Hatu had landed where the corner of the building almost met the gate wall. A small child might have been able to slip through the gap, but not a grown man. He assumed that the remaining gate was for local security, not military defense, for an invading army would have had to fight its way through the entire city to reach this position, and leveling the house behind him would most certainly take less time than battering down that old gate with a ram.

He looked at the rear of the building, suddenly concerned about how he was going to get back to Bodai, and realized that a pile of refuse and broken masonry had created a makeshift wall between where he stood near the edge of the building and the edge of the plateau. Hatu tried to inspect it as best he could in the dim light of the gate lamps and soon hoped that he did not have to depart in a hurry. Then he spied a sturdy-looking small crate, or more correctly a large wooden box. He gingerly moved toward it, as he had no idea what he might be stepping on among the debris, and his role as a beggar boy demanded he wear poor footwear. He was relieved to find the box met his requirements; it was sturdy enough that he could stand on it and boost himself back onto the roof when he needed to take his leave.

Hatu removed it as quietly as he could, hoisted it over his head, and slowly returned to the edge of the building, keeping the closest guard in sight through the narrow gap as best he could. He was far enough away from the corner of the gate wall that as long as the guard didn't completely turn around Hatu would remain unseen. All he needed to do was not make noise, Hatu reminded himself. The guard looked half-asleep and Hatu could hear him muttering with his companion on the other side of the gate, though he still couldn't make out the words.

Hatu reached the wall and set the crate down. Moving back a step, he judged that if he got a decent start he could hop on the crate and reach the eaves; then he'd be able to pull himself up to the roof. He let out a breath of relief, though he still wondered how quietly he could accomplish the feat. Then again, he considered, if he was in a hurry, stealth was probably not required.

He glanced around, considering how best to get nearer to the cathedral. He'd already risked tripping over debris and building materials, so he thought staying as far away from the building as he could and seeking a clear route to it was best. He made his way slowly to the verge of the plateau, painfully aware that the rooftops below hidden in the darkness were far enough down to ensure his rapid demise should he slip. The light from the castle walls, cast by torches set about ten feet apart, provided little illumination, and the half-built cathedral looked like some ill-defined monster crouching in the darkness. It was cool and damp, as the ocean air brought in enough mist to make seeing more difficult than usual. Good for escaping detection, but terrible for finding one's way.

Hatu wondered what possible reason Bodai had for sending him up here, unless he was trying to get his student caught, for Hatushaly saw no opportunity to observe the citadel at this point and the cathedral appeared empty. He supposed the old master wanted him to crawl around the half-finished building in case secret rooms or strange additions were being built, but how he was supposed to recognize them was a mystery to Hatu. He knew nothing of construction, never having apprenticed in any of the building trades, save occasionally helping to repair a hut in a village, and beyond personal instruments of combat, large weaponry was as much of a mystery to him as masonry and scaffold-ing. He could have tripped over an unassembled bal-lista and had no idea what it was. And one empty room looked much like another, rarely revealing any special purpose.

A large pallet of masonry, a table, and a huge box of tools and supplies lay between Hatu and the completed entrance to the cathedral. Below the table, which was empty, sat a long box containing papers that Hatu as-sumed were plans for the cathedral. For a moment he considered inspecting them as best he could in the faint light from the street below, though he doubted he would learn much. Never having worked around this scale of building, he'd never studied plans before. He considered taking them, then decided it was better to leave them undisturbed. Hatu was wondering about the safest way to creep into the building site when he heard a voice call out faintly.

Hatu ducked behind the tall stack of facing stones—marble or granite slabs, he couldn't be sure which—and heard the voice grow louder as someone approached. It was calling out a name. He chanced a quick glance and saw one man approaching from the keep and another exiting the cathedral to greet him. When they met, he could make out what was being said, but Hatu didn't recognize the language. It was naggingly familiar, a few words here and there were almost recognizable, but he was not able to grasp what was said.

Again, Hatu glanced around the corner of the stone blocks and saw the two men pause and continue their conversation before the half-constructed entrance to the cathedral. One carried a partially shuttered lantern, emitting just enough light to let them step safely through the clutter of rock and debris, but not easily spied from any distance.

Hatu felt the hair rise on his neck and arms as he realized that the style of one of the two men—dark clothing, head covering, and soft footwear—looked familiar. He looked like a sicari!

His companion seemed to be wearing something akin to the fashion of the church official he and Bodai had met at the docks.

Hatu remained motionless and hoped he did nothing to betray his presence. If there were sicari here, he would be dead the moment they discovered him.

The two men entered the cathedral, and when they had disappeared into the darkness Hatu crouched low and forced himself to be calm. He concentrated on slowing his breathing, which in turn slowed his heart, which had for a few moments felt as if it were about to burst through his chest. As he relaxed, he recognized just how close he had come to panic. Without his training, he most likely would have been dead now.

Hatu considered his options. He could return at once and inform Bodai of what he had seen, but he knew that the old master would ask many questions for which he had no answers, and he would, in all likelihood, be ordered to return. He realized he had only one option.

Hatu continued trying to stay composed. He had no idea if the two men were already deep within the structure or just inside the entrance, so he ruled out following them directly through the dark, half-finished doorway and instead moved quickly and silently to crouch behind a segment of unfinished wall on the right side of the door. He heard the voices fading and the faint tread of boots on the stone floor as the two men walked deeper into the cathedral.

Hatu took a step to his left and peered in at the corner of the cathedral doorway. When it was completed, Hatu imagined the frame would be hung with some massive wooden thing, at least twenty feet across, given the size of the opening. The faint light from the men's lanterns was moving further away, indicating that the two men were moving deeper inside the massive building.

He quickly tossed aside following them through the door. Since he had no idea what sort of obstacles, what potential cover, or how many other people might lie in the gloom inside, it was too risky.

He moved quickly to the left corner of the cathedral and peered around it. The connecting wall was still a low course of stones just high enough for Hatu to hide behind. He ducked and began to walk just outside the wall on a parallel course to what he judged to be the one taken by the two men from the doorway.

Hatu tried to ignore the fact that any mistake on his part would likely result in his death. The main purpose of his training, like that of all students of Coaltachin, was not to be detected. He focused on employing every trick and skill he had learned so far.

Duck-walking, as it was called, was difficult even for a gifted youngster like Hatu; his thighs and hips were protesting painfully when he heard the voices again from within the shadows and paused gratefully. He straightened slowly and glanced over his shoulder, memorizing the way, in case he found himself leaving this location in a hurry. There was just enough light that he could see darker shapes in the gloom, with an occasional reflection from a source in the city below.

Hatu knew there were tools and stones piled by the corner he had just passed, so if he had to flee and not run face-first into them, he might survive. If he could get clear of this cathedral, reach the crates he had placed near the gate across the main road, and reach the first roof . . . Hatu left the thought unfinished. Dwelling on too many things at once caused mistakes, like doing something stupid that was not conducive to calm observation and invisibility.

He could still hear the faint voices of the men some distance away. The darkness was a blessing and a curse. He could barely see where to put his feet, but it sheltered him from scrutiny. Hatu turned his head slightly, trying to detect the direction from which the voices originated.

He took a deep breath and let it out slowly as he pulled himself atop the low stone course. Hatu assumed that more stones were added each day, and he silently thanked whatever deities were listening that he wasn't trying this the following week. He lowered himself gingerly to the floor inside the cathedral, then stopped to listen again.

Large stone pillars that would eventually support the ceiling rose from the stone floor, and from their size Hatu guessed the roof was going to be very high up and very heavy. Each pillar was three feet thick, wide enough for him to hide behind if he was careful.

He moved as cautiously as possible, hoping the occasional noise from the street below the citadel and the early night rustling of nocturnal animals and birds would mask whatever sounds he might make: dislodging a forgotten tool, hunk of stone, or loose lump of dried mortar. It made his movements seem impossibly slow, but Hatu knew he was making steady progress toward the two mysterious men.

The voices grew more distinct as he neared the two men, and he could now make out a third voice. He positioned himself behind a pillar and listened for a moment, then he crouched down and looked around the stonework. Hatu saw figures faintly outlined in the glow from a brazier. Four men knelt around the fire, speaking quietly with the two men Hatu had followed.

The brazier was one typically used for cooking and heating, a small earthenware dish hard-fired to withstand the heat of the coals and designed to give off little light; on Coaltachin it was called a hibachi. It helped Hatu detect movement but provided no great detail; from where he watched, it appeared that the four men wore black, or at least very dark, clothing, but he could barely make out shapes, let alone identification marks.

He judged the usefulness of lingering here: despite feeling a nagging familiarity toward the language, he could not understand what was being said, and he could hear only half of the conversation because the men kept their voices low.

Then Hatu heard a word he recognized. It was immediately repeated by one of the men he had followed, but his inflection made it a question. Hatu's heart skipped and he forced himself to calm in order to focus on what was being said. Squatting as low as he could, he peered further around the corner, and suddenly understood what he was hearing.

He pulled back around the corner and flattened himself against the stonework, panic threatening to rise inside as his heart began to pound. He forced himself to stillness, keeping his breathing slow, rather than deep, a calming practice he'd learned early. Once he fully had control of himself, he peered around the corner of the pillar. His training had taught him that if anyone looked his way they wouldn't be staring at the floor. He would then freeze and hope it was dark enough to hide. If it wasn't dark enough, he'd know it only moments later.

Then one of the kneeling men stood and walked to a low course of stones waiting to be hoisted up onto the growing wall and opened a shuttered lantern.

Hatu froze, his cheek hard against the cold floor, fighting every instinct he had not to pull out of sight. He had been taught to hide behind as much cover as possible, but every fiber of his being wanted to bolt and run as fast as he could. He knew movement in low light drew the eye, while an odd shape in the gloom was less likely to garner attention. From the perspective of those in the room, should someone glance his way, his head would seem nothing more than an odd-shaped stone, but any movement would give him away. He forced himself to believe in the sense of this mantra, and slowly he realized he was safe; none of the men were looking his way. Then he slowly and silently let out his breath and continued to watch them.

The man holding the lantern returned to the group and removed a folded paper from within a leather packet. He handed it to one of the two men Hatu had followed. Hatu felt the hair on his neck rise a second time. The four men around the brazier were also dressed like sicari, the armed assassins and spies of Coaltachin, but with slight differences, which were numerous enough to make Hatu certain they were not from his home nation.

Again the men spoke, and the man with the document pointed to it in response and repeated the phrase containing words that Hatu recognized.

Hatu stayed motionless, to remain part of a murky landscape. He knew that he had to leave as soon as possible and report to the false monk waiting for him.

The man holding the paper returned it to the packet and closed the shutter on the lamp. Hatu seized the moment to move and hide once again behind the pillar.

He knew that even a small change of illumination would force the eyes of those in the room to adjust and cause a brief moment of darkness; he had a very good chance to remain unseen. But he also knew that any change in light would not keep him from being heard should he make any sound.

Back to the stone, he forced his protesting knees to push him upright, and when he was standing, his back to the sheltering pillar, he settled his mind for a moment, took control of his breathing, then stepped, deeper into the darkness.

He retraced his steps as slowly and with as much control as he could muster. As he moved further from the gathered men, each new yard fueled his desire to simply leap over the low wall and run; only discipline gained from lifelong lessons prevented him from giving in to the impulse. When Hatu reached the wall near the unfinished doorway, he eased himself over and down, landing lightly on the balls of his feet.

He tried to stay clear of any line of sight from within through the huge door opening but moved quickly, one step shy of a run, until he saw the crate he had left next to the building. He risked three fast steps and a jump onto the box, grabbed the eaves of the roof, and pulled himself up. If the guards at the gate noticed any noise, Hatu would be off across the roofs of the next three buildings before they had the chance to climb up and investigate.

Hatu reached the edge of the final roof, and with no sign of pursuit, he sat. His heart felt as if it might pound out of his chest and he could barely breathe. He took some time to steady himself and, when he was ready, lowered himself to the ground and rounded the corner into the street that would return him to the market and the burned-out temple beyond. The beggar boy walked at a good pace, fast enough to look like someone with purpose: the sort of behavior that often kept petty thieves, pickpockets, and thugs from approaching, that hinted they would do well to seek easier prey. Even a ragged beggar boy might have something worth stealing. It was early enough in the night that people still moved through the streets and the evicted drunks hadn't yet started wandering.

It felt as if it took hours for Hatu to find his way back to Master Bodai, but he knew it was more like minutes. Even with people on the streets, in most cities a lone figure at this time of night was likely to draw the attention of the town watch, and this city seemed under even more scrutiny than most, so he had taken his time and paused often to ensure he wasn't seen.

When Hatu passed through the burned-out door

he found the false monk stirring something in a pot above a small fire. Bodai took one look at Hatu's face, ignored the heat, and used his stirring stick to over-turn the clay pot and extinguish the fire. "What?" he asked calmly.

Hatu hunkered down. "I gained entrance to the citadel grounds and, before seeking a way in, set off to inspect the cathedral as you instructed. I spied two men making their way into the unfinished building.

"They spoke a tongue I did not recognize at first. One was dressed like that church soldier at the docks, an officer or an official, but he met with five other men in hiding, dressed like sicari."

Bodai held up his hand, and Hatu ceased speaking. "Like sicari?"

"I could not see much, but there were differences."

"Describe them."

Hatu paused, collecting his thoughts. "Their head covers were not like the ones our men wear. They looked more like turbans"—he made a wrapping motion around his own head—"not the big ones like the traders from—"

"Enough," interrupted Bodai. "What else?"

"I could see little, but one opened a shuttered lantern briefly and I could see that their clothing was looser than that of our sicari, with a wide belt and an over-vest, I think; it was very dark. And by then I could understand some of what they said."

Bodai tilted his head, much as a dog might when lis-tening. "Go on."

"They spoke our tongue, master. But with an accent unlike any I've heard before. It was thick and alien to my ear."

"Describe it."

Hatu said, "At first I could not make it out, for they . . ." He paused, then continued. "Seem to swal-low the sounds rather than speak them as we do." Bodai nodded. "They held the sound 'o' in the back of their throat, so it wasn't made clear."

Bodai said, "Did they shorten their words?"

Hatu's eyes widened. "Yes, that is it! That is why I had trouble until my ear became used to the sound. They spoke as if they had rocks in their cheeks!"

Bodai let out a slow sigh. He nodded slightly, then began gathering his scant goods and putting them in his travel bag and said, "What else?"

Hatu continued. "They spoke of meetings, mes-sages, and much of the meaning was hidden, but they knew of what they spoke. They said only one word I understood clearly; they repeated it twice, and that was the word I recognized first."

"What did they say?"

"Your name, 'Bodai.' They took out what must have been a map, as each man was given a gate to watch, and one stationed at the docks. The man from the church said he'd send others to go with the five sicari, and other men would be sent for."

"We go now," said Bodai, standing up.

Hatu grabbed his go-bag and followed Bodai out of the building. They moved toward the docks but turned to the east at the small plaza. "There is a place we must visit before we are found," said Bodai as they walked quickly. "For if they do not see us try to leave tomorrow, they will begin searching the city in earnest." He looked around as they reached an empty corner and lowered his voice. "But should ill befall me, or we get separated, you must get back to Coaltachin. You know how to seek a ship?"

Hatu said, "Yes, seeking an island to the east."

Bodai nodded once in affirmation. "Seek out Zusara, and tell him what you told me." Hatu nodded, despite the fact that the prospect of meeting the most powerful master in Coaltachin alone only added to his worry.

"The men you took for sicari, they are from Azhante. Speak that name back to me."

"Azhante," repeated Hatu.

"Now, do not speak that name to anyone but Master

Zusara or me; not even to another master. Do you understand?"

Hatushaly said, "Yes, master."

He glanced down at Hatu, then motioned for him to follow.

Seeing no one around, Bodai asked, "What else did you see?"

A sudden memory struck Hatu. "Badges, I think. They wore small badges shaped differently from any I've seen. I only remember them because of how they flashed in the lantern light."

Bodai nodded. "Black lacquered badges, which is why they caught light. It keeps infiltrators from—" He stopped and looking at Hatu, said, "Never mind. You should know only what you need to know, and you know a bit more than that already."

The two moved with the purpose of people on their way to a destination, perhaps a bit late, hence their quickened pace. Hatu stayed one step behind Bodai as a beggar boy would, showing respect for a holy man.

Glancing continuously from side to side, Bodai quietly asked, "Where are those men from?"

"Azhante," replied Hatu. Being questioned so soon about that name informed Hatu that Bodai considered it to be critical.

Reaching a corner, they turned, and Bodai stopped before the first door on the right, opposite a backwash inlet from the harbor, covered in drifting refuse, dead fish, and other flotsam. Bodai struck the door once, waited, then struck once more, waited again, then struck three times.

The door opened to reveal a pair of armed men, weapons drawn. Bodai said, "We need to travel to an island in the east." The men stepped aside and put away their blades, and Bodai and Hatu entered.

A lantern rested on a table in a sparsely furnished room. Two chairs had been positioned against one wall, and the cold fireplace on the back wall lay next to a door with a dark curtain. "A ship leaves on the morning tide," said one of the two men.

"Getting to the docks might prove a problem," said Bodai. "Apparently both the king and the Church are looking for us. Someone must have realized who I was after we left the docks this morning."

The man who had spoken looked at his silent companion and said, "Never easy, is it?"

The second man shook his head.

The first man brought over the two chairs and said, "Sit. We need to find some lads, then we'll move you. We'll come up with a plan before morning. Hungry?"

Hatu nodded and Bodai said, "I was about to eat when we had to bolt." He sat and let out a quiet sigh of relief.

"I'll get you something from the back. Bread's fresh and we have cold meat and cheese."

"A feast," said Bodai lightly.

Hatu realized that he now held his entire body taut, as if he had clenched his fist and the feeling had spread from his head to his toes. He took a slow breath and tried to relax. He failed.

Bodai glanced at him and nodded once, as if he understood. Then he said, "We wait."

As a freighter made ready to depart the harbor, the sailors on deck saw a colorful procession making its way toward the boarding plank. A gaudy palanquin carried by six large slaves and followed by half a dozen retainers, all heavily armed, reached the gangplank and was lowered. Its gauze curtain was pulled aside to reveal an obese man with a massive black beard and flowing oiled locks to his shoulders; he descended the carriage as a young man in fine robes placed a step before him.

As Hatu extended his hand to help his master from the litter, Bodai spoke through the enormous false beard, "When attempting to evade those who seek you, it's often wise to look exactly like someone they do not have to seek."

Hatu was exhausted from the fear of being discovered, and from spending the night having his skin dyed to make him look like a southern islander, but the sight of Bodai wrapped in an entire roll of linen to double his weight, wearing the outlandish dress his agents had found for him, was still amusing.

He followed Bodai up the gangway as their retinue of hastily gathered agents departed, to scatter quickly throughout the city. Hatu found the theater absurd but looked forward to describing the humorous event to Hava and Donte someday, assuming he lived long enough to see them again.

4

New Considerations
and an Old Friend

Declan sat quietly while enjoying a mug of ale. The forge had been busy since he accomplished his masterpiece as they caught up on some work put aside while the sword was completed. But finally, the tools, plowshares, and horseshoes had been finished, and by three o'clock, Declan had fulfilled the work. There were still a few small tasks, but nothing pressing, and Edvalt had pointedly told Declan to leave early and to begin to consider his choices.

He had removed his dirty tunic and trousers, soaked through with sweat, and had poured buckets of well water over his head to clean up as best he could. Edvalt had commandeered the wooden tub for a proper scrubbing and once he had rinsed away most of the soot and grime, Declan decided he could wait for a day to bathe properly. He settled for a quick swim in the ocean, washing the salt water away with a bucket of fresh, determined to get his proper bath soon.

They had not spoken of Declan's options since he finished the sword for Baron Bartholomy, but the decision hung over the new master smith's every waking moment. While Declan had always known this day would come, and that he would be ready to set out and create his own future, he suddenly felt as if it had taken him by surprise. He realized that thinking about it and living it were quite different.

Edvalt had made it clear that once Baron Bartholomy had paid for his sword, the old smith would consider retirement. Good smiths were able to live better than most common men, but even they rarely earned the opportunity to retire, and often lived with their sons or daughters until death arrived to claim them. Some earned enough goodwill from a village that the people provided for their dotage, but that was rare. A few, like Edvalt, were good enough to be able to plan for the day they could no longer do justice to their craft. They earned enough coin to buy food for their remaining years and live in a quiet cottage on the edge of a town, or rent a small loft in a city.

Declan knew that Edvalt and Mila would not move in with their daughter and her husband. The old smith still had years of work left in him, but he was getting to an age when he would welcome a gentler pace. Declan understood that. Over the course of Declan's life he had seen Edvalt maintain his skill, but he knew that his pace was slowing. Tasks that used to take an hour now took longer. Even with a talented apprentice like Jusan, Edvalt's productivity had fallen a little.

Soon, it would reduce significantly. It was a simple fact of life. If he lived in a big city, a craftsman like Edvalt could still do well, fashioning small, valuable items, mostly armor and arms, but here in Oncon? For every sword commissioned, he had to make hundreds of horseshoes and bridal bits, repair wagon tongues and wheel rims, fix or fashion rakes or hoes, and create all the other village items that devoured the days and returned little in payment.

Declan weighed his choices. Edvalt would expect an answer soon, perhaps even within days. He knew that should he stay and buy the smithy, the transition would be an easy one, for he would simply continue to work as he had all his life, paying Edvalt a portion of his due until he owned the smithy outright. It was an appealing plan, for this was the only home he had ever really known.

Yet there was a curiosity within him, a desire to see

some of the world. Garn was a vast place with diverse peoples and foreign ways. Not only were there many alien places on the twin continents and the surrounding islands, there were distant lands across the sea few men had visited. During Declan's life, many travelers had passed through Oncon and they had piqued his interest about such imagined destinations.

A master smith, even one as young as Declan, would be assured a good life and prosperity in the right town, and with the patronage of a local baron he might even expect wealth. Who knew if there were master smiths beyond the sea? Or even if anyone across the oceans knew of jewel steel?

The lure of the unknown and the comfort of the familiar pulled at him equally. He let out a slight sigh and realized that though he would have to decide between them soon, he did not have to make a decision this very minute.

Marius, the proprietor of the room that passed for a tavern in the village, three tables and a tiny bar where only four close friends could stand, came over and said, "Bit early for you, Declan."

"Edvalt . . . ," he began, then decided not to go into detail and finished, ". . . gave Jusan and me the afternoon to ourselves. Work's been hard and I thought an ale would soften the evening."

"Well, I guess," answered Marius. He was a slender man of fading years, as close to a man of means as one might find in this village. He had a steady business in ale and wine but also lent money, and as a result owned tiny interests in several local enterprises; and while Oncon had no formal inn, for a few coppers, Marius would allow travelers to sleep on the floor of the tavern room, or in the shed. He even traded in some luxuries, if asked, and had items shipped in from nearby cities. "You want another?" he asked.

Declan regarded his half-finished ale and considered the question. He wasn't much of a drinking man, and on the rare occasions he had overindulged, he had always awakened sick and miserable. Declan shook his head and said, "I'm good."

The sound of a wagon rolling up before the inn caught Declan's attention just as a familiar voice shouted, "Marius! Get your saggy ass out here and help me unload!"

"Rozalee!" said Declan with a laugh.

Marius looked annoyed, because he knew heavy lifting would be involved. "Declan, help that harridan unload and your ale is free."

Declan nodded and said, "One more after we're done, for both of us?"

With a feigned resignation Marius agreed, and

Declan hurried outside to see one of his favorite people climbing down from the wagon's seat. Rozalee stood almost as tall as Declan, her face lined by the sun and the wind, nights sleeping out in fair weather and foul, and most of all from laughing. Rozalee laughed a great deal.

She wore a floppy, wide-brimmed hat, secured by a chin tie, and she cast it back as she threw her arms around Declan and hugged him hard without ceremony, lifting him off the ground. She was not a heavy woman, but she was muscular from years of driving mules, loading and unloading wagons. She grabbed his buttocks playfully, with both hands, and squeezed hard. "How's my favorite apprentice smith?" she asked as she let Declan go.

Laughing as he disentangled himself, Declan said, "It's been years since I was an apprentice, Roz."

Smacking his ass, she said, "I wasn't talking about you, fool. I meant Jusan. He's turning into a lovely young man."

Declan laughed again as he moved to the rear of the wagon. It was a converted dray Declan had worked on a few times. The sides and rear boards could be removed if Rozalee needed to lash down large crates or other cargo, as they could be held in place by the iron bolts Edvalt had fashioned for it years ago. With the sides and rear boards attached, a variety of goods could be transported.

Rozalee untied a series of ropes threaded through the iron eyelets set in the heavy oiled canvas on top of the wagon. With a nimble leap she mounted the cart and rolled back the covering. Declan admired the way she moved.

No one would call Rozalee pretty—she was somewhat long-faced and her unremarkable light brown hair was now turning grey—but she possessed a confidence that attracted men like honey drew bears, and she was open about her appreciation of the attention.

She handed down the first crate to Declan, who put it next to the doorway. From the aroma it contained some variety of fresh fruit. Besides the berries found in the hills, fruit was rare in Oncon and Marius charged a lot for it. Edvalt's wife, Mila, had been threatening to plant fruit trees behind their home for years but never had; everyone knew that this close to the sea, there was too much salt in the soil to grow anything but the heartiest of plants.

When they had unloaded three more cases, Rozalee said, "That's the last of the fruit, I think until next spring." She handed Declan a large crate of meat and said, "Freshly butchered, but needs to go into the cold cellar now."

Declan nodded and lifted the heavy crate onto his shoulder. Mutton and chicken were usually available in the village, and pork after piglets were weaned, but beef had to be shipped in: another rarity that Marius charged well for.

Declan entered the inn to find Marius conspicuously absent—the tavern keeper avoided heavy lifting as much as possible—then he moved through the small common room to the rear yard. The only structure in the ill-kept yard was a ramshackle run-in shed rarely used for horses; the few that did end up in Oncon were usually stabled at Edvalt's place. To the left of the inn door, steps led down to the cold cellar located deep under the building. Once again Declan felt annoyed that Marius was too stingy to have built a staircase inside the inn, but quickly dismissed the feeling: it was like being upset with the tide for rising in the afternoon; it was simply the man's nature.

Declan set down the crate and opened the unlatched wooden door, admitting just enough light so he could see. He carried the crate down the steps into the underground cellar, found a cool back corner for the meat, and set the crate down. A quick glance around told him Marius wasn't stocking much that wasn't local. He moved a crate of withering vegetables near the door so it would be used before turning completely. Marius wasted nothing, so Declan knew the tavern stew should be avoided for the next two or three days.

He returned to the wagon and carried several more crates down to the cold cellar, then, when he was finished, Declan found Rozalee tossing the canvas into the wagon bed. As she raised the tailgate and locked it down, she said, "You heading back to the smithy?"

"I'm finishing my ale and have one for you. Marius is buying."

"Then I'm drinking," Rozalee said with a chuckle. She climbed up to the driver's seat and turned the mules around. The animals had been to Oncon village numerous times and knew that they were only a short journey from being unhitched from their traces, watered, and fed, so the often-recalcitrant animals were eager to please as she drove off.

Declan nursed his ale until Rozalee came back. He fetched two fresh mugs of ale from Marius, who passed them over the bar with a scowl but said nothing.

Once he was seated opposite Rozalee, he asked, "What news?"

After taking a long pull of the ale, she wiped her mouth with the back of her hand and said, "The usual. War in the east; Sandura is moving against a couple of the free lords who have done something to displease

Lodavico. And rumors of bandits, emboldened by the turmoil, raiding in the Covenant."

Declan nodded. "You're not the first to warn us. Though, there's not much booty in the Covenant, so I don't see the reason."

"Food, rape, a few trinkets, and little risk . . ." She paused, then said, "Consider the men who would be tempted by that."

Declan shrugged. "You're widely traveled, you've seen much. I only know what I've experienced here. Still, you hear things. The king of Sandura can dare much in his little wars, but the first ruler to move on the Narrows will find three other kings and most of the free barons opposing him." He tried not to grin but couldn't help himself.

Rozalee's eyes narrowed. "You've been in a bit of an odd mood since I got here. I've not heard you use this tone before. What has happened?"

Declan tried not to smile. "I finished my master-piece. A few days ago, Edvalt gave me a master's rank."

Rozalee stood and leaned across the table, grabbing Declan's face between her hands, and gave him a deep kiss. Sitting down, she slapped her hand on the table and said, "I am going to fuck you tonight. Jusan can wait until my next visit."

Declan didn't know what to do other than laugh.

Like several of the young men in the region, he had lost his virginity to Rozalee. It had been a rite of passage, and Rozalee was generous in her gifts but not profligate. She had rebuffed more advances than she had accepted; when she chose a young man, it was considered a mark of honor.

Declan stopped laughing and said, "You are serious."

She nodded. "You're a good man, Declan. And truth to tell, I've missed you lately."

Feeling emboldened by the drink, he said, "I've never asked, well, because stories precede you, but . . . your husband, doesn't he care about . . . this?" He made a small hand motion between himself and Rozalee.

She replied, "My husband, if you must know, was an old man when he took me for his wife and I had barely matured enough to bear children. That was twenty-five years ago. Now he's content to nod off after a massive midday meal and several cups of wine. His cock might rise occasionally and require the attention of one of the town girls, but many are willing because he has wealth and is generous." She leaned forward and whispered, "To keep them from telling anyone he lasts but a minute, then falls back to sleep."

Rozalee looked sad. "It was never a meaningful union. We never had children." Then she brightened. "But I have been given the freedom to travel, as he hates to leave home; conduct our business, as he has no head for it; and do as I please with whomever I please." She squeezed his hand and stared into his eyes and said, "What troubles you?"

Declan said, "Do I stay, or go?"

"Now the town has two master smiths, and needs but one."

"The truth is it needs only a journeyman, which will be Jusan in a few more years, and while he's not brilliant, he is good enough. We rarely receive commission for arms or weapons, so much of what Edvalt has taught is . . ." He shrugged. "I liked learning the craft of armory, but the art of making steel . . ." He sighed. "It's a difficult skill, and has little value when most who come to the smith need only a plow blade mended or a wagon rim replaced . . ." He shrugged again, letting his sentences finish themselves. "It's the craft of it that I like." He let his gaze wander past her, as if trying to peer into the future.

"To go, or to stay," she echoed. Again putting her hand on his, she said, "Have you taken to a particular girl here?"

Declan laughed. "I have not. Most fathers in Oncon would love to see their daughters married to the smith, almost as much as they would the miller over in Trosh.

In a village of fishermen and vegetable farmers, I will be considered a wealthy man in time."

"So no fun?"

He gave a small smile and said, "I didn't say that, but a little fun during a drunken festival is not a betrothal, and I don't know if I'm interested yet. A wife, children . . ." He shrugged.

She studied his face, then said, "You will be. It's buried in your nature to be a husband and father." She sat back. "But you are the type to settle down first, so you can provide well for them. If you leave, have you put away enough to start your own smithy?"

"A little, and Edvalt will no doubt make a small gift of coin to me; it's a smiths' tradition." He looked at her, admiring how she was still the most attractive woman he knew. She had an uncommon bearing and, despite her age, a muscled and strong, lithe body. "And you?" Declan asked. "Have you enough put by?"

She laughed loudly, then turned toward Marius and waved for two more mugs. "Are you worried for me?"

He shrugged. "You travel alone in dangerous times. Your husband is an old man, as you say. Things can happen."

"You're a sweet man at heart, Declan. My husband never had a head for business. So when I married him, I made a bargain with Jack."

Declan said, "His name is Jack? I just realized in all the years I've known you, you've never spoken his name."

With a wry smile Rozalee said, "I try not to. Anyway, I learned the business and after a few years convinced him to let me travel with him. A year later I was traveling without him. I built up the business, so it was easy to convince him he needed to stay at home and take care of things there. To this day I don't think he realizes that I only did it to spend as little time with him as possible." She stopped speaking when Marius brought over their mugs.

The old innkeeper said, "That's the last of it, unless you want to pay me." He turned and left, leaving Rozalee and Declan laughing.

Rozalee continued. "I run the business, Declan. Jack sits around and occasionally takes a shipping order from a local merchant, but I set the rates and collect the money. I allot him spending money, but Jack has no idea how well we do, year to year. And he really doesn't care so long as he can buy drinks, shoddy trinkets for easily impressed young girls, and new clothing now and again. I've put by for my future. Should the need arise, I could stop working today and have enough to live on for the rest of my life."

He only nodded, finding none of this surprising.

"Have you given thought to where you'll go?" she asked him.

"I've never been anywhere much, just up the road a bit and back. You've traveled. What do you think?" he asked.

She thought on it a moment, then said, "West, then up the coast. There are many decent towns on the western coast; it's prosperous, trade is growing, and it's as far from the eastern wars as you can get without a ship."

"West is as good a direction as any, I suppose," he replied.

Rozalee said, "You should probably get back to the smithy unless you plan on being drunk tonight. I need a bath and a meal." She sniffed playfully in his direction, then said, "You could use a proper bath, as well."

Declan drained his mug and stood up, feeling slightly wobbly. He conceded she was right; he was one or two more mugs from intoxication. As he left, anticipating her finding him in the smithy later, she reached out and took his wrist. "You will leave, Declan," she said quietly. "If not shortly, soon enough." Then using a lighter tone, she said, "And you better tell me where you end up."

Realizing he had been told to bathe, and that meant she was serious about what she said about her plans for him later, Declan walked with a slight stagger on his way back to the smithy and felt that this was indeed the very best time of his life.

5

A Parting and Trials

Hava stalked the girl like a cat, placing each step purposefully and shifting her balance so she could move in any direction and not let her opponent dictate her choices. The young women both held battle staffs, able to inflict serious damage if unleashed on an unarmored opponent, but not usually lethal, if the skull wasn't the target. Hava watched her rival, waiting for an opening.

The day was unusually hot, so perspiration drenched both girls, despite a slight breeze from the ocean. All the students wore fighting clothes: loose-fitting trousers and a short-sleeved, split-front tunic, one side closed over the other, secured by a wide cloth belt knotted on the left hip.

The training area was makeshift: a meadow above

the beach, which was divided by a stream that fed into a river and emptied into the sea a mile further down the slope. For reasons not shared with the students, several masters had traveled to Corbara, the main port in Coaltachin, and each had brought along their oldest pupils. While the teachers did whatever they had come here to do, the youths had been given over to a pair of local preceptors to continue their training. This was the second day of exercises, and the students were now completely bored.

There were no classes, only training. Beneath the routine of exercise and combat, Hava felt as if something was about to happen; she sensed a tension in the two preceptors, who seemed to be waiting for something. The students had been housed in the local school, now crowded with all the newcomers, but last night, the usual gossip and joking had been absent, as if they all shared some unnamed expectation.

The older students were routinely sent away when they were finished with their schooling, but this trip felt different. Something was amiss, and Hava couldn't guess what it might be, but at this moment she had no attention to spare for speculation: this was her third match of the day, she was bone tired, and every bit of her concentration was focused on her opponent.

The preceptor had paired Hava with a girl named

Nessa, from another school on a nearby island. She didn't know the girl well, though they had trained together on two previous occasions when the students from different schools got together to spar. Sparring with Nessa felt like facing herself to Hava, as Nessa was also slender, fast, and athletic, but there the similarities between the young women ended, for Nessa was also one of the most beautiful girls Hava had seen, a fact often reinforced by quiet remarks from the boys. Although she was long legged, like Hava, Nessa's hips and breasts were fuller, giving her a slightly more curvaceous physique. Her honey-brown hair was sun streaked, and her green eyes were striking in her tanned, slightly freckled face. Her ample lips were now tightly pursed in concentration.

Hava had been told that Nessa was one of the best fighting students in her village. While they had trained together, this was the first time they'd faced each other in a match. Nessa might have been the best in her school, Hava thought as she circled the girl slowly, waiting for her to make the first move, but no matter how much the boys—and a few of the girls—might have admired her, Nessa was never going to become a sicari. In Hava's less than generous estimation, the young woman was stupid when it came to combat: she needed instructions repeated and often didn't follow them, and her fighting style was entirely predictable.

To test the theory, Hava feigned a left sweep at Nessa's feet, and the girl acted as Hava expected, jumping straight back to put more distance between herself and her opponent. Hava had been lingering over certain moves, portraying herself as slow, and attacking the girl from above, inviting Nessa to jump over the sweeping staff and get closer. So either Nessa was far smarter than Hava thought, and knew it was a trap, or she was as poor a fighter as Hava judged.

Nessa was fast and she reacted quickly, but Hava knew that was the sum of the girl's talents as she moved back to ready herself for a counterattack. She decided that most of Nessa's training must have been against opponents of even lesser talents, who didn't possess Donte's strength or Hatu's speed.

Realizing that she was tiring of the exercise, Hava feinted again, this time making a spearing move with the butt of her staff, and as she anticipated, Nessa blocked and thrust downward to her left. Hava then spun to her own left and brought up her staff against the right side of Nessa's neck, poised to deliver a stunning blow to the head.

"Halt!" shouted a woman named Elana. Both students stepped back and turned to face the instructor.

Elana said, "Hava, you know blows to the head are not permitted."

Hava nodded. "Yes, mistress. That is why I halted the blow rather than knock Nessa to the ground."

With a slightly sour, slightly amused expression, the preceptor said, "You've made your point. I give you this match." She glanced at the angle of the sun above the meadow and said, "We are done for today. Bathe at the river and assemble for a meal at the school in an hour."

The combined classes had been assembled on the north side of the island just outside of the city of Corbara, scattered across the field in small mixed groups under the supervision of lower-ranked instructors, those who would someday be preceptors. The preceptors were with the masters in the city, where matters of importance were being discussed.

The local school was just up the hill from the training meadow. The day was hot and the students quickly headed down to the stream, many stripping off their fighting togs as they hurried toward the water.

Hava and Nessa reached the bank together and stripped off their garments. As they waded into the shallow creek, stooping to splash water over themselves, Nessa said, "You fight well."

Hava paused for a moment, considering a truthful

response or pointless compliment, and chose a combination. "You're very fast," she said, "as fast as anyone I've fought but Hatu."

"I remember him," said Nessa, settling into the cool water, resting on her back, leaning on her elbows. "He's the . . . foreign boy?"

Hava nodded as she duplicated Nessa's position, deftly moving away the few sharp pebbles until there were only smooth ones beneath her. She looked around and realized she missed Hatu. "He's a . . . friend."

Nessa smiled and cocked her head slightly. "What about your other friend, the big one?"

"Donte? He's traveling." *He's traveling* was a code not to ask questions, for it meant Donte was on a mission of some sort for a master.

Nessa ignored the warning and said, "Oh, really?"

Hava, finding herself on the verge of disliking the girl and fighting off her irritation, cut off further inquiry by saying, "He left yesterday." And now she missed Donte, as well, and found her irritation toward Nessa growing.

Nessa sighed, luxuriating in the cool water. Hava looked beyond the young woman's curves to see some of the boys casting glances in their direction, despite other nude girls standing beside them. Hava took a deep breath and then let it out slowly. *Boys,* she thought. Nessa was easily the most beautiful girl here, but to Hava she was little more than the girls sent to the brothels to listen for rumors from drunken travelers.

"You're the best fighter I've met," said Nessa absently. "Of the girls, of course."

Hava's brow furrowed a little and she echoed, "Of course." She had decided to push aside her growing dislike for the girl; someday she might find herself working with Nessa. She might never become a sicari, but Nessa's beauty predicted that she would end up on the arm of someone influential, even very powerful. And she might even surprise Hava and become a *noconochi*, a special female assassin. Finally, Hava decided to offer some advice. "You know, you rely too much on your speed. You fall into a pattern."

Nessa made a sour expression. "I know. I only win because I'm faster than most. I really don't care. I only fight because they make me."

Hava was astonished at this remark and found herself unable to speak. Being able to fight for one's life was a core skill for any student who wished to serve the nation. She could understand someone like Hatu, perhaps, as an outlander, not holding quite the same beliefs as she did, but for a girl of Coaltachin, who had come so far in her training . . . ? Any student who betrayed such an attitude within the hearing of Master Facaria would have been sent away from his school within days, to be used as a worker, sold as a slave to an outbound trader, or even killed. Either Nessa's master was more lax in his training than Master Facaria, or they had already decided that her fate lay along another path. If she was not the fool she appeared to be, but as cunning as she was beautiful, maybe she would become a *noconochi*, and a poisoned drink, or a dagger in the night, would be her weapon of choice. Maybe, thought Hava, her master had already decided that was her course.

As if sensing Hava's surprise, Nessa said, "I can defend myself but have no desire to ever need that skill." She smiled as she stretched and sat up, glancing over her shoulder to where the boys still tried not to be obvious about staring at her, while other students splashed and shouted a little further on. "Boys," said Nessa, "they are so easy." Then, letting her gaze follow the lines of Hava's body, she said, "Girls, too." She leaned forward, her smile predatory. "We have other weapons besides a staff or blade." She lowered her voice and asked, "Have you been with a woman yet?"

Hava kept her expression calm, unwilling to betray any feeling to this girl. It didn't matter if she was merely seeking a reaction or if she was revealing sexual interest; both were met with a mask of indifference. "It is forbidden," said Hava calmly.

Nessa laughed, and several of the boys glanced in her direction. She smiled and waved at them, and they quickly turned away. "As I said, so easy." She looked again at Hava. "Yes, forbidden." Her smile hinted at subjects Hava preferred not to pursue.

Sex between students was strictly prohibited. No reason had ever been given for the rule, but over the years the more intelligent ones had pieced together the reasoning. Hava had discussed it with Donte and Hatu when they were younger; Donte had predictably made jokes, but Hatu seemed uncomfortable talking about sex. She found that odd as it wasn't forbidden to talk about it and sex was often discussed openly at the school, and living close to island farms, she'd been watching animals mate since before she understood what it was.

Most students thought the ban on sex was to avoid pregnancies, but Hava knew there were ways to prevent that from happening. Its true purpose was subtler, more about the forming of relationships and bonds, and to prevent any that might be placed ahead of loyalty to the family, clan, or nation. Hatu was often lost during such talk, as he was a foreigner. When they were much younger, Hava, Donte, and other students had asked the instructors about Hatu's origins, but silence or a switch across the back of the legs quickly communicated that this question was not to be raised, ever.

Hava pushed aside those thoughts. Now completely annoyed with Nessa, she stood and said, "I'm going back to the school to wait for food."

Nessa looked a little surprised but shrugged.

Hava dressed quickly, picked up her practice staff, and walked toward the school. Reaching the classroom, she spied a familiar figure resting with his back against the wall, his travel pack used as a makeshift pillow.

Hatu dozed in the afternoon heat. Hava poked him lightly in the leg with the tip of her staff. His eyes opened at once, his body tense until he saw who it was and sighed. "What made you decide you must wake me?"

She squatted next to him, a playful smile on her face, and said, "I'm bored. I need someone to amuse me." Then she hit him on the shoulder. "When did you get back?"

"This morning. Master Bodai told me to return here, and you were out there"—he waved toward the training yard—"and I did not want to risk being ordered to fight. I'm too tired. I had the night watch on the ship. I need sleep." He leaned back and closed his eyes.

She hit him again. "I said I need amusement," she demanded in a joking fashion.

Looking slightly annoyed, he stifled a yawn and said, "Did Donte stop being funny?"

"He's traveling."

Hatu sat up fully. "When?"

"Yesterday. Master Facaria brought the older students here—"

"The Council meets," interrupted Hatu.

"Where have you been?"

Hatu softly said, "Traveling." Hava rarely let her emotions betray her, but the expression on her face communicated much to Hatu. "Sorry," he added.

She gave one curt nod of understanding, though clearly she didn't like it. Hatu sensed her irritation and said, "Did I do something to annoy you?"

She frowned as she sat down next to him, and then let out a somewhat dramatic sigh. Hatu raised an eyebrow. "No," she said after a moment. "I'm just . . . tired, and there's this girl who put me in a bad mood."

"Girl?" Hatu sat up straighter, adjusting his position against the wall and giving his friend his full attention.

"It's nothing," said Hava, looking Hatu in the eyes. "I let her put me in a bad mood."

Hatu nodded once, an emphatic agreement. "Good, because no one puts you anywhere."

Her eyes widened a bit, then she laughed. She suddenly leaned forward and kissed his cheek. "I've missed you, you bonehead."

His brow furrowed. "Really?"

She hit him in the shoulder again, this time just hard enough to cause him to pull away. "What?" he asked.

"Yes, really." Then she narrowed her gaze and gave him a look he had come to know well since they were children: for the moment at least, this topic of discussion was closed. Finally she said, "I wonder how much longer we're going to be here."

Hatu said, "Not long is my guess." He weighed what he could and couldn't share with her, then said, "You know I was called out of the warehouse by Master Bodai?"

She nodded.

"I traveled with him." Hava's expression told him that he was stating the obvious given how long they'd been gone. He continued, "I . . . we were on our way back and . . ." He again considered what he could tell her, took a breath, then said, "Master Bodai sent word to the other masters to meet us here when we arrived, at dawn."

"So you spoke to the Council?" Her eyes widened slightly as the Council had almost a mythic status to the students of Coaltachin.

"No," said Hatu. "I just waited around outside all

morning, then a while ago Master Bodai told me to come here and wait. It's just that whatever they . . ." He shrugged without finishing the thought. "I think most of us will go back to school."

Hava reached out and put her hand on his shoulder. "I don't think so."

"Why?"

"Because we were sent back after you left with Master Bodai. Master Facaria summoned only the older students—Donte, myself, and three others—to come with him to this meeting. The younger students stayed home. That's the way it was for all the schools. Only the eldest are here. Before we left the school, we were told to put all our belongings in our go-bags."

Hatu looked troubled. Hava said, "Wait," stood up, and crossed the room. She rummaged through her bag and came back with a smaller cloth sack. "You don't keep much, but I grabbed this for you just in case."

He opened the sack and found a few of his personal items, mementos mostly: a broken practice blade he had kept as a child for good luck, a particularly pretty stone he'd found in a stream, a large spool of good thread he had purloined from a booth years before, a well-made metal spoon, and a ribbon. He glanced up at Hava and said, "Thank you. These are just . . . things, but you were very thoughtful." He looked at her as if seeing her in an entirely different way.

"We're friends," she said, "and Donte was too busy being Donte to remember you were already gone." She sat down again and sighed. "We were only back for a short while before we returned here."

Hatu nodded. "We were only—" He stopped himself from telling Hava they had been in Sandura. "We were only ashore for one day before we turned around and headed back. I've been at sea for the entire time since I left."

He settled back and his tone turned contemplative. "It's odd, but we've been told all our lives that . . . that the school isn't home, just a place to learn before we go and do whatever it is we're told to do—"

She interrupted. "But it is home." Shaking her head slightly, she said, "It's more home than my parents' hut. You and Donte are more like brothers than my brothers are. I can barely remember their faces."

Hatu felt a stab of concern. If they were no longer to be students, and were to be sent out into the world on missions like the one from which he had just returned, would that mean he'd not see Hava again? That idea felt like a kick to the stomach.

He saw a look of concern pass over her face as she said, "What?"

He was silent, then, almost whispering, he said, "Nothing, really. Just an odd thought." The other students returning to the training floor to await their call to a meal interrupted further conversation. Hava sat back against the wall, next to Hatu. After a moment, she gently patted his hand.

Neither spoke for a while.

Nessa entered with a group of boys behind her and noticed the friends. She nodded at Hava, and gave Hatu an appraising look, but said nothing.

"You really don't like her," Hatu said, studying Hava's expression.

"How can you tell?"

"I know that face. Others might not see it, but something about her . . ."

Hava looked down, avoiding eye contact, and said, "She's different. Something about her makes me very . . . uneasy."

"How?"

"I can't tell you, but look at how the boys flock around her." She lifted her head and indicated across the room where Nessa was surrounded by admirers.

"They just want her," said Hatu dismissively. "Even though it is forbidden."

"People always want what's forbidden. Don't you?"

Hatu smiled. "There are better girls," he said, looking at Hava.

Hava stared at him for a moment, then she looked away. Softly she said, "She's lazy."

Hatu shrugged as Hava glanced sideways at him. "She's going to end up married to someone important, in some foreign land probably, and she's going to spend her life sending messages to the Council. She can be lazy as long as she's clever."

Hava considered that. "Maybe she can be clever, but to me she seems obvious."

A thought struck Hatu. "I wonder if we all appear obvious to others."

Hava laughed softly. "Perhaps." She shook her head slightly. "It would prove a useful tool, having people underestimate you."

Food was brought to them and the students ate in relative silence, as they had been trained to do when in a school, especially when surrounded by others not well-known to them. This was one of the many habits drilled into them since infancy.

As the meal ended, Bodai and Facaria entered the room with another pair of men unknown to Hatu and Hava. Facaria came to where Hava and Hatu had been eating; they were now both on their feet with their hands clasped before them. He spoke to Hava. "You have ended your schooling and are now to spend time in other places. Go outside to where the other girls are gathering and wait for further instruction." She grabbed her bag and barely had time to give Hatu a slight nod, as close as they would be allowed to a proper goodbye.

The ache returned to his gut as the thought that he might not see Hava again for a long time, or ever again, struck him once more, and he was barely able to focus his attention when Master Facaria said, "You're to go to the harbor. Look for a light boat named *Fair Charmer*. The captain expects you, and three other lads and will be leaving with you on the evening tide. You'll be told what you need to know when you arrive. Go."

Hatu hesitated for only a moment, then grabbed his bag and hurried out the door. Outside the school's entrance, a path led down to a road that would take him easily to the harbor. Hava stood nearby, next to Nessa and four other girls; she noticed him and smiled. He raised his hand slightly and gave her a small farewell wave, then, shutting out the sudden cold that gripped his core, turned his attention to getting to the harbor before the ship sailed.

He could hear other boys hurrying out of the school and following his trail, but he refused to look back. He pushed aside the familiar rising anger as he tightened his jaw and tried not to think of Hava.

Hatushaly stood silently on a corner in the city of Numerset, knowing what was expected of him, and calm and confident in that knowledge. He was in the Washa District, home to merchants who catered to the noble and wealthy people of the city. Hatu attempted to blend in as well as a ragged boy could in a city littered with urchins.

He had docked two weeks before, was met by the local crew captain, and was taken to a warehouse. Donte had been a welcome sight on his arrival, and within minutes of talking to his old friend, Hatu knew his school days were truly over. He had thought they were over when Hava was sent away and Master Facaria sent him here, but he was now starting his real work for Coaltachin; he was a fully fledged criminal. While he welcomed the reunion with Donte, it only deepened his concern that he might never see Hava again, and that raised feelings he could not sort out.

He took a deep breath and scanned the crowd. Today he was part of a four-boy team, a "boosting crew," and his role was that of the "stall." It was his task to interrupt the progress of a well-to-do member of the crowd, for only a moment or two, allowing the "cutter" to liberate his purse while the target's attention was diverted. The cutter was the most practiced member of the crew, chosen for their swift hands and reflexes, and able to slice a coat and snatch a coin pouch from a pocket, or separate a purse from a belt, without notice. Within seconds the cutter would hand his prize and his blade to the "bag," who would dart away as quickly as possible. The handoff was known as the "toss." Today, Donte was the bag.

Should the victim, or the "mark," notice and be quick enough to catch up with the cutter, the boy would not have the purse or blade in his possession, making any accusation impossible to prove.

The fourth boy, the "eye," would signal a likely mark. He would wander about the stalls of the market looking for someone with a full purse and lax attention, the type who might not notice a missing purse until the boys removed themselves to another venue.

Hatu shifted uneasily; the eye had not yet signaled them, despite passing by several promising-looking marks. It was as if he was waiting for someone specific. Hatu began to feel a familiar discomfort, that he was unaware of something important.

Then came the signal: the eye, a boy named Jolen, took off his cap and wiped his brow as a stout merchant in fine robes walked past him. Hatu moved without hesitation.

He saw that the mark carried his belt purse on his right, indicating he was a left-handed man, as wise men kept their off hand close to their purse. Hatu veered slightly to bring himself to the man's left side, then stumbled in front of him, drawing the man's attention for an instant. Hatu took the opportunity to make eye contact and started to beg.

"Please, sir, have you a coin to spare? I'm an orphan and haven't eaten in days!"

Brendant, the cutter, was in position to take the purse and dart away, but instead he drew his dagger and plunged it deep into the man's stomach. Hatu saw the boy push upward, under the rib cage and deep into the man's liver. The mark would bleed out within minutes. All the man could do was gasp, barely making a sound as his knees began to buckle.

The eye shouted, "Long gone!" and the boys took off at a run, as fast as they could move, darting through the crowd toward the docks.

They were half a block away before the first shout of alarm went up behind them. Brendant motioned for the others to follow him into an alley, where he stripped off his jacket to reveal a ragged short-sleeved shirt beneath. He put the jacket behind a pile of rubbish and motioned for the others to follow suit.

Hatu glanced at Brendant. "Crib?"

With one shake of his head Brendant indicated that they were not returning to their base. "Open water," was all he said in response, and the other three began modifying their clothing for their new roles.

Hatu pulled off his jacket and was about to toss it on the pile when Brendant said, "Don't leave your thing."

Hatu nodded. He retrieved a round metal tin from an inside pocket of his jacket and slipped it under his shirt, above his belt. He knew it would be annoying, but it was vital that he didn't forget what the other young men called "his thing." It was a pomade to darken his hair to a more common brown-red shade. It resisted water and washing, so he only needed to apply it every few days.

In less than two minutes, four young sailors ambled out of the alley and walked calmly away from the murder scene toward the docks as the alarm spread through the market like a ripple in a pond.

Hatu felt anger rising and forced it back down. No one had told him this wasn't a simple purse cut, and he was doubly angry, as he had been forced to abandon the first pair of boots that had fit him in almost a year. But most of all he now felt uncertain, as he had many times since his childhood. Brendant wasn't a common crew boy, he was a man who looked younger than his years, an experienced sicari, for no common crewmember would be tasked with an assassination.

The four sailors moved calmly through the crowd, their meaningless banter lost in the noise of the streets. Donte regaled Hatu with his speculations on a barmaid, and Hatu focused on him just enough to grunt affirmation or inquiry without saying a word.

He tried to make sense of what had just happened. This particular crew had been working in Numerset for more than a year before Donte and Hatu joined them, and they had established themselves among the ruffians and cutpurses of the city. Each crew spent half their time fighting for their right to participate in the local criminal bounty.

They had arrived from Coaltachin one by one and found each other slowly, blending in with the hundreds of nameless people cast by fate into poverty. They had found a small neighborhood gang and, after a few fights to demonstrate their prowess, had quickly taken over and built it into one of the most efficient crews in the city. With other captains, they had formed their numerous crews into what was called a regime and together had effectively taken control of crime in the region. Regimes reported directly to one of the masters in Coaltachin, who coordinated with the other masters in the Council.

The boys and girls who showed talent were allowed to remain, while those who proved a liability to the gang had been cut loose, allowed to perish, be captured, or join another gang. Hatu's crew had shown themselves to be ruthless since his arrival.

Occasionally, as had occurred the day prior, a coded message would arrive for Brendant, who would then inform the others as to the task. Hatu, Jolen, and Donte knew without being told that his instructions came from the clan leaders, the Council.

Brendant's crew, which currently numbered about twenty-five boys and girls, generated gold for Coaltachin. That gold was turned over to him every day. There was a captain at every level, so their context created a variety of titles. Brendant was a crew captain; he had an under-captain named Jadique who ruled in his absence, and who would, Hatu supposed, take over now that Brendant was fleeing the city.

Brendant's crew had become one of the most proficient in the city's network, and as such was well rewarded. Hatu had saved his share, not squandering it on gambling, women, drugs, or drink. He occasionally allowed himself a good meal at an inn near the eastern gate, as he enjoyed his privacy and, in his estimation, none of the crew except Donte offered him the prospect of good company, but that was the extent of his self-indulgence. When he could steal away, he traded his coins for small gems through a trader he trusted. He had a small pouch sewn into his trousers, which he could grab quickly should the need arise. He estimated he could live for a year or more on what he had saved. Another year here, and he would be able to support himself in a meager fashion for years to come.

There were as many as a dozen crews in the city regime; the boys and girls were divided into various-sized companies, depending on need. Most of them were involved with petty, but lucrative, street crime, while crews of larger boys acted as enforcers, and kept discipline within the other gangs as well as keeping local criminals out of the more profitable neighborhoods. The entire city was under the authority of the regime master. Not every member of every crew was from Coaltachin, but every key member belonged to them. Most of the locals didn't know they worked for the Council. They didn't even know where their bosses were from. The wall of secrecy, the barrier to knowledge, was absolute, and every member of Hatu's group from the home island knew that to violate that pledge was a death sentence to all involved.

It was Brendant's responsibility to see that the gold

was shipped back to the Council. After permitted deductions, he passed the payment to a particular dockworker who would in turn pass it to the appropriate ship's captain bound for Coaltachin. A certain amount was expected from them each month, and although Hatu did not know what the level was, to fall short would earn punishment, perhaps dire if warranted, so Brendant's crew ensured they were never short. More than one greedy lad had ended up in the bay with ears and nose removed, or fingers chopped off, as a warning to others.

But their tasks—a burglary of a warehouse, the robbing of a courier, or in this case, an assassination—served ends none of the boys understood; it wasn't considered necessary for them to understand why particular targets were chosen, which frustrated Hatu further. Others might have had the temperament for blind obedience, but it chafed his very being. He was beginning to consider what it would mean to leave the land of his upbringing and venture into a world beyond the one he knew. Half of his thinking was born of curiosity, but the other half was the child of frustration; the constant edge of rage within him never let go.

One thing Hatu had never spoken of, even with Hava or Donte, was his sense of being different, of not being entirely of Coaltachin, despite its being the only home he had known. Hatu understood from his earliest days that he would eventually leave. No one told him, but he knew he was not from Coaltachin, and the admonitions never to speak of his origins applied to him as much as to the other children. He would never rise to the Quelli Nascosti. Not knowing where fate would take him also fueled his ever-present anger. Two feelings arose when he dwelt on his unique position: fear, from not understanding why he would be allowed to leave knowing as much as he did about the Kingdom of Night, and frustrated anger, from not knowing why he was different and how this could be allowed. He was certain he would not die for what he had learned, because if that was to be the case, why train him in the first place? This was the one nagging mystery that Hatu forced aside when it arose in his mind. There was no point in speculating, and he knew eventually he would learn the mysteries of his origins and purpose.

As the boosting crew reached the end of the closest dock, a worker nodded to Brendant and made a sign that Hatu recognized, one identifying the man as an agent of the gang. With a single nod he indicated which ship was their destination and the four young men hurried up a gangway that was pulled in just seconds after Hatu's bare feet touched the deck.

They set to work without being told. Hatu and Donte

climbed the rigging, for they were the most gifted at the tricky and dangerous work to be done aloft. Jolen and Brendant joined the deck crew. Sheets were hauled, sails unfurled, and the ship gently eased away from the waterfront.

Numerset had no proper harbor, simply a long quay sheltered somewhat by an ancient rock breakwater in desperate need of repair. In foul weather ships were anchored offshore, heavily battened at every joint to keep afloat, for left at the quay they risked being smashed against the rocks beneath the landfill upon which it had been built. But in clement weather the long quay allowed for a quick departure, with no need of a pilot.

The ship was a xebec with the name *Nelani* painted across her stern; she was a narrow three-master lateen-rigged vessel, built for speed and to carry small precious cargo rather than bulk. The *Nelani* was a coaster, not a deep-water ship, but in the islands you were rarely out of sight of land for more than half a day at speed. These shallow-draft ships ran less risk from the unexpected shoals and hidden reefs, and there were many harbors against sudden storms.

With Donte positioned at the other end of the foot rope, Hatu unlashed one of the three large sails, then scampered up the ratlines to secure the top of the boom. Lateen sails were designed to be trimmed easily but still needed to be secured against sudden changes in wind direction.

Hatu saw Donte smiling at him and found it irritating. He knew Donte was amused by his confusion over recent events, and often wondered why they were still friends. They were the most unlikely pairing and had been drawn to each other as children, but neither could explain why they had remained close; at times Donte amused Hatu and at other times his friend angered him.

When the three sails were unfurled and secured, the young men grabbed ropes and shimmied down to the deck. Getting the ship under way did not allow time for conversation, but even when the work was done, with so many ears close by, discussion was unwise. There was an invisible hierarchy in Coaltachin, and one never knew who was privy to what information. Since childhood, the students destined to serve at higher position, and even those who joined the lower ranks of the hidden ones, were taught to be cautious about who might be listening.

A quick survey of the decks gave Hatu no clear indication of what was expected of him next, so he made his way down the companionway to the deck below. They reached one of two small tables at the far end of the crew's quarters. Twelve hammocks indicated that this vessel was a "short runner," one that traveled short distances with a light crew. Unlike bigger ships, the *Nelani* had no large cabins for captain and mates, only a large curtain defined fore and aft, and the captain and a single mate would sleep behind the curtain. Hatu also expected short runs meant two shifts of six men each, rather than three shifts of four. Six crewmen above on a ship this size meant a relatively easy cruise.

Their two companions appeared shortly after Hatu arrived, and when they were seated, Donte asked, "Any ideas?"

Brendant shook his head. "I just got the word to take care of that fat merchant, flee the city, and return to home."

"Home," muttered Hatu.

"You have a problem?" asked Brendant in a challenging tone.

Hatu paused briefly to gauge the look in Brendant's eyes. The leader of this crew was obviously upset about something else, too, but had not confided in any of the others. As a sicari he lived in a different world most of the time, and probably disliked working with boys who were fresh from school. His eyes assessed Hatu.

Hatu leaned back against the bulkhead and muttered, "Just tossed some really good boots away, is all."

Brendant took that at face value and said, "I expect we'll learn what this is all about when we get home."

Jolen, usually the quietest of the four, said, "If they care to let us know."

"That's the way it is," replied Brendant.

The captain came down the ladder and approached their table. "I don't know what you lot are about and I don't care to know," he began, his tone not inviting commentary or answer. "I was just told to set sail the moment you came aboard and make for home." He paused for a moment and looked from face to face, evaluating them. "You two," he said, pointing to Donte and Hatu, "get up on deck with the day crew." To the others, he said, "You are night watch. Sleep on the deck." He motioned to the floor below the table. "The hammocks are for my boys. Watch, after the evening meal." Then he turned his back on them and climbed the ladder in the companionway to the deck above.

"Well, we've been told," said Donte with a rueful smile. He gently hit Hatu in the shoulder with the back of his hand and inclined his head toward the ladder. "Let's go." He rose and Hatu followed, as Jolen and Brendant started looking for a place to bed down out of the way of those who would soon be coming below.

Once on deck, Donte said, "Something's going on. The captain wasn't pleased with us."

Hatu nodded. "Something."

The ship's mate motioned them over and said, "You lads, up above. Need extra eyes."

"Trouble?" asked Donte.

A smack to the back of Donte's head clearly indicated that the mate didn't wish to be questioned and the two young men quickly climbed the rigging, Donte on the mainmast, Hatu climbing the aft-set mizzen. The small coast-hugger had nothing like the crow's nests found on larger ships, just a simple circular platform on each mast large enough for a man to sit or stand on. Lookouts tended to alternate sitting and standing as neither was comfortable and muscles became stiff and achy if a man lingered in either position too long.

Both Hatu and Donte chose to stand at first, as sitting on the wooden perch with their legs wrapped around the mast tended to be hard on legs and arse even after a short time. Donte spoke loud enough for Hatu to hear, but not loud enough to be overheard by those below. "A lot of people seem angry we're here."

"If the captain, first mate, and Brendant equal a lot of people, I guess you're right."

"Well, you're angry because of your boots; that makes four."

Hatu couldn't help but laugh.

"And I'm also angry, because I was going to spend this night with Florinda."

Hatu laughed again. Florinda was the most recent tavern girl Donte had been trying to charm since he'd reached the city. Hatu had lost track of how many had come before her. Donte had vanished for several nights over the last two weeks, so Hatu had assumed his charm had worked.

Both young men fell silent, as they knew further conversation could divert their attention from their first duty: to sweep the horizon for any sign of approaching trouble. The hours passed slowly.

Near sunset, Donte said, "Hatu, to the northeast!"

Hatu looked in the direction Donte pointed and after a moment three dark specks resolved against the approaching gloom of evening. "Sails!" he shouted.

"Where away?" came the instant response from the captain on the deck below.

"Northeast, by two points north, coming up fast!" In the seconds of their exchange, the spots had become clear enough that Hatu knew the three ships were coming straight at them.

"Break out the banner!" shouted the captain.

Hatu looked at Donte, who returned his expression of ignorance. Within a minute, a black banner had been hauled aloft and was fluttering in the evening. It displayed a yellow circle with a red stripe running through it, from top to bottom: the symbol of a ship of Coaltachin.

Hatu's eyes narrowed as he looked at his friend and again Donte's expression mirrored his own confusion. That banner was flown rarely, as the ships of Coaltachin were seldom revealed, but when they did it was to warn potential attackers away; this close to the home island the promise of unrelenting revenge caused most corsairs to veer off.

The three ships kept their course.

"They're still coming, Captain!" Hatu shouted down to the deck.

Hatu could not hear what the captain said to his first mate, but he could imagine. Few who sailed this part of the world would invite confrontation with Coaltachin, but those who did were among the deadliest adversaries the island nation had.

From the deck came a shout: "Trim to lee, turn about!"

Without hesitation, Hatu and the other sailors aloft readied the large booms to swing, as the captain had decided to flee. Every man aboard was a trained fighter, some, like Brendant, among the most deadly imaginable, but the strength of Coaltachin was not overt conflict when it could be avoided. It was stealth, surprise, and trickery. Hatu knew the captain would confront one ship without thought, two perhaps, but three was more than enough cause to seek an escape.

Donte was moving as quickly as Hatu, reading the wrenching gibe that would almost certainly mean hanging on to the yard sheets for dear life. The rudder was pulled hard, and the ship heeled over, and then righted itself so abruptly that any man not holding tight risked being thrown over the side or to the deck below. He couldn't spare a glance to see if Donte was hanging on but knew his friend was as experienced at sailing as he was.

Securing the ropes once they came around, Hatu did spare a glance at the three approaching ships. It would be a race. They were smaller than the *Nelani* but perhaps had enough sail to draft and were fast enough to overtake her. He had only a rough idea where they were, but guessed at least half a dozen islands were scattered close together on the heading the captain had chosen. They sat south of an open expanse of water called the Clearing, a region without islands, on either side of which the islands were known as the North or South Islands. They were heading deeper into the South Islands, which were mostly uninhabited and considered a dangerous region.

If the captain could tack around one of the islands and shield his ship from observation for as little as ten minutes, he had a chance to lose their pursuit in the archipelago, then make his way north again, across the Clearing and into far more friendly territory.

It was late afternoon and the sun would be setting in less than two hours. Hatu shimmied down a sheet to the deck. He calculated that they faced an hour of stern chase before they were overtaken, but should the captain find an island to shelter behind, they could lay up in the darkness and steal away later.

"Islands," shouted Donte from above, pointing ahead.

Hatu looked to the stern and saw the captain instructing the man on the tiller to come to a new heading. Someone said, "Weapons," and without bothering to see who had given the order, Hatu hurried to the forecastle with the other deckhands. Large hinged doors were pulled open to reveal a weapons cache to rival a garrison. Swords, pikes, shields, bows, and quivers full of arrows lay inside. Hatu hesitated, letting the other crewmembers arm themselves first. A number of men chose melee weapons, and only one a bow. Glancing up to where Donte still sat as lookout, Hatu grabbed two hip quivers, putting both over his shoulder, then two bows.

He climbed quickly up the ratlines and, reaching the top, handed a bow and quiver to his friend. "Thanks," said Donte. "I see we don't have many archers."

"Three, apparently," said Hatu, tossing his head toward the other bowman on the foremast. Hatu kept his eyes on the approaching ships and forced himself to calm. Hitting a moving target when you were stationary was difficult enough; hitting one when your perch was pitching with ocean swells was doubly difficult. He knew he'd be lucky to hit anyone below, but he could trouble the enemy enough to prevent them casting grapples.

Hatu settled in to wait. Glancing down at the decks, he appreciated the discipline shown by the Coaltachin crew. It would be some time before the other ships overtook the *Nelani,* if they did at all, and now was the time to conserve energy when possible, not waste it in anticipation of a fight that might never come. In less than an hour the sun would set and then within minutes either they would be in a fight almost certain to end in the death of every man aboard, or they would elude their pursuers. Either outcome was likely, so Hatu waited and tried to stay calm.

The minutes passed slowly, and with a bow slung across his back and a quiver at his hip, Hatu adjusted the sheets as ordered and kept his eyes on the horizon. Fighting other boys was one thing, and even gang fights were nothing he feared, but he'd never fought aboard a ship, and these were likely to be experienced pirates who knew every trick of oceangoing combat.

As the sun lowered and the pursuing ships neared, Hatu felt the dampness in the air increase and he looked toward the bow. They were heading into mist. Not a proper fog, but a twilight thickening of the air as the temperature cooled, common to these islands. A night haze was forming that would burn off the next morning as temperatures rose again. Anything that helped obscure the vision of those who followed was welcome.

The captain corrected their course loudly enough to be understood, but he didn't shout. The pursuing ships were close enough that even the faint chance of being heard was to be avoided.

The *Nelani* heeled over to starboard and Hatu saw the captain was planning a circular course around a nearing island. He saw another dark shape behind it, another small landmass. Hatu trusted that the captain knew these waters and returned his attention to those who followed their ship.

Suddenly they heeled over as the wind snapped in from another quarter, a slight shift, but enough to have the crew aloft scrambling to trim the sails.

Hatu looked aft and saw they were now out of sight

of those in pursuit. The order to alter course yet again, and reef the sails, came from below: the captain was cutting their speed and knew where he wanted to be when those ships overtook the *Nelani.*

For a xebec, reefing meant adjusting the boom position and gathering in sail rather than gathering a true reef found in a square rig, so Hatu rode the boom as it slowly descended, pulling in yards of fabric and tucking it away to be lashed down when the boom stopped. The ship slowed and he saw that the captain was bringing her in close to the rocks. They were going to hide.

They were in a narrow channel and Hatu fervently hoped the captain knew his way about these rocks. When the boom had been lowered to a few feet above the deck, it stopped moving, and Hatu and other sailors secured it. Orders were now being given by hand signs and anything that made a lot of noise was stowed, lashed down, or muffled with rags. To lower the sails completely would cause the ship to drift; the loose sheets, tackle, and shrouds to rattle; and the timbers to creak and groan. This way enough tension was maintained to keep relatively quiet and hope the sounds of the surf would mask the little noise that must be made.

The seconds dragged and the men could hear their hearts pounding.

Hatu had sailed enough to know he was no true

sailor; he could act the part and perform the duties, but the currents and winds, knowing a ship by its sound and the feel of wood beneath his feet, were all beyond him. He had to trust that the masters had put no fool in charge of this ship. All he could do now was wait and be ready to fight.

A movement; then a darker shadow against the distant gloom: the hint of a sail passing before the narrow line of sight between the two islands, barely more than a flicker; then came another, and then a third. Hatu suppressed a shiver, for he had felt the ships pass rather than seen them, and that troubled him in a way he could not express.

More painful minutes passed, then the captain spoke in a whisper and a sailor turned to relay the order. "We shelter here. Cap says he won't risk turning around in the dark. We've given them the slip and so we'll head out at dawn. Now, reef in the sails fully and we'll drop the sea anchor. Then stay at your post, but take some rest."

Hatu realized that he'd been holding his breath and let it out silently. He felt a slight jerk on the yard, so he reefed in the sail fully then quietly lashed down the yard. The anchor was let out as silently as possible, with agonizing slowness.

At last all was still.

6

Unequal Talents

Hava sat, trying to appear calm, but she shifted her weight slightly, from side to side, as if the mat were uncomfortable. It wasn't, but she was annoyed and bored by the lesson and that made her unusually restless.

The sexual part of her training had been a little difficult, and she was trying to resolve being told how to behave with how she felt about these acts. A constant frustration had lingered with her throughout the month she had spent with the Powdered Women and she was starting to wonder if this was how Hatushaly felt. He certainly seemed vexed much of the time.

She was also annoyed at how her thoughts had turned to him again. Thinking of him, and, to a lesser extent, Donte, was pointless, as she knew it was possible she might never see either of her friends again. Even though Coaltachin did not have the huge population of the greater kingdoms, or even some of the more powerful baronies, they were scattered over half the world. The thought caused her more distress than she could explain, but she had known all her life that this might be her future; Donte was destined to become a master if he didn't sabotage himself, and while she couldn't explain how she knew, Hava felt that Hatu's fate would take him far from their school in Master Facaria's small village. Still, the inevitability of something didn't make it any easier to deal with when it arrived, she decided.

The current lesson focused on how to be a noconochi: a beautiful woman who could flatter without appearing obvious or obsequious. All of it was lost on Hava. Some students seemed to have a knack for flirting and praising in just the right fashion, but she did not. She wondered how she was supposed to laugh at a poor witticism or bad joke if she wasn't even able to recognize it as at least a feeble attempt at humor. She also found it hard to be quick to respond, most of the time having to pause in order to think of an answer. She had no facility for being glib; it was not part of her nature. She was good at straight talk, as Hatu and Donte would tell anyone, but banter was lost on her.

She didn't mind silence, but when it came time to make conversation she wanted to talk about something, anything, as long as it was interesting.

Early on, she had thought the actual sex might be the most demanding part of the training, but aside from the pain of losing her virginity it had largely become banal. She knew of sex before arriving here, and by the time she lay beneath a man the actual experience of it was the only thing she found alien. Since that first time there had been moments when she had been delighted to discover things about her own body and how it responded. And she took pleasure in learning any new thing: she appreciated how her more experienced teachers listened to what she told them and helped her become proficient at every sex act required. Apparently, being a good sex partner required a level of self-knowledge that most men and women seemed to lack in Coaltachin, or perhaps all of Garn, from what the instructors said.

Hava found sex with the female instructors and other girl students most difficult to endure; she appreciated female beauty and some acts were pleasant enough, but for the most part she preferred the hard, angled bodies of men. Well, some men anyway. A few of her partners had been as difficult for her as the women had been.

Trying to return her attention to the lesson, she was

wryly amused that once again Nessa had placed herself directly in front of the instructor, an older but still attractive woman named Mistress Mulray, who was head of the school. Nessa seemed determined at all costs to be the best student, even though it was not a competition. And it appeared that over the last month the instructors had been perfectly aware of Nessa's bids for attention.

Hava couldn't gauge Mistress Mulray's age but assumed her to be just old enough to be her mother, perhaps thirty-five, maybe even forty years old. She was still fit and trim when most women of Coaltachin had been worn down by hard work and the birth of multiple children, and she carried herself with a bearing that spoke of authority.

In Corbara, Hava had occasionally caught sight of women like Mulray, borne in litters or walking with a retinue: wives or mistresses of wealthy foreign merchants and travelers. As a child Hava had thought these women almost not human, but creatures of mythic beauty and grace. It hadn't been until she was older that Hava had learned about cosmetics, hair coloring, and clothing designed to flatter. Still, to be taught by a woman like this had intrigued Hava for a while. And there was an air of command about Mistress Mulray that she had not seen in the foreign women visiting

Corbara, an authority rooted in her ability more than her station. Her dark hair framed an olive face; she had dark eyes and full lips. It was her eyes that hinted at a strength that was unusual in most of the women Hava had met. That strength, beneath all the art of seduction and manipulating men and women, was echoed to a lesser degree by the other women instructors; all were adept, but none matched Mistress Mulray. She made every lesson look effortless, until the students tried to duplicate what she taught. Her combination of beauty and power had greatly intrigued Hava for the first few weeks. Now the novelty had worn off, and Hava wondered if all of these well-clothed, painted women had been like Nessa when they were her age.

Nessa showed rapt attention to the lecture, and again Hava wondered why she seemed determined to be the best at everything. Hava was delighted to let her be, as it kept Nessa from pestering her. Nessa wasn't someone Hava cared to spend time with, but for some reason Nessa seemed determined to curry favor with a handful of girls, some of whom had taken to following her as if she led her own crew.

One night, they had been learning how to drink without quickly becoming drunk quickly, which involved knowing the types of food to be eaten, or the oils that coated the throat and stomach to slow intoxication. Despite instruction, the entire class had for the most part become drunk. It had led to something close to an impromptu orgy, which, while expressly forbidden, Hava was convinced had been part of the exercise. Despite the sex no one was punished for it the next day, nor was it even mentioned. Hava took it as an example of losing control while thinking one was still in control. The many hangovers and tortured stomachs the next day were object lessons in self-delusion.

She had managed to fend off the advances of several of the boys and girls, but as things began to wind down that night, Nessa had tried to slip under Hava's blanket. Hava had feigned sleep and kept her blanket wrapped tightly around her.

Nessa had reeked of wine, sweat, and sex, the combination of which repulsed Hava. Finally she threw an elbow that caught Nessa in the side of the neck with just enough force to make it clear her attentions were not welcome. After that, Nessa had seemed uninterested in Hava to the point of ignoring her, which was fine with Hava.

The lesson came to an end, and the students, mostly girls, rose to leave, but before Hava could reach the door Mistress Mulray waved her over.

When the two of them were alone, Mulray said, "We should talk." She motioned for Hava to follow and led her down a long hall with half a dozen doors on each side. Hava knew that behind each door was a room in which students and instructors practiced many of the things that had been introduced in the lectures.

Reaching Mulray's quarters, Hava stood silently at the door until the instructor waved her in and indicated for her to sit on a cushion on the opposite side of a small table. In the corner were a sleeping mat, pillows, another small table, and a wardrobe snug against the wall, the instructor's personal space.

Hava sat and regarded the older woman. Mulray stared at Hava for a long, silent minute, then spoke. "You're not very good at any of this, are you?"

Hava sighed. "I guess not, mistress."

"Some women have no skill at being a noconochi, but most can become a common woman, even a coarse one with guile if needed, but you . . . ? I'm at a loss. Why were you sent here?"

Hava was caught off guard by the question and paused before answering. "I do not know, mistress. Master Facaria told me to come here, so I did."

Mulray nodded slowly. "Who are your people, your family?"

"Farmers," said Hava without hesitation. "My father and my two older brothers—"

"You are not the eldest?"

"I am the eldest girl," responded Hava.

"So Facaria picked you but not your brothers?"

Hava's slight shrug indicated she hadn't considered that remarkable. "He came to our farm one day and watched us."

"Watched you?" Now Mistress Mulray looked interested. "Say on."

"I don't think my father expected his visit. I was little, so I had no idea he was someone important. He talked to me and gave me a sweet. He chatted with my brothers."

"What did he talk about?"

"I don't remember, mistress. I was little."

Mulray nodded. "Why did he pick you, I wonder."

Hava tilted her head as if considering the question. Then she said, "I was the fastest girl in our village. Best fighter, too. And maybe because my father needed my brothers on the farm?"

Mulray narrowed her eyes. "Best fighter?"

Hava said, "I used to get into fights. I wouldn't let the older children bully me. I got beaten a lot but always fought back, and finally they left me alone."

"Ah," said Mulray, as if that explained everything. She smiled. "I think we both know your time here is over. You may have learned a thing or two that will prove useful if you can learn to flatter people who don't deserve it, but for the most part you're ill-suited for our particular training."

Hava felt a rush of conflicting feelings: relief she might not have to continue having sex with strangers and pretending she liked it, but also a touch of panic.

Mulray considered her. "What troubles you?"

"It's just . . ." Hava paused. "I don't understand why I have failed. Am I not pretty enough?"

Mulray seemed surprised by the question, then laughed. "No, it's not that. If you remained here, when we began teaching grooming . . ." She looked Hava in the eye. "Nessa will spend years, perhaps most of her life, being the plaything of some powerful man or woman, perhaps several. She feels compelled to curry favor and approval, as she is by birth that sort of woman. It can lead to great personal gain for some, but it is also a trap for others.

"Young women such as yourself, well, let us say we can make you beautiful or not, as it suits us. We have girls and boys working in taverns, brothels, we have camp followers, many of them easily move from one place to another. If we need you to be the daughter of an innkeeper in a distant city like Abala or Sandura, that is who you will be for a long time, or . . ." She let the thought go unfinished. "Nessa may find herself spending years with a man she despises, and wealth and position will do nothing to lessen that loathing." She regarded Hava gravely. "Before you came to us, did boys try to have sex with you? Or girls?"

Hava seemed untroubled by the question. "I understood the rules. No sex."

"Few girls your age arrive here having obeyed that rule entirely. Fewer boys."

Hava said, "My father told me to always follow the rules."

"Do you?"

"Generally. I have these . . . had these friends, and sometimes . . . I got punished for being with them." She laughed slightly. "The truth is I never would have done some of those things alone, but being with them . . ." She shrugged.

"You miss them," said Mulray. It wasn't a question.

"I . . . do," admitted Hava. "We're taught not to expect to be with our fellow students after school, but . . . it's hard."

The shift in Mulray's posture communicated to Hava that the discussion was over. "I still am uncertain why Facaria chose you for this training, but I'm sure he had his reasons." She rose from her seat and Hava followed suit. "You can ask him, if you like, when you see him. I'm sending you back to his little town on Morasel. You have no place here."

Not knowing what else to say, Hava bowed and asked, "Should I continue to the next class?"

"No. Take the rest of the day for yourself. I'll arrange for you to leave tomorrow. There's a trader who brings food up from the town and he'll be here later. He unloads, spends the night in the kitchen, and leaves first thing in the morning. You'll go with him to an inn by the docks and we'll arrange passage to Corbara and on to Morasel."

Hava bowed in respect, then left Mistress Mulray's apartment and moved slowly down the hall, uncertain of what to do with the rest of the day. Sounds from behind closed doors and naked bodies visible through open ones made it clear that afternoon instruction had begun. She found nothing arousing in the sight of naked young men and women engaged in their various acts, and for a moment wondered if there was something wrong with her.

A sudden rush of uncertainty caused her to feel angry, and being angry made her think of Hatushaly. She stopped for a moment, glanced through a partially opened door, and saw one of the sex instructors on her knees pleasuring one of the students, a muscular young man she knew only vaguely. The juxtaposition of that image with thoughts of Hatu was unsettling. The thought of having sex with Hatu lingered for a moment, and she pushed it aside. She had no better friend . . . and since coming to Facaria's school she had been forbidden such musing. Hava resumed walking, wondering if she should just return to the girls' quarters and take a nap.

But she wasn't remotely tired: indeed, she felt charged up, annoyed. Hatu was a strange boy and always had been. A good friend, yes, but hardly handsome with his oddly colored hair and freckled face. Still, she liked his smile, which he didn't show enough.

And why didn't she feel that way about Donte? He was by any measure a better-looking boy, with his broad shoulders and ready grin, and the wild thatch of unruly dark hair he managed somehow to make look rakish. She forced herself to calm. Maybe it was as simple as missing her friends, and it was impossible to be in this school with the Powdered Women and not think of sex.

But thinking of Donte made her realize she was hungry. She immediately decided the kitchen was her destination.

There she found the cooks and helpers lugging produce in from outside. They ignored her until the head cook saw her grabbing an apple and yelled, "No food! You miss a meal, and you go hungry. That's the rule."

Hava grinned, suddenly feeling as if she were once

again with Donte and Hatu, stealing food from Facaria's kitchen when no one was looking. She darted past the cook, out of the door, and dodged through a crowd of people unloading boxes from a large oxen-pulled wagon.

She jogged across the training ground, to the base of a grassy hillock, the shouts of the angry cook fading behind her, and found herself suddenly happy. As she bit into the juicy red fruit, she wondered at the feeling of a burden being lifted from her.

The years of training, friendship with two boys— one decidedly odd and the other perhaps the most confident person she knew—and her ability to excel at most anything she put her mind to combined to reassure her that although she wasn't good at seduction, flattery, and pretending to enjoy sex with strangers, there was nothing wrong with her.

Suddenly it hit her that she wouldn't have any problem with having sex with Hatu or Donte—not that she currently wanted to, but she would almost certainly have done much better had they been her training partners. Given her recent experience, it seemed a bit odd to fancy having sex with people you liked. Yet, there it was.

One assistant instructor, named Hector, had made her laugh, and she'd had the best sex with him since arriving; he made sex fun. The other instructors, far

less so, and one, a fellow named Almos, had almost repulsed her. He was so devoid of feeling it had been like
a cook preparing a meal, or a carpenter fashioning a
crate thoughtlessly after years of practice.

She began to understand why she wasn't cut out for
the life of a Powdered Woman, one who used her body
as an assassin's weapon. She would return to Master
Facaria and speak plainly with him. She would be a
gifted sicari, if he allowed that. If not . . . ? She'd worry
about that problem when it presented itself.

Glancing at the sun, she judged she had the pleasure
of lazing away at least three more hours before supper
would be served. Taking stock of her surroundings,
Hava realized she had never been beyond this small
meadow beneath the grassy hill, except for morning
and afternoon exercises every day.

Keeping fit here was a decidedly different concept
than at school on Morasel. She finished her apple and
tossed the core into nearby weeds. Perhaps an apple
tree might sprout there, she thought happily.

She decided to hike up the hill to see what the island
looked like. She had only a vague concept of where
she was. On the passage here, students had been kept
belowdecks. She had done far less traveling than Donte
or Hatu and knew little of the sailor's craft. The con-
finement had exasperated her further because she knew

she was physically able to perform duties above deck. She was certain Hatu and Donte had exaggerated the rigors of working on a ship, but even if their complaints about hard work and long hours had been true, she knew she was up to it. There were a few things either of them could do better than her—Donte was stronger, and Hatu a bit faster—but she had bested both of them enough times to judge the three of them equals.

Hava climbed the hill and discovered a lovely view of the west side of the island. Behind her more hills rose, blocking the landscape beyond, but from where she stood she could see for miles. Perhaps now that she was free of studies, she might return and watch the sunset.

She sat on the grass and felt the sea breeze, which rose every afternoon at about this time. The resident staff had mentioned that in a few weeks the rainy season would arrive and the weather would alternate between thundershowers and sunshine. She wouldn't be here to see that.

Hava lost track of time as she let her thoughts wander, and after a while felt the onset of drowsiness.

She stood up, shaking off the tired feeling; she wouldn't permit herself to fall asleep and miss a second meal. She walked over the crest of the hill, the boundary between the trimmed meadow grass and the tall grass and brush, treading carefully, as there were loose rocks among the tall grass that would trip up the unwary and she did not want to be limping back to the school with a twisted ankle.

A short distance away something caught her eye. Hava was not a trained tracker by any means, but she'd spent enough time in the wilderness with those who were to recognize that someone had been up here recently. The tall grass had been disturbed, and a good many stalks had been bent or broken to make a small clearing behind a thin curtain of intact stalks; the ground had been cleared of rocks, so someone could sit comfortably. She looked back and saw it was a good position to watch the school of the Powdered Women.

She knelt and observed the stalks and thought that whoever had made the clearing had been here recently, as there was still some moisture in the bent grasses, and if memory served, those would have dried out within a day or so of being damaged. The broken ones were dry, so she estimated someone had been here within the previous day.

She couldn't see what would be gained by spying from this vantage point, given the distance, except perhaps the coming and going of deliveries, like the one today, or the arrival of other visitors, or new students. Nothing within the building could be seen.

She looked carefully at the verge of the meadow and halfway down the hill she saw something a bit strange. Hurrying down there, she discovered a second observation point, one that provided a different enough perspective that she was now certain someone was spying on the school.

Hava felt a sudden sense of urgency to alert one of the instructors, but before she did, she was determined to make a complete survey of the verge around the meadow, to see how many more observation points could be found. She started down the hill again, and was halfway between the second observation site and the edge of the school's tree grove when a sound alerted her to the fact that she was not alone.

Taking a quick step into the tall grasses, Hava crouched. If she had been observed coming down the hill, this would do her no good, but if she hadn't perhaps she could continue to avoid detection and discover who was out here. No guards were ever placed around the schools in Coaltachin, as those islands that housed them were controlled completely by the nation and few foreigners were permitted to set foot on them. Those who lived here knew better than to trouble anyone at the school. The Powdered Women were under the full protection of the Council, and students from every master were trained here. So, if someone had secretly come ashore, they must have been foreign, but why had they come and for whom were they spying?

"What are you doing, girl?" said a friendly voice from behind Hava.

She turned and saw a man standing in the grass. He was of middle height and average girth, nondescript in most ways, with short-cropped, light brown hair. He wore a simple tunic and trousers, and woven sandals. He seemed to be without weapons, but carried a large black satchel secured by a strap across his chest and over his left shoulder. "You hiding from someone?" he asked, a grin on his face.

Hava returned the smile and said, "My father. I came with him from the town and didn't feel like unloading his wagon." She waved down to the rear of the kitchen, where the delivery was just about finished. "He's got enough help from the kitchen folk," she said, exaggerating her island accent enough to sound like the farm girls from home.

"Ha," the man said. "Avoiding work? I can understand that. I've done that a time or two myself."

"Who are you?" she asked as innocently as she could, resisting the urge to flutter her lashes as she'd seen other girls do, knowing she could not be convincing. Instead she strove for a wide-eyed look.

"I'm Mareed," he answered. "I live on the other side of the hill." He patted his satchel. "I'm an artist."

She feigned wonder. "Really? I've never met an artist. What does that mean?"

"I draw." He opened the top of the satchel and drew out a large piece of paper. She reached for it but he pulled it back. "Sorry, but paper like this is rare and I want to keep it from damage."

She attempted to look crestfallen. "Sorry," she said.

"That's all right." He held out the paper so she could see a drawing of the hill and woods, with clouds over a distant sea.

"Oh, that's nice," she said.

"When I've finished I'll use colors on it and then hang it on the wall for visitors to see."

"How interesting," said Hava.

He took off the satchel, working the strap over his neck while carefully holding the paper in one hand. He then opened it wide to replace the drawing. Hava looked into the satchel while Mareed carefully put the paper back into place. "Why here?" she asked as innocently as possible. "Why not closer to the ocean? Doesn't the school building block your view?"

"School?" he said. "I wondered what that was.

"No," he continued, "I just draw—" He suddenly lunged for her, a small blade in his left hand.

Hava had expected the attack and expertly stepped inside his strike, using her right arm as a block. The worst that would happen was that she'd be cut on the arm or shoulder, but the blow wouldn't be fatal. Years of combat training had taught her to ignore the impulse to leap back, exposing her torso and neck to a potentially killing slice.

She threw all her weight into an upward blow using the heel of her left hand, smashing it up into the man's nose. She knew that he would be stunned and blinded for a moment.

Hava felt his blood flow over her hand as she reached down and gripped Mareed's left wrist with her right hand, but felt him yank back, blind but anticipating her next move.

She tried to follow, stepping behind his right leg with her own, letting him trip backward as she struck his face again. A hot pain on her upper right arm told her she'd paid a price for that move but at that moment she was in a fighting state: heart pounding, senses extended, alert and not even thinking about what she was doing, just doing it from years of hand-to-hand training.

Mareed tried to roll to his right, only to be greeted with the toe of Hava's foot under his chin. The one thing she was better at than any student in the school was kicking. Donte and Hatu had complained more than once of the pain she inflicted with her wheel kicks, and she had seen the bruises she'd left on them.

Her attacker fell back and Hava kicked him a second time, but he managed to grab on to her foot and twisted, causing her to fall. She hit the ground and rolled, turning and coming to her feet as he struggled to get up, still half blinded by tears and blood from a smashed nose and a kick to the head.

She started another kick but saw him roll away, anticipating it, and so let her momentum turn her halfway. Spying a large rock, she continued rolling forward as he came to his feet, grabbing the rock as she passed.

It was clear to Hava that Mareed was a trained fighter, and only his underestimating her had kept her alive. He had expected a simple town girl who needed to be silenced, but instead he was faced with a girl trained to be a skilled killer.

She weighed throwing the rock but decided that if she failed to render him unconscious, she would leave herself unarmed. She cursed the rule that forbade weapons being carried at school and admitted she now understood why Donte was always armed, no matter where he was.

Mareed circled slowly, seeking to cut off any route Hava might choose if she decided to run. He held his knife ready to cut or thrust and kept himself prepared should she attack first.

Hava waited for Mareed to move. Her best choice was to use her speed and agility to counter his attack, hopefully ending with a solid blow with the rock, hard enough to render him unconscious or break bones. And she knew she probably had only one chance.

Time seemed to slow for Hava, and in a quick internal dialogue she asked herself what his best move would be. She instantly decided that he would force her down the hill backward, hoping she would trip or lose her balance, even for an instant, and give him an opening.

Without further thought, she feigned a stumble, and as she had hoped, Mareed seized the opportunity to attack. She started flailing her right arm, then as he lunged she wheeled to her right, keeping her left leg in place; as he went past her—his blade perilously close even as she moved away—Hava brought the rock down as hard as she could on the back of his head.

There was a loud crack and the shock ran up her arm. Mareed crumpled facedown into the dirt. His entire body shuddered and he went still.

Hava circled away in case he was pretending, but when she saw his face she knew he was truly dead. His eyes were open and fixed.

She stood for a moment, nearly panting, and then started to shake. Despite years of combat training, assorted bumps and bruises, and the occasional bleeding wound, this had been her first real contest with her life hanging in the balance, and the reality of that struck hard.

For a full minute she just stood staring at the dead man, feeling the need to alternately laugh and cry, and then she felt sick. She turned her head and vomited up the apple she had eaten a little earlier. Spitting the sour taste from her mouth, she turned and walked down the hill, and across the meadow.

As she reached the now-empty wagon, the driver glanced at Hava, then suddenly fixed her with a stare. "You're bleeding, girl!"

She looked at her right arm and realized her tunic sleeve was crimson with blood and it was now flowing around the rock she still held. "I guess I am," she said. Suddenly her legs gave out. "I think I need to rest a little," she said.

Hava was on the verge of losing consciousness when strong hands gripped her and helped her rise. Her attention sharpened a little and she realized two of the burlier male helpers were guiding her inside.

They sat her on a stool beside a table in the kitchen and Hava's focus faded. A sharp pain in her right arm revived her and she realized that one of the instructors was sewing her cut, making careful tiny stitches. Standing behind her was Mistress Mulray. "What happened?"

"A man on the hill was spying on the school. He attacked me and I killed him."

With a gesture of her head, Mulray indicated that two male kitchen staff should go and investigate. It dawned on Hava that the reason there were no guards at the school was that every member of this household was a trained sicari, and the students were only slightly less deadly. For some reason it had never occurred to her before, but now it seemed obvious.

Hava was handed a mug of juice. "Drink," the instructor said. "You've lost blood."

The pungent sweet taste told her she had been given a large mug of pomace grape juice before it was drained of the lees and fermented into wine. In her still unfocused state she wondered why she hadn't known there was a vineyard nearby.

The juice helped to revive her a bit and she remained silent until the instructor stitching her arm finished. "Tincture," the woman said, and applied a liquid that burned. "That will keep it from festering," she told Hava as she bandaged her arm. "The wound is long but not deep. Still, keep it covered for a few days and if it itches, don't scratch. Let it heal and put on a fresh bandage in three days."

The instructor stood and left Hava alone with Mistress Mulray. "Now, tell me what happened."

Feeling less groggy, Hava recounted the entire encounter as best she could. By the time she had finished one of the two aides had returned with the large canvas satchel. He said, "We found the body. We searched and found the blade and this." He handed Mistress Mulray a black lacquered badge with a metal pin.

Mulray's eyes widened enough for Hava to know that the sight of the badge alarmed her. The older woman motioned for the satchel to be opened and its contents dumped on the table.

More than a dozen pieces of paper fell out, along with charcoal sticks and erasing rubber. Hava said, "He said he was drawing clouds or . . . something. But the other smaller ones are drawings of faces."

Mulray looked at them and Hava saw blood drain from her features. "These are students," she said.

Hava's expression was one of open confusion. "Why—?"

Mulray held up her hand and said, "Get Hava's go-bag from the student barracks. She sleeps in a quiet room tonight."

She looked at Hava and said, "Rest. I'll have food

sent to you. I do not want you leaving your room or speaking to any other students. You will return to Coaltachin, and I'll have further instructions for you tomorrow."

Mulray departed, and seeing no reason to stay, Hava stood and followed an instructor to one of the many small rooms in the school. She nodded thanks to her companion, who closed the door. Hava lay down and while her mind was still trying to comprehend what had happened, she fell asleep.

Hava awoke as the door opened. She had slept until dinner, risen to eat, and then quickly fallen asleep again. As predicted her wound was sore and starting to itch. A young girl at the door said, "It's time to go."

Hava rose and realized she'd slept in her clothing, and from the angle of the sun coming through the window that it was later than first light. She hurried through the school and as she was about to turn toward the kitchen, the girl guiding her said, "No, this way."

Hava followed, trying and failing to recall the girl's name, until they reached the door leading to the stabling yard outside. There, a fine two-horse carriage waited, with a high front seat for the driver; behind him the square body of the wagon housed a bench seat with side boards to keep passengers from falling out, with an opening on either side above a single step held in place by fancy ironwork.

Hava hadn't seen its like before and was impressed by the size of the large spoke wheels. Mistress Mulray waited under a canvas covering held above her by a latticework of intricately carved wooden supports. The older woman beckoned Hava to get in, and she complied, sitting next to the mistress and holding her go-bag in her lap. "How are you feeling this morning?" asked Mulray as the driver flicked the reins and the horses began to move forward.

Hava said, "I slept a lot and my arm hurts, but not so much I can't ignore it."

Mulray smiled. "You're a bit of a surprise."

Hava didn't know how to respond, so she remained silent. After a moment, Mulray said, "I let you sleep because you needed it, and I wished to speak with you alone. Rather than wait for a ship, I've ordered one to set sail the moment you're aboard. I have documents for the captain and will give them to him in person." She looked at Hava and said, "Now, we have some time to continue our conversation. I would like you to recount what happened with that . . . artist, now that you're a little more lucid and may recall details you missed yesterday."

Hava repeated her narrative, adding a few details she

had missed, and when she was done, Mulray reached over and patted her hand. "You were perfect, given the circumstances."

Stunned, but trying not to show it, Hava looked away, contemplating the lovely morning as they rode down the hill to the town and harbor beyond. Finally she said, "Thank you. If I'm truthful, I had no plan. I just . . . acted."

"As it should be, Hava," said the older woman. "You've been trained to act in certain ways without thinking—to do what needs to be done." Mulray paused for a moment, keeping her hand on Hava's. "Master Facaria is a very . . . traditional man. He has his detractors, but he often sees things the rest of us miss."

Hava noticed the *us* and realized that not only was Mulray in charge of the school, the leader of the Powdered Women, she was of equal rank to the male masters.

"Here is what you must understand," Mistress Mulray continued. "First, no one must hear of what occurred yesterday; no one. You may only speak about it with members of the Council. If they do not ask to speak with you about this, you will forget everything; yesterday was without incident. Do I make myself clear?"

"Yes, mistress."

"Good." Mulray looked squarely at Hava and added, "There's one thing I must say. You asked if you weren't pretty enough to be a Powdered Woman. Men seek many things, and most men can be blinded by beauty. A woman like Nessa will have powerful men competing to get her into their beds. Some might marry her, should they be able, but in the end, she is to them nothing more than a thing, a prize to be paraded before other men. That is the secret of her strength; she will hear many secrets because some drunken fool wishes to impress her, or believes he loves her and can rely on her confidence. She will always betray them and serve Coaltachin."

Mulray paused, then said, "A man who sees you for what you truly are is rare. Facaria is such a man, and so he understands this. We women live at the sufferance of foolish men who are blinded by beauty. Facaria, and the few men like him, know better. Listen to him, and ignore those who treat us as if we are possessions, trophies for their power and prowess. They are men who can be manipulated and used: they are prey to be gutted."

Mulray fell silent for a few moments. At last she said, "There will be times when you will feel alone and need to know who your true allies are. Train yourself to separate the false from the true. Can you do that?"

Hava was uncertain how to answer.

Seeing the girl hesitate, Mulray said, "Do you know anyone who would put his life at risk to save yours?"

Without hesitation, Hava answered, "Yes."

"Who?"

"A boy I know," said Hava, thinking of Hatu.

Mulray said, "You had no lovers before coming here; you said you were a girl who follows the rules. So, he is a friend?"

"Hatushaly," said Hava. "He would risk his life for me, I think."

"Think or know?"

Hava considered for a moment, then said, "I know."

"Ah," said Mulray. "Knowing there is someone like that out there, even if they are miles away from you, or it's been ages since you've seen them, that can make a difference." She tapped the side of her head with her forefinger. "Knowing it, yes, that can make a difference."

They rode silently as they passed a lumbering oxcart, and Hava returned the driver's wave while Mulray ignored him. For the rest of the journey, the head of the Powdered Women occasionally made seemingly inconsequential small talk, interspersed with long periods of silence.

Finally they reached the seaside town where Hava

had landed only a month earlier. The carriage rolled through the town, the name of which was still unknown to Hava, a situation she didn't find surprising: few foreigners had set foot on this island since the creation of the school of the Powdered Women, so the town needed no official name.

As the carriage rolled to a stop, a dockworker hurried over to assist Mistress Mulray as she stepped down. She waved him away, making it clear his help was unnecessary as she easily descended, despite wearing a long narrow skirt.

Hava, in her usual trousers, had even less need of help. She shouldered her go-bag and followed Mulray to the end of the docks, where a small, fast ship waited. When they reached the gangway they were spied by a heavyset man who hurried to meet them, touching his forelock with his right finger in a casual salute. "Good to see you again, Mistress Mulray."

"You as well, Captain." Mulray indicated Hava. "She will be your only passenger, and this is your only cargo." She handed him a large sealed pouch. "As fast as you can to Corbara, and see personally that this reaches Master Zusara."

"Understood," he said, taking the pouch.

Turning to Hava, she said, "The captain will deliver you safely to Corbara and arrange passage from there to Morasel. Try to remember what you've learned here, you'll find some of it useful."

"I will," replied Hava.

Mulray bit her lower lip as she thought for a moment, a fact Hava found revealing: Mulray had something to say to her but was considering how to say it. Then Mulray said, "I was wrong on one thing."

"What, mistress?"

"I know exactly why Master Facaria sent you here."

Hava's eyes widened slightly.

Leaning forward, Mulray spoke softly into Hava's ear. "So you would learn with certainty what you should never become."

Hava was speechless, and Mulray walked back to the carriage.

Hava finally turned to the captain, who said, "You must be something special, girl."

"My name is Hava," she said as he turned toward the gangway.

"And I am Captain Joshua," he replied. "It's a quick trip; the winds blow favorably and strong this time of the year. We have a cabin for you."

As she followed him up the gangway, Hava said, "Captain Joshua, I want to work. I will grow bored with nothing to do."

"Work?" said the captain, looking over his shoulder

as he stepped down onto the ship's deck. "What, you want to be a pirate?"

Hava's gaze narrowed under her furrowed brow. "Pirate? Why pirate?"

"Because the only women crewing ships on this ocean are pirates; they have a funny liking for it."

Hava said, "I'm fit and I learn quickly. I'll go mad if I have to sit around with nothing to do."

The captain laughed. "Well, if you can deal with a rough crew—"

"I can," she said firmly. "This isn't my first ship's passage."

"Well, then, Hava the Pirate you shall be. I'll have someone show you where to stow your gear, and you'll berth in your cabin, not with the crew," he said. "And I'd advise you to eat alone: the men can put a starving man off his meal with the way they go at chow." He motioned to a crewman who looked only a few years older than Hava. "This is Hava," he said to the sailor. To Hava, Captain Joshua said, "This is Daniel; he'll show you your quarters and then start your education." Looking back at Daniel, he said, "This young lady would like to become a pirate, so you'll train her. When she's on deck, she's a recruit."

The blond youth broke into a broad smile. "Prettiest recruit I've ever seen, Captain."

"Belay that. Pass the word, she's under Master Zusara's protection."

All hint of humor fled Daniel's face at the mention of the leader of the Council. "Sir," said the young man. He turned to Hava and spoke deferentially, "Follow me and I'll show you around."

As Hava followed Daniel, wondering what it meant to be under the protection of the most powerful man in Coaltachin, she heard the captain bark, "Make ready to set sail. Cast off all lines!"

Hava tried not to grin. She was going to learn how to be a sailor!

7

An Incident on the Covenant Road

The next day found Declan up early, as the sun was rising and Oncon lay shrouded in morning fog. He had bid Roz goodbye as she started her journey home, checked the banked fire in the forge, ensured the water buckets were full, then picked up his masterpiece and began to ready it for its buyer. Word had reached them that Baron Bartholomy would arrive soon to finalize the purchase of his sword.

As the sun brightened the eastern horizon, Declan sat on a sturdy hitching rail carefully polishing his masterpiece. It was the only tangible evidence that he had been made a master smith. He had to remind himself that, yes, it had indeed happened, and Edvalt was waiting for him to make his choice, to stay or to leave.

Not for the first time, Declan considered the irony of Edvalt's mastery of weapons making. He seemed to find making weapons, especially swords, distasteful, yet he was brilliant at it.

Early in his apprenticeship, Declan had begun to realize that as gifted a smith as Edvalt was, weapons were the true measure of such gifts. Blades for scythes and perfect tines on rakes reflected good craft, but swords and pole arms reflected art. Farming tools and wagon repairs required no mastery of the fire and the folding of steel. Most common smiths were content to buy their materials from a monger, ready-forged into low-grade steel.

A smith could work his entire life devoted to simple iron repairs and never once fold steel as Declan had the day before. Despite the chance that his apprentice might never again find the need to forge a weapon like it, Edvalt had seemed almost desperate to pass on his knowledge. Declan was young enough he couldn't imagine feeling that way, though he conceded that he might someday, should he father a son.

Still, fate had brought Declan to learn from a true great master, if such a rank existed. Over the years, as Declan had served his master, word of Edvalt's skill had traveled, and despite their living in the Covenant, more commissions for arms had come. Declan did not know yet how to measure what he'd learned from Edvalt, but he suspected he had reached a lofty rank because of his teacher and that only a handful of smiths were in his position.

He looked at his masterpiece and realized that it would be painful to see Baron Bartholomy take it away. Declan would know it was his, though Bartholomy would credit Edvalt with its fashioning. Declan was at peace with that; he owed everything he was and knew to Edvalt.

Then there was Roz. She had fulfilled her promise and the sex had been more intense than any he had ever known. However, the best part of the night had been the conversation afterward, an intimacy Declan had never before experienced. He had felt a deep peace and there was, for lack of a better word, trust in it, space where ideas and feelings could flow.

Roz had been up before first light, shaking off the straw from the stable they had used for bedding, and as the false dawn brightened the eastern sky, she had driven her wagons up the hill to the main road.

Declan had felt a pang of regret watching her leave. It wasn't just the sex, though she was the best lover he had known. Bedding the town girls was a pleasure he declined more often than accepted. Roz had set something of a standard they couldn't equal. He chuckled to himself as he imagined that it must be a little like the deep passionate love the taletellers sang about: lovers separated by some dire circumstance, who either conquer all or die tragically depending on the tale.

Declan saw himself as no hero, nor Roz as any damsel, but he knew his feelings for her were a bit more than perhaps he cared to admit, even to himself. She was almost old enough to be his mother, and he suspected she had lovers all over the East Lands, in the past even a few here in Oncon; he had a sense of who they might be, though he had never inquired.

It was because she made him feel differently about things, but mostly about himself. He wasn't quite sure why, but he sensed these different feelings were important and something he needed to better understand. Certainly before he settled down and wed. No matter who she might be, the woman who became his wife would need to make him feel the way Roz did.

Declan was not by nature an introspective man, yet for the first time in his life he found himself with a great deal to ponder. In his easy conversation with Roz the previous night, he had come to understand that he would leave Oncon sooner, rather than later. He would not buy Edvalt's smithy.

Edvalt, despite his protests, still had many years of good work before him. Declan knew him well enough to know that a retirement sitting around Marius's miserable excuse for an inn was not in his nature—mostly because, except for a few hours in the evening when the weather was good, it was usually empty. Sitting on a stool on the beach, fishing beyond the breakers, was not a pastime the old smith would enjoy for long. Mila might at last convince him to plant some fruit trees behind the house, but Declan couldn't see Edvalt as a grower or gardener.

No, Edvalt was the sort of man who would work until he could not. Declan couldn't imagine anything after that, because Edvalt was a man to whom work was life, and life was work. Deep in his heart, Declan knew that if the old smith were to cease working, it would be his first step toward welcoming death. Thinking about age, infirmity, and death caused Declan's mood to darken, so he turned his mind to the moment, concentrating on the sword he had fashioned the day before.

As the morning sun rose above the horizon, Declan inspected the blade. He had never finished one of this quality—Edvalt had always seen to the task before—and saw that the metal resisted polishing more than common steel. It was the nature of the thing, Declan assumed; he had experienced it in the final finishing at the forge, when he also recognized that setting the edge to give it sharpness was actually more delicate a task than he had anticipated. There he had to act quickly to set the edge, but now he could take his time with the polish.

Which was fine with the newly anointed master smith, for Baron Bartholomy was two days away from appearing to claim it; Declan would put the blade away when the day's work began and return to it in the evening, slowly but surely polishing the blade to gleam like a jewel in the sunlight.

Jusan appeared at the door. Often upon arising, he did small tasks for Mila before meeting Edvalt's needs. He waved at Declan and shouted, "Berries!"

Declan laughed, for the summer berries grew on the lower hills and Jusan would be gone for half a day, which would annoy Edvalt, though he would never voice that displeasure to his wife.

A few moments later, Edvalt emerged out of the little house. Seeing the retreating back of his apprentice, he asked, "Berries?"

Declan nodded.

"Well, I must remind Mila that she's going to have to start taking care of these tasks herself if you leave us, as then it will just be Jusan and me."

"I wish you luck with that," said Declan.

"Right," agreed Edvalt. "How's the polish coming?"

Declan handed him the blade. Edvalt flipped it in his hand, turned it toward the rising sun, and inspected the finish.

"Slow going, this steel," he said, handing the sword back to Declan.

Before Declan could reply, Jusan came back into sight, scurrying down the small road that led to the highway. "Riders!" he shouted, just as the sound of hoofbeats in the distance reached them. "Armed riders!"

"Oathmen or mercenaries?" asked Edvalt.

"I see badges of Sandura, but no tabards nor uniforms; they look like mercenaries."

Edvalt nodded once and said, "Bring me my sword." Jusan ran off and returned moments later with two swords. The young apprentice threw a two-handed longsword to Edvalt and pulled a shorter broadsword out of its scabbard, which he tossed aside. Edvalt said, "We start no fights, but be ready for one."

Edvalt glanced at Declan, who quickly twirled the newly minted sword, testing its balance again. Edvalt's expression asked if the new master smith was prepared to fight.

Declan nodded once. Neither he nor Jusan had faced an armed man in combat before, yet Edvalt had trained them to be as competent with a weapon as the men who would wield them, for it was a poor smith who didn't know how his wares were to be used. Declan had joined a few fistfights as a youth, as had Jusan, so they both knew how to stand up for themselves, but armed combat was another thing altogether.

Declan knew he had the skill to fight, he just didn't know yet if he had the stomach for it. Jusan looked frightened, but he was a resolute boy and would stand his ground.

Riders appeared on the short road down from the highway. A trio of horsemen moved purposefully toward the smithy. A clutch of men on foot halted at the verge of the road, waiting.

The riders reined in a half a dozen paces before the smith. The leader glanced at Jusan and Edvalt, then at Declan. He looked at the forge and bellows, then said to Edvalt, "It's an odd smith who greets a stranger with his weapon drawn."

Ignoring the banter, Edvalt said, "State your business."

Pointing at Declan, then Jusan, the man said, "That's what we require. Sturdy lads who can wield a sword." The men behind chuckled, and the leader said, "Or try to learn."

"He was my journeyman, now he's a master smith,"

said Edvalt. The blacksmith held his sword in his right hand, the flat on his shoulder, a fashion that suggested he was willing to use it but was not looking for conflict.

"You a warrior, then, smith?" asked the lead rider.

Declan studied the men. The leader, a slender, nervous-looking man with dark hair and eyes, sat astride a grey gelding, the best of a poor group of mounts. Declan assayed the other two horses, judging them perhaps days away from being unfit; one had an obvious bone spavin that would have the animal limping soon, and the other a hitch in its movement that suggested a ruptured tendon or an abscessed hoof. The men looked equally woebegone, their equipment little better than what ghouls might glean from the fallen in battle to sell at market.

One rider wore a jack jerkin—a heavily quilted cloth double folded to stop all but a direct hit—the other metal scale sewn to jack. The leader wore a well-made, if damaged, overshirt of linked chain. All of them wore a band of dark red cloth with a single yellow slash tied around their left arms: the mark of Sandura. If they truly served a king, they were of the lowest rank: hired swords, not oathmen. More likely they were slavers pretending to be a press gang for Sandura.

Declan glanced at Edvalt, who nodded slightly, and the apprentice knew what his master did not say: these men were skilled in warcraft and unpredictable. Declan nodded in return he was ready.

Edvalt answered, "I've fought, in younger days." Glancing again at Declan he added, "And it's a poor forger of weapons who doesn't understand their use."

The leader was silent, as if appraising the risk. "We have the king's writ to take recruits."

Quietly, Edvalt said, "Not here. A quarter mile back where the roads meet, where the black oak stands, is a wooden sign upon which is inscribed the Emblem of the Covenant. The five crowns—" He halted. Old habits die hard, he conceded; it hadn't been five crowns for almost seventeen years. "The four crowns," he amended, "concede this road." He pointed to where the men, whom Edvalt now knew to be conscripts for San- dura's army, waited. "The Narrows Covenant covers all surrounding lands! Your king has no writ here!"

The leader glanced at the men beside him, as if trying to gauge the balance between risk and reward. Edvalt, while older, was still a powerful figure and had the poise of a seasoned warrior. Jusan was large for his age and seemed ready for a brawl, his expression one of determination, wary, but without fear. Declan was a tall, strong-looking young man, and his purchase price would be that of three lesser boys, especially if the buyer needed a smith. All three men stood with hands on swords, ready to enforce their demand. Edvalt added, "You may not be oathmen to the king of Sandura, but you act in his name; would you have Lodavico named oath breaker?"

The leader of the mercenaries silently weighed his options for a moment. "Truth to tell, old man, we're not strictly Lodavico's men. He's just paying more these days than anyone else!" He suddenly shouted and drove his heels into his horse's flanks. The animal leapt forward, knocking Edvalt off balance and the smith stumbled backward before getting his feet under him and throwing his weight forward to unleash a blow at the rider.

The rider turned as Jusan and Declan prepared for the others to attack. Edvalt didn't hesitate and lashed out with his own sword, striking so hard he completely severed the man's right leg below the knee and sliced through the stirrup leathers and girth, cutting into the horse's side and causing it to buck and thrash, and almost kick Edvalt in the process.

Blood fountained from the rider's severed leg as he screamed and was thrown from the horse, high into the air, before hitting the ground with a painful thud, his saddle falling with him.

The horse bucked again, then bolted in pain and ran straight at the other riders, causing them to split up.

The lead rider lay screaming for a moment, gripping uselessly at his leg, his blood spewing. Declan knew that if someone didn't get a tourniquet on him soon, the man would bleed to death in minutes. He lifted his own sword, ignoring the dying man a few feet away, and watched the other riders.

They glanced at each other and it was clear there was no obvious second in command. Neither of them seemed certain what to do next. Edvalt said evenly, "Slavers! You best turn around and leave the Covenant. We'll not go quietly, nor will the lads in the village down the road. You'll have nothing but blood and pain for your labors."

Still the riders hesitated. Then in a commanding tone Edvalt shouted, "Leave now!"

Looking at their unconscious leader bleeding out on the ground, the man closest to Edvalt said, "What about him?"

"We'll bury him. Now go!"

The riders sat motionless for a moment, until one turned his animal and the other followed. Edvalt motioned for Jusan and Declan to stand next to him. Without taking his eyes off the road above the smithy, he said, "They'll be back with the others. And this time they'll come down the hill at a charge." He glanced around and then started to jog toward the house. "Follow me."

Declan spared a glance at the fallen rider, who now lay motionless; his eyes were fixed on a point in space above him and held no sign of life.

They reached the door of his home as Edvalt's wife appeared. "I saw," she said. Mila was sun-browned and tiny, but as tough as old leather in Declan's opinion. Her hair had been fair when she was younger, but the blonde had turned to white over the last ten years.

"Then to the village as fast as you can, old woman, and fetch armed lads and whichever old men wish to keep their sons free of these slavers."

Without comment, she hurried toward the heart of the village, running like a girl a third her age.

Edvalt said, "Declan, the sword."

Declan knew he was being told not to let that blade fall into the hands of these mercenaries. He glanced at it. Unfinished and only partly polished, it looked an average blade. Until it was finished few would recognize its worth. Still, a skilled swordsman would only have to feel the balance and test the edge to know it was a fine weapon, and any smith of repute who gave it a polish would recognize it for the treasure it was.

"The lads from the village will be here shortly," said

Edvalt. "But we're probably going to have to do some hurting until then. You boys ready?"

He glanced from Declan to Jusan, then returned his attention to the road. Both nodded once.

"Now, in a minute or two they'll come racing down that road with the boys on foot trying to stay close. If they're smart, they'll come at once, but they don't look like they have the wits the old gods gave fish, so the horses are likely to be a fair bit in front; try to dodge away at the last." Both young men had worked with enough horses to have a very good idea how it would feel to be run over by one. "Get your backs to a wall and just keep them off you until the village lads get here."

As predicted, the two riders came galloping down the short road to the smithy and Declan readied his sword. He'd never faced a man in a real fight, and his heart pounded. He tried to remember everything Edvalt had taught him over the years, but his mind was awash with conflicting thoughts, almost all of which were swept away by a sudden urge to turn and flee.

He could feel his knees shake, and perspiration poured from his face and back as if he were again at the forge, but this time it reeked of fear. He hesitated, almost a moment too long, as one rider veered toward him with his sword back, ready to lop off Declan's head, then suddenly he was moving.

The rider swung low and Declan only kept his head by chance, as the man held his sword raised to the left side, and he inadvertently deflected the blow. He staggered as he felt shock run through his arms and was abruptly slammed by the side of the horse. It was a glancing strike, but it knocked him back and he felt the air explode out of his lungs from the impact with the wall of the smithy.

Fury rose up and fear fled as he saw the rider turn his mount, urging it forward again. Declan set himself, then ducked and unloaded a low blow that took the horse's left foreleg out from under him. The rider yelled in a mix of rage and shock as he was sent flying over his horse's withers, and Declan turned and ran to where he had struck the dirt. Declan dodged around the screaming, thrashing mount and charged at the horseman. The rider was attempting to roll to his feet when Declan swung hard in an upward blow and cut deep into the man's throat. Blood spurted like a fountain and for a brief instant Declan felt his sword held, then he yanked it back and turned to survey the fight.

His gaze narrowed, and with unexpected clarity he could see every aspect of the struggle. Jusan and Edvalt were besieged by another rider, though they'd positioned themselves near the side of the house, so the horse was more of a hindrance to the man's getting close than a threat to the two smiths.

Declan sensed more than heard the first of the fighters on foot as he attacked and spun as the man bore down on him. He saw the coming blow this time, as clearly as he had when practicing with Edvalt, and took it on the strongest part of his own sword: the shock taken and returned, so the attacker's arm recoiled as he turned the wrong way, opening himself to a quick counterthrust. Declan twisted his wrist and extended his arm, gutting the unarmored warrior like a fish. The man fell, and Declan ended his life with one plunge of the blade.

The fear of the first moments of combat was washed away in a rush of energy unlike anything Declan had known in his life. He had no sense of his own mortality, only a certainty he would come through this struggle victoriously. He spun in place, seeking his next opponent, and saw the scene had barely changed from before the man attacked; time itself seemed to have slowed.

He rushed to Edvalt's aid as the old smith protected Jusan from the remaining rider; the boy had been injured and stood with his back against the wall of their hut. Blood flowed down one arm. With a leap, Declan grabbed the collar of the rearmost rider's leather jerkin from behind and dragged him from his saddle. Edvalt was instantly on the fallen man and had his sword into his throat before Declan was fully on his feet. The horse shied and ran, and Declan saw every detail, as the warriors on foot continued to arrive. For a moment Declan wondered what had taken them so long to reach the struggle.

He pushed the thought aside and turned to face seven armed men who slowly fanned out in front of him. From their expressions and the lack of leadership, Declan could tell not one of them wished to be the first into the fray. With a glance, he saw Edvalt crouched and ready for the attack.

Declan laughed, and three of the men stepped back. The young smith suddenly took a single leap forward, wheeled, and threw a blow at one man's head, and saw him fall back, almost losing his footing as he retreated. Then two men attacked and Declan found himself moving with a precision and speed he would not have imagined he possessed, despite hours of practice with Edvalt. He took one man's strike on his own blade with ease, then spun and struck the other man across the throat before he brought his own sword up and continued in a full circle to strike the first man in the back, knocking him to his knees.

Edvalt hurried forward and finished the man while Declan turned to face another. The three men who had retreated needed no more excuses to quit the struggle, and they turned and fled. The last two men standing saw Mila leading the villagers toward them, many holding old weapons or farm tools, but all yelling and ready for a fight, and they took off, only a few moments behind those already running up the road.

Declan hesitated for a moment as he considered giving chase, but Edvalt's voice cut through the air. "Help me!"

He saw that the old smith was also wounded, a deep cut in one side, but Edvalt ignored his injury as he knelt beside Jusan, who had collapsed to the ground, his back against the wall of the smithy.

Declan had seen enough injuries to know that Jusan's was serious. He ran to the house and grabbed kitchen rags, then hurried back to find that some of the village men were giving chase to the slavers, while others were putting down the two dying horses. A few had gathered around Mila and Edvalt, who were tending to Jusan. The young apprentice was white faced and his vision went in and out of focus, but he was still conscious.

Declan handed the rags to Mila, who placed them firmly on Jusan's left side. "The blood's red," she said, "so if we can stop this bleeding, he should live." Declan knew that if the blood had been dark, it would have meant the boy's liver or other organ had been pierced and Jusan would have been dying.

Declan knelt beside Edvalt to inspect his left side. "Nasty," he said as he saw the long slash across the old man's ribs.

"I've had worse," said the smith.

"Get me my sewing," ordered Mila, and Declan hurried into the house. His heart was pounding and he flexed his hands as if he was struggling to gain control of himself. His mind raced as if he were still in combat, yet he also felt an odd calm that kept him focused. He moved to where Mila kept her sewing basket, a tightly woven wicker rectangle with a cleverly hinged lid, in two strides. One benefit of being married to a smith was an abundant supply of needles, the sale of which had contributed in no small part to Edvalt's prosperity over the years.

He carried the basket out to Mila, who took it and efficiently pulled out a large needle and threaded it. "We need to brine the wound," she said.

Edvalt kept his hand pressed against his side as he settled down into a more comfortable position. Mila said to Declan, "Get salt, a half handful, and a half-filled pitcher of water. Mix it good and bring it here."

Again Declan headed into the house and did as he was asked. He returned with a half-filled pitcher of salted water. Seaside folk had long ago learned that, for reasons known only to the gods, wounds that were bathed in seawater festered less often than those bathed in freshwater. As it was too far to run to the sea, salting freshwater did as well. It didn't mean Jusan wouldn't get a festering wound and die, but it bettered his chances.

The youngster screamed weakly and thrashed about as Mila bathed his wound. Declan had to hold him in place as the old woman began to sew. Jusan gritted his teeth and tried not to cry out, but he could barely restrain himself. At last Mila tied off the stitches and said, "That's as good as it can be done; he's in the hands of the gods now. Carry him inside," she told Declan.

As the newly minted master smith did so, Mila turned her attention to her husband, who repeated, "I've had worse."

With a snort of derision, she answered, "I've given you worse."

Declan laid Jusan down on his own bed; the younger apprentice usually slept in the smithy, but he'd rest better on a proper cot. The boy's head lolled and his eyes were closed, but he was breathing easily, so Declan knew that Jusan slept. He returned outside to find the village men approaching with a dozen or more freed captives, and driving a trio of wagons.

A fisherman named Rees hiked his thumb over his shoulder toward the following prisoners and said, "We have trouble, Edvalt."

Wincing as his wife finished sewing him up, the old smith said, "Really?"

"I mean, more's coming." Rees knelt before the smith, his leathery tanned face and bald, sunburned pate glistening with perspiration. "The lads we cut loose tell of slavers moving in groups, fanning out to comb through the Covenant. Seems old Lodavico of Sandura is replenishing his armies. Lost a bunch of soldiers in the last year, something to do with destroying all of Ithrace's former allies. Since he betrayed Langene all those years ago, he seems to think the Covenant doesn't mean anything. Sandura's army might well be heading this way, but before that"—he pointed a thumb back toward the corpses of the slavers—"this lot are already behaving like no truce exists around the Narrows."

Edvalt leaned back against the side of the smithy, saying nothing for a long minute as he considered what he had heard. Rees began to speak, but Edvalt held up his hand. "I'm thinking," was all he said.

There was no official government in Oncon. As in many villages in the Covenant, the locals governed themselves by consensus, which at times led to some very rough justice, but for large part the system worked. Edvalt was looked on by the villagers as a natural leader, in part because of his position: the smith was the most important man in the village, and he knew more about the outside world than any other resident. Some even suggested he had been a soldier, perhaps one of rank.

Finally Edvalt said, "We should brace for trouble, then." He motioned to Declan to help him to his feet. Once upright, he stood for a moment, testing how steady he was. He brushed away Declan's offer of help and said, "I'm fine."

Such was the respect for Edvalt's opinion on important matters that the villagers gathered around him remained silent. A few helped the freed captives settle in under the shade of the smithy and house, while everyone waited.

Finally Edvalt spoke. "Did any of the slavers escape?"

Rees stood and looked at the other villagers. "Did you chase them all down?"

A man named Flet stood on his toes and spoke over the heads of his neighbors. He said, "A couple got up the road. We let them go when they turned east and kept running. They'll not be back soon."

"No," said Edvalt, "not soon, but they will be

back." He grunted with discomfort and said, "They'll be coming for these"—he pointed to the prisoners sitting a short way off—"and any others they can take."

"What should we do?" asked a woman named Thea. She was a widow with one grown son who cared for her. She added, "If they take my boy, I'll starve."

Edvalt shook his head. "No, Thea. We're not the sort of community to let you starve, but you're right. They'll take your boy, and other lads, like Declan and Jusan."

"So what do we do?" asked Rees, echoing the widow's concerns.

"Well, first thing," said Edvalt, "might be some valuables in those wagons." Two of the villagers turned to inspect the carts. Then he pointed to the captives. "And we feed this lot before they die on us."

He moved away from the building, again brushing off Declan's attempt to help him. "I've got a cut, lad. I'm not dying."

He got to the center of the clearing, where he could look down toward the rest of the village, and said, "We must be careful, for if we're not, those murdering bastards might just start killing before we can get organized."

He held up his hand for silence, anticipating the flood of questions that began, and after a moment he said, "Here's what we do: All the boys and young men have to leave the village. We have three, maybe four days to get them away. The slavers have a company commander somewhere. He won't take kindly to losing men and captives. If those two who got away find him tonight, he'll call in his other squads, and they'll gather by tomorrow night. Another day to get here . . . Three days, maybe four," he repeated.

"What will we do about the crops?" asked one of the farmers. "With the boys gone, we'll lose more than half."

"The fishermen can help out. With fewer mouths to feed they don't need to make a catch every day. When the crops are in, the farmers can learn to haul nets.

"The boys don't need to be gone forever, just for a few weeks. Head some of them down to Newbay. That should be far enough away and we can send word by boat if the slavers head that way. If they find only old men and women, small children, maybe they'll give up combing the villages."

"What about the girls?" asked a woman, putting her hand on her daughter's shoulder, a girl of fourteen years.

Edvalt nodded. "Yes, they should go as well. If these bastards are looking for fighting men and don't find any here, they may instead look for women to sell, or at least make use of. They may also burn a few huts in the bargain. Let's give them as little reason to kill us as we can." Then with anger he added, "But be ready to fight and kill them if you must."

The men tried to look determined, but all knew only the men and women over fifty and children would be left if the young men and women fled. "Some of the boys should go with all the girls to Covenant Green. There's that order of holy women there."

"Nuns," supplied a village woman.

"Yes, they're the type that feed lepers and takes care of madmen," offered another.

"Yes, go to . . . What do they call it?"

"The Abbey of Hope," supplied the first woman.

"Good name," said Edvalt. "Tell whoever is in charge what happened here and ask that they shelter the girls until we send word it's safe for them to return. The boys can help out around the town for food or chance coming back. The slavers should be here and gone by then."

At the last, Edvalt didn't sound convincing.

"What about them?" asked another fisherman, indicating the freed prisoners.

Edvalt looked at the ragged men, ranging from their late teens to their early thirties. All showed signs of beatings and starvation. "What do you want?" he asked the prisoner closest to him.

"Something to eat would do," he answered, and a few of the villagers laughed. "And then I want to go home."

"Where's home?" asked Edvalt.

"Marquensas. I'm a teamster. We took a cargo of fruit to the market at Dunkeep, and on the way back we got taken by those murderers."

"Dunkeep?" said a villager. "That's in Ilcomen!"

The teamster nodded. "I mentioned that as we were being chained up. Didn't seem to impress the slavers." He motioned toward the wagons and said, "One of those up there is mine, or rather was my master's. He died trying to fight them off."

"Well, it's yours now," said Edvalt. "Let's feed these boys," he said to the villagers. "After we eat, let's meet here and organize. We've got to get ready. This trouble is far from over."

As the villagers began to help the freed captives, Edvalt motioned for the teamster to stay. "We'll feed you soon, but I think we can help each other. What's your name?"

"Ratigan."

Edvalt laughed and winced from the pain that caused in his side. "You're called Rat, I would wager."

The man's brows narrowed. He looked whipcord tough, slender but muscular, and Declan could see why the slavers had taken him: with training he might prove a good warrior. "Not since I was a boy of eleven and beat Jono Bolles senseless for it," he replied with a note of challenge in his voice.

"Well, Ratigan," said Edvalt, clapping him on his shoulder, "we're all friends here; else we're dead men. Come along and I'll tell you what I have in mind."

Ratigan entered the hut after Mila and Declan, and was followed by Edvalt.

The old woman uncovered a food chest, pulled out bread baked the day before, and cut off a large slice. "Got salted fish and some cheese, too," she said. The starving man nodded as he bit into the drying bread.

"Now," said Edvalt, "I've got a lad in that cot too weak to walk, and we have to have him away in a day or two at the most; I think I know a way that will benefit us all."

"How?" asked Ratigan.

"I want you to take my former journeyman"—he pointed at Declan—"and his apprentice—"

"My apprentice?" interrupted Declan.

"Your apprentice," said Edvalt with a nod. "If we survive the coming days, I can always find another lad to train up. I was going to sell you this smithy if you'd a mind to stay, but if slavers are making free and the Covenant is being ignored, there may be no smithy in a few more days. And if they do burn this place to the ground, Mila and I will have to start over somewhere else." He didn't look terribly distressed at that prospect; Declan knew Edvalt was frugal and had secreted away enough gold that starting over should not be a problem. Declan also realized that Edvalt didn't wish for Declan to buy the smithy; he might have said he was ready to retire, but truly he wasn't, even if he hadn't understood that until this moment. Edvalt would likely welcome the challenge of rebuilding. Declan found the irony delicious and welcomed the decision's being taken out of his hands. No, for Edvalt, starting over would not be a problem; living through the next few days, on the other hand, might be.

"I want you to take the smaller anvil, my second-best set of tools, and that box of sand." Declan's eyebrows rose slightly, but he said nothing. In a softer voice Edvalt said, "Keep that sword you're almost finished with." He leaned forward and whispered to Declan, "My gut tells me when Baron Bartholomy arrives—if he arrives here—he's only going to find smoking rubble."

Declan looked his former master in the eye and said, "Hope for the best—"

"Expect the worst," finished Edvalt. Resuming a normal tone, Edvalt said, "Accompany Ratigan to Marquensas. I promised Baron Daylon that should I find an apprentice whom I judged to be my equal, I would send that lad to him." Before Declan could object to being elevated to Edvalt's equal, the older smith held up his hand and cut him off. "In his own way the baron is a fair man. If you take his service, he'll treat you well. If you don't wish to, that's likely fine. Seek out a town or village nearby in need of a smith and establish yourself. Sandura may be bold here in the Covenant, but I'll bet Lodavico is years away from taking on the likes of Baron Daylon. I'll give you a bit of gold so you can purchase or rent a building. You'll know what you need to do from there, lad.

"You're a fine smith, Declan. Best apprentice I've ever had, and you've the makings of a fine swordsman from what I saw today. Either way, you need to be out on your own. Jusan's a fair apprentice and you'll sort him out as well as I would.

"Now, that's an end to it."

Declan knew his former master well enough to accept that if Edvalt said that was the end of it, it was indeed the end. He nodded once and left the hungry driver wolfing down food, as Edvalt rested.

Declan stepped outside as a man named Posey waved to him. "Declan! You need to see this."

Posey stood at the side of the lead horse on the first wagon and as soon as Declan neared, he turned and hurried past the second to the third. Declan hesitated when he saw the first mule. He then hurried to confirm his suspicion, and his spine went cold as he recognized the last wagon. "Roz?" he asked softly.

"No sign of her," answered Posey.

Declan saw two of the former captives sitting in the shade of the smithy; the young men were wolfing down food given to them by one of the townsfolk, and he hurried over to them. "Do you know what happened to the woman driving that mule team?" he asked.

Both men nodded. One with a badly-bandaged face spoke through a mouthful of bread. "Ran into her just before we got here. She was coming down the road . . ." He shook his head, realizing that detail was pointless. "Anyway, her wagon was empty and they said she was too old to be sold to a brothel, so they decided to have some fun with her."

The other man nodded. "She put up a fight, I can tell you that. She had her knife out and was off her wagon before the first rider could dismount. She neutered him like a calf and left him screaming like a frightened little girl as he bled to death."

The bandaged man said, "She held two others at bay, then turned the blade on herself."

The second man added, "She was not going to be raped: she made that clear. Took her own life rather than give in to the bastards."

Declan felt dizzy. A painful, hot hole replaced his stomach. He stood motionless for a moment, then asked, "Where?"

"About an hour up the road," said the first man. "They left her there, beside the road, alongside the lad she killed."

Declan felt a stab of cold in his stomach and pushed aside any thought that Roz might be dead. Until he saw her with his own eyes . . . He turned and silently walked into the smithy. A moment later he returned with a shovel in his hand and walked to the first wagon. Leaping onto the buckboard, he took the reins and urged the horses to move and turn the wagon around.

Posey asked, "Where are you off to, Declan?"

Eyes fixed forward, he answered, "To say goodbye to a friend." With a flick of the reins he started the wagon up the road.

Declan drove the mules hard, and given the contrary nature of the beasts, they surprised him in their willingness to be hurried. Unlike horses, he found mules tended to be smart and take the path of least resistance given the opportunity to choose, but they would not budge if you overloaded them, which was why teamsters like Roz, who were not usually in a hurry, preferred them to horses.

Circling carrion birds showed Declan where to go,

and as he rounded a curve in the road he almost shouted in relief. Roz sat with her back against a rock, waving a blade weakly at two buzzards that seemed unwilling to wait for her to die. Declan chased them away and knelt beside her. Roz smiled weakly and said, "About time," then passed out.

He quickly examined her wound and found she had deceived the slavers by cutting widely but not deeply. The cut had soaked her tunic and trousers quickly: they were covered in enough blood to make the slavers confident she was dead, but not enough to kill her quickly. Declan took off his shirt and used her dagger to cut it into rude bandages, and then did his best to stanch the fresh blood seeping from the caked wound. He lifted her into the wagon as gently as he could and tried to position her comfortably between the sacks of goods to keep her from too rough a ride, but he knew time was of the essence.

As he turned the wagon and urged the mules to their fastest pace, relief at Roz's survival battled with his fear that he would be too slow getting her into Mila's care. The day was not even half over, but since the morning his life had changed more than he could have possibly imagined just hours before.

8

An Unexpected Change of Tide

Hatu's attention began to drift and he shook himself alert. The greatest trap of being lookout in a situation such as this was lulling oneself into a false sense of calm. The other risk was having an overactive imagination and seeing things in the dark that weren't there. An advantage of their position was that they'd almost certainly hear another ship approaching before they saw it. So listening was key.

It was still easy for the mind to wander every few moments, and for Hatu that meant revisiting old slights and unanswered questions, or the face of a girl.

He felt himself stir thinking of Hava and pushed aside the image of her at the bathing pools. Lately he had been thinking of her as more than simply a friend. That last day at the school near Corbara, something unspoken had passed between them, something different, and Hatu found it both arousing and disturbing. He didn't fully understand it, but it had led to his missing her.

Yet without much bidding, thoughts of her returned: memories of their years growing up, and their odd friendship.

She was the only student who could best him in training. He usually beat her in combat, though once in a while she had anticipated his moves and defeated him, so he could never take a match with her for granted. The same held true for Donte, for with any bout involving strength, he won over everyone on the island, but in other competitions Hava and Hatu won their fair share. The one place she always was victorious was the long races. Hatu could beat her in dashes, but if they were running cross-country, she always ended up in the lead. Donte teased Hatu mercilessly about that, claiming that Hatu couldn't beat her because he was too intent on staring at her arse. Donte ignored the fact that he couldn't beat Hava either. And while he would never admit it to Donte, he did think Hava had as fine an arse as any he had ever seen. She wasn't exactly what most of the boys would have called pretty, but Hatu liked the way she looked, and always had.

Refusing to admit his attraction to her was important to him, especially when he competed against her and Donte watched. He was supposed to feel toward her as one would feel toward a sister, and yet somehow that had changed just before they separated; it bothered Hatu in ways he had no words for. Anything beyond friendship was forbidden, and he might never see her again anyway, a possibility that at times brought him close to rage.

His embarrassment over Donte's teasing had caused him to focus on besting Hava in every contest they had, which only made him less effective at winning. He shook himself out of his reverie. If he wasn't thinking about her body and face, he still fixated on her—that gentle kiss on the cheek, the feel of her hand on his—and so he used his rising anger to force the memories aside. He needed to stay alert.

All was still quiet, the gentle lapping of the waves on the shore the only sound breaking the silence. The weather on Garn was mostly predictable in these latitudes; more extreme weather was common in the deeper oceans. Here, currents between the islands were far more worthy of concern than any sudden storms or surging tides. The currents were constant, until they were not, as reefs broke apart and sand shifted, and suddenly a safe narrow passage became treacherous.

The moon rose before dawn, as it did this time of year. The tides would shift gently to the east, and perhaps the weather would change a little. The weather in these waters this time of year was rarely violent, though when storms did come, they tended to be wild and life threatening. Out at sea, few vessels could survive the rare heavy storms, and sheltering from them was the only safe option.

The moon lightened the horizon and for a moment Hatu wondered at it. According to one of the masters at home, Master Tagaga, the moon was either very small and close to them, or very large and far away. He concluded that it was probably the latter, because it moved so slowly across the sky. Hatu was mildly curious as to how he had come to that conclusion, but not enough to ask Master Tagaga; the teacher tended to talk at great length, more so when he was drinking, and he was rarely as entertaining as Master Bodai.

Still, those lectures had stirred Hatu's imagination, making the young man wonder about things he had not considered before. Independent thinking and asking too many questions were not behaviors encouraged among students who might someday join the Quelli Nascosti. Had he been Coaltachin born, he'd have been halfway up their ranks by now, if the masters judged him favorably. Hatu knew he'd never be a sicari; he wondered what his fate would be.

It troubled him, but at times he felt relief; obedience was paramount, and giving your life for Coaltachin was a very real possibility. He knew he was different from the other students—no one else shared his ruddy-cheeked complexion and copper-gold hair—but it was more than just where he was born. Hatu didn't know how he had come to the school or who his people were. He'd been taught to ask few questions, and only then when instructed.

There had been subtle signs, things he had only begun to recognize in the last year or so, that told him that he was different: He had been protected in ways other students were not. He was exposed to the risks of training but had been sheltered from grievous harm. Occasionally a student would be seriously injured and unable to train further; they were rarely killed, but it did happen. Hatu's instructors had always found a way to lessen his risk. He did not know why, and as with so many other things in his life, that only frustrated him and made him angry.

He tried to focus on the horizon, but the dark sea and sky were blending, and staring into a dusky void brought images to his mind. Unbidden, Hava returned to his thoughts, and he recounted their lives at the school. As children they had played and trained together. Like Donte, she had been in his life every day until their missions away from their home island of Morasel had separated them.

He remembered the first time that being close to her had stiffened his flesh and the embarrassment he'd felt, for it was that time of maturation when he was still a boy but a man's body was coming into form. Donte had been his ally, defending his friend at the bathing pool from the depredations of the other boys. Now Hatu wondered if Donte had been sheltering him from their mocking or sheltering the other boys from Hatu's potential rage. Hava was not the only girl to cause such a reaction, and he was not the only boy of their age to react to a girl in that way. The instructors were dismissive when questioned; they said they would outgrow such things and simply reminded them of the rules against having sex.

Hatu wasn't concerned about breaking the rules and knew Hava never would, but he was concerned that she might see him become aroused by her when they were naked in the bathing pool or during training. He wanted nothing to change their friendship.

He shook off his musing and just resigned himself to missing Hava.

He glanced over at Donte and saw he was alert and still watching for anything in the gloom that might herald a threat.

Hatu tried to concentrate on the task at hand, but something kept pulling his thoughts back to Hava, perhaps because he was returning to their home island and there was a slight chance he might see her again. He wondered why he felt such a void when he thought of her; perhaps because he had believed she would always be there, and then suddenly she wasn't. A part of him had been removed when he saw her the last time, as he hurried to the docks in Corbara.

Then, something changed.

Hatu's instincts warned him that danger was upon them. He glanced at Donte, who was staring into the darkness to the west; it was easy to be lulled into watching the moon rise and ignore any threat out of the gloom.

Donte was barely visible in the faint moonlight, a dim chiaroscuro lightly outlined on one side, but Hatu could see his attention snap toward him. Donte nodded once. He had felt something, too.

Just as Hatu was about to shout a warning, he heard the sound of water erupting on both sides of the ship, followed by the sound of heavy bodies landing on the deck. Looking down between the gathered sails and in the dark, he could only make out the shapes of strange men moving oddly across the decks; they seemed to be undulating rather than crawling. Despite that, they were swift.

Men who had been asleep on deck were roused in moments, and then the screaming began. Hatu looked over at Donte, whose eyes were wide enough to reflect the rising moonlight, and he shook his head in a silent admonition not to move.

More men began to scream.

Hatu froze in shock for a moment. These were men of Coaltachin, hardened fighters no matter what role they played now. They were unyielding and not easily frightened, yet the sounds from below were of utter, primal terror.

In the faint light from the moon, Hatu could only see shapes below, made more obscure by the frantic action. The men seemed to be writhing on the decks, trying to escape what attacked them: beings somewhat larger than men and moving with inhuman speed. He saw a creature reach a deckhand, strike him down or embrace him, then launch itself into the air, arcing into the water with a loud splash. Hatu looked over to Donte and saw the vague image of his friend made motionless by the horror unfolding below.

Confusion crushed Hatu, rendering him unable to

think. He tried to peer further into the darkness, willing himself to see what was occurring below. He felt panic rising as the unseen horror drove his imagination into a primitive place, turning him into a cornered prey animal. Not being able to see was worse than seeing, as the sounds indicated that his crew were being completely overwhelmed. The cries of rage and anger common in battle were absent, replaced by a collective wail of pure terror that would have been impossible for Hatu to imagine moments before.

He again looked over at Donte and from what little he could make out in the darkness, his friend was as rooted by fear as he was.

Donte sensed Hatu looking in his direction and pointed downward, then made a motion with his hand, again indicating they should stay right where they were. Whatever the things on deck were, their undulating movement didn't suggest that they could climb the rigging, and Hatu was of no mind to argue with Donte's logic.

The sounds of terror fell away as the men below were killed or swept up and carried into the sea. Muffled screams were the last sounds the two lads in the rigging heard from the deck, followed by a pair of splashes into the sea. Then silence fell.

Hatu remained motionless, afraid that whatever

horror had visited those below still lurked. He could hear the gentle lapping of the waves on the shore and the faint sounds of creaking wood as the ship rocked mildly, causing loose rigging and tackle to fill the night with occasional rattling.

Time dragged as the moon rose higher and its faint light gradually gave more clarity to what had occurred below. The decks glistened with water and blood, and Hatu suspected that when dawn came, the bodies strewn about would be seen clearly.

Silence overwhelmed him. He was terrified to move, yet every instinct told him to climb down, leap over the side, and make the short swim to shore, to get as far away from this place as he could. He kept looking at Donte, who would occasionally look back. Neither lad was willing to leave their seemingly safe perch yet.

Hours dragged by.

The false dawn in the east brought light enough to see the carnage below Hatu and Donte in shades of black and grey. The two youngsters sensed it was time to climb down and decide what to do next. They descended gingerly, their lingering terror keeping them as quiet as possible.

Once on the deck, they could see body parts and blood everywhere, but not one recognizable face. It was as if those not carried away had been literally torn to pieces and those pieces scattered in every direction.

Donte's face was ashen as he whispered, "What do we do?"

Hatu understood his friend's reticence to speak loudly. "I don't know," he replied in hushed tones as he glanced around. He felt that if he looked long enough at the bloody work, it might somehow make sense. "Is anyone else left alive?"

"I don't think so," said Donte. "It's been quiet for a long time, haven't heard a sound. It sounded like those things got below, down the companionway."

"What were they?"

Hatu said, "Matron Mona told us sea stories. Ocean men, maybe."

Donte said, "Ocean men? Sea naga? Water demons?" He looked to the east as the sun edged above the horizon. "They are just stories." His expression showed his refusal to accept the possibility that mythical creatures had attacked the ship and killed or abducted everyone but them.

"This is not a story!" snapped Hatu, pointing at the carnage surrounding them. He instantly lowered his voice. "I don't know," he said. "Whatever those things were, they were big and they came out of the water, and they dragged half the crew into the sea."

"Why did they take them?" Donte asked, as if somehow Hatu could make sense of this for them both.

"I don't know!" Hatu kept his voice down, but his tone revealed that his anger was now threatening to break the surface. "I have had the same training as you. Why would I know when you don't?"

Donte lowered his eyes, shaking his head as if he couldn't bear to consider a myth come to life. "What do we do?" he repeated.

Hatu looked around and said, "We can't sail this by ourselves. So we need to find another way to get to Coaltachin."

"A boat?" said Donte, pointing at the gig hanging off the stern. "We could manage that."

"To where?" asked Hatu.

"Anywhere but here," replied his friend.

"Do you know where we are?"

Hatu considered. "Roughly. I sailed with Master Bodai and with Master Cardina on a few short trips, before we were sent to Numerset. I thought I knew where we were before we turned south and ran from those three ships." He pointed in a northerly direction. "If we go that way, we should find The Clearing and, in a day or two, ship traffic."

"Let's go," said Donte.

"What about those things?"

"Maybe they sleep during the day, like bats or owls. They didn't attack until night."

"Let's hope you're right," said Hatu as he started to climb the stairs to the stern castle. Then he halted.

"What?" asked Donte.

"I'm going below."

"Why?" Donte grabbed his arm.

"Food, water, whatever else we might need. Start getting that boat ready."

Donte nodded. His expression communicated that he was more than content to cede the visit below to his friend. Hatu hurried down the companionway and pulled aside the heavy canvas curtain that separated the crew bunks from the captain and mate's quarters.

Hatu moved to the captain's bunk and opened the footlocker next to it. He had no idea what to expect but judged that if there was anything important inside, and he didn't bring it home, he'd be held responsible.

Inside, he discovered the captain's papers, along with a heavy pouch of coins. If they survived their attempt to get home, he would give all of the coins to whichever master they met first. Donte might object, but Hatu had learned at an early age that not giving those higher up their due was a quick way to end up floating facedown somewhere. At the bottom of the chest, under the captain's clothing, he found a canvas pouch. It felt like further papers were contained within, but it was sewn shut and sealed with wax. The waterproof material told Hatu it contained something important, something the captain, and whoever he was giving this to, wanted to remain undamaged. He swept up the papers and the sealed pouch, and put them inside a larger waxed leather pouch. His haul should stay dry unless they encountered far worse weather than expected in this region at this time of the year.

A quick look in the galley made him gag, as he found the first severed head. A galley boy named Chou stared at him with blank eyes. Hatu grabbed a bag and filled it with hard bread, dried fruit, and jerky. No variety, but enough to keep him and Donte fed and strong enough to row for a week or more, should they need to.

Putting thoughts of the waiting dangers aside, Hatu grabbed a couple of shirts hanging from nails and two heavy coats; the weather at sea could turn suddenly, even during the mild season.

He reached the top of the stern castle as Donte released the second davit pin; all they needed to do was untie the ropes and lower the gig. It was a narrow, light boat, but it had a short mast and a sail, as well as oars, so they should be able to conserve their strength at times, if the journey proved a long one.

"I wish we had more water," said Hatu as he put the food and water he had fetched from below into the boat. "We've got full barrels, but most of the crockery in the kitchen is smashed." He held up two stoppered bottles. "This is all I could find," he said, and handed them to Donte. "I'll fetch some water skins."

He hurried down below for a second time and returned with two filled water skins. "There may be one or two more, but I couldn't find them; too much of a mess to dig through. We'll have to nurse the water."

Donte said, "There are other islands close by. When we've shed this place, we'll put in somewhere green and look for water."

Hatu shrugged an agreement and reached for the rope at his end of the boat. Glancing at his friend, who gave a single nod, they began to lower the boat at a steady rate.

They let the gig down slowly, being careful not to tip it. Its narrow design facilitated speed when rowing or sailing, but it wasn't intended to carry a lot of cargo. What they had pillaged from below would leave them barely enough room to sail or row, but losing any of their provisions could be the difference between living and dying on their voyage.

The davits had been fitted with monkey-jaw clamps. If they pulled on the ropes slightly, the clamps released and the young men could play out the ropes slowly. If they released the ropes suddenly, the monkey jaws would clamp shut and prevent the gig from breaking loose. The danger of the process was that if one rope was released as the other was held, the bow or stern might tip downward and launch all of the provisions into the ocean.

Just as the keel neared the water's surface, two huge forms erupted from the sea, one next to Hatu, the other next to Donte. They looked manlike, with large eyes and heavy brows, but no hair grew upon their pates and gill-like slits quivered where their noses should have been as water drained from them. Their skin was very pale, as if denied sunlight, and below their waists long serpentlike tails churned the water to keep them in place. Massive arms reached out as Hatu and Donte tried to turn away, but their attempt to flee was blocked by the ship's stern, and the creature's limbs encompassed the two young men.

For a brief instant Hatu saw the morning sky above, then he and Donte were plunged below the water's surface.

9

A Hint of Things More Dire

The two wagons rolled through the narrow city gates after Ratigan exchanged words with one of the soldiers there. The man appeared a little more intelligent than the others, and after hearing about the recent events in Declan's village, he decided that a full report was required for the king, who was away at his summer castle on the coast, a few days' travel from Ilagan. They parked the wagons in the shade near the wall and a court scribe arrived within an hour. Declan and Ratigan gave their accounts while Roz and Jusan slept in the wagons. Declan had argued that he should take Roz to her home and then return and share his tale, but the soldier in charge of the gate detail wouldn't have any of it. He only released them when the scribe was certain he had recorded all the useful information they had to offer.

Roz awoke just before they started moving again and Declan gave her a long drink of water. She was recovering slowly from her loss of blood and he held her head while she sipped from the cup he offered.

"Where . . . ?" she whispered.

"Almost home," he replied.

"'S good," she responded, then her eyes closed and she fell asleep again.

Declan moved Roz's wagon out behind Ratigan's and reflected on the unexpected changes in his life. Just days before he had been agonizing over staying in Oncon or leaving home, and suddenly fate had taken the decision away from him completely.

Their journey had been a tiresome one. It had taken them ten days to get to Ilagan, when six or seven would have been the norm, for Declan had refused to wake Jusan and Roz at first light the day after the attack and continued letting them sleep late every morning after.

The tedium didn't help Declan with his worries. Would the raiders return? Would their home ever be safe? For even if the village was left untouched, there was no guarantee of safety. If the Covenant was being ignored by the nobles after the years of relative calm since the betrayal of the Firemanes, it wouldn't be wise to return until it was known who claimed Oncon and who would protect it, or until the Covenant was restored. In the kingdoms, villages the size of Oncon were never this far from the protection of a city, or at least a garrison of some sort.

Declan had worked enough around horses and mules to be able to drive Roz's wagon smoothly as she rested in the back, while Jusan rode in the back of Ratigan's cart. Having no second driver to switch with meant that at the end of the day, the two healthy young men were more than ready for rest, and they were forced to split the night watch until they were within distance of an Ilcomen garrison.

Declan had come to know Ratigan better as they camped beside the road each night. The young smith found the teamster an occasionally pleasant but often annoying travel companion, as he seemed overly anxious to be on his way. When pressed as to the reason for his haste, he was evasive, and Declan decided it was probably to do with the business of his master's death.

Declan and Ratigan had almost come to blows on the second day of traveling together, but the driver backed away when Declan stood firm, determined to care more for Roz and Jusan than for the driver's urgent need to get back to Marquensas. Declan insisted on letting them sleep until after the sun rose, rather than move at first light, for traveling in the wagon beds was hardly restful, then made them stop for a long break at midday and make an early camp in the afternoon. Once they were out of the Covenant and into the kingdom of Ilcomen, their journey was without incident.

Roz and Jusan were both recovering slowly, and the four travelers had finally reached Ilagan, Ilcomen's capital, the largest trading center in the kingdom and Roz's home. As they moved toward her estate, Declan studied the confusing view before him.

The city had clearly grown up around an ancient hill fort and spread out below the acropolis. The surrounding countryside was predominately flat, so the tor and keep in the center of the city dominated the view. Ilagan was crowded, busy, and smelled bad, but Declan could see that the city was a major commerce center. It was as if every single available spot on any street or byway held a merchant stall, or a table, or a simple rug on the ground displaying whatever wares were being offered.

They made a slow journey through the city, as the crowds filling the streets grudgingly gave way to the wagon. Impatient, Ratigan was disinclined to care about knocking people into the mud, and Declan stood ready for a brawl as they left shaking fists and shouted insults in their wake.

Ratigan had passed through this city several times, and as the driver didn't seem to be worried by the offended citizen's outrage, Declan thought that pushing through must be normal behavior in the city. By the time they reached Roz's home, the young smith had concluded two things: he now understood why Roz traveled so much, and he would never establish a smithy anywhere near this pest-ridden hole. It was just too crowded, too noisy, and it reeked. Stone channels ran down the center of the streets to serve as sewers; night pots were emptied into them, sometimes their contents thrown from the higher floors of buildings. The stench of human waste and rotting refuse nearly overpowered the country lad not used to such pungent odors. He decided that the city builders must have relied on the frequent rains in this region to keep the city's fly population under control.

They started moving uphill in the direction of the keep, and Declan noticed a decline in the stench, flies, and market sounds. They were replaced by the more familiar ring of hammer on steel from a nearby smithy and other sounds of industry.

The small group finally reached their destination, a

large open yard with an iron gate that could be locked at night. There was a large warehouse on the left and what appeared to be an office on the right; a massive stable and wagon repair shop lay opposite the gate.

Seeing the familiar wagon enter driven by a stranger, the workers in the yard hurried to investigate. Declan asked them to let Jusan sleep in the wagon yard under Ratigan's care while he spoke to Roz's husband. Their home was in a large building behind the stable yard; it held offices on the lower floor and their residence on the second and third.

Roz's husband, Jack, met them at the door and looked stricken as servants rushed to take Roz from the workers carrying her.

Roz looked exhausted, but she managed a slight smile as she gave Declan a painful hug, whispering her thanks, before allowing their servants to help her upstairs, walking feebly.

Declan followed Jack into a room he suspected was used for business as well as having a social function. A desk against the far wall suggested just that, and there were comfortable-looking chairs and several small tables scattered around. Along the wall opposite the door ran a large bookcase, with several leather-bound volumes separated by carved stone bookends, and a few decorative items. Declan had no idea what they were for except to look nice, but they appeared costly, being of polished stone and precious metal. He thought one at the end resembled a bird of some sort. Jack indicated that Declan should sit and said, "Please excuse me a moment while I see to my wife."

Before Declan could answer, Jack was out of the room and heading upstairs. He was much like Roz had described him, yet Declan found other qualities in the man that she'd never mentioned. Her husband was heavyset with a balding pate, but he'd let the fringe of hair above his ears and around the back of his head grow to his shoulders. Declan had seen many types of traveler through Oncon and had long since acknowledged that he didn't understand the fashions of those with means, and had no desire to. Jack wore a velvet red sleeveless over-jacket, soft leather breeches, and very polished boots that looked as if they'd never seen mud.

Declan spent a few minutes alone, finding nothing in the room to occupy his interests, beyond trying to puzzle out what those stone and metal carvings on the shelves might represent, but enjoying the feel of the very comfortable chair after spending days on a wagon seat with no back.

A few minutes later Jack returned and said, "The servants are bathing her. I've sent for a healer to look at her wound, but for now she seems . . ." He sat down, his face ashen. "Pray, tell me what happened . . ."

"Declan," provided the young blacksmith.

A young serving girl appeared at the door. Declan thought she was very pretty, almost boyish with her petite frame, but her large cornflower-blue eyes were made all the more striking by her raven hair under a white lace cap. She certainly was as unlike Roz as any girl could be, and perhaps that was the reason she was here while Roz was on the road. Declan pushed aside speculation as Jack instructed her to fetch some wine and glasses. Declan started to object, not wishing to prolong the uncomfortable meeting any more than necessary, but Jack waved away the protestation.

"So?" asked Jack. "How did my wife come to be in this condition?"

Declan explained what had happened as best he could without touching on his personal relationship with Roz. He glossed over everything until the arrival of the slavers, and as he told the story about seeking out Roz after the fight, Jack's eyes welled with tears and his complexion turned even paler. His hand visibly trembled as he sipped his wine, and as Declan finished, he put the glass down and covered his face for a long moment as his shoulders shook slightly. Declan felt embarrassed, not because Roz's husband was weeping, but because he didn't have any idea what to say.

Finally he said, "She . . . she was very brave."

Jack nodded his head from behind his hands and, after another long moment, took a gasping breath and said, "She is extraordinary. I don't deserve her." He was taking the news of Roz's injury much harder than Declan had expected; his feelings for her were obviously much deeper than she had led Declan to believe. Finally, he took a deep breath and asked, "You're one of her young men, then?"

Declan said, "I . . . pardon?"

Jack waved his hand, letting the serving girl refill his goblet. "We have an arrangement, Roz and I. We ask no questions, but I . . . let's say I think you're the type of lad she enjoys spending time with." He glanced at the girl, who smiled back at him, and he said, "We deny each other nothing."

Jack took a long pull on his wine and waved away a second refill; with a small gesture he indicated that the girl should depart.

"I've got friends waiting for me," said Declan, standing.

"And I've kept you from your travels, I fear, and I should look in on my wife." He stood up. "How can I repay you?"

Declan was taken slightly aback. "Repay me? Roz is my friend. There is no debt."

Jack smiled in an almost fatherly fashion and said, "I see why she chose you." He motioned toward the door and walked with Declan. "Know this. Should you ever need anything that it is within my power to grant, you shall have it." Declan started to object, but Jack put up his palm and cut him off. "Not as repayment of a debt, but . . . out of friendship."

He extended his hand and Declan took it.

Declan left and stood outside the closed door for a moment. This experience, as much as any he'd had since leaving Oncon, told him that he knew little of the world beyond that village. While he felt concern for Roz's recovery, he knew she would live, and Declan found himself relieved to be leaving Ilagan.

He climbed aboard the wagon and Ratigan nodded toward Jusan, who was sleeping soundly. "Let's be off," said the teamster, his voice unusually low. Declan realized that, despite several annoying traits, the young driver seemed a good man at heart.

As they drove through the city, on their way to Marquensas, Declan decided once again that he didn't know Roz as well as he had thought. He still wrestled with conflicting feelings for her, but when all was said and done, he was only left with the sense that much of what she had told him over the years was invention.

Roz certainly knew how to please a man in bed, and she had taught Declan most of what he knew about pleasing a woman, but he had never imagined being her man. She was, after all, already wed, was past the age to want children, and traveled so much, but he was certain he would happily wed someone like her, someone younger, but still of like mood—and with no other young men awaiting her pleasure.

He tried to put his confusion behind him as he judged whether or not he would meet Roz again someday. He decided that if he did, he would ask questions as the mood dictated, and that pondering them now was a waste of effort.

Still, it had been his first visit to any city of size, and he had found the experience interesting. Now that he and Ratigan were in one wagon, they could talk more freely. "Is it always this crowded here?"

Ratigan laughed. "This is the quiet season. King Bucohan and his court are at the seaside, away from the stench and the flies, so all the mad royal business has moved someplace else for a while. It will be this way for another month, until the king returns." He glanced at Declan. "You should have been here in spring for the wool fair." Grinning, he said, "Traders from hundreds of miles around flock here to buy and sell massive amounts of wool! They ship it all over the continent and across the Anoke and Semalon Seas. Over the fair, the city's population grows three- or fourfold; over fifty thousand people pass through here."

Ratigan went on to explain that it was not a single fair, but rather a series of weekly events that took place across six of the surrounding towns. Merchants moved their wares around as buyers came and went, but because most of the commerce passed through Ilagan, it was known as the Ilagan Wool Fair.

After leaving Ilagan, their journey through Ilcomen proceeded without incident. They stopped for a night at a proper inn in the town of Lovan, one of the trade centers and also quiet this time of the year. Jusan was recovering well enough that Declan acceded to Ratigan's request to make an earlier start each day. They progressed slowly through Ilcomen until reaching the border of Marquensas.

Jusan's youthful vigor was offset by the exertions of traveling in a freight wagon, wedged among bundles of rags and Declan's tools and anvil. Like Roz, Ratigan and his master had been hauling fruit when the slavers assaulted them. Their cargo had long since turned and been tossed out of the wagon, save for one bag of oranges, which Jusan used as an unforgiving pillow.

Days passed as they moved closer to the coast, and as they passed an ancient pile of stones, Ratigan said, "That marks the border. We are now in Marquensas."

Declan felt a slight shudder run through him as they passed the marker. Perhaps it was his imagination, but something felt different as they entered the barony. A few hours later, he saw the landscape changing and realized that regardless of his imagined sense, Marquensas was a very different place from Ilcomen.

Trees had appeared on the horizon and as they neared them, Declan could see further copses scattered along the roadside, but the hills rising to the east were clearly covered with forests. There was a spectacular wealth in lumber here and it appeared carefully tended. Logging roads ran down to meet the widening highway, and traders and travelers appeared with mounting frequency; a few were heading toward Ilagan, but most of them were lumber wagons heading in the same direction as they were. Because of the amount of finished lumber heading toward Marquenet, Declan assumed there must be a water-driven sawmill somewhere nearby, or a very big center with a large number of woodcutters.

By the end of the day they had passed three villages surrounded by small farms, and these more familiar sights told Declan that it was a happy and prosperous community. The children laughed and played until sunset, rather than wearily finishing their work, which meant there was plenty of food to go around. Their clothing was well kept and none of them wore rags. The smell of food cooking on the fires made both Declan and Ratigan acknowledge their hunger and even woke Jusan up.

"Food?" said the young apprentice, his eyes looking bright and clear for the first time since the attack.

"We'll camp soon," said Declan. "Rest now."

"It's hard to rest with all this bouncing around," complained the youth, but he soon dozed off while Declan and Ratigan shook their heads and chuckled.

They camped between villages that night, but Declan knew he was not far from an inn and a proper bath and bed when they reached the city. Jusan stayed awake for most of the evening, and promised he was well enough for an early start the next day, then promptly fell asleep after their meal.

The next morning they passed through the first town of any great size they'd seen in Marquensas. "This is Aoldomon," said Ratigan. "I usually don't stop here. My late master didn't stop here; didn't like the inn and the innkeeper, for some reason. Besides, we always carried enough provisions to reach Ilagan."

"When will we reach Marquenet?"

"Around midday."

Declan sat back and nodded.

They reached the first city gate just after noon as Ratigan had predicted, and were halted by a guard. He inspected the anvil and tools alongside Jusan and the bag of oranges and waved them through. As Ratigan started to move the wagon forward, a sergeant came forth and said, "You're Milrose's man?"

Ratigan reined in the team and said, "Yes."

"Didn't I see you two drive out together less than a month ago?"

Ratigan sighed, and Declan knew that he was anticipating trouble. "My master is dead. Murdered by slavers."

"Where?" asked the sergeant, a look of concern on his face.

"In the Covenant," answered Ratigan.

After a moment, the man said, "That's one for the baron, then. See that you go there first, boy."

Ratigan's good judgment overcame his desire to get back to his master's business. He said, "Yes, Sergeant," and urged the team forward.

As they wended their way through the streets, Declan could see the ancient keep, Caer Marquenet, on top of a steep hill in the center of the ancient city.

Declan decided that it made sense that most cities grew up around forts that were on top of hills, or at least it seemed that way to him. Apart from its acropolis, Marquenet was unlike Ilagan and other towns he had glimpsed on this journey. It was a city of plastered walls, white in the noon sun, with tiled roofs of red, grey, and blue, and cobbles that also showed their colors when not covered by dust or mud. The streets they used were narrow, but Ratigan knew the city as well as he knew his own face and easily navigated a course that skirted the worst of the city traffic. Glancing to the west, Declan could see throngs of people on a larger street jostling their way past carts and wagons while Ratigan proceeded unimpeded toward the castle.

They cleared the narrow street, which emptied into a large market square, and Ratigan said, "Now things get slower. Keep an eye out for trouble."

"What sort of trouble?" asked Declan.

"Any sort," said Ratigan. "There are all manner of mountebanks, thieves, and thugs in the market."

Jusan looked up from his makeshift bed and said, "I see soldiers over there."

"Aye," replied Ratigan. "City Watch. They're the worst of them."

They moved slowly to the right and Declan saw

a vast area covered with stalls and tents; they were erected in what at first appeared to be a haphazard fashion, but after a while resolved into an intersection of two walkways, encircled by a broad road into which all the streets in this area of the city terminated.

"Docks are to the west," said Ratigan. "Freight from all manner of places arrives there, and the local fishermen deliver their catch there in the evenings. I used to work near there, for my master brokered the delivery of fish as well as fruit. The orchards run for miles to the north of the city. The east is farmland, some of the best in the world, so I've been told. And we just came through the hill country. The Wild Border, we call it."

"Didn't seem so wild when we passed through," said Jusan.

"I don't know why it's called that, boy. It just is."

Declan said, "Probably an old story."

"Almost certainly," said Ratigan. "There's an old story for most things. I pay them no mind. I have other concerns."

Declan said, "You've been getting more agitated since we came within two days of here. What is it?"

"My master's dead and I have no claim on this team; if some bunghole city magistrate doesn't like my looks, I might well be blamed for my master's death. But my master had no family in this city, and I put my life and freedom at risk for his business, so I'm as entitled to make a claim on it as any man. Aren't I?"

"Yes," agreed Declan, deciding not to pursue the matter further. He had traveled with the teamster long enough to know that any hint of disagreement would only make things worse. It was in Ratigan's nature to take a well-intended remark and put the worst interpretation on it when he was in a dark mood.

They made their way slowly through the press of the crowd, toward the broad northwest road that led up the hill to the keep. Declan looked around at the metalwork on display and saw a lot of decently made kitchen items: pots, knives, metal plates, and other simple but profitable goods. A few weapons merchants also displayed their wares, which, from a distance, Declan judged to be fair. He saw a few of the men at those booths take note of their wagon as it passed, seeing the large anvil and tools peeking over the edge of their boxes.

Ratigan saw Declan's reaction to those glances and said, "No doubt, before sunset, every blacksmith, metalworker, weapons crafter, and armorer will know a new smith is in the city."

"Is that a problem?"

"Could be." Ratigan shrugged. "We'll see."

Leaving the market and moving up the hill, Declan noticed that the buildings, inns, and other businesses looked a bit more prosperous. He decided they must be the longest established, since anyone who built anything after the keep was finished would have tried to stay close to the safety of the fortification.

Jusan had regained much of his usual self and said, "Must be nice living up here. Air is fresh."

Declan was used to the lad's condensed manner of speaking, having practically raised him as a younger brother. "Very nice," said Declan.

"What are you two going on about?" asked Ratigan.

"Jusan was saying that it's nice up here on this hill. The air doesn't stink."

"Gets a breeze off the ocean most days," said Ratigan. "It can get hot and damp down in the city sometimes, that's for certain." He clucked his tongue and urged the horses on as they came to the summit of the road; another hundred feet of flat road lay before them, running straight toward the merchants' gate in the keep wall.

Declan said, "We felt the ocean breeze where we grew up; cool, but carrying a lot of dead fish." He inclined his head and added, "This smells different."

Ratigan took a deep breath and nodded, as much of an agreement as Declan was likely to get from the contentious man.

The wagon slowed as they reached the outer wall surrounding the baron's keep. Two massive wooden

gates with iron bands and hinges faced them, surrounded by a large square barbican with a double iron
portcullis, which was currently raised. From the look
of it, Declan guessed it hadn't been used defensively
in years, perhaps not in any living man's lifetime. He
wondered if it would even submit to being lowered,
there was so much rust in evidence. His curiosity made
him wish for a moment to climb up and inspect the
chains and pull mechanism, though he knew that was
never likely to happen.

Two guards waited; they wore the now-familiar tabards of Marquensas, a golden rose on a light blue field.
Both held up their hands as one of them said, "Your
business?"

Before Ratigan could answer, Declan said, "Your
lads at the city gate ordered us here when they heard
our tale of slavers in the Covenant, wearing the colors
of Sandura. Do we tell you our story?"

The two sentries exchanged glances, and one turned
and called over his shoulder, "Sergeant! Merchant's
gate!"

The call was echoed by other soldiers and a few
minutes later an old soldier in a long surcoat with three
chevrons sewn above his heart ambled into view. He
demanded, "What is this?"

"A report of slavers in the Covenant, sergeant," said one of the soldiers, tilting his head at Declan.

The sergeant shook his head slightly as if being presented with a problem he'd rather not deal with, but approached to inspect the three young men in the wagon. Declan had met a fair number of soldiers over the years, for many escorted nobles who needed their horses shod or their gear repaired as they passed through Oncon. Declan had seen this sergeant before, or at least half a dozen men like him, and judged him a stern, no-nonsense type. He had a grey beard and his hair reached his collar, and while his muscle now ran to fat around his girth, Declan had no doubt the man was still very dangerous in a brawl. Finally, the old soldier said, "What tale is this?"

Declan glanced at Ratigan, silencing him before the teamster could speak. "I come from the village of Oncon, in the Covenant near the Ilcomen border." He gave them a concise report about the attack of the slavers.

The old sergeant sighed again, then said, "My lord will wish to hear this. Leave your wagon there." He pointed to a spot just inside the gate. After Ratigan had moved the wagon, the sergeant motioned to Declan. "You, follow me."

Declan climbed down and followed the sergeant

through the large bailey that surrounded the ancient keep. As they rounded the corner, he could see that a two-story building had been added to the original six-story tower, and that some other new outbuildings also nestled against the wall. Their need to hold a defensive position had apparently lessened with time, as over the centuries the city grew to surround the home of the first ruler of Marquensas.

As they turned another corner, they walked into the marshaling yard. The stables lay against the north wall of the fortification, and the soldiers' commons against the west wall.

Declan saw a man and a boy dressed in tunics and trousers standing before two horses being readied for a ride. The sandy-haired man nodded at the sergeant and said, "What's this about?"

"News from the Covenant, my lord." He waved at Declan.

From the honorific, Declan assumed that the man was Baron Dumarch, and that the boy was his son. There was a resemblance: the boy appeared to be about eighteen years old, his shoulders had begun to broaden, and his carriage was very similar to the older man's.

Declan gave an awkward half bow, then said, "Slavers have raided the village of Oncon, my lord. They wore the colors of Sandura."

"When was this?" asked Daylon.

"Over three weeks ago, my lord," answered Declan. "My apprentice was almost killed in the fight and so we had to travel slowly. The village has been abandoned; everyone has dispersed. I do not know if the slavers returned, or if the village stands."

The baron's son appeared on the verge of asking a question, but his father raised his hand and silenced him. Baron Daylon appraised Declan for a moment, then said, "Apprentice? What is your trade?"

"I'm a smith, my lord."

"What do you fashion?"

"Whatever my lord requires." As Declan answered, another man appeared from around the corner and approached them. His clothing marked him as a man of stature but not a noble. Declan had seen his like before traveling with nobility; this man was a highly placed adviser or servant. Declan studied him silently, as there was something oddly familiar about him, though Declan was certain they had never met.

"Weapons, armor?" asked Daylon as the man came to his side.

"Yes, my lord." The newcomer said to Declan, "You look young to be an armorer."

"I am . . . ," said Declan. "Sir."

"Balven is my body man," said the baron.

Declan inclined his head. "Sir, I know I am young, but I am a master smith. The raid occurred just after I finished my masterpiece, my lord."

"Master," echoed Daylon. "I have my own smith in residence, but should . . . trouble come our way, we're likely to need every able smith in Marquensas." He stared at Declan for a long moment, then asked, "Do I know you?"

Declan was taken by surprise. "I think not, my lord. This is my first journey outside the Covenant, and I would most certainly have remembered had you passed through our village."

"There's a look about you; something familiar." He studied the young smith some more, then said, "Perhaps you remind me of someone.

"Now, another question: you could have chosen many destinations after leaving the Covenant, so why here?"

"The man who owned the wagon that we arrived in, Milrose, he was of Marquensas. He was killed when the raiders took his wagon and driver; I believe they were hauling fruit to Dunkeep. We freed Ratigan, the driver, and he felt the need to return here."

Daylon turned to his son and said, "Wait here. We will have to delay our ride for a few more minutes."

The youngster looked disappointed but said nothing. Daylon said, "I would see this wagon." He walked past the sergeant, Balven, and Declan, who all turned and followed him.

Reaching the wagon, he looked it over and said to Ratigan, "You're Milrose's man?"

Ratigan tugged his forelock and bowed his head. "Yes, my lord."

"I recognize the name," added Balven.

Daylon nodded. "Tell me what happened."

Ratigan glanced at Declan, who remained impassive, then said, "Well, we were just coming out of Ilcomen, heading through the Covenant to Far Avaran, where we had a buyer for a wagonload of oranges and pears. We were in a hurry, you know, because the fresher they are, the higher the price. Usually only takes a week of fast travel.

"Got just outside of Ilagan, near Dunkeep, maybe half a day away, when the slavers jumped us. They killed Master Milrose and dumped half of the fruit on the roadside. Wanted the wagon for captives. So they loaded me up with half a dozen other miserable wretches and off we went. I was only with them for two days before they ran into Declan and the other villagers in Oncon. Killed every one of those bastards and . . . well, I knew I'd best come back to tell you about it, my lord. And then there's the business of the wagon and its team."

"Did Milrose have any family?"

"A daughter, but she's married to a tailor over in Julland Town, raising kids."

Baron Daylon was silent for a moment, then turned to Balven. "I want a fast rider ready to travel to Ilcomen in an hour. I'll have a message for King Bucohan. He might not know that slavers were bold enough to raid across his border and into the Covenant."

Balven said, "Yes, my lord," and, with a slight nod to the sergeant, indicated that he should see to the order. The sergeant hurried away.

Daylon shouted after him, "And tell my son we're postponing the ride today."

Looking at Ratigan, he said, "A tailor's wife needs no wagon, and you did us a service by reporting this. Keep it, and should any other carter or teamster dispute your right, tell them I sanctioned it. Be your own master."

"Thank you, my lord," said Ratigan, obviously pleased. Declan knew that the cost of a good wagon and team was more than Ratigan could earn in three years as a driver.

Declan said, "One last thing, my lord."

"Yes?" said Daylon, turning to Declan.

"My master said that I needed to see you to honor his pledge."

"Who was your master?"

"Edvalt Tasman."

Daylon looked at his half brother, who raised an eyebrow and gave him a short nod. Daylon was silent for a moment, then said, "He was as gifted a smith as I've ever known. I made him promise he'd send me his best apprentice. So, that would be you?"

"He judged me fit to be named master," said Declan. "I was an orphan and he was like a father to me, and so because of that, I honor his pledge to you, my lord."

Daylon was again silent, then he said, "You tell me this more from duty than from any desire to seek service."

"Truth to tell, my lord, I promised him I would do this, but my ambition is to set up my own forge and be my own man."

Daylon smiled. "Much like your master, it seems." Balven nodded in agreement. "When you've settled somewhere, hopefully within our borders, send word to the sergeant of your whereabouts: we may possibly need your service."

"I will, my lord."

Declan mounted the wagon and Ratigan turned the horses, heading toward the gate and out of the marshaling yard.

As the wagon drew away, Balven turned to his half

brother and said, "You thought you recognized him?" His tone was slightly mocking.

"Do you recognize him?" asked the baron.

With a half laugh, Balven put his hand on the baron's shoulder and said, "Daylon, that boy looks more like our father than you or I."

Daylon's eyes widened as recognition struck. "Another bastard brother?"

Balven said, "You didn't think there was only one of us out there, did you?"

"Now that you've said it, no, not really; I just never thought I'd meet another."

"Well, after the fit your mother threw when Father brought me here, I suspected he'd leave his other bastards where they were, but I always thought we might chance upon one sooner or later." Gazing after the wagon, Balven said, "Father certainly had an eye for the ladies."

"This is true," said Daylon, then he fell silent.

After a moment, Balven said, "You're thinking."

"I do, upon occasion," the baron answered dryly. "Let's not mention the boy's identity to anyone. It may hold some advantage for us in the future, but if not, let's make sure the young smith doesn't become a disadvantage."

"As you wish," said Balven with a slight bow, "my lord."

"Now, I need to send missives to Bucohan and a few other nobles, to apprise them of Lodavico's latest nonsense. I was content to ignore his idiocy as long as he kept it in the east, but now it's coming too close to our borders."

Balven nodded agreement and walked back to the keep with his half brother. He took a moment to glance over his shoulder at the retreating wagon and then returned his attention to his brother. "The smith?"

"Keep track of him. If he's as good as Edvalt, I would like him to make weapons for us rather than our neighbors. Besides, you're likely not the only one who will notice the family resemblance."

Balven said nothing as they mounted the steps into the keep.

10

In the Crimson Depths

Hatu awoke suddenly, in pain and darkness. It took him a few moments to organize his thoughts enough to remember that he had been on a boat with Donte before he was pulled under the sea by monstrous sea creatures. The abrasions on his body smarted from being exposed to salt water, and several deep bruises throbbed. He blinked and saw dark shapes moving in the gloom.

He shook his head as he realized that he was bound by his wrists, shackled to chains hanging from the ceiling; his shoulders ached and felt as if they might be separating. Hatu looked up, barely able to see the upper limit of the dark, wet cave. He saw a glow coming from the pools of water scattered around the large cave, and from pockets in the walls, and recognized it as some kind of phosphorescent algae. It gave off just enough light to cast shadows and faint patches of illumination. He looked up again and, as his eyes adjusted, began to make out further details: the chains were threaded through a heavy iron ring attached to the ceiling by a massive bolt.

To his left, an unconscious figure dangled limply from another pair of shackles. Hatu got his feet under him and discovered he could move but barely a couple of inches once he stood upright. A shorter man would have been literally hanging from the chains. He ignored the chill in his legs from the ankle-deep water and stood as tall as he was able, moving his arms a little. It eased the deep pain in his shoulders slightly and he moved them gently; as circulation returned they throbbed, but he could tell nothing was dislocated or seriously injured.

A deep moan echoed from some distance away, and he could hear the sound of lapping water. Hatu looked to his right and saw another chain hanging empty, and possibly a fourth beyond it, but he couldn't be certain.

He stood on tiptoes, which eased his shoulder joints further. When the pain faded, he gripped the chains with his hands and pulled slightly, causing a popping sound in both shoulders, loud in his ears against the relative quiet of the cave. He felt instant relief and moved as best he could under the circumstances.

Then the calm was sundered by a cry from within the deep gloom: a weak wail of pure pain and terror. Hatu had heard many men scream since his boyhood, so he understood the differences. He'd heard men shout out in pain as their wounds were treated, or some bellow their outrage, or give savage voice to battle lust, but this cry was . . .

The sound ended in a gasping echo, like a man sucking in his last breath, followed by a loud anguished sigh trailing off into silence. For the first time in his life Hatu was visited by a fear that settled into his bones, one that turned him colder than any wet cave ever could. He gritted his teeth so they wouldn't chatter, his mind racing like an animal seeking escape. For a long time, no coherent thought was possible.

Hatu let his feet go limp; the painful jolt he felt as he once again hung from the ceiling was enough to banish his mindless terror and gave him space to replace it with more useful outrage. Another crucial lesson taught by every master and teacher from his earliest memory was that you were never without hope until your very last breath. He tugged against his chains a few more times and judged that trying to force them was totally futile, so instead he turned his mind to his surroundings and to those who had captured him.

He could see no one else besides Donte's still figure on his left, though at least half of the cavern was hidden from his view by deep shadows or utter darkness. Hatu turned to look at his friend and whispered, "Donte?"

Donte hung motionless, not stirring. Hatu could just make out a wound on his friend's head: a scalp cut that had bled freely and bathed one side of his face, neck, and shoulder. He knew from their training that scalp wounds often looked worse than they were, but also worried that Donte's limp form suggested the cut may have come from a hard strike. A blow that had caused him to be unconscious for this long might be killing him silently. His education had included tending the wounded, and head wounds were often the most difficult to understand and treat; a man might take a blow to the head and seem to be on his way to recovery, only to then die suddenly. Master Bodai had watched healers cut into the heads of dead men to learn about the causes of such things, only to come away as baffled as before. He had surmised that the damage was probably obscured by the inspection, the evidence destroyed as the healer cracked open the skull.

Hatu spoke Donte's name again, but his friend remained silent. He could see Donte's chest moving slightly, so at least he knew he was breathing.

Hatu forced his mind from mindless terror as he tried to make sense of their surroundings and look for an escape. He had little concept of where they were, but before he allowed himself to be overwhelmed by other problems, his first task was to free himself of these shackles. He'd heard of sicari who'd been trained to dislocate their thumbs and slip their hands through such bindings. He moved his fingers and thumbs around, realizing he had no idea how to go about such a feat. He tugged and pulled, but whatever the trick, he knew it was beyond him.

Hatu gave a single tug on the chains, knowing it was just a vain attempt at discovering a last-second escape, as distant voices broke the silence. He decided to feign unconsciousness, and perhaps learn something.

The voices resolved into soft-spoken female tones, speaking a language unfamiliar to Hatu. As they neared, he could feel their presence even with his head down and eyes closed.

"This one pretends." The woman spoke in the trade language of the isles. "Isn't that so, boy?"

Hatu saw no benefit in prolonging the pretense and risking the consequences, and so opened his eyes, standing as best he could.

The two women were dressed in similar red robes with their hoods tossed back. The twinkling light of the phosphorescent pools made discerning details difficult at first. The play of shadows across their faces disguised them until Hatu's eyes adjusted to the play of the light.

One of the women was perhaps older than Hatu by only a few years. The other was of such an age that she could have been her mother, or maybe an older sister, but there was no resemblance between them. The younger woman had plain, angular features that Hatu imagined might turn beautiful as her temperament added patina and tone. She looked at her companion, then back at him suddenly, and Hatu only saw madness in her widening eyes.

The older woman possessed surprisingly normal features and a pleasant smile, though, given his current situation and how the ship had been attacked, Hatu assumed her geniality to be a mask. The two women had obviously played some role in the onslaught, and it involved magic of the darkest sort. The creatures that had attacked the ship were not from a drunken seaman's tale to get others to buy drinks. Those man-shaped things were surely the product of something powerful and evil.

"Ah," said the older woman. "The last two from

that accursed ship. What to do?" Looking at her companion, she asked, "Meat, mate, or swimmer?"

The younger woman regarded Hatu and said, "He is not pretty enough. Meat." She then approached Donte and said, "This one is pretty." She examined his head wound and said, "Mate, if he recovers." With a petulant tone she added, "I have not had my fun in a long time, Madda. I haven't made a daughter!"

The one she called Madda said, "You're young, Sabina. You want your fun all the time and neglect your duties; all you think of is mating and daughters." She cast a disapproving look at the younger woman. "There was a day, before my youth, when girls like you were also meat. There were more of us then, and we ruled this ocean." Her voice fell off as she finished, "Be thankful times changed."

The younger woman's rapacious expression twisted into one of anger and resentment as the reprimand struck her like a physical blow. She scowled, and Hatu decided there was nothing attractive about her sharp features. The woman called Madda would have to be cautious of this one.

The first woman ran her hands down Donte's chest and fondled his groin. "He's big," she said, smiling with an evil gleam in her eyes.

"If he regains his wits you can mate, then meat."

"Mate," the one named Sabina whispered. "No meat; it's too pretty."

Madda began to say something and then stopped. She leaned close to Hatu, close enough for him to get a good look at her face, and he realized that whatever opinions he had formed were now secondary to something he had never felt before: a strong, overwhelming aura. He was seized by a nearly mindless desire to get as far from the woman as he could, and found himself pulling back on the chains that suspended him, hard enough to fully extend his arms and brush his back against the wall behind him. Fear, followed closely by rising anger, overtook him.

An animal whimper escaped Hatu and he turned his face as she reached up to touch his cheek. He clenched his eyes tightly, then his eyes snapped open, locking his gaze to her. As she was about to touch his face, she yanked her hand away, hissing as if in pain. Then he heard her say, "Go, bring Hadona here."

"What—" the younger woman started to complain.

"Bring Hadona here!" shouted the older woman, and the tone and volume of her voice made it clear there would be no more argument.

The young woman hurried off and Madda whispered, "Who are you, youngling?"

Hatu said nothing, his mind now consumed with a

fear that had reduced him to a quivering animal. His only one desire was to be anywhere else but in this cave with this woman. Anger rose with that fear, just a moment behind it.

"Fear drives the beast," muttered Madda. Hatu felt her grab his chin and yank his head around, so that his nose almost touched hers.

He mustered every iota of discipline he could find and kept silent, determined not to let his fear give this woman any more advantage than she already possessed.

Suddenly, a rush of energy coursed through him, and he relaxed. He stared into her eyes and was rewarded as she pulled away slightly, released his chin, and stepped away. "You are more than you seem," she whispered.

Hatu thought he detected a note of fear in her words but said nothing. His lessons had taught him that his best chance for survival was to keep calm and never stop looking for a way out. One master had even gone so far as to tell him, "If you fall from a cliff toward rocks below, screaming mindlessly means certain death. If, in those last few seconds, you turn your mind to finding a way out, you'll likely still die, but you give yourself a chance to survive." It had been said in semi-jest, but there was a kernel of truth in that admonition.

The woman was reacting strongly to him, as if she could almost feel the rising anger within him, directed at her like a weapon, and perhaps that played to his advantage.

As she withdrew another half step, Hatu stole a glimpse at his friend still hanging limply from his chains. At least Donte was spared this terror, he thought. His continued lack of movement led Hatu to the conclusion that he'd never recover from the blow to his head. Anger drove out the remaining fear and Hatu considered that should he somehow survive this captivity, he dreaded telling Master Kugal that his grandson was dead. The nearly comic probability of that outcome almost tipped Hatu into a sense of giddiness that he recognized as being a short step away from hysteria. From fear or rage, mindless hysteria was no choice at all, so he used every trick learned since boyhood to force himself into as calm a state as possible.

Over Madda's shoulder, Hatu saw a group of women emerge slowly out of the gloom; they surrounded an old, bent woman but kept a respectful distance from her. The young woman Sabina preceded the elder.

Hatu blinked to focus until the woman blocking most of his view stepped aside and bowed. "Hadona," she said in greeting. "It's this one." She indicated Hatu.

If the other women repelled Hatu, Hadona totally repulsed him. She was not only ugly and wizened, her shoulders rounded by the weight of her years and her face little more than parchment stretched over bone, but evil flowed from her like a palpable miasma, a cloud that surrounded her and grew stronger as she neared.

She stepped before Hatu and muttered, "What is this?"

"He is why I asked for you," answered Madda. "I sense—"

"Fire," interrupted the old woman as she moved closer to Hatu. He could see every detail of her face; she was ancient, but the light in her eyes seemed timeless, and she wore the expression of a cunning feral cat calculating how best to snag its prey. Hadona reached out, but her fingertips only hovered over Hatu's chest.

"Who are you?" she whispered, and put her hand over Hatu's eyes.

He fell into a dark place where shadows moved against darker shadows, and images rose out of them, but of a sort he had never seen before, like the impressions left when he closed his eyes against a sudden brightness. The streaks of color resolved into fluid shapes: faces from his past rose and fell away, shifting into other images, constantly morphing and turning.

As if in a waking dream, he remembered.

The fight had erupted over some imagined slight, two boys trading barbed comments for no reason other than boredom. Hatu didn't even know what the first remark had been, or who had made it. The confrontation had caught his attention only after it had escalated to insults and pushes.

He and Donte stood among the onlookers who had gathered in the otherwise empty warehouse. It was a hot day, the takings had been lower than the masters expected, and every street thief, gang basher, pickpocket, and lookout was on edge. It didn't matter what the reasons were; people were always punished by the leaders for a low take.

There were two types of street gangs operating throughout the nations of South Tembria, in the hundreds of ports scattered among the two thousand or so islands to the east of the continent. A few of the key ones were controlled completely by the Quelli Nascosti of Coaltachin; others, like this one, were infiltrated by members of the The Hidden.

Hatu glanced at Donte, who, with a tiny shake of his head, indicated they should both stay out of this fight. Their current gang called themselves the Black Spiders, and they would otherwise have been beneath notice, save that recently they had been aggressively expanding their activities, and that had come to the notice of the Council in Coaltachin. Hatu and Donte had been placed there to discover the identity of the Black Widow, their leader. Local gangs were allowed to operate as long as they didn't get too ambitious. Whoever this Black Widow was, she had intruded upon operations controlled by Coaltachin.

It was Hatu and Donte's first mission together—smaller boys were less likely to be suspect—and the crew boss who oversaw them was blocks away, so it was critical they make no error that would jeopardize their safety. It had taken them a few weeks to insinuate themselves into this crew and get a sense of the Spiders' overall organization. Donte had a lead, and if it panned out, they'd have the Widow's identity and could send a message home: the trigger that would likely result in the Black Widow's eventual elimination, and her gang's being scattered or absorbed. This fight might be just the opportunity to—

"No," a voice came into Hatu's mind. "Further back. You're more than a mere street thug."

A flash of light, a sliver of darkness, and he was back on his home island again. Heat bathed the students as they struggled to master the task before them. The art of being silent was being driven home by this morning's practice—the lesson Hatu hated the most. He did not mind standing on one leg—he was strong and had good balance—nor remaining silent, but he found it nearly impossible to empty his mind, whatever that was supposed to mean.

He was almost eleven years old and his mind raced even then. He wanted to know things, understand how they worked or why they were . . . how they were. There were so many unanswered questions in his mind, but to speak to a trainer without first being spoken to was forbidden. Any infraction brought forth the switch or a leather strap. So, he kept silent and remained frustrated, and the years of silent obedience masked low burning anger, always there deeply hidden.

"No," came the voice of Hadona, "further."

Another lightning flash, more darkness, and Hatu was in the village below the school. Part of his mind knew it wasn't real, and for a brief moment he fought against the compulsion to obey the reality offered to him, but he didn't really understand how to resist it, and so was swept back even further.

Hatu saw the dog and without knowing why, he felt afraid. He wanted to cry out and run away, but even by five years old, he had been trained not to cry or voice any distress. A tiny whimper was all he let escape.

He had been playing with some colored stones that one of the matrons had given to him while she hung the washing out to dry. Other children played nearby, occupied with various things to keep them out of trouble, but he was the closest to the road.

Hatu stood and hurried to where the matron pegged clothing to a line and tugged on her skirt. Looking down, she raised one eyebrow in question and he pointed toward the dog.

She instantly dropped the washing and scooped Hatu up into her arms. Looking around, she saw a pair of farmworkers walking down the road from the tableland and shouted to them, "Mad dog!" Then she carried Hatu toward the other children.

Over the matron's shoulder, Hatu watched as the men, who carried a rake and a pitchfork, saw the dog behaving strangely and hurried to put it down.

"No . . . something else."

There were no words this time. His vision was jumbled, and random memories came in and out of focus. Light and shadows dominated his thoughts, and Hatu found himself fighting to give words to concepts. He was tiny.

His existence knew touch, smell, lights, and shadows, warmth or the absence of it, hunger or suckling contentment. And yet, there was more, too; for in the brief moments between nursing and sleeping he felt other things course through his mind, things he did not yet understand, even though he felt certain the understanding would eventually come. They were energies that felt apart from the world of sensation and perception that he was growing into, and he welcomed the attachment to what he would later come to think of as "the other."

This was also the moment he lost "the other," and without words to describe its loss, Hatu only felt a deep void, a faint reverberation of something important lost, an echo that would lie at the root of his constant sense of frustration and anger.

"There you are," came a voice. "These are the things I must know."

Someone picked him up, and loud noises close by startled him. He began to cry but a hand covered his mouth and muffled the sound. He heard voices speak words he didn't understand in his memory, though he understood them now as he relived this memory.

"They're killing the babies! Take him and flee."

"Where?" A voice spoke very close to him, perhaps the person who clutched him against her chest. He felt soft warmth and could hear a heart pounding.

"To the stream from the lake; follow it down the gully into the valley. It looks like it ends at the falls but there's a trail that continues on the right side. Follow it down to the coast. Then down to where his father fights. See if anyone survived. If not, hide the child as best you . . ." The voices and images faded.

Hatu came alert, chilled to the bone, his teeth chattering. The evil crone peered into his eyes and again he felt alien sensations course through him, as if a storm approached and was causing all the hair on his arms and head to stand up. She chanted and he heard words he almost understood. The ache faded from his shoulders and he not only felt revived, but his strength returned in a rush. She waved her hand and the feeling of well-being faded. She whispered, "He is gods-touched. He is a creature of vengeance. He has magic sleeping within him."

"Kill him," said Sabina. "Meat!"

"No!" said Hadona. She looked as if she was about to strike the younger woman, who pulled back, cringing slightly. "You would invite destruction upon all of the Sisters of the Deep." Hadona then turned to look at Madda. "He is a thing of power, a weapon to be used. We cannot have it used against us, but whoever kills him will unleash fury beyond imagining. He must die far from here, and not by our hands." She was silent for a long moment, then said, "Have the swimmers put him back."

"What of the other one?" asked Madda.

Hadona looked at Sabina. "Keep him for your toy.

Maybe a first daughter will teach you things no one else seems able to."

As Madda laughed, Hadona said, "Call the swimmers and get him away, now!"

Hatu glanced at his friend still hanging limply, wishing he could speak a goodbye, then Hadona waved her hand before his face, and darkness suddenly overwhelmed him again.

11

A Quick Instruction and Introduction

The wagon was less than a block south of Caer Marquenet's main gate when a group of men stopped in the middle of the street and blocked their passage. The three older men at their center held large hammers, marking them as blacksmiths. "Who here calls himself a smith?" demanded the man at the front, a burly, blond-haired fellow with massive shoulders.

Declan nodded, his face a neutral mask. "That would be me."

"Boys said there was a new fellow in the city, heading to the caer with an anvil and tools in the back of his wagon. Get down and we'll talk."

Some locals paused to witness the potential confrontation between the three young men in the wagon and the half a dozen blacksmiths with their apprentices, eighteen in number.

Declan turned to Jusan and Ratigan and said, "It will be fine," and he climbed down. He motioned to Jusan. "My sword."

Jusan handed it down and Declan belted it around his waist before he slowly walked to stand before the self-appointed leader of the mob. "Now, what is it?" he asked, keeping his tone quiet.

"We have some standards in Marquenet."

"You're a guild?" asked Declan.

"No," said the blond smith. "Baron Dumarch doesn't allow guilds, but he is more honorable than most lords, and we follow his example; we offer good work for fair pay, and we don't let just any common journeyman"—he leaned forward, inspecting Declan—"who's only just finished his apprenticeship wander in and lower prices and quality. We have a tradition in Marquenet."

"Some standards, you said," replied Declan.

The blond smith nodded. Declan judged that his stance was a threat implied, not an open challenge. Still, a potential confrontation was but moments away. Declan smiled slightly, nodded, and said, "Standards are good."

"What are you called?"

"Declan, and you?"

"Gildy."

"Do you speak for all the smiths in the city, Gildy?"

The large man let his hammer slide through his hand until he gripped it under the iron head, then he crossed his arms and said, "For the sake of this discussion, yes, I do." Gildy's face tightened as if he expected trouble. The men arrayed behind him looked ready to brawl as well.

Declan nodded. "Well, to begin, I'd not undercut anyone's prices, and I haven't even decided where I want to set up shop yet. I had a message for the baron, and now that it has been delivered, I think I'll head out of the city and look for a town or village that is in need of a smith. There is obviously no shortage here."

Gildy relaxed slightly, hearing that. He nodded, acknowledging Declan's intent. The men behind him stood a bit more at ease, as well.

"And lastly, I'm not a journeyman. I'm a master smith."

Gildy's brow furrowed and said, "Master, you say? You don't look like you have the age."

"I was taught by the best."

"Who?"

"Edvalt Tasman, at the forge in Oncon."

Gildy looked over his shoulder and another smith nodded and said, "We know that name from when he was the baron's man. He's . . . very good."

Declan pulled his sword, and before anyone could react, he reversed it and handed it hilt first to Gildy. "This is my masterpiece."

Gildy regarded the unpolished sword for a moment and then took it from Declan. "Doesn't look like . . ." He felt the heft and balance, then looked more closely. He ran his thumb slowly along the fuller, thick raised center of the blade, then held it out and looked down it. "Balances well," he said softly. "Very well." He again brought it close to his eyes and rubbed its edge, revealing a slight sheen. The other smiths and apprentices fell silent as Gildy continued to judge the blade—thrusting, taking blocking positions, and cutting broadly, as if in combat.

Finally, he went past Declan and put the blade flat on the wheel of the wagon. He lightly tapped it with his hammer, which produced a ringing tone, and held the blade up closer to his ear.

"Damn me," he said softly.

Gildy turned to look at Declan, an unspoken question on his face, and after a brief second, Declan nodded.

"*It's a jewel of a thing,*" Gildy said so only Declan could hear.

Again Declan nodded, but said nothing.

Handing the sword back, the large man said, "Tell me of its fashioning."

"I built the furnace, clay atop stone; stoked the coals; and chose the iron. I mixed the coal ash and iron sand and judged the slag by color. I folded the steel—"

"How many folds?"

Declan smiled slightly. "Twelve."

Gildy nodded. "It's a fine weapon. Needs a polish."

Declan scabbarded his sword and said, "Didn't want it looking too conspicuous."

Gildy laughed. "Well, modest, too." He turned to the others and said, "Declan is who he claims, if he indeed made that sword, and since he's given us no reason to doubt him, this, lads, may be the youngest master smith you'll ever see!" He clapped Declan on the shoulder in a friendly manner.

The others hesitated for a moment, and then the mood changed; several of the men nodded at Declan in greeting. Gildy said, "Set up your shop where you will, but come by and have a drink before you leave the city, and I'll tell you how things get done around here, so you don't cause any ruckus with your fellow smiths." He pointed south and said, "Three streets down there's a clothier at the sign of a black-and-white sheep. Turn right and you'll find my forge on the left side of the street a short way down."

Declan held out his hand and said, "Fair enough."

They shook, and then Gildy turned and said, "Need to get back to work, boys."

When the knot of smiths and apprentices had departed, Declan climbed back on the wagon. Ratigan said, "You did well. There's no tougher bunch in the city than the smiths, 'cept maybe the teamsters. Get on their wrong side and things can turn very grim."

"You didn't think to inform me of their . . . fraternity before we arrived?"

Ratigan shrugged, flicked the reins, and got the horses moving again before he said, "Didn't see the need. You never mentioned where you intended to go after we talked to the baron."

Declan sighed. "I guess that's right." He looked around as the wagon headed down the road back toward the market. "Where are we going?"

"I don't know about you and the boy," said Ratigan, "but I'm heading for the market to see if anything needs hauling. When we get there, I'd be pleased to help you unload that anvil and your tools."

Declan looked at the driver, then laughed. "I imagine you would." Then he lost his smile. "I'm going to require your services a while longer, until I find a proper site for a forge."

"I need to earn some coin, Declan," said Ratigan crossly. "I have horses to feed and they're growing lean on the grazing we've done since leaving Oncon. They require grain. Grain requires money."

Declan said, "I'll buy you some grain and toss in a couple of silver coins, but I can't just stand on the roadside and use my tools. I need a proper forge or a place to build one."

Ratigan nodded. It was clear he wasn't going to shed Declan and Jusan easily, and despite his self-serving nature, he also knew that he owed his freedom, even his life, to the villagers of Oncon, and the two men with him were at the heart of his liberation. He was silent for a while, then said, "There's usually someone at the market who might be of help."

They wended their way through the busy streets to an intersection a block away from the market. Ratigan navigated them easily through a narrow back street to a large open area filled with horses, wagons, carts, and a few pack animals. He found a place he could easily leave, parked the wagon, and jumped down, motioning for Declan to follow. Turning to Jusan he said, "You'd best keep an eye on things here. No one will bother you in daytime, but if no one watches the wagon, those tools will likely be missing when we get back."

Declan looked at Jusan and said, "Rest here and I'll be back shortly."

Jusan, who was almost at full health, looked annoyed at being left behind but said nothing and only nodded.

Declan walked beside Ratigan to the market. As they approached the first booth, the smith asked, "Would leaving my tools there really be a problem?"

"Maybe not. Nobody bothers horses and wagons, but something that can be lifted out and carried away?" He shrugged, then pointed. "There she is."

The "she" was a stocky, middle-aged woman wearing a bright blue head scarf, from which strands and curls of shocking orange hair tried to escape. Sunburned cheeks and freckles dominated her round face, and her very large frame was clad in a simple scoop-neck, sleeveless top and a huge bright blue skirt that swept along the ground. She stood behind two younger women, a slender dark-skinned girl with sharp features, and a curvaceous blonde who bore a slight resemblance to the large woman behind her. Declan thought the blonde was as pretty as any girl he had ever seen.

"Hey, Kalanora!" Ratigan shouted in greeting.

The large woman's eyes narrowed as she saw Ratigan approaching. "Don't waste my time or pester my girls, Ratigan!" Then a puzzled expression crossed her puffy face and her eyes widened. "Weren't you off somewhere with Milrose?"

Ratigan ignored the harsh tone of her first remark and answered her question. "Milrose is dead. We got hit by slavers near the Ilcomen-Covenant border."

"Hmmm," was all Kalanora said as she looked down her nose at the driver in a manner that suggested she believed that whatever ill had befallen his master, it was probably Ratigan's fault.

"Who's your friend?" Kalanora asked, turning an appraising gaze on Declan, as if she was disinclined to give any companion of Ratigan's the benefit of the doubt. Declan was certain the two had history.

Before Ratigan could answer, a loud blast of a horn and the beat of several drums in unison filled the market, quickly followed by a babble of voices, and Declan and the others turned toward the source of the tumult.

Kalanora spoke loudly. "Now what is it?"

Ratigan and Declan moved toward the sound, and through the crowd they saw a procession traveling into the marketplace from the south. Half a dozen men in dark grey robes, with their hoods thrown back, had entered the square; their advance had slowed as the crowd gave way sedately, despite the clamor from the drums and brass horn.

Behind the men came a stranger-looking vehicle than any Declan had ever seen, and he had fixed wheels and axles on every type of carriage, wagon, and cart known on the continent. It was pulled by six draft horses; he couldn't see the wheels or detail below the upper half of the wagon due to the crowd, but the upper half alone was odd enough to catch Declan's attention.

It looked like a hay wagon, but with its high sides cut down and a large platform fixed on top. A sturdy wooden chair, almost a throne, had been nailed to the platform, and on it sat an elderly man wearing a black robe and a red skullcap who appeared to be doing his best not to fall off. He had a pale, pinched face, and his eyes darted around, as if he was searching for something in the crowd. His smile looked feigned, and more like he was in pain, and he was making an odd gesture with his right hand, holding it upright and moving it around slightly. Declan thought it looked as if the old man was giving some sort of benediction to the crowd.

The strange wagon lurched and groaned. Without looking at it, Declan could tell it had a fixed axle, and so visited every bump in the road upon the hindquarters of whichever dignitary sat on the silly contraption. Still, the man's rictus smile remained fixed.

"Who is that?" asked Ratigan and Kalanora at almost exactly the same moment.

Declan only shrugged, while Ratigan said, "I think we'll soon find out. They're stopping."

To the consternation of several merchants, the horn was blown one last time, followed by a ruffle of drums, and the procession halted in the midst of potential buyers. Then a man who walked before the team drawing the odd wagon shouted, "Silence!"

The command only brought forth a louder babble of angry voices and again came the command to fall silent. After a minute of jeering, the noise fell away until replaced by a low murmur of curious chatting and whispering.

Seeing that it was as close to silence as he was likely to get, the speaker shouted, "By order of the One, to each state and nation, a holy guide has been dispatched. In each state and nation a prelature is to be established in the capital city, in which will reside a man of high office, tasked with overseeing the spiritual well-being of the people, and with leading the hunt for heretics.

"You are now in the presence of Marquensas's prelate, His Excellency Episkopos Hosa."

"That's an odd name," said Kalanora.

The crowd muttered, not entirely sure what was expected of them. The Church of the One had grown in power over the last hundred years, displacing other faiths through political maneuvering, clever alliances, and outright bullying and bribery. They had been more aggressive over the last thirty years, and bloodshed had been replaced by political manipulation of the highest order. The Church claimed their rise was due to the supremacy of their god, and that it was proof that their faith was the only true faith.

Edvalt had told Declan that when he was a boy, an uneasy peace had existed between most of the faiths, but since then he had seen this new church systematically destroy the others. Only a few minor faiths were still tolerated, and those had cleverly adapted so they could claim to worship the same god.

"Well, I guess we've got someone else to tell us how to live our lives," said Kalanora with a snort of disgust.

The speaker raised his voice again. "The prelature is established in the building on West Hill. It was consecrated last night after the episkopos blessed the building and a dozen heretics were burned at the stake. Prayer services begin at sunrise and end at sundown. The faithful are always welcome."

The drivers, who stood to either side of the horses,

as both flipped the reins, urging the horses forward, and the procession began their exit from the market, apparently heading to another market on their way back to West Hill.

"West Hill?" said Ratigan. "That's what they were doing with that building?" He glanced at Declan. "Used to be the Temple of Othan, goddess of oceans and weather. Every sailor in the city would say a prayer there before leaving on a voyage, back when I was a boy."

"They took it over two years ago." Kalanora hit Ratigan lightly on the back of the head. "And if you didn't spend all your time drinking and bothering good girls, you'd know that, Ratigan." He turned and looked daggers at her, rubbing the back of his head, as she continued. "They converted the temple to the One. It's now called a church. They conducted rituals, burned a lot of incense and a few heretics. The entire quarter fairly reeked of sage, balsam, and myrrh for weeks"—she lowered her voice—"to hide the stench of burned flesh, I expect." Returning to her normal speaking voice, Kalanora continued. "And that chanting . . ." She shook her head as the procession left the market. "Well, at least we know *episkopos* is a title of some sort, and not a name."

Returning to Kalanora's stall, Ratigan said, "Better one priest than ten telling us what to do, I should think."

"You're too young to understand," said Kalanora. "Hell, even I'm too young and I'm older than you." She half laughed, half snorted as they moved behind the table where her daughters waited. "When I was a child, some of the old churches still had influence, but they also had this . . . I guess you could call it respect. You could make offerings and sacrifices to whichever god you fancied and people rarely noticed or cared.

"Now, if you so much as mutter the name of an old god around one of the black robes, you end up tied to a stake on a stack of kindling. Even the followers of Tathan are saying that the sun god was only a harbinger of the One, spreading light, getting the righteous prepared for the coming of the word." She sighed. "Clever actually—they got to keep their jobs as long as they shared the money."

Declan said nothing. He had thought little about faith, as there weren't any temples or shrines in Oncon, and it was difficult to reach the ones in Ilcomen. He'd only been in a few over the years, when traveling with Edvalt, who would occasionally stop and toss a few coins into the priest's box to receive a blessing. Declan didn't pretend to understand matters of faith. Mostly he didn't care.

Kalanora let out a long sigh of resignation. Then her

eyes narrowed and she said, "Again, what's your business, Ratigan?"

"My friend Declan is a smith. He's looking to set up a forge. I told him if anyone knew where he could best position himself in Marquensas it would be Kalanora."

"Smith, huh?" she muttered as she looked Declan up and down. Her daughters visibly brightened and, smiling, became more attentive, as a good smith could afford a family and provide for them year-round. As they started to step forward, Kalanora waved them back without looking. "Any good?"

Declan nodded.

"Well, Marquensas has more smiths than a dog has fleas, especially here in the city. So, no matter how good you are, there are established smiths who are as good as you here, and pulling trade from them won't win you friends."

"That's why we came to you, Kalanora," said Ratigan with what Declan could only call a false smile.

Kalanora raised one corner of her mouth in a dismissive expression but turned to Declan. "There's an empty forge near the frontier. Can be dangerous country sometimes, but you look like the sort of lad who can care for himself."

Again, Declan nodded.

She was silent for a moment and then glanced at Ratigan. "This isn't a favor, Ratigan."

Declan reached into his belt and removed his coin purse. He took out two silver Ilcomen coins and handed them to her. She glanced down as she took them and nodded. "Go north, along the coast, past Lord Dumarch's villa at the headlands, then take the road that heads inland from the village of Pashtar. Three days' steady travel and you'll find a town called Beran's Hill. Nice little place. Northernmost town in Marquensas, so it can be a little lively up there, even dangerous, as I said, but it's a busy trade route. Their smith died a few weeks ago, I was told, so unless someone else has squatted there, the forge is empty. Go to the Inn of the Three Stars and ask for the owner, Leon. He holds the widow's rights to the forge. Tell him I sent you and make him a decent offer for the widow and you'll have a nice forge on a busy trading route. You may have to toss out a squatter, if Leon hasn't already, but you'll have no easier start than there. I hear it's a dandy forge. You can't do better than that unless you're working for the nobility."

Declan nodded and said, "Thank you," as he handed her another silver coin.

She glanced at it, nodded once, then said, "Now

go away. I have business to conduct and there's been enough interruptions for one day."

Ratigan grinned evilly and said, "See you soon, Kalanora. Love the new hair color."

Kalanora muttered, "That bitch Clothild swore it would be just like when I was young. Now I look like my head's growing carrots!" She lost her harsh look and laughed. "I wear the scarf so people won't think I'm the Firemane baby!"

Ratigan backed away and said, "Little old for that assumption, aren't you?"

She immediately lost her good humor.

Ratigan bowed slightly, staying. out of her reach.

Declan nodded thanks, and noticed that both of the girls watched them as they left. When they were out of sight, Declan said, "Firemane baby?"

Ratigan said, "Where did you grow up?"

"Oncon."

"I guess that explains it," said the teamster as they headed back toward Ratigan's wagon. "Used to be five grand kingdoms. Now there are four. Ithrace's king was called Firemane, because of his red hair. All his line had it. A kind of coppery gold shot through with sunshine, according to the stories. The tale is that every Firemane was killed save a baby who some servant carried away. Anyway, there was also a curse or something to do with the death of the last Firemane."

"Last? I thought you said there was a baby who lived?"

"That's just a story," answered Ratigan.

As they neared the wagon, Ratigan said, "On the other hand, there's been enough bad stuff happening in the east since that king's death . . . Maybe there really was a curse." He stopped for a minute, then said, "But if there was a child . . . ?" He shrugged. "The other four kings would pay a handsome bounty for it; grown boy or girl now, I expect. Now, anything else you want to know about?"

"Those girls?"

Ratigan grinned as they resumed walking. "The dark one's called Mina, the fair one's Phaedra. Different fathers, as you can tell from the looks. Mina's mean and Phaedra's sweet, but get a few cups of wine in them, and both know how to have a good time."

Declan frowned. He realized they might offer him a similar sort of relationship to the one he had with Roz, but he had feelings for her. He gave Ratigan a disapproving look for a second, then shrugged.

Ratigan stopped again and looked at Declan. "Why? They can be fun; getting them away from Kalanora is the problem."

"I don't know. Just . . ." He fell silent, thinking of everything that had happened recently, from becoming a master smith to his last night with Roz and talking to her husband, all of it. His confusion was still there, but he knew it would eventually fade. "Nothing really," said Declan as he resumed their walk.

Finally, as they turned the corner leading to the open yard where the wagon waited, he said, "I'm a master smith now. I'm about to open a new forge. I should be settling down."

Ratigan laughed. "You haven't had much time with the girls, then." He slapped the younger man on the back playfully, a gesture Declan endured silently. "Those girls are just sport for the night, not future mothers." He paused and reconsidered. "Let me say that differently: they are almost certain to become mothers, more likely sooner rather than later, but they are not of the type to make good wives."

Declan kept his face a mask. Arguing with Ratigan wasted too much time and energy. He also knew from talking to travelers that a lot of men felt that way toward the women they encountered. But he was a village lad and had grown up in a place where mothers taught their daughters to be a certain way—even those daughters who didn't listen; he'd bedded a few of those who didn't listen to their mothers—and he thought of Edvalt and Mila, and the other older couples in Oncon . . . maybe he was just a village boy out in a different world. Either way, Declan didn't care for the feeling listening to Ratigan gave him. Meeting Jack after bedding Roz had made him uneasy, and now he realized he was trying to rethink how he should feel about women . . . and he was totally lost. At least Ratigan was firm in his opinions, crass as they were.

"You're going to be the only smith in town. Many mothers would love to marry off their daughters to a smith. Most towns, your only rival would be the miller or a very successful trader. So, wait a bit and see what kind of place Beran's Hill turns out to be. If you don't like the girls there, save up a little gold, head back here, and see if there's a shopkeeper's daughter who suits you better."

Declan paused as he considered what Ratigan had just said, and then laughed. "Ratigan, you surprise me."

The teamster stopped and looked at Declan. "Why?"

"For such an ill-tempered fellow, you show depth; that was actually very sound advice. I thank you."

Ratigan looked at Declan and for a moment couldn't seem to decide if he'd just been insulted or complimented, then he also laughed. "I do have my moments," he replied, and they resumed their walk.

They reached the wagon and found Jusan awake.

"Been nothing but quiet around here," he said to Declan. "What now?"

Declan turned to Ratigan. "Is there a safe place to keep my tools and anvil tonight?"

"My old master's yard. Unless someone beat us there with news of his demise, Milrose's house should be locked." He reached into a belt purse and pulled out a key. "And I can get in."

Declan took out some coins and said, "I'm going to go find Gildy and ask him a few questions, then meet you at Milrose's place. Buy some grain for your horses, and some food for us. We leave for Beran's Hill at dawn."

Ratigan told Declan how to find Milrose's shop, then looked at Jusan as Declan walked away and said, "He takes charge, doesn't he?"

Jusan's color had returned, and for the first time since his injury, he laughed. "You have no idea. But he is a man to trust. He was a better big brother to me than my own big brother."

Ratigan climbed onto the seat of the wagon, urged the horses to turn around, and started off toward his late master's shop.

Declan returned to the market and could feel the tempo of the place was slowing. It was perhaps two hours to sundown and people who needed to be home to prepare meals or tend to children had already departed.

After questioning a few locals, Declan was fairly clear on where he needed to go, and less than half an hour later found himself at the door of Gildy's forge. The large blond man stood above a wheel rim, hammering it to a wooden wheel. Seeing no apprentice at hand, Declan steadied the wheel so Gildy could finish quickly.

When he was done Gildy said, "Thanks. I sent my boy off to fetch some coal and thought to complete this myself. Not as nimble as I once was." He smiled as he wiped his brow with a rag. "Now, what brings you here?"

Looking around to make sure they weren't overheard, Declan said, "You said to come by and we'd talk about how things get done here. I'm leaving tomorrow, so here I am."

Gildy laughed. "Help me put this on that wagon over there and we'll get a drink."

Declan did as he was asked and by the time they were finished Gildy's apprentice had appeared with a scuttle filled with coal. Gildy instructed him in what he wanted done, then said to Declan, "There's a little inn at the corner, where most of us gather at the end of the day." He glanced at the angle of the sun and said, "It's a little early, but that's good, as there are a few things I'd like to discuss without being overheard."

"Right," said Declan.

Gildy pointed to the sword at Declan's side. "That is true jewel steel?"

Declan nodded.

Gildy grinned, his face still beaded with perspiration. "Most smiths would have polished that to a mirror and hung it on the wall to boast about it."

Declan inclined his head slightly and shrugged. "My master was not about boasting."

"I know of Edvalt. Did he tell you much about his early life?"

"Some," said Declan, offering no more.

"Well, he knew weapons, that's a fact. Maybe the best around, from what I remember. I was only a young journeyman when he was the baron's armorer. I only caught a glimpse or two of him before . . ."

"Before the Betrayal," Declan finished. He knew that Gildy could only mean the betrayal that ended the Five Kingdoms when he was a boy. The Betrayal was a topic few openly referred to; it was behind them now, and any who spoke of it were mindful of who might be listening. Baron Daylon might not have cared what common folk thought, but the Church of the One had ears everywhere, it seemed.

Gildy nodded. "As I said, Edvalt was in service to Baron Daylon. I worked at another forge here in the city, still learning what I needed to know to get my own place." He made a gesture as they walked out the door of the smithy, motioning for Declan to follow. "Now, what do you want to know?"

"Whatever it was that you wanted to tell me in private," said Declan.

"We've just discussed most of it. There are maybe three smiths in Marquensas who can make jewel steel, four now with your arrival—not that there's much call for weapons so fine. I'm the only one in this city. That you can, and that Edvalt was your master, marks you as finely trained, and not a lot of the lads around here are anxious to have a better smith show up. Making rims for wagon wheels"—he hiked his thumb over his shoulder, took off his apron, and hung it on a nail in the wall before he continued— "that will feed the family, but weapons and armor are still the best source of gold. It's been peaceful enough around here for the last ten years, but on the frontier things are lively, so there's a steady call for weapons. And I hear that back east things are getting nastier by the month, but so far it's still quiet around here.

"So, those of us in Marquenet, we just get by, which

is why everyone's a little anxious about arrivals such as yourself."

"That doesn't quite explain the welcome," said Declan.

"Well, the boys are also concerned about someone with little talent offering lower prices. It reflects badly on the rest of us if we don't chase them off."

"You're beginning to sound like a guild."

Gildy smiled and then quickly let it fade. His brow furrowed a little as he said, "Not a proper one. Baron Dumarch wouldn't let a guild organize; besides, as I said earlier, he's a fair enough man who's true to his word, so we've no need to make it formal. We stay in touch with each other and make sure any steel made in Marquenet is not a bad reflection on any of us. The ironmongers know better than to bring poor-quality ore to the city."

Declan nodded. "Fair."

Gildy said, "Now, I need a flagon; there's nothing left to speak of that can't be overheard safely."

Declan again nodded as they continued walking.

Gildy glanced at him and said, "Don't talk much, do you?"

A slightly embarrassed smile accompanied Declan's reply, "No more than I must, I guess." Declan could be as voluble as the next fellow in comfortable surroundings and with a jack of ale in hand, but in a strange city, finding his way, he felt it better to listen than talk.

Gildy led him to a small inn two streets away from his shop and found a table. It was a little early in the day for most businesses to close, so the room wasn't crowded yet. An obliging barmaid brought over two large flagons of ale, and Gildy finished off a long pull by wiping the back of his hand across his mouth before saying, "So, then, what else can I do for you, Declan?"

"Tell me about Beran's Hill?"

Gildy tilted his head a bit and said, "Beran's Hill? Interesting place. Might be just the spot for an enterprising youngster like yourself." He leaned forward, elbows on the table. "No smith, I hear; people there have to make a day's journey or more to get things fixed, or wait until some tinker comes by with a cart." He sat back after taking a second drink. "Used to be a smith there by the name of Walter; Walter the Smith."

Declan said nothing. He would also be called Declan the Smith or Declan Smith: he was a bastard and would therefore be known by his trade, not his father's name.

"He was one mean old man, Walt Smith, though I hear his missus is a nice enough woman," said Gildy. "Beran's Hill is on a crossing of trade routes that skirt most civilized places, and a few roads that lead to a few where no timid soul would go. Quite a lot of smuggling going on up there. The road to reach the town cuts through the Wilds twice."

"So it's dangerous?"

"It's called The Wilds for a reason. The Baron's half portion has been fairly quiet for years; he sends troops up there once in a while if things get too troublesome, but the eastern half earns its name.

"Besides, most places can be dangerous, Declan. For some reason the baron's put no garrison in Beran's Hill; some speculate he's looking the other way so that trade can go east without paying duty, though that makes little sense, or he has some other reason. It can be dangerous there at times. That fancy sword you cobbled up? Can you use it?"

"If need be."

"Good, because the question isn't 'Is Beran's Hill dangerous?,' it's 'How dangerous a place is it?'"

Declan smiled. "So how dangerous is it?"

"It's pretty rough-and-tumble. You're from the Covenant, yes? That's where I heard Edvalt went."

"Yes, I grew up in Oncon."

"Used to be a pretty peaceful place, with every king ready to hang anyone who started trouble."

"Until recently, yes."

"So where'd you learn to handle a sword?"

"Edvalt always said it was a poor smith who didn't

know what his customers needed. So he taught me to use weapons, ride horses, work a team, even plow. I can cook a bit as well, so I know pots and kettles." Declan paused. "Still, with weapons you've got even more wagered on knowing how they work."

"Truth, that, but there's a difference between knowing and being good. You good?"

"Good enough."

Gildy said, "Then you should be all right in Beran's Hill. You'll get some rough traders and drunk caravan guards most of the time, but once in a while some very dangerous types will pass through the town, the kind you can't talk to, except with blood and steel. So most of the lads who've taken residence there are tough, able to defend the town."

Declan only nodded, thinking of his encounter with the slavers. Had Edvalt not been there, Declan was fairly certain he and Jusan would now be dead or in chains. He decided that having neighbors who could defend the town was a good thing.

Declan asked a few more questions, specifically about prices for the more common wares made by smiths in this part of the world; he was surprised at some of the variations, but most amounts came close to what Edvalt charged in Oncon.

Gildy drained his flagon. "Well, I'm for home and

a cleanup. My wife objects to me eating without washing my face and hands first. Not sure how she got that fancy notion, but one thing my father taught me is a happy wife means a happy life." He laughed at his own rhyme, then said, "Or at least it's a lot less vexing than what stubborn men endure, if you take my meaning."

"I think I do," said Declan with a smile. "The drinks are on me."

"Of course they are," said Gildy with a laugh. Declan shook hands with Gildy and watched him leave. He sat for a few minutes thinking about his journey. Declan was not by nature a reflective person. He took each day as it came, but the recent changes in his life had been so momentous that he had to stop and wonder about what fate had put before him. He was looking at himself more and asking questions he had never considered before. He took a drink from his half-empty mug, feeling slightly bemused and a little anxious about how his life was changing, and without his having a great deal of choice in the matter.

He'd always known that someday he'd be a master smith. Edvalt had made that plain early on, praising him when he earned it, chiding him when he deserved it, but telling Declan he had a talent few smiths possessed. The young smith had never taken special pride in that, counting it a fair assessment of his abilities. He wondered at times why what came naturally to him seemed such a challenge for Jusan.

Jusan made up with hard work what he lacked in talent, and though it took him longer to master things, once he knew something, he didn't forget it. Declan was convinced that Jusan would become a master, too, just by dint of effort. He might be ten or fifteen years older than Declan was now, but he'd have his own forge eventually. After determination, Jusan's biggest asset was his meticulousness. He might have been slower than Declan at the forge, but in the end his work matched up well.

Declan finished his drink and stood up. The barmaid looked over with a smile, as if asking if he'd like anything else. He shook his head slightly and departed.

He found his way easily back to the shop of Ratigan's former master. He entered a small yard and saw the horses were in their stalls, happily eating grain from a trough; they had also been combed and cleaned. Whatever Declan thought of him, Ratigan clearly cared for them. Declan had seen enough neglected animals in need of shoeing to know these were healthy, and had watched the teamster do what he could for them every night while on the road. Ratigan might have had unfortunate ideas regarding women—Declan was amused when thinking of what

Roz would say to him—but he apparently took care of his responsibilities.

The young smith entered the modest house that had served as Milrose's office and found Jusan and Ratigan sitting at a table in a small room at the back. "There you are," said Ratigan. He indicated a chair in the corner and invited Declan to pull it up and join them.

On the table rested a meat pie, a large pitcher of ale, and half a round of cheese, or what was left of it; only a large slice and the empty rind remained.

"Sorry about the bread, we ate it," said Ratigan.

Jusan looked embarrassed and echoed the apology. "Sorry."

Declan waved that away and set to work on the pie. He'd had enough ale, so eyeing the pump in the corner he said, "Does that work?"

Ratigan nodded, so Declan grabbed an empty cup, rinsed it, and filled it. Sitting down, he said, "Never seen a pump inside before."

Ratigan said, "See them a fair bit in the cities. Cost some to pipe in from the nearest well, but it's very handy. Saved my master a lot of time not having to haul buckets."

Declan noticed a bruise on Ratigan's face and said, "Where'd you get that?"

"One of the neighbors decided that since Milrose

wasn't coming back, he'd just move in. I had to move him back out."

Declan said, "You all settled in, then?"

"More or less. I'll tell that fool in the morning that I'm coming back and not to try to move in again. Nothing worth stealing here except the horses and wagon, and those'll be under me. I'll see if anyone needs anything dropped off on the way to Beran's Hill 'cause we got a bit of extra room. That'll make a little more coin. See if anything needs to be hauled back here, too."

"Enterprising," said Declan.

The three young men finished eating and turned in. Ratigan conceded the only bed to Jusan without protest, and Declan's opinion of him rose again.

12

Adrift and Alone

Banging wood was the first thing Hatu sensed, the sound cutting through his hazy consciousness. He came fully awake and felt himself sway as he realized that he was back in the gig from which he and Donte had been seized. He looked up.

The small boat was still tethered to the ship's stanchions; the water lapped just below the keel. Nothing had changed. Provisions still sat beneath the sail, which was ready to be hoisted, and the oars were neatly tucked to one side.

He moved to sit up and every inch of him protested. Besides the expected pain of bruises and ache of joints stretched by chains, there was another feeling: he felt like the very fiber of his being had been insulted, and an echo of pain from the shocking energy that had flowed through him still lingered. He forced himself to sit up, then moved his head over the side of the boat as sudden dry heaving wracked his body. He had nothing to throw up, but his stomach spasmed three times before he could catch his breath.

Hatu was still as he waited for the pain, nausea, and sudden bout of dizziness to subside. He kept breathing slowly, trying to absorb the horrors he had somehow survived.

Donte. Hatu knew that as long as he lived he would never be free of the image of his friend hanging motionless, seemingly lifeless. Hatu's heart sank further as he remembered that even if Donte were revived, the thing in the cave (he couldn't think of her as a woman) would then use him. He felt tears rising and wiped them away. He had never felt this alone in his entire life and employed the mental toughness that had been beaten into him to force his mind away from helplessness. Even if Donte survived with relatively little damage, Hatu had no way of finding out where he was, let alone mounting a rescue. He might as well have been dead; perhaps that was even a better fate than what might lie before him.

Hatu knew that letting despair overwhelm him was as sure a path to death as the one he had just escaped. Why he had been freed, and what that evil witch had meant by his being a vessel of power, were mysteries he'd have to put aside.

His first duty was survival. But on the heels of that recognition came the question, *Why did she let me go?* He had repeatedly pushed it aside. He had no idea what power and danger they had been talking about. His desire to find out what that evil witch meant was another reason he wanted to return with the armies of Coaltachin. Every thought needed to be turned to surviving and getting there.

Hatu needed to find a friendly port. He had an approximate idea where he was, now that he was back at the ship. He calculated how fast the ship was moving under full sail and its heading before the captain put into the cove he mistakenly thought would shelter them. Hatu roughly reckoned his course. He knew that tacking a small boat against the prevailing wind and rowing when he must would probably get him to The Clearing in three or four days, as long as he didn't get lost among the countless islands in this region. He had provisions enough for a week or more, and once he made his way home he could share what had happened.

Once his duty was discharged he could turn his mind to the questions raised in that slimy pit of evil. He now had names for the strange feelings and sense of disconnection he'd experienced since childhood.

Power, magic, and destiny formed the reawakened part of him that had been slumbering inside since just after his birth. He would learn its true nature and master it.

He had no idea where the Sisters of the Deep resided, near or far from here, or on which heading, or even an inkling of how long he had been unconscious while carried there and back. It might be the masters of Coaltachin would wish to seek them out, or more likely they'd count the ship and crew—including Donte—as a loss and turn to other business. But even if fate did not permit a swift return, he'd come back here someday, find that evil cesspit, and burn out every inch of it. He would show them he was indeed gods-touched.

The boat was leaking and it was only the morning of the second day. Hatu had tied off the rudder and tried to take a rest before sunrise, only to wake up a couple of hours later ankle-deep in water.

Hatu didn't know if the captain had been remiss in keeping the boat trim, or if the damage had been caused by its banging against the ship's stern while he was a captive, or if it was a combination of the two, but the boards on the starboard side had loosened just above the waterline, so seawater came in each time the boat dipped. It was a slow leak, and Hatu managed to keep the boards above the waterline on a long port tack, but if he had to come about, water seeped in quickly and he had to turn about and tie off the sail to the rudder: an old trick he had learned very young. Then he had to bail out the water, but the problem was he had nothing to bail with, so he could only get a bit out with his cupped hands before having to return to minding the tiller and sail.

The solution he'd been taught was simple: Hatu should find an island, pull the boat onto the shore, find some tar or resinlike substance, and use whatever else he could find, including torn clothing, to make battens and seal up the two worst leaks. A few minor ones did not look likely to become worse absent violent weather, in which case he would most likely sink to his death anyway, so he could ignore them.

The problem was that he was sailing through a series of sandy atolls with no vegetation to speak of besides tough grass and shrubs. A few of the larger ones might support bougainvillea trees or other flowering plants, and a coconut tree could improve his chances of avoiding starvation, but while the fibers and leaves could be used as rude caulking, he still needed a sticky water-resistant substitute to fix the battens to the leaking boards. Plant resins would suffice for a short while, but what he really needed was tar.

Hatu did his best to navigate the treacherous rings of coral. While most of the atolls were visible, there were reefs just below the surface that demanded his constant attention. Twice during the first day he had lowered sail and rowed, but doing so took on more water and the fatigue was wearing him down. He'd lost track of how long it had been since he had last slept.

The weather hadn't been Hatu's friend, either. While this region rarely got truly cold, it could become cool, and wet clothing and the constant breezes chilled him. He knew he needed to find shelter, and soon. He was thankful for the heavy jacket he had grabbed before he'd been taken—and even more thankful the witches hadn't removed it—but it wasn't enough. The other jacket, lying soaked with brine in the bottom of the boat, was a constant reminder of Donte's fate.

He was also low on water. One of the ship's barrels would have been welcome now, even though it would never fit in the boat. Had Donte been with him, they would have proven more efficient at sailing the boat, but now Hatu knew they simply hadn't known how much water they would need. He tried not to punish himself for being inexperienced and not seeing the future, but it was his nature to be harsh with himself, so it was a struggle.

The dry, constant wind drained Hatu's body of

moisture as fast as it took his warmth. Chapped lips were a constant reminder that water was scarce and vital. He could survive without food for days, but lack of water could kill him in hours without shade on a hot day. He took out half a dried biscuit and realized his provisions were down to its other half and a questionable hunk of salted pork. He crunched the biscuit between his teeth, hard enough that he could feel his jaw pop slightly as he tried to crush it. He needed to finish the pork soon, for while it was heavily salted, it was usually stored in the relative cool of the room next to the galley but had been sitting under a simple waxed tarpaulin since he departed, and for however long he and Donte had been held. He instantly pushed the image of Donte out of his mind, as he needed to focus all of his energy on surviving.

At midday he saw something flickering in the distance, off to port, and he tied off the halyard to the tiller through an iron eyelet, causing the wind to steer the boat and take him closer, as he needed to bail out more water. By the time he had drained a sufficient amount of water to stem sinking for a few more hours, he could see that the flickering was a flock of seabirds. They could have been following a ship, or hovering over the floating carcass of a large sea creature or a school of fish near the surface, or they could have meant land. A ship or island would do, he said silently.

Sensing his rising desperation, Hatu countered it by taking a quick inventory and checking his position as best he could. He knew he should be leaving the coral reefs, which were east of where the witches had captured him. He wondered for a moment whether the three pursuing ships had been in league with the witches, for Hatu now realized that his captain had taken the only course left open to him: a turn to the west away from the coral and into . . . He pushed the thought aside as fanciful. There was nothing about those evil women that even hinted at a link to something as prosaic as pirates or slavers, and it seemed that they had little use for men anyway, beyond breeding daughters, creating those monsters that served them . . . or food. He shuddered slightly and pushed away any more speculation on Donte's fate.

The birds turned out to be a flock of terns, diving on anchovies or other small fish. The birds were migratory, but at this time of the year they would be nesting. Hatu felt buoyed by that, for it made it more likely that their colonies would be on an island close by, and that meant water, or at least eggs, as unlike most birds, terns were content to lay their eggs on the ground. The potential for any source of food or water gave him renewed energy.

Hatu saw a faint green spot of land on the horizon and, from the angle of the sun, judged he should reach it before evening. He trimmed his sail, caught a favorable wind, and bore down on his destination at good speed. As he neared, he looked for a decent landing and saw swells moving toward a long beach. The even rolling breakers on the sand were evidence of the lack of rocks, and so Hatu put about and lowered the sail, preferring to row in the last few hundred yards. He was surprised at the exertion it required and judged himself closer to complete exhaustion than he had realized.

The combers that would become breakers picked up the boat and helped move him toward the beach. At the right moment, Hatu shipped his oars and jumped to the stern, pulling up hard on the rudder and yanking it free of the collars that locked it in place, to prevent its being damaged by the sand when they finally beached.

His weight in the stern picked up the bow and the boat slid easily onto the shore. Hatu hurried forward and pulled the boat in further, so it wouldn't wash back out to sea. High and low tides were small here this time of the month, for reasons that Master Bodai had once explained, calling it a neap tide, and Hatu now couldn't remember. He'd check on the boat again later, but for the moment his first order of business was water, then food.

The island proved bigger than Hatu had first thought, and he could see hilltops just above the tree line. He carried a long knife, the only weapon among the various things he and Donte had pillaged from the ship, as well as empty water bags. He uttered a silent prayer to any god that might be listening that he'd not have to use it for defense, as he felt weaker now than he had during any time in his life. He had nursed his food, but the lack of water over the last few days was taking its toll.

Hatu left the sand and felt damp soil beneath his feet as he moved inland, a good sign, for it meant there was groundwater close to the surface. He paused every so often to listen to the forest sounds, trying to discern if running water was nearby. Climbing a few small hillocks, he saw what looked to be a damp trail, and in a few minutes found a pool of water fed slowly from a dripping ledge above. He knelt but resisted the urge to drink and instead brought a handful of water to his nose. He had been told that stagnant or very slow-running pools often caused stomach illness, and sometimes, fatally so. The water had a bitter, moldy odor, so Hatu cast it aside and wiped his hand on his trousers. He looked for a way to climb further up and spotted a faint rocky pathway through the thinning trees.

Stepping gingerly on the slippery rocks that fashioned a primitive stairway, Hatu finally heard the gurgling sound of running water as his head cleared the overhang.

With an upwelling of relief, he saw a small stream running down an incline near the wet ledge. Hatu didn't hesitate, but half-crawled, half-flung himself over the ledge of rock and stuck his face into the little bubbling stream. He drank deeply. Then caution took over as he remembered a warning that drinking too much, too quickly, could cause a man to pass out or vomit up the water.

He took a deep breath and slowly counted to ten as he felt the water begin to revive him, then he leaned over and drank slowly for a bit. He repeated this until he felt all hints of his previous thirst fade. He then took stock of his surroundings as he filled his water skin.

Hatu wanted to stay near the beach, so that repairing the boat would be easier, but he also needed to be near water and, he hoped, food. He had been frugal with the rations in the boat, and had perhaps two or even three days of food left if he was careful, but hunger was his constant companion and reminder that his time without aid was coming to an end.

An hour of daylight remained, so Hatu spent half of it exploring the area around the pool. Tracks indicated animals were in abundance—and saw no obvious predator's tracks—and many used a watering hole that was further down the slope on the opposite side of the island. He'd weigh the option of moving his boat to that side of the island the next day. It would be closer to the water source than where he'd pulled in. And the beach below appeared as free of rocks and other dangers as where he'd landed.

On the way back to his boat he stumbled across a bush covered in fresh tanaberries, bittersweet to the taste, but providing enough sustenance to extend his stay on the island for an extra day or two if need be. He picked a large handful, marked the location in his memory, and followed the trail through the woods, eventually reaching the edge of the beach.

A quick check to ensure his boat was still secure, and Hatu returned to the edge of the woods to make a camp. Having a fire was a double-edged sword, for while it was vital for warmth and to cook food, it was also a beacon for anyone sailing along this coast. After his recent experience, he was inclined to distrust anyone who might sight his fire from a passing ship. He knew he was probably safe from those who had taken him, but he felt fearful.

Still, keeping a cold camp when your kit was also damp was an invitation to illness, especially when weakened. Weighing his options, Hatu decided illness was a worse possibility than the chance of unwanted discovery. He had pillaged flint and steel from the ship, and combined with dry tinder, he had a brisk little campfire going in short order.

He ate his handful of tanaberries and what was left of the dried meat and hard cheese, rolled up his extra jacket—Donte's jacket—and moved close enough to the dwindling fire to keep warm while he tried to sleep.

Fatigue and flashing images warred within him as he tried to find a comfortable position in the sand; as he finally drifted off, his last thoughts were of being very tiny and held close by someone who was very frightened.

It took three days, but Hatu at last found a sealant for repairing his boat. He'd managed to eat enough berries and a few other plants as well as a clutch of tern eggs to restore some of his energy. He would stock up before he left but first he had to repair the major leaks.

A cove to the north of where he'd come ashore was strewn with large chunks of tar. The islands were a mix of coral atolls and volcanic rocks, and he guessed that somewhere close by an underwater vent spewed hot lava and thick oil. The molten rock would cool quickly in the water, but the hot oil would become the thick tar. Sometimes it sank, but sometimes it contained enough gas bubbles to cause it to rise and drift on the tide. He'd spotted it easily, as he'd seen tar sands and tar rocks all his life. The matrons had scolded him many times for returning from the beach with black feet. Half a dozen chunks would provide more sealant than he needed. He would cut up Donte's jacket to make the batten and then seal it with hot tar. He wasn't that confident about how well it would work, but he had seen no hint of a ship or boat anywhere on the horizon the entire time he'd been on the island, so being rescued from this beach seemed unlikely. Hatu now found his fear of being discovered was outweighed by his need to find a way home.

He roughly knew where he was, and had a general idea where the shipping lanes to the north were and a rough estimate of how long it would take to get there. He knew if he were careful, he'd return the gig to seaworthiness and stand a chance of reaching the Clearing.

Hatu had grown up on an island, so he knew how to fish and had a good idea of what plants he could eat. He'd build up a store of dried fish and fruit, fill his water skins, and be off when the boat was finished.

The days wore on as he labored to make his boat seaworthy again, and while he labored thoughts came to him unbidden. He saw new images as he tried to sleep, and as he attempted to caulk his boat with the rude battens, questions arose.

Who was the woman who had clutched him to her breast when he was tiny? Hatu thought it was a woman, but he wasn't sure. Where were they going? What did that evil witch mean when she called him "gods-touched"? And why was he spared when all of his shipmates died?

At last his work was finished, and Hatu knew it was time to leave. He realized he had been wrong in his first estimate about where his boat had drifted to, and so his estimation of how much time it would take to reach the Clearing was also simply wrong. He might need to sail and row for as much as another week to reach the Clearing, and who knew what other problems he might encounter along the way?

Launching his boat as the tide retreated gave him a small advantage getting into deeper water. Hatu remembered a talk by Master Tagaga, who knew more about sailing than anyone Hatu had met. He had said that the moon affected the tides. Another time Master Bodai said this was so because it tugged gently upon the sea when it was distant, but was strong when it was close. He had also said something about what the tides would be like if there was no moon at all, or if the moon was bigger than it was, but Master Bodai had lost him completely by that point. Hatu did know that you ran the risk of meeting more weather when the moon was big in the sky than when it wasn't. And he wanted to take advantage of any circumstance of benefit that presented itself. Now he wished he had paid closer attention.

The tide carried him easily offshore, and after a few minutes Hatu was satisfied that his repairs would hold for a time. How long remained to be seen.

He raised sail and began his tack around the island, using the morning sun to set his course.

Three days of sailing brought him to a cluster of small islands, high peaks of volcanic origin, lush with vegetation. He spent half a day gathering more fruit and spent the night sleeping beside a banked fire.

Just before dawn he awoke to the familiar sound of a ship nearby, the creaking of planks and the rattle of tackle. His gig was lying snug in the sand where he'd left it, so he jumped to his feet to see where the sounds originated. In the lightening gloom he made out the shape of a ship close enough to the shore that the sound of its passing echoed across the calm water and above the low sound of small breakers.

For a moment Hatu considered shouting or lighting a torch, but an unexpected chill ran up his back and gave him pause. The lateen sail coming into focus as the sky lightened could belong to one of the ships that had driven his own into these waters. Grateful for the still-gloomy predawn that lessened his chances of his being seen by a lookout, he was also irked that he couldn't make out further details and be certain he was avoiding peril rather than letting rescue pass him by.

Within a few more moments the shape of the ship vanished into the still-dark west. Hatu sat and let out a breath. He was going to sail north this morning, anyway, so being up an hour before dawn was not that much of an additional hardship. His water skins were full, he'd found enough fruit to last another week, and he spent his last day fishing, and had caught and dried fish for another week beyond that.

He obliterated all signs of his presence, as he had been taught by his masters, and when the sky to the east proclaimed that the sun was but minutes away, he pushed off the beach and got his boat beyond the breakers before he clambered aboard. It was going to be a warm day and he'd dry quickly enough.

A week of sailing between small islands put Hatu where he thought he should be, though he'd had to put in twice for water, more often than he had anticipated. Seawater seeped in around his battens but not enough to cause him concern at this point. Still, once in the Clearing, he would need to find a passing ship or both types of water would become a problem.

At midday of the eighth day since leaving the first little island, Hatu saw a sail off to port. He judged that he must be very close to the southern boundary of the Clearing, as he hadn't seen any land ahead since he awoke. He watched as the sail grew slowly and realized he would soon be seen by anyone on board. He weighed the risk of being found by pirates against the risk of staying alone in the boat, and decided that this close to the south side of the Clearing, his chances of surviving the former were better, given that most of the pirates in these waters worked for the masters on Coaltachin.

When the ship was nearer, he stood and began waving his coat in the air. After a few minutes he saw it alter its course to intercept him.

He lowered his own sail and waited.

When the ship drew close enough, he heard a voice shout, "Who are you?"

There were no clear markings on the freight hauler, which was larger than the *Nelani*. They could have been smugglers, pirates, or honest traders, but he had been given clear instructions how to deal with unknown ships at sea. Hatu cried out, "My ship was lost with all my companions. I can work for passage."

"I have a full crew," came the reply as the ship bore down on him. "Where are you bound?"

"To an island east of here," was the reply he'd been told to give. It was a code indicating he was of Coaltachin, and should any of his people on board hear that, they would know that he needed aid getting home.

"Lots of islands to the east of here," said the man, whom Hatu could now see at the bow of the ship. "Does it have a name?"

"Any port will do," he said, knowing he was speaking to someone who was not of Coaltachin.

"I've got a full crew," repeated the man Hatu assumed was the captain. "But I can't let a man drown. You'll work for no pay to the next port, then you're on your own."

"Fair enough," said Hatu. "I have a large pouch for the owner of my lost ship. Can I bring it aboard?" Bringing the captain's papers from the *Nelani* was a risk, as he knew the captain of this vessel might want to examine the contents of the package.

The captain ordered a line thrown to Hatu, who quickly secured it to his boat's bow, letting himself be pulled along. "What's in it?"

"Papers," said Hatu, quickly adding, "I can't read, but they might be important. My captain was careful about such things."

Another line was dropped and next to it a rope ladder. "Tie it on and come aboard."

The rope to his gig was cut and the big leather pouch was on the deck before Hatu was halfway up the ladder. As he climbed over the railing, one of the sailors working nearby said just loud enough for him to hear, "I know that island."

His response told Hatu that the sailor was one of his people, even if the ship's captain wasn't. He felt relief knowing another man of Coaltachin was on board. He tried not to stare but cast a lingering glance, coming away with the impression that the speaker was a young man, less than thirty years of age, dark of hair and eyes, broad of shoulder, but otherwise unremarkable. He returned his attention to the captain.

The captain was portly, his muscle turned to fat by years of eating like a young man long past a young man's time. He said, "I'm Donis, captain of the *Isabela,* and this is my mate, Landon." The man standing beside the captain gave one nod. "We'll put your trunk in the hold so you can return it to your master when you're home. You're aboard an honest ship with an honest crew and no one will make free with your master's papers. Now, Landon will tell you your duties."

The captain turned away and the first mate asked, "You know this type of ship?"

Hatu regarded the hard-looking older man, who judged him as he stood there. The ship was a tidy vessel: three small masts, the fore and main square rigged; the fore held a single foresail, the main a mainsail and a topsail, and the aft a gaff spanker. "I've sailed her like," answered Hatu.

"Turn to, and find a berth below. You'll work night watch."

It was what Hatu expected, but he'd be glad for a few hours' rest before work. He spared a glance at the sailor who'd spoken to him, but the man was gone from sight.

He went below.

Hatu found an empty hammock and got a few hours' sleep before being roused by the change of watch. He followed his newfound shipmates to the deck and as he left the companionway the sailor who had spoken to him pulled him aside. "What ship?" he asked quietly.

"*Nelani*," Hatu answered. "Every hand lost, but me."

"We'll speak later. I'm Costa." Costa then vanished down the companionway.

Hatu was hungry but knew he'd be told when he could eat. He looked around and saw the first mate motioning with his chin that Hatu was to go aloft. At night, unless the wind shifted, he'd double as lookout as well as yard crew. It was the most miserable job on a ship like this, even in mild weather, but as a castaway seeking passage, it was the best he could expect.

He found himself mostly standing lookout as the ship was driven by a following wind and the sails needed little trimming beyond tightening and loosening stays.

He realized he was half-asleep when a stirring to his right snapped his attention to a figure climbing out to his yard along the foot rope. It was Costa. "We're bound for Halazane," he said without preamble. "There's a ship waiting for me, heading home. Once we get aboard we'll have a long talk. Until then, we do not know one another."

His manner and tone made Hatu judge him to be a captain at the least, if not a master. He vanished back into the darkness, leaving Hatu alone with his many thoughts.

13

A Short Journey and a Strange Event

The morning after Declan's meeting with the baron, Ratigan's wagon headed out of the north gate with two boxes of goods added to Declan's belongings. They traveled through the city's faubourg, nearby small farms, then climbed slowly up into farmland. To the west the farms ran to bluffs overlooking the ocean, according to Ratigan. Declan had lived with farmers and fishermen his entire life and recognized the lush land through which they rolled.

During the first day they passed through groves and fields, and twice came close enough to the coast to catch a glimpse of the ocean on the western horizon. At sundown they made a roadside camp and Declan said, "I'll take middle watch."

"No need," said Ratigan. "No bandits this close to the city; not a lot of wildlife either. This is a very civilized land, my friend."

"Really?"

"Not like the old Covenant, but almost as peaceful. Baron Dumarch keeps things quiet. He has patrols traveling these roads all the time. We'll probably see more than one before we're done."

"It's amazing how rich this land is, Ratigan," said Declan as he unrolled his bedding. "How's he hung on to it?"

"I'm a teamster, not a noble," said Ratigan. "With clever noble business, I expect. I traveled since I was barely as tall as that wheel"—he hiked his thumb over his shoulder, indicating the rear wheel of the wagon—"and I know he's well thought of outside of Marquensas, too. From what I hear, that high opinion was well earned and he's a dangerous enough soldier that even kings treat him with respect. Rich enough to be a king in his own right, too." Nodding for emphasis, Ratigan added, "Respect: that's a good thing to have." Declan returned the nod.

"I'll take care of the horses. Break out the food,

and don't eat all the bread!" said the teamster with a laugh.

Jusan laughed, too and said, "No problem. We have four loaves."

They ate and bedded down, and the night passed uneventfully.

As they continued northward, Declan continued to be impressed by the abundance of Baron Dumarch's demesne, the thick woodlands rich with game, the rivers and lakes abundant with fish. Well-tended pastures and lush meadows lay on each side as they rolled by. Declan almost felt a sense of loss when the wagon crested a dell and Ratigan said, "That's Beran's Hill ahead."

The lushness of Marquensas had started to fall away a few hours before they reached this point; the trees had thinned out and the grass plains west of the road had given way to scrub and patches of sandy ground. From what Declan knew of farming, this more arid soil could be worked but would require much more effort for a lower yield; he understood why it was left uncultivated given how close it was to far better land just a few miles to the south.

As the wagon crested the road, Declan noticed a few solitary farms, and from the faint stench on the breeze, he could tell hogs were kept somewhere to the west. He assumed that this town was close enough to good farmland that food was not a problem, but he wondered why anyone would choose to live here.

As they reached the southern boundary of the town itself, the answer to that question became apparent. The hill that gave the town its name sat across five converging roads. Declan could see a number of wagons, riders, and coaches moving along the four other roads. "Why is the road into Marquenet so quiet?"

"Compared to other cities, Marquenet isn't on the way to any other place. You only go there because you want to go there," answered Ratigan. "Marquensas has four cities with better harbors than Marquenet. Here, you will see the trade from six landlocked holdfasts." He waved to the west. "And from there comes most of the goods that travel by sea, because the baron of Port Colos charges much less duty than Baron Dumarch. Everyone leaves Beran's Hill alone, for it's not a wealthy place, but a trade hub that serves everyone."

Declan nodded as if he completely understood what Ratigan said, but in truth he knew little about commerce except where it applied to his very narrow professional interests. He knew to buy iron when prices were low, if one had the means, and likewise for charcoal. Other than that, and knowing the general prices for his wares, he was lost when it came to matters of commerce.

They entered the large town and Ratigan expertly navigated his way through the busy streets. Declan felt a little disoriented, for many of the buildings lacked signs of any kind. He was used to that in Oncon, but at home he had known every building in the village, and in the cities through which they had traveled, most places of business had signs indicating their trade, even if they were rudely rendered, but here there were none. Finally he said to Ratigan, "How do you know where you're going?"

"Just watch what folk leave with, food, leather goods, clothing, and remember where you saw it." He shrugged as if this were an inconsequential issue.

The teamster made two quick stops to unload his modest cargo before they arrived in front of a large inn displaying a sign with three stars of white painted on a black square. Ratigan negotiated a sharp corner and drove the wagon safely into a small stabling yard behind the inn.

Jusan was again given the task of protecting the wagon; Declan was pleased to see he was now fully recovered from his injuries and thought that a few days of good food and hard work would strengthen him.

Declan followed Ratigan into the dark inn and they

stood inside the door for a moment as their eyes adjusted to the gloom. The room had only one entrance and one large window on the north wall; candles flickered on the bar and tables. Customers ate or drank quietly, but the inn was not crowded. Declan expected that would change as the afternoon wore on and people stopped in after work.

Ratigan and Declan moved to the bar, where a large man with an improbably thick thatch of greying black hair stood watching them. When they reached the bar, he said, "What will it be?"

Ratigan said, "You Leon?"

"I am."

"Kalanora in Marquenet said you'd be the man to see about a forge; you hold the widow's rights to it?"

"You a smith?" asked the barman.

Ratigan indicated Declan, who nodded, saying nothing.

"I am and I do," said the barman. "If Kalanora sent you, you're not here to waste my time. But it's a very prosperous and big forge for a newly minted journeyman."

Declan said, "I became a master this month and am seeking a good place to make a home."

The innkeeper took out three large cups and a black bottle from behind the bar. "Can't discuss business properly without a drink or two," he observed. "First round is mine. After that, you pay."

He poured a small shot of amber liquid into each cup, then said, "Good health and fair dealings!" Then he tossed the drink back.

Declan had never seen this type of spirit. He wasn't much of one for getting drunk, though like most young men, he had learned that lesson the hard way. Now he had one or two ales at most; he had tried some wine but wasn't entirely sure he cared for it. He sniffed once and was greeted with an aroma that reminded him of the solvent he used to clean grease from tools after packing an axle. Declan saw Ratigan toss back his drink and followed suit.

An unexpected hot sensation greeted his tongue and he tried to swallow. The liquid burned his throat, bringing tears to his eyes; he gasped, inhaling a tiny bit of the burning liquid, and started coughing.

Leon tried not to laugh as Ratigan slapped Declan on the back.

"Never had a whisky before, eh, lad?" asked Leon.

Red-faced and trying to breathe, Declan shook his head and finished coughing. "What did you call that?" he asked.

"Whisky. It's made in the north by the Kes'tun; savages without a doubt, but in the barbaric tongue that passes for their language, it means 'the water of life.'"

Declan's eyes stopped tearing. "If you say so."

"I do, and they do," said Leon, pouring another round. "This time, sip until you get used to the sting; you'll find it grows on you."

Not wishing to offend a man he was about to negotiate with, Declan sipped the drink. It still burned, but now that he expected it, he didn't inhale and send himself into another fit of coughing. The taste was acidic and made him want to spit it out, but instead he swallowed. His eyes continued to water.

"As I said," continued Leon, "it'll grow on you."

Declan thought that unlikely, though a warm glow seemed to be spreading through his stomach. He nodded.

"Now, before we commence with business, you should have a look at the place, I expect." He turned and shouted at a door to the rear. "Gwen!"

A few moments later a girl came through the door wiping her hands on her apron. "What, Da?"

"Take this lad down to the Widow Smith's place and let him poke around for a bit. He's thinking of buying it." To Declan he said, "This is my daughter, Gwendolyn. Gwen, this is Declan."

She gave him a quick, appraising look, then smiled. "Declan," she repeated as if to cement his name in her mind. "Come on, then, Declan." She stretched out his name as "Dec . . . lan," as if liking the sound. She smiled, nodded, and with an inclination of her head indicated that he should follow her out the door. He did, assessing her as he followed.

She was pretty, and like her father she had thick, dark hair, which shone like a raven's wing in the sun when she loosened the grey head scarf she had worn while in the kitchen. Her figure was somewhat masked by her dress; it was big across the bodice and swept along the ground, an old garment often mended, but tidy. He wondered if it had originally belonged to another.

She glanced over her shoulder and said, "Smith, is it?"

He nodded, beginning to feel the effects of the whisky, and said, "Yes. Looking to set up a forge."

"This one will need some work. Not sure how much. I know nothing of forges."

Declan was feeling a little off balance, because of the whisky, but also because he found the girl surprisingly attractive. There was something about her that put him in mind of Rozalee. He had no idea what, as they looked nothing alike; she was young and full figured while Roz was past her youth and slender to the point of being skinny. But it was an attitude; the way Gwen carried herself, perhaps? Or maybe he simply wanted to be reminded of how he had felt with Rozalee.

He pushed the notion aside and turned his attention to the moment. As they wended their way through the busy town, Declan was forced to dodge people in the streets to avoid running into them. He asked, "Is it always this crowded?"

She laughed. "Worse. When a big caravan arrives, every inn can be full." She glanced up at him and said, "If you're not lax, you'll do well here."

"Who's been fixing things since the old smith died?"

"My dad's chased away a few squatters. There are a couple of tinkers in town who can fix things well enough to get someone on the road again, but if you make an offer, you'll soon have more work than you know what to do with." She turned a corner and said, "Here we are."

Declan took one glance at the smithy and knew it would do. As he approached he began assessing what needed to be fixed, and before he opened the forge doors, he knew he could turn it into the equal of Edvalt's place. There was already a small rear door, and he calculated it would be relatively simple to fashion a heavy shade to block out light. He would need to close the massive forge doors, blocking out the outside light when working on steel, but that could wait; he doubted he'd be getting many weapons orders as the Baron of Marquensas had Gildy and a host of other smiths closer to hand, so very fine weapons were unlikely to be in demand. He knew how to make a very serviceable weapon without having to smelt jeweled steel.

The smithy had a large yard, which was good, for he might need to repair multiple wagons if they arrived in caravans. The main doors were large and would admit plenty of daylight when needed. He opened the right side. "How are the nights here?" he asked Gwen.

"Meaning?" she asked.

"I mean the weather, especially in winter."

"We're a bit off the coast, but it's all downhill from here to the sea. Keeps things a bit more even, I've been told. So, nights in winter get cold, but not bitter. Go east for a day or two and you'll find foothills that occasionally get dusted with snow, but I've only seen snow on the ground twice here." She paused and considered, then added, "But it can get wet. We've had seasons rainy enough to drown a duck."

He laughed at that and she smiled.

"I think I'll cut a smaller door into this big one. On cold days and colder nights the last thing I want to be doing is standing in an open doorway if I don't need to. Beran's Hill's further north than where I'm from, so I didn't think the nights would be any more gentle, likely far less so."

"Work a lot at night, do you?"

He shrugged. "Sometimes, to finish a job on time, it's what you have to do."

Declan swung the door aside and entered. The forge was old but had been well tended; the stone had endured many fires so Declan didn't have to worry. Edvalt had cautioned him about using new stone for repairing a forge; moisture often became trapped inside the porous rocks and heating them could produce enough steam to make them explode. He saw a pile of aged stones in the corner and nodded his approval. The old smith had kept replacements near the heat, so they'd be dry if he needed them.

"What was this smith's name? Walter?"

"Walter," answered Gwen with a nod. "Walter the Smith."

"He kept an orderly forge." Declan inspected the large bellows hanging on chains linked to iron rings that traveled on iron rods so they could be moved into position over the fire as needed. "Nice," he said, looking closely at the bellows. "This leather is going to have to be replaced sooner rather than later," Declan muttered to himself.

"Is that a problem?"

He looked at her and smiled. "Using leather around a forge is always a problem. The heat dries it very quickly. I might change this for cured canvas if I can find some." He looked at Gwen. "How far to the coast?"

"Three days' travel by cart. Half that on a horse."

"Good. I can get what I need from a sail maker." He moved away from the bellows. "Until then I'll get some neat's-foot oil to condition and protect the leather." He took another look around and nodded. "This will be a fine smithy when I'm done." That made Gwen smile, and Declan found himself returning the smile without thought.

"Come see the house," she said.

"House?"

"Out back." She took his hand, leading him through the rear door. He had expected to see a small home, like Edvalt's, with perhaps two rooms, but the house in front of him was large by Oncon standards. It stood two floors high; the high roof of the smithy—so the massive bellows could be hoisted—blocked the sight of the home from the road. Gwen led him inside and said, "It needs a proper clean. The widow went down to a village on the other side of Marquenet to live with her sister. It's why my da is selling it for her." She continued to hold Declan's hand, a fact he was acutely conscious of.

The house was tidy, like the forge; well kept and had a big table in the kitchen. There was a small room in the back where Jusan could sleep, a big improvement over his usual sleeping mat by the forge. Upstairs were two bedrooms; the bigger one had a compact sun porch. A door permitted Declan to stand on it and look down on what appeared to be a garden.

Gwen said, "That will take a little work, pulling weeds and planting vegetables. But Widow Smith always had fresh carrots, cabbage, and turnips for stew; she thought it worth the effort."

Declan took a deep breath. This was much more than he had expected. The forge he could manage, but with this house, too . . . He said, "Did your father tell you what the widow wants for the forge and house?"

"No, but it shouldn't be a problem," she answered with a smile.

He looked around a bit more, then said, "Let's go talk to your father."

She nodded and echoed, "Let's."

They walked back toward the inn and Gwen asked, "So it's just you?"

"What?" He glanced down at her and saw her studying him. "I . . . Oh, my apprentice is in the wagon, watching our baggage. He'll be living there, too."

"I mean no family?"

"No, just me. I'm an orphan, I guess. Never knew my parents. My master raised me. Can't remember living anyplace before that. Edvalt said he took me in because I was large for my age and he thought he could turn me into a good smith. Gave him fifteen years of service and a bit."

"That's a long time."

Softly, Declan replied, "I guess; now it seems but a moment."

The pedestrian traffic was beginning to increase as the business day was winding down and shoppers were anxious to finish up before hurrying home. The two young people dodged around a crowd carrying all manner of items and Declan said, "Most smiths work as much as twenty-five years before becoming a master. Edvalt said I have the gift." He cut himself off. He wasn't overly given to talking, but he found himself almost prattling to the girl for no reason he could think of. "I guess I do, else he wouldn't have given me a master's rank." Realizing he was now boasting, he quickly added, "Maybe not that gifted, but a lot of hard work." He decided to stop talking about himself.

She smiled.

"So, you've always lived here?" Declan asked.

"Born," she said with an emphatic nod. "My da was working crops and driving stock up and down from the meadows, doing all manner of things, when he met my ma. She made him settle down. They saved and built the inn themselves. I was tiny then, so it's the only home I've known."

"Your ma? She work the inn?"

"She passed," said Gwen, her voice softening. "Fever took her five years back." Glancing sideways at Declan, she smiled again. "I think Ma would have liked you."

Declan was momentarily at a loss for words. He recognized flirting, but this was something else. He realized that despite knowing Roz and village girls in Oncon, he really had no idea what to expect from this innkeeper's daughter. It felt like nothing more than an appraisal, and it made him feel both flattered and a little intimidated. She was absolutely the most attractive woman he had met.

They reached the inn and entered. Declan saw that Ratigan had switched to ale as he spoke with Leon. The innkeeper looked up as Declan reached the bar and asked, "You like it?"

"Looks all right," said Declan, trying not to appear too eager, and still a little flustered by Gwen's apparent interest. It was a far finer smithy than he had hoped for. "What is the widow's price?"

"One full weight of gold," said Leon.

Declan's face remained impassive, but it was three times the gold he carried. With the vast number of kingdoms, holdfasts, and city-states across the continents and islands, coins were universally accounted by quality and weight. Declan carried a third of a weight, roughly sixty coins of not-quite-uniform size, which was the equivalent of two months' or more earnings for a master smith. A full weight would equal half a year's work, with nothing left over for food, iron, coal, or any other necessity.

Finally Declan said, "That's a lot."

"It's a nice smithy," replied Leon. "Walter put a lot of years into it, built up a tidy little home behind it. Good location."

Declan realized that despite any affection Leon might have held for the Widow Smith, he was also getting a commission. He said, "If I agree to that price, what are the terms?"

Leon looked surprised. "Terms?"

"You didn't expect a master smith to wander in carrying a full weight of gold, did you?"

Leon stroked his chin. "Now that you mention it, I guess I did." He looked at Declan and said, "What do you propose?"

"I can give the widow thirty gold coins, a sixth of a weight, and . . . four coins a month until the full weight is paid."

Leon glanced at his daughter, who was staring at him intensely, her eyes narrowing as if daring him to say no to the offer. She nodded her head slightly.

He looked at Declan and said, "I think the widow will agree to that." He reached out and they shook hands. "Move your gear in, and I'll send word and your gold to the widow."

Ratigan said, "I'm returning to Marquenet as soon as I pick up a load. I'll carry them for you."

Leon glanced at Declan, who nodded his assent that Ratigan could be trusted. Declan said to the teamster, "If you've finished your drink, let's take Jusan down to the smithy and unload the wagon." Ratigan nodded and took a final pull from his flagon.

Declan bid goodbye to Leon and Gwen, who took his hand and held it slightly longer than he expected her to before letting it go.

Outside, they mounted the wagon and Declan said to Jusan, "We have a smithy."

Jusan grinned and asked, "A good one?"

"A very good one," replied Declan.

Ratigan laughed. "From the way that girl looked at you, you're buying more than just a smithy, Declan. You'll be a family man in no time, I'll wager."

Declan glanced at Ratigan and then at Jusan, who with a laugh asked, "What girl?"

Declan shrugged slightly and quietly to himself said, "That might not be a bad thing."

14

A Short Respite and Revelations

Hatu sipped a bitter coffee, a small pot purchased for an even smaller copper coin at a dockside inn in Halazane. He'd left the *Isabela* the afternoon before and had portered the captain's chest himself, unwilling to let anyone else handle it. Costa had given him the name of the ship on which they were to meet, the *Sasa Muti*. It was an odd name, meaning "holy tree" in the language of the Kes'tun people. What made it doubly odd was that the Sinyowai were horsemen from the grassy plains of South Tembria. There must have been a story behind its christening, and perhaps he'd remember to ask someone on the voyage home.

The *Sasa Muti* sailed on the evening tide, so Hatu

had the day to rest, eat, and recover a bit. He was young and healthy, but the travails of the last month had taken their toll and he probably needed a few more days. No doubt he'd be questioned once he boarded the ship, and after that, he'd almost certainly be put to work.

He'd taken the little coin he'd saved and spent some of it on a bath with clean hot water, and on having his filthy clothes washed while he soaked. Hatu spent most of his days dirty, for the urchin or peasant-boy roles he usually played often required filth. It didn't mean that he enjoyed the constant stench and having itchy skin. He couldn't help but doze as he bathed and had to be roused when it was time to leave. The attendant who scrubbed his head and shoulders seemed disappointed when he chose not to pay her for sex, too. He would have enjoyed it, but he didn't have enough coin to be pleasured and find an affordable inn.

Hatu had purchased a sleeping mat in a paneled-off area of this inn, shared by strangers and with no real privacy. He slept next to the dead captain's chest, which he'd placed against the wall.

During the first night Hatu awakened twice, and both times found himself pressed against the sea trunk, dagger in hand, in a room undisturbed save for snoring. He had willed himself back to restfulness using the mind-calming exercises taught to him as a child.

His sleep had been troubled since the witches who had called themselves Sisters of the Deep had freed him, but these disturbing dreams were different from the nightmares and sleep terrors he had experienced during childhood. He remembered no coherent images or memories upon awakening, just a nearly overwhelming sense of approaching doom coupled with a deep feeling of hopelessness. The visions had lessened while he was aboard the *Isabela* as hard work brought Hatu a numb, deep sleep, only slightly troubled by terrors.

He'd used what coin he had left to buy a rude breakfast of porridge, half an apple, and a slice of cheese, keeping a hard bread roll for later in the day, and was now lingering over his coffee. It left a sharp aftertaste, but it was bracing and he needed to stay awake until the chest was aboard. If the *Sasa Muti* sailed at evening tide, he would only be in the way, or put to work, if he arrived more than an hour before they put out to sea.

The inn had two floors of common space and Hatu's table was on a balcony overlooking the harbor. He had never visited this port before, as his stints as a sailor had been short, if intense. There was no man in service to the masters of Coaltachin who could not pass as a common sailor, even if it was as a poor one; it was a vital skill for an island nation. If you weren't crew, you were a passenger, and passengers were objects of curiosity. Crew were part of the ship and hardly noticed, especially on short haulers with constant turnover. Sailing provided an easy way for agents of the nation to move between the hundreds of important islands in the region.

Hatu was savoring the nature of this city, if *savoring* was the right word. He had traveled enough to realize that all ports smelled basically the same: sea salt on the breeze, a damp mix of mildew, rotting fish, and sewage. Cheap inns, rarely cleaned, added the reek of spilled alcohol, unwashed bodies, piss and shit, and a general moldiness. But the scent of each city also had its own signature, and Halazane held a hint of spices in the air, as it appeared to be a nexus for traders from the surrounding islands. One of the few things that took away Hatu's frustration and anger was his delight in discovering new things. He knew that all information was potentially useful, even if its use wasn't immediately apparent.

One of the things that every boy and girl raised on the home island took for granted was the training they received in many different trades and traditions. An agent of the Quelli Nascosti might need to pass as a servant, a traveling peddler, or a skilled worker, and every child still in training was a potential sicari. Hatu, not yet seventeen years of age, could masquerade as an apprentice in several trades; he knew leather working and dyeing, smithing and weaving. The beauty of being a young agent with modest skills was the ability to seek work in several trades and use the excuse of poor training from an untalented former master.

Hatu sighed as he wrestled with his memories. Trying to reconcile what he now thought of as his *normal* memories with the visions he had endured since that witch was in his mind struck him hard, a struggle with no obvious outcome, but the conflict was oddly intriguing, too. He felt things he could put no name to, yet they left him with a sense of approaching change, as if what he had glimpsed of his earliest memories was somehow at the root of his lifelong frustrations. Somewhere there was an answer, something that would make sense out of the things he had battled against since he was a toddler. It was a faint hope, but whatever happened in the future, something had changed. The feeling he had that something was closed off had changed abruptly, and he was now curious as to what he would find inside.

Hatu took a measured breath. It would take time to understand, and who knew how much of that he would have. He had to reach home, see whichever master was present, and give a full accounting of his days since leaving Numerset. He attempted to order the events in his mind, beginning with the assassination of the unnamed merchant—unnamed to him, at least; he accepted that he might never know why the man was killed.

He also knew that the news he carried might not earn him any thanks from the masters, especially Kugal when he learned that Hatu had survived and his favorite grandson, Donte, hadn't. It didn't matter that Hatu felt his loss, too; the masters and captains rarely showed concern for their underlings. Even Master Kugal's displays of affection for his only remaining grandson, Donte, had been spare.

Thinking of Donte made Hatu think of Hava, and he couldn't help but sigh. Now that his friend was gone, he missed Hava more than ever, and in a way he had never felt before. She had intruded on his thoughts at the oddest moments since the *Isabela* had rescued him. He took a deep slow breath and attempted to put her out of his mind, and stem the growing ache inside.

He failed.

His memory returned to the first time he had seen her; she had been the most pugnacious girl in his group, unafraid to confront anyone, even boys twice her size. Even at that first sight of her, he had been drawn to her; something in her manner touched him, as if he'd found someone who could understand him.

When not being instructed, students on Coaltachin were left to their own devices, which meant establishing a pecking order. Hava stood out because she was a little taller, thinner, and had unusual auburn hair, so she attracted bullies. She quickly established that she could take care of herself, and after receiving a couple of bloodied noses and one broken arm, the larger boys left her alone. She quickly attracted attention among the girls and extended her protection to them as needed, though otherwise she had just two friends, Donte and him. It had always been the three of them.

Hatu had his own unique appearance to deal with, and while he was not the most gifted fighter among the boys, when his anger did surface, he could become deadly. He'd almost beaten a larger boy to death with his bare hands until pulled away by one of the instructors. After that, the other boys gave him a wide berth. Donte could be an instigator at times, but he seemed to sense when Hatu was approaching the limit of his patience and could intervene, even if he couldn't see any limits for himself. Hava had the ability to calm him like no other, to make him forget his sometimes senseless anger.

Several significant things happened during that time in his life: He started to realize that he was treated slightly differently from the other students and he had grown somewhat isolated because of the distance that difference created.

And he had become even more aware of Hava.

The sense of alienation and his changing feelings for one of his two best friends caused him hours of fretting, as Matron Naniana used to call his low-level, constant worry. She would chide, or attempt to joke him out of it, but all she succeeded in doing was forcing Hatu to hide his feelings even deeper.

The special treatment he received, his not fully understanding his place, those were the concerns that nettled him most. The loss of Donte had made it worse, and now he felt Hava's absence as a constant pain that was impossible to ignore unless he was busy. Hatu looked down and discovered he was tightly gripping the rail of the balcony, and he willed himself to slowly let it go.

Sipping the last of his coffee, he observed the market below and the harborside beyond it. Hatu was nearly seventeen years old, and almost counted a man by most nations on Garn, but he'd traveled and seen more than perhaps nine out of ten of the people he now looked down at. Some might have been merchants or sailors who'd traveled among these islands, perhaps even to the east coast of South Tembria, but he had been further than that twice before his sixteenth birthday, whatever day that might have been. He had been told he was an orphan, and his birthday had been arbitrarily placed on the sixth day of the

Month of the Falling Stars in the Coaltachin calendar, so tradition and passages associated with age could be observed. It was probably close enough to his true day of birth, so there was little difference. Still, it was just another thing about himself that Hatu would have liked to know. Then he recognized a bit of irony, perhaps even humor, in that; like many who traveled, he had to reconcile the local year, month, and day to his native calendar and found often he was days off by the time he returned home. He could return on what he thought was his birthday only to discover it had occurred days before, so what did the date on the calendar matter?

He sighed as he tried to let go of all the perplexing thoughts in his head and looked down at his empty coffee mug. He didn't want any more, so he put it down next to the small pot and decided what to do with the rest of his day. Sitting around getting angry over things he could not control was pointless. Longing for the sight of Hava was even more pointless. He might never lay eyes on her again.

The chest sitting at Hatu's feet had precluded any sort of exploration of the city; wandering around with it on his shoulder would attract too much unwanted attention. A porter on his way to the docks carrying a burden was unremarkable, so his choices were fairly obvious: to waste the day in this inn and deepen his frustration and anger, or to get to the ship early. He sighed with resignation as he took one last long look at the city below. He was acquainted with street life enough to know it was unlikely that he'd find something diverting or unusual enough in Halazane to warrant the effort of losing it.

He gazed at the tableau of the busy market and harbor before him. Hatu had seen a dozen or more others like it during his five years of missions, and they blurred in his recollection; he was uncertain if he could name them, let alone recall anything memorable about most of them. There had been one market that held a stall where spiced meat on a skewer would be carved off and eaten on a bed of rice, covered with a wonderful brown sauce. He suddenly felt angry that he couldn't identify the place, as he might never have the chance to eat that dish again.

The realization was disappointing, but the anger that came with it was all too familiar. Hatu closed his eyes for a moment and remembered one of the exercises taught him by Master Kugal to calm him. Many situations demanded calm, no matter what was occurring; his life could even depend on it.

His wariness about being put to work on the ship was finally overcome by boredom. Hatu hoisted the chest onto his shoulder, glad it was small and not burdened with heavy contents, and made his way down the stairs to the street leading to the harbor.

He wended his way through the market, noticing small differences in the style of garments, food, and jewelry offered, as well as the array of tools and weapons. He saw a light silk scarf with a clever print pattern and wondered if Hava might like it.

Hava! He could not keep his mind from returning to her. He needed to get aboard that ship and get to work.

She dogged his thoughts, haunted his dreams, and he was unable to stop it. He even recalled the first time she aroused him, to his utter embarrassment, and how Donte dared any of the other boys to make fun of his stiff flesh. Hatu had just knelt down in the cold stream, hiding as best he could.

Male and female students had bathed together in streams near the village for as long as Hatu could remember, or occasionally at one of the communal bathhouses. It was a pleasure everyone looked forward to, for bathing was sometimes impossible for days at a time, and itchy skin and the smell of sour clothing often became a constant companion. Hatu had seen Hava and the other girls naked many times, but that time had been different. Even when just remembering, he still felt the embarrassment.

It had happened during the time his body started to change, when he began to see hair under his arms and around his cock; he had looked for a beard, but it was late in coming, as he was fair. One day the changes were something to simply ignore, and the next he was suddenly painfully aware of how differently girls were looking at him, especially Hava. Since they were little more than babies, he had never been shy around her, and along with Donte she was the closest person in the world to him, so the change had almost made him burst into tears of frustration, for he didn't understand it and couldn't talk to her about it.

When he broached the subject with the matrons, they told him to speak to the male instructors, but they had only told him about sex. No one had understood that he wanted to speak about feelings.

That frustration confused things even more, as it always did for Hatu, and made it even harder to speak of how he felt with anyone, even Donte, and especially Hava. That reticence began to change how he behaved with her.

As he dodged through the growing crowds, his mind went back to another day, after his shoulders had started to broaden, his voice to deepen, and when his appreciation of girls had completely changed.

They had been undergoing combat training. The

students of the Quelli Nascosti were grounded in every hand-to-hand combat style known, both the traditional and less-than-traditional ones. Using everyday objects as weapons had earned Hatu and the others a good deal of minor injuries. He didn't mind; instead he learned and became one of the best impromptu fighters in his class.

That day they had been training in stick fighting, a fair foundation for hand weapons of all kinds. Hatu had been paired with Hava for the third round and she defeated him soundly. Donte took him aside and said, "What is going on with you? It's not that she's beating you; I know she's good." He glanced at Hava as she took up a position before her next opponent. "It's that she's beating you so easily."

"I don't know," Hatu had admitted, his voice revealing his frustration.

Donte had taken a long moment to study his friend, then his eyes widened and he looked from Hatu to Hava and back again. Finally he had said, "Ah, now I see. We'll talk later."

As the day had worn on, they'd progressed from stick fighting to hand-to-hand combat, which always resulted in skinned knuckles, black eyes, bloody noses, and a general bad mood among the students. The instructors had paired Hava and Hatu once more, and with an easy block, she stepped inside his guard and hit him so that he lost his footing and landed hard, striking the back of his head on the stones sharply enough to daze him.

He didn't remember getting to his feet or moving to lean against a wall but suddenly found himself there, faint lights dancing in his vision. He vaguely recalled Donte saying, "You walked into that one. She's making you a crazy man."

Hatu would never admit to Donte that he was right, but he knew it was true. Something about Hava now made his chest constrict and his stomach hurt; it made him want to laugh and cry at the same time. He did not understand the feelings, and as was the case with everything in Hatu's life, what he didn't understand simply angered him.

Donte had finished his talk with Hatu by saying, "You can't have her. You know the rules. So forget it, think of her as your sister! Get your mind right."

From that day on, any fighting or other contests with Hava were hit and miss. Sometimes he could, as Donte said, get his mind right and win. And other days, it was as if he were trying to move through water, hip deep, or run uphill on sand, and she would always be one move ahead of him. There seemed no obvious pattern, so Hatu was convinced it was about focus; when he wasn't mentally ready, she knew him well enough to sense it and take advantage. He repressed a slight smile at the realization that the older they got, the more aware he was of her as a woman, the more often she took advantage and beat him. For she was gifted enough that he had to be totally engaged in the contest to best her. In reality, there was not that big a difference between their combat skills. And, grudgingly, he conceded she was a better archer than he was.

Hatu felt grief rising as his thoughts shifted from Hava to Donte, and on the heels of grief would come anger, so he pushed the memories away and turned his attention back to his immediate surroundings. He had become lost in his reverie for several blocks and that was a gross violation of his training.

Abruptly, Hatu realized he was being stalked through the market. Highly trained, despite being lost in thought over a girl, he realized he'd already seen the man dressed in a blue jacket and black flop hat in the crowd, and he now kept a steady pace off to Hatu's left, flanking him. The market was a maze of pathways with stalls set up in a rough set of lanes across the square. Hatu made a sudden turn between two stalls and turned again suddenly on the next pathway through the market, then stepped behind a table on which a variety of charms were displayed. He saw the man who had followed him continue on past, missing Hatu's second turn.

Hatu doubled back the way he had come and took

an indirect course to the harbor, checking regularly to see if he was again being followed. He reached the dock and found the *Sasa Muti.*

He climbed the gangplank and waited at the top to be noticed. A sailor finally took note of him and said, "What's it then?"

"I was told to come here by Costa."

The man looked a bit curious but said, "Wait."

Hatu's wait was a short one as Costa soon emerged from the companionway in the stern. The *Sasa Muti* was a square-rigged, two-masted lateen. He let his gaze travel from the high and long stern castle to the stout prow; she was a deepwater sailer. Amidst the shallow-draft coast huggers, she stood out like a swan in a school of ducks. Whatever curiosity Hatu might have had about her being in a relatively shallow port left when Costa said, "Where have you been?" He didn't wait for an answer as he motioned for a nearby sailor to take the chest Hatu carried. "My cabin," he instructed the man. Unlike before, the broad-shouldered man wasn't wearing the clothing of a common sailor, but was dressed in well-made, but not ostentatious, garb: fine trousers and tunic, well-cared-for riding boots, and an over-vest of black leather.

Hatu knew what authority in the Quelli Nascosti looked like when he encountered it. This man might have played the role of common sailor on the last ship, but here he was definitely someone of rank. Costa pulled Hatu to the bow of the ship and looked around. "I want to be able to see anyone who might hear us," he said quietly. "I expected you last night."

Hatu blinked as he considered his answer. Excuses were rarely tolerated, and blaming a superior was rarely wise, but in this case he decided candor was his best choice. "You didn't make that clear to me when we left the *Nelani*, else I would have come straightaway."

Costa studied him, then smiled slightly. "Not afraid? That's good, and you're probably right. I should have made myself clear." Hatu noticed he kept glaring upward slightly, as if Hatu had something on his head. "Did anything unusual happen?"

"Someone followed me through the market, but I lost him," said Hatu. "I'm not certain why; it was crowded and nothing about the chest looks like it could be valuable." He shrugged.

Costa studied him for a long moment, then said, "It's that damn hair of yours. It's like a beacon."

Without thought, Hatu reached up and touched his hair. Costa knocked his hand away and said, "Don't call attention to it."

"What about my hair?" asked Hatu. "I lost my coloring gel."

Costa's brown eyes widened and he raised his brows as he said, "Gel? What about—" He stopped and narrowed his gaze and said, "Who is your village master?"

"Facaria," Hatu replied.

A pained expression visited Costa's face for an instant, as he looked heavenward, then he returned his gaze to Hatu. "That explains it. He's very . . . traditional. No gossip, rumors, or unfounded information under his watch." Costa said, "I'll get more gel before we cast off. Once we're home, you and I will visit Master Facaria and—" He interrupted himself and asked, "How old are you?"

"Seventeen years on my next birthing day."

"When is that?"

"The sixth day of the Month of the Falling Stars, by the old accounting."

"Not that far away," said Costa, putting his hand on Hatu's shoulder. "You were probably noticed because it was the first time you've been out on a bright day with clean hair." He pointed to the stern. "My cabin lies to the right side of the captain's. Go there now and wait. I will find you a darkening gel personally. Now go."

Hatu did as he was instructed. If Costa was going to have words with his village master, the man was indeed important. As he hurried along to the stern cabins, he wondered what this business with his hair was all about.

———

As he had anticipated, once his hair was properly disguised again, Hatu was immediately put to work stowing cargo, and by the packed hold, he judged that Halazane was the ship's final stop on a long voyage home. Ships that were under the control, directly or indirectly, of the Quelli Nascosti were rarely permitted to dock on the home island, so Hatu could finally feel some measure of safety when the ship set out that evening.

After a quick meal, Hatu was summoned to Costa's cabin. The big man waved for the youth to sit on a chest opposite his bunk, which put Hatu close enough to the older man to make him a little uncomfortable. Maintaining a respectful distance was always part of the students' training.

"Master Facaria?" asked Costa.

Hatu nodded.

"So, what were you planning on doing when we reach Coaltachin?"

"Give over the captain's chest and tell the first master I found what happened."

Pointing to himself with his thumb, the man who had called himself Costa said, "Tell me what happened, boy. I am Master Reza."

Hatu knew it must be true, for no other man in Coaltachin would dare claim to be that man. His father was

Master Zusara, the closest thing Coaltachin had to a king, as he led the Council. He was also the head of the most powerful family in the nation, controlling more regimes and able to summon more soldiers and sicari than any two masters combined. Reza was one of three strong sons who protected their family's interests; each controlled a regime larger than the smaller families in the nation.

Zusara was first among equals, it was said, and what he lacked in official authority he more than made up for by using his influence. If a close vote was called in the Council, it was his that carried the most weight, and while some claimed he was simply good at forging consensus, Hatu remembered Facaria had once said that while no man could ever become king of Coaltachin, Zusara had come closer than anyone else in history. He was also something of a legend because he rarely left his home and seemed reclusive. He was like a spider at the center of its vast web: the master always knew what was occurring at its edge, without ever leaving its heart.

Hatu began his story with the killing of the merchant and his flight from Numerset, but when he came to describing the attack on the ship and he and Donte's attempt to flee in the longboat, he felt deep feelings stir. A profound ache rose up and threatened to break his calm as he started to recall his conversation with the head witch, Madda. He found himself fighting back tears and his voice grew thick with emotion when he described Donte's fate and the discussion between Madda and Sabina. Before he knew it, tears were coursing down his face.

Reza leaned back, resting against the bulkhead behind him, saying nothing until Hatu reached the end of his story. He allowed the young man a moment to regain control.

Quietly, Reza said, "You did well, but there are now more questions than there were before. I'll take you to my father and summon Facaria. The Council will want to hear this. And you should remember as much as you can about these Sisters of the Deep." He waited to see if Hatu would say anything and then indicated that the youth was dismissed with a nod of his head.

Hatu left the cabin and made his way to the crew bunks belowdecks. He wondered what Reza had meant by "more questions," but as he was both emotionally drained and work fatigued he let the curiosity fade away, found an empty hammock, and lay down. Within minutes, he was fast asleep.

15

An Unexpected Visit and Rumors of War

Daylon tossed the reins of his mount to a lackey as he nodded to his son. "Good ride," he complimented the lad.

Marius was his second son, two years younger than Daylon's heir, Wilton. His little ones were daughters, Linnaya, who would be playing with dolls somewhere in the keep, and the baby, Betina.

Balven appeared as Daylon expected, tousled his nephew's hair, and said, "Catch anything?"

The boy laughed and made a face. "We weren't hunting. Just riding."

As the boy started to hand the reins to another lackey, Daylon said, "Tend your own horse, Marius."

The youngster gave his father a dark look but said nothing as he followed the lackey. His father called after him, "When you're as expert at caring for your animal as John over there"—he indicated the groom who had taken his own horse—"then you can have someone else do it. If you can't care for your mount in the field, who will do it? If you don't know what they need, how will you know your retainers are caring for them correctly?"

"Yes, Father," came the annoyed response.

When the boy was out of sight, Balven laughed. "God, he reminds me of you at that age."

"A god?" asked Daylon. "Which one?"

Balven held up his hands, as if surrendering, and in a theatrical tone said, "Please, my lord, it's but a simple expression; don't have me whipped."

"Used to be 'gods' when we were boys."

"Anyone who thinks that the temples and churches of the old gods are returning is foolish, my lord," said Balven quietly as he moved closer to his half brother. Almost whispering, he said, "And it invites the accusation of heresy." He paused for a moment and added, "You've not opposed the One Church, but you've also not embraced them. It's starting to be noticed."

"You have a recommendation?" Daylon asked, knowing his half brother most certainly did.

"Build them a shrine. A tidy little shrine off in the corner of the keep somewhere; and make sure the icons of other gods are gone before one of their . . . what do they call them? Episkopos, yes. Before one of their censer-swinging, low-chanting, obnoxious prelates comes to consecrate the shrine. Have them visit on whatever holy day seems appropriate and you'll avoid that quick burning."

Daylon nodded. "I suspect it feels like a very slow burning to those tied to those stakes. Very well, see to it." Looking past his body man's shoulder he said, "Who's here?"

Balven turned to see Daylon take stock of the extra horses being cared for in the stable and nodded. "Baron Rodrigo of the Copper Hills arrived while you were out."

"Unlike him to appear without prior notice," said Daylon. "Where is he?"

"He's either in the great hall, chatting with Baroness Linnet, or in the kitchen molesting one of the girls."

"How long's he been here?" asked Daylon as he turned and began walking toward the main entrance of the keep.

Quickly falling in next to his half brother, Balven said, "Less than an hour."

"He's still flirting with my wife, then. He won't

begin plaguing the household girls until he's had a cup or two of wine."

The two men hurried into the keep and entered the great hall. Daylon saw his wife, Baroness Linnet, enduring Baron Rodrigo's attempts at charm. She suffered his banter with a fixed smile that reminded Daylon of the painted masks worn by players at the fair. Upon seeing her husband she brightened noticeably and said, "Here he is!" to Rodrigo.

Linnet was Daylon's second wife, as political a marriage as could be arranged. She was kin to three of the four current kings of Garn and counted half a dozen barons as her relatives. His first wife, Marie, had died in childbirth beside their stillborn son; she had been the love of his life, a fact Linnet had known since the day of their first meeting. Daylon still grieved for Marie.

While their marriage held no great passion, Linnet and Daylon had come to know each other well; they accepted one another's flaws and accommodated the needs of their marriage and their family's alliance. It was a comfortable relationship; he paid her enough attention that she felt no need to seek it elsewhere, and he had even abandoned his habit of bedding common girls when away from his castle. In most ways Daylon considered it a happy marriage, though he was occasionally visited by fits of melancholy when thoughts of Marie came unbidden to him; they had been so young when they met, who knew if he would have felt the same, this many years later, had she lived. He pushed aside morbid introspection and conceded that Linnet tried hard and succeeded in being a good baron's wife.

She was a striking woman in her thirties, a full seventeen years younger than her husband, her dark hair showing the first hints of grey. Her eyes were green and when she stared at him, Daylon found them piercing. She had never been what he counted pretty, but her figure was still trim and her angular features were unusual, and could be beautiful when she smiled and laughed. Their sex life after four children was still a pleasure, if not as active as it had been when they were younger. By Daylon's estimation, she was still a few years from taking a younger lover, and he wasn't sure if that would bring him anger or relief.

Certainly Rodrigo found her attractive enough, and Daylon played at being jealous when it suited his mood, always confusing the Baron of the Copper Hills. Daylon had discovered how much he liked confusing Rodrigo years before, and rarely felt guilty for doing so.

Daylon extended his hand and the men shook as Linnet rose and said, "Well, now that you're back I'll leave you to your man talk." As she started to sweep from the room, she asked, "Should I send in another pitcher of wine?"

Reflexively, Daylon glanced through a window at the height of the sun and judged it close enough to supper that indulging wouldn't leave him snoring an hour before his normal bedtime. He nodded and Linnet departed.

Balven waited until the servant appeared with the wine and waved the girl away as he took it, filled Daylon's flagon, and topped up Rodrigo's.

After taking a sip, Daylon said, "So, what brings you to Marquenet so unexpectedly?"

"I'm in need of a master weapons maker. You remember Brembol?"

"Fine master of his craft," said Daylon.

"Only better man I've seen was that fellow you used to have; what was his name?"

"Edvalt," said Balven without hesitation.

"Yes," said Daylon, glancing at his half brother. "Edvalt Tasman."

"Whatever happened to him?" asked Rodrigo.

"He earned his freedom." Daylon was silent for a moment, then continued. "After the battle." The Baron drained his flagon as if to dull the memory.

Rodrigo needed no clarification of which battle Daylon referred to. They had rarely spoken of that great betrayal, both keeping their own counsel on how they felt about the destruction of the king of Ithrace, but when they needed to reference it, they always called it "the battle."

"Well," said Rodrigo, "old Brembol is dead."

"Dead?" Daylon motioned for his cup to be refilled and Balven obliged. "He wasn't that old."

"No," agreed Rodrigo. "He wasn't, but his liver certainly was, given his love of strong drink. He preferred whisky, and lots of it. His apprentice found him one morning last week at his table, forehead on the wood, a half-filled cup of whisky clutched in his right hand."

"You must have another good weapon-smith in Copper Hills," said Daylon.

"I have many fine ones, if you need a wagon wheel banded or a plow blade fashioned. While a few of them are adequate at making simple weapons for the rabble who may answer my oathmen's call, I prefer the best I can find for my castellans and household. There seems to be a shortage of fine weapons makers, these days."

"And why this sudden need for fine weapons?"

Rodrigo had known Daylon for years and understood his relationship with Balven, so he felt free to speak his mind. "It's been quiet these last few years, but you know another war is coming."

Daylon shrugged noncommittally. "War is a constant risk in our time."

Rodrigo took a long pull of his wine and indicated that Balven should again refill his cup. Daylon's body man obliged and the lord of the Copper Hills said, "I've never understood your desire to act coy, Daylon. You're not some falsely shy nobleman's daughter trying to cozen a suitor into believing she hasn't ridden the stable boy's cock a dozen times. You read the winds of change better than any man I know." He drank again, then wiped his mouth with the back of his hand. "It was you who told me, after that miserable battle on the cliffs at Answearie, that we should not think of . . ." Rodrigo paused, looking frustrated. "Hell, I don't remember exactly what you said; I try to put the Betrayal out of my mind as much as I can, but I know you commented on the long game. You were thinking of the future.

"Well, that future will come soon. Lodavico is readying for another war, or I'm as stupid as they come. He's stopped invading his neighbors and converted how many? Five, six baronies are now part of Sandura or indirectly controlled by Lodavico. I don't know how many free barons he's converted to oathmen, but the border raiding in the east has gotten worse. It's as certain as I sit here that many of those 'raiders' and 'bandits' are Sandura's men."

Daylon fell silent, taking a long sip of wine. Finally he said, "I just heard a report of a raid into the Covenant, near the Narrows."

"Sandura?" asked Rodrigo.

"According to the story I heard, they weren't who they claimed to be. Slavers perhaps, but clearly intending to sell young men to Sandura as soldiers."

Rodrigo's face became a mask of puzzlement. "Drafting soldiers is tricky. You just create a happy band of deserters at the first opportunity. My father taught me a little military history, and he made it clear that having both sworn men and unwilling levies serve together was a bad notion, forcing you to have one part of your army guarding another part while a war rages on."

"Your father was right. Press men for ships, yes, as you only have to keep guard on them in port, but in the chaos of a battle? Worse, if the battle swings against you, such men may switch sides."

"Something besides soldiers, then? For slave labor?"

"Perhaps," agreed Daylon. He glanced at Balven, who indicated with a slight nod that he understood his brother's wishes: by tonight dispatches would be carried east to agents employed to gain information and return it as quickly as possible. With luck, within a month Daylon would have a decent idea of what Sandura was doing with these captured men.

Rodrigo accepted another glass of wine from Balven. "What worries me most are his links to the Church of the One God," he said. "They have certainly reordered the . . . order of things." He laughed at his own clumsy turn of phrase.

Daylon smiled. "Something to be worried about."

"I try to be tolerant—as a boy I dropped more than a few coins in various offering plates, as my father taught me—but this 'most holy king' thing Lodavico has been given by the Church . . ."

Dryly and quietly Balven said, "Can't have come cheaply."

Glancing at Balven, then back to his host, Rodrigo said, "It's more than the gold, Daylon. He's given offense to those who still hold ties with the old temples and churches, declaring war on them, if not overtly, and he has ordered the destruction of all temples and churches in Sandura that are not of the One God."

"Now, that I hadn't heard," said Daylon. "I'm not surprised, but still . . ." He sat silently for a minute, then said, "I believe your instincts are correct, my old friend."

Balven said, "If you'll indulge me, my lord, I fail to see how King Lodavico's pledging allegiance to the One God benefits him."

Daylon said, "It gives him the excuse he didn't have before."

Rodrigo said, "Daylon, you're a king in all but name. You've taken this wonderful barony your father left you and made it richer, stronger, and more influential. You could declare yourself king and demand an equal voice to Lodavico; none of the remaining kings would oppose you openly."

Daylon laughed. "Just openly?"

"Perhaps," amended Rodrigo.

"And give Lodavico and Mazika an excuse to do here what they did to Ithrace? They'd need less manipulation and fewer lies. The blessing of the church and the promise of tearing Marquensas apart would be enough for half the barons on Garn to line up alongside them."

"So what do you plan to do? We both know war is coming." Seeing Daylon's expressionless mask, Rodrigo added, "So, you have a plan, but you're not in a trusting mood, I see."

Daylon said, "We've been friends for many years and I trust you more than any man not of my blood, but some discussions are premature, and this would be one of them. Now, back to the question of finding you a decent weapons maker . . ."

"Do you have one you're willing to let me poach?"

"Perhaps. You brought up Edvalt, and by coincidence one of his apprentices, now a master by rank, was here just a few days ago."

"Is he still in the city?" asked Rodrigo, now very interested.

Before Daylon could answer, Balven said, "No, he left the city."

Daylon looked at his half brother and said, "He did?"

Balven inclined his head slightly. "I knew you'd want some word of his whereabouts, so I had him followed." He nodded toward Rodrigo, but also in the direction of the far wall, with its maps, its journals, and all the notes the baron had compiled on the coming conflict.

Daylon said, "So then, where has he gone?"

"One of our agents overheard him speaking with a local rumormonger, a woman named Kalanora, then he found a smith named Gildy. He's heading to a newly vacant smithy in Beran's Hill."

Daylon said, "Interesting choice," in a noncommittal tone.

Rodrigo said, "I'll seek him there."

"Do me a favor?" asked Daylon. "I don't think he will take your service, as he has already rejected mine, but employ him while you seek another weapons master for your keep. I would welcome your judgment on the quality of his workmanship.

"Now," said Daylon, rising, "I need to change out of these dusty clothes and ready myself for dinner."

"I could use a bath as well," said Rodrigo, standing up. "Could you send someone along . . . ?"

Daylon glanced at Balven, who nodded. "I'll attend to that."

Daylon waved Rodrigo off, and his half brother turned to escort the Baron of the Copper Hills to a guest room.

Alone for a moment, Daylon Dumarch, the most powerful free baron on all of Garn, tried to order his thoughts. If Rodrigo was alarmed by the events occurring in the east—by Sandura flexing its muscle—then things were moving at a faster pace than he had anticipated.

That posed two problems for Daylon: the first was that he wasn't quite ready to openly challenge Lodavico, and the second, the far more worrisome involvement of the Church in politics. The order had been flirting with power since Daylon was a boy, but now they flaunted it. Why they might have allied themselves openly with Sandura was a mystery to Daylon. As soon as Balven returned they'd discuss what messages needed to be sent to their agents in the east.

Still, better to have a problem at his doorstep than an army, Daylon thought as he moved toward his quarters and clean clothing.

16

Hints of Truth
and Dark Designs

The voyage aboard the *Sasa Muti* was uneventful, save for a little unseasonable rain on the second day. Reza had sent word ahead on a swifter boat, for they were fully loaded and slow, and he wanted Hatu's report safely in his father's hands should some misfortune befall them. Ten days after setting sail, they came within sight of Coaltachin's main anchorage in the city of Corbara, known as Safe Harbor, but also by a variety of other names depending on who was sailing into the port. The locals simply called it "the Harbor" or "the City" when speaking to outlanders.

Being vague was one of the many tricks employed by the people of Coaltachin to ensure uncertainty among potential enemies. Only trusted visitors and those of Coaltachin knew that Safe Harbor was part of Corbara.

Hatu looked from north to south, taking in the details of the harbor, but found himself empty of any emotion regarding the place. It wasn't a void, but he did feel an absence of any sense of home here, any loyalty or affinity. It was just a place to be, and only marginally safer than being out in the world.

They made straight for one of the more important docks. Hatu was unsurprised, given which master was aboard. Two horses waited at the bottom of the ramp. Master Reza said nothing about the captain's chest, so Hatu assumed the matter was settled and that it would find its way to whatever destination the Council considered appropriate.

Reza spared Hatu a brief glance to see he was mounted and urged his horse forward. Hatu had ridden before but was hardly an expert, so he struggled to keep pace until Reza slowed to make his way through the press of the town.

Hatu had passed through Safe Harbor several times, but he had never lingered here, so he was quickly lost and focused on keeping Master Reza's back clearly in sight. They rode up a hill past some prosperous-looking shops and an inn, and then came to a winding road that led to a clearing. There stood a simple wooden post with an iron ring, and Reza dismounted and tied off his horse's reins, Hatu following suit a moment later.

Reza said, "We walk," as he pointed to a narrow path that vanished into a thick stand of trees.

Hatu followed Reza up a narrow pathway that led to a slender bridge over a lively stream, past a small grove of fruit trees and a well, and ended at a three-step porch leading up to a modest building. It was little more than a large hut, perched on wooden pilings. Hatu entered through the door after Reza, who said, "Father, this is the boy Hatushaly."

A man of late middle years looked up from where he sat on a cushion on the floor and set aside the document he had been reading. "Welcome home, my son," he said to Reza; then he motioned to Hatu. "Stand over here where I can see you better."

Hatu had met many masters, and traveled with a few, like Bodai, and felt he understood his position with them. But Master Zusara was a legend in Coaltachin.

So Hatu was surprised to find him something of a disappointment. He had expected some figure of myth, a powerful man, perhaps even magical, but instead he saw a fairly nondescript man in his late fifties or early sixties before him, dressed in a plain grey tunic and trousers, with woven sandals on his feet, and sporting no rings or other jewelry. Had Hatu passed him in the market, he would have barely noticed Zusara.

As he moved to the indicated spot, Hatu realized that was probably intentional, and part of his genius. He had been taught, when learning to mark targets in the market, that many men felt the need to call attention to themselves with fine clothing, ostentatious displays of wealth, and retinues of servants. But Master Zusara was not such a man. Hatu stood motionless, silently waiting.

Looking at Reza, Zusara asked, "Has he reached manhood?"

Reza shrugged, then said, "The day is to be upon him next month." Then he added, "Yet he appears but two years older than my youngest son."

Master Zusara nodded. "A little broader of shoulder, perhaps, but yes, they seem of like age." He silently looked at Hatushaly, then asked, "So, why is he here? Why bring me a child?"

"A ship was lost and all hands, save one." He gestured to Hatu. "I think this is a story the Council needs to hear firsthand."

Zusara's face showed a small expression of surprise, and Hatu reckoned this father put much faith in his son's judgment. "Then we shall summon the Council."

He put down the scroll he had been holding and said, "I read your message. It was even more cryptic than usual. Some of what you shared disturbed me . . ." Zusara studied his son's face for a moment. "I expect that what you didn't share will prove even more disturbing. I sent word to the other members of the Council that you would be arriving soon and they should be ready to come on short notice. Most are at their homes, though . . ." He glanced at Hatu. "It doesn't matter where the other two are. Five may serve as well as seven if the Council needs a judgment. I shall send word and we will hear this story tomorrow morning."

He stood up stiffly, and Hatu realized Zusara was older than he had first thought, or perhaps suffering from injuries gained in years gone by. "Come," he said to Hatu. "I shall show you a room. You will dine with me tonight and meet the Council tomorrow."

Reza nodded and said, "We will need Master Facaria as well; I shall send word."

"That old woman? Very well, if we need him here, send for him. He'll either preen like a peacock to the Council over the invite or complain about the need to travel all night. We shall see which Facaria appears tomorrow."

Reza inclined his head slightly in agreement and turned without speaking to Hatu. Hatu hesitated a moment, then entered a hallway behind the most powerful master on the island, and in the entire nation of Coaltachin, and heard a deep sigh escape from the old man.

Toward the back of the house was a tiny room containing a mat with a simple cloth coverlet, a table, and an unlit candle in a holder.

"Rest," instructed Zusara, motioning Hatu into the room. "It should be clean. If the water rises during the rainy season, this is the part of the house that gets drenched, and it can make things smell of mildew, but my wife . . ." He smiled. "That's for another time. Tonight, you will tell me your tale over supper and I shall craft your words for the ears of the Council so we may do what's best." Turning his back, he said, "I shall send for you. Rest now."

Hatu wondered what was coming next but decided to take Zusara's suggestion and lay down. He felt a familiar nervousness, a cross between concern, even a bit of fear, and frustration, which he willed away. He was tired to his bones, so sleep was quick to arrive.

Hatu awoke to the sound of footsteps and saw a woman move aside the curtains that had allowed the room a bit of privacy. She spoke softly and with a modest smile said, "My husband asks you to join him at supper."

Uncertain what to say beyond, "Thank you," Hatu

rose quickly from the sleeping mat and moved past her, down the short hall to the room where he first had encountered Master Zusara.

Zusara sat on cushions before a low table. A delicious smell rose from a large tureen resting upon it. Hatu glanced at Master Zusara, who indicated that the young man should sit as he moved to the opposite side of the table. A moment later, Zusara's wife appeared with a tray of fruit, bread, and a large square of cheese.

Master Zusara said nothing as she cut the bread and cheese into portions small enough to be eaten easily, left the fruit on the platter, and then ladled the soup into deep bowls. She left without a word having been spoken by anyone.

Hatu watched her depart and said, "Your wife is not eating?"

Master Zusara waved his hand in a dismissive gesture. "She knows to leave men to men's business."

Hatu let that remark sink in for a moment; he considered himself a man but still endured many people looking at him as if he was still a boy. And since he'd mixed with Hava and other strong girls his entire life, he wasn't entirely sure what men's business meant. Lacking anything intelligent to say, he smiled. "Sir," he finally said, as neutrally as he could manage.

The old master smiled. "You have been away too

long, I see." Hatu nodded. "You've picked up foreign ideas. We can discuss women later if you'd like."

The remark startled Hatu a little; his tone was almost fatherly.

"You appear troubled," Master Zusara observed.

"I . . . would like to say something to please you, sir, but in truth I am only now beginning to learn things a man should know."

"Ah." Zusara studied the young man's face for a moment. "And what else?"

"I would appreciate your wisdom on any subject, but this thing I . . ."

"Survived? Endured?"

"Yes," said Hatu.

"Tell me of it, then, and we'll talk of other things later."

Hatu began his tale slowly, trying to frame every moment in such a way that he shared the horror without overstating it. He had been taught that the truth required no embellishment, but forgetting details was also a fault.

When Hatu began recounting the part of the narrative when he had awoken in the cave next to the unconscious Donte, feelings started to rise within and he was forced to pause several times to collect himself. "I was terrified, if I'm to be truthful, master. I know

I should have . . ." He was on the verge of tears and forced himself to keep silent. Master Zusara's face remained expressionless and he offered no comment; his silence gave permission to Hatu to take as much time as he needed.

"I have thought about it again and again; was there something I could have done? I didn't even know where they held Donte, and I don't know what I could have done had I known. In the end, I just thought I must get home." He gulped back a sob and willed himself to calm. Zusara gave him further time to compose himself.

"Home," said the old master quietly. There was something thoughtful about his tone, though Hatu couldn't say why.

Finally, Master Zusara said, "You've had time to think on all this, obviously."

"Sir," said Hatu, nodding his head in agreement.

"Why do you think you were spared?"

Hatu shook his head and remained silent for a second before he said, "I do not know."

"Think on that some more, because tomorrow the Council will be here and you will need to tell the tale again." He narrowed his gaze and said, "And that will be the first question you are asked."

The rest of the meal passed mostly in silence as the sun lowered beyond the horizon. Zusara asked him a few questions about where he had traveled and what trades and skills he was familiar with, responding to his last answer with, "You've trained in more trades than most your age. Is there one that you preferred?"

Hatu thought it was an odd question; the skills were simply part of the false identities he used when needed. He shrugged and said, "Perhaps being a tinker. I do like fixing things, working with my hands. It's straight-forward."

As he stood, Master Zusara said, "We need to take a short walk."

Hatu stopped himself from asking where they were going, because when a master told you something, you did not question it. He got to his feet as the old man moved to the door.

"There are torches over there," Zusara told him, pointing to a large container just to the left of the door. "Fetch two."

When he had done as instructed, Hatu held them while the master struck flint and steel, showering one of the torches with sparks. It caught a small flame and Hatu turned it slowly, spreading the fire, then lit the second torch from the first. "Always keep a ready torch against the darkness," said Zusara. "Seep oil or light tar will alight with the tiniest ember."

He guided Hatu down the steps to the path that

led to the town road, but instead of turning downhill, Zusara motioned for Hatu to follow him past where the road appeared to end. It did in fact continue but was used so little, the stretch beyond Zusara's home was overgrown and hidden from view. The master casually pushed aside fronds and tall grasses that bowed over the narrow path, and after a few minutes, Hatu realized the road had truly ended, and they now followed nothing more than a track.

As the sky darkened and the torches became the primary source of illumination, Hatu studied his surroundings, looking for his way out—a practice born of habit. It would be easy to lose one's path in the darkness.

"So, about those foreign customs I spoke of. What do you know of women?" asked Zusara, ending the silence.

The question took Hatu aback for a moment, until he realized the master referred to his earlier question about why the master's wife had left them alone.

Hatu weighed his answer before speaking. "I remember the imposing matrons who raised me when I was tiny, and a few of the girls in class sometimes bested me in training. I see many powerful women when I travel. I see them in the village near the harbor here, and in all the other nations . . . I have heard the names of baronesses in North Tembria, women of position and authority, yet I have never heard of women of rank here in Coaltachin."

Master Zusara nodded and said, "Because we have none. In the outside world, women are never important in warfare, and in politics only to forge alliances between powerful families. At best, they are bargaining chips in an important game of chance. Oh, they can comfort a man and give him relief, but at worst they are distracting and dangerous. The only truly noble thing women are capable of is giving us sons."

Hatu nodded, having absolutely no idea what Zusara was getting at. He waited and then, after a long moment, said, "I am not certain I understand, master."

"Have you had a woman?"

The young man found the question a little off-putting, though he couldn't put name to the reason. "Yes, master. A few times." The truth was Hatu had only been with one girl, a barmaid in Numerset, just days before the merchant's murder. Later he had discovered that Donte had paid her to be his first. He was still embarrassed by the entire thing, yet knew boasting about women seemed to be an important pastime to the other young men. He shrugged, trying to look unconcerned, though Master Zusara wasn't looking at him. Hatu knew that there must have been something of consequence in this topic, even if he didn't grasp much of what the master was saying, or the discussion wouldn't have been causing him such discomfort.

Zusara halted, turned, and looked at him appraisingly. "During your travels, have you desired many women?"

Hatu hesitated, then said, "I'm not sure how to answer, sir. There were girls who drew my eye, a few who I would have liked to have had sex with, and a few with whom I did." He tried to speak as if it was of no matter, afraid that to be caught out in a lie about women would be a bad outcome of this seemingly offhand discussion. Some part of him realized that no matter how casual a conversation with Zusara might seem, nothing he said was without significance. Hatu just hadn't grasped what that significance was yet.

Zusara said, "No matter. All things in their own time." He let out an audible sigh, then said, "What passes between a man and his wife may not be noble, but it is very important." He put his hand on Hatu's shoulder. "This is why the common people of Coaltachin are like those of other nations: boy meets girl, they think they are in love, they marry and have children . . .

"But between the Quelli Nascosti, marriages are arranged. Older, wiser men pick the wives of their sons, nephews, and grandsons. If the boy is an orphan, his master will decide for him.

"It is done this way because the wife must make the husband strong, and the husband must make the wife strong in turn, matching two equally valuable, but different, strengths. It is too important to our future to leave such a choice to the whims of youthful feelings. Do you know why?"

Hatu shook his head. "No, master."

"Because the greatest service we do for our kin, and our nation, is to make sure that we stay strong. Our children must be as strong, or stronger, than their parents."

Hatu was surprised when the master sighed audibly, revealing a hint of frustration. "At least that's how it is supposed to be. There have been the occasional . . . bad choices."

Hatu was now completely confused. He failed to see the point of this conversation but said nothing.

"So you have been with a woman?" Hatu was pleased that in the torchlight, the master couldn't see his blush and witness his embarrassment, but the question appeared rhetorical as Zusara laughed. "Village girls?" Hatu nodded, furthering his deceit. He tried to reassure himself he was only being a little dishonest with Zusara.

Zusara smiled as if remembering his own youth, then patted Hatu on the shoulder, turned, and resumed walking. "One of the hardest things for a boy to learn when becoming a man is to master his desires.

"Some young men desire gold. Some desire power. Some desire drug-granted dreams or the pleasure of strong spirits. Other men cannot resist games of chance." He glanced back at Hatu as if ensuring he was listening. "Those who do not master such . . . *cravings* are . . . weeded out. They make a family weak."

Continuing their slow walk, Zusara nodded as he said, "Almost everyone desires the touch of another." He looked forward and shrugged. "Men, women, it doesn't matter, it is the most common desire of all. Nature doesn't care who you bed; nature just wants children." He chuckled. "Even those who seek out others like themselves, men seeking men, women with women . . . many of them desire someone to carry on their name." He nodded and added, "Some of the best people at raising children are like that." Then he shook his head slightly, as if confounded by the very topic he had raised. "In the end we can say this: had our parents not succumbed to their desire, we wouldn't be here, would we?"

"I think . . . ," Hatu began before he realized that he really didn't know what to think. He looked at the master.

"My point, boy, is that you must be cautious of

desire and even more of attachments, of caring too much about those around you." He stopped again, turned, and regarded Hatu. "It is easy to forget you are not truly one of us."

Hatu stopped. "I do not understand, sir."

"No, you do not." Zusara studied the boy's face. "You are a charge of the Quelli Nascosti. We cared for you, raised you, and taught you. But you are not one of us."

He was different; the single most powerful man in the nation had now openly acknowledged something that Hatu had known intuitively since he was young. He decided to give voice to the question that had nagged him most of his life: "Then who am I?"

"That is what we will now attempt to find out," said Zusara, once again resuming their climb up the narrow road. "Fate has provided you with a different path, Hatu, but you will find that what we have taught you here will serve you wherever that fortune takes you."

"That is a lot to consider," Hatu said softly, almost a whisper.

"This is indeed much for a young man to absorb," said Zusara, tapping Hatu on the shoulder. "Today shall be the last day you live as you have; with your manhood day approaching, this was soon to be true anyway, so what does it matter if you and I decide a few weeks early?"

Hatu was still confused by Zusara's rambling discourse but was now convinced that somewhere in all this discussion of men and women, family, and the rest lurked something very important to his future. He let go of the need to understand every phrase and word, and decided to wait for it to come together and make sense. He nodded to the old man.

"Now, back to women." Zusara paused again and held up a finger to emphasize his point. Hatu stopped as well. "Women who give you sons . . . they are worth much. Wives . . ." He sighed. "A man's wife . . ." Again he halted, as if still unsure where he wanted the talk to go. Finally, he took a deep breath and said, "Well, try not to care for a woman too much; it makes things difficult. It was a hard lesson I learned and passed along to my sons. Reza learned it best." He looked out at the horizon, as if lost for a moment in memory. Then he shrugged as if indicating something was implied there that Hatu didn't understand. "Just try not to care; it makes hard choices easier."

As they started walking again up the hillside path, Hatu thought about the master's wife and couldn't imagine how the quiet, soft-spoken woman ever made Zusara's life difficult.

"You fall asleep in their arms and you get used to that"—Zusara paused and let out a quiet sigh—"and that is where the difficulty begins. They whisper in your ear after dark . . ." The old man waved a finger as if warding off some evil. "Therein lies the danger."

Then his tone brightened. "Not all women are problems. Many do what they're told without complaint. And there are a few who are strong enough to train; those girls are very valuable."

Without thought, Hatu said, "Hava."

Zusara blinked in the torchlight, then asked, "Who is Hava?"

"A girl . . ." He let his voice drop a bit. "She was the best fighter . . . as good as Donte. We are . . . were friends."

"Hmmm." Zusara looked at Hatu for a silent moment, then said, "You like her." It was not a question.

"She's a friend," he repeated, trying to make it sound matter-of-fact when he could barely hold his emotions in check at the mention of her name. He'd ached to see her since losing Donte and had never felt this alone in his life. If Hatu wasn't vigilant, the terror of what he had endured with the Sisters of the Deep would overwhelm him. He now managed it in the same fashion in which he managed the constant anger that had been with him all his life, but it was never easy.

Zusara made a dismissive noise. Returning to their trek, he said, "You grow used to a wife. Mine has given me four sons, three still living. You know my youngest, Reza . . ." Hatu waited while the master collected his thoughts. "Over the years, you become accustomed to having the same woman around. If you do not send her from your bed once you've enjoyed her, as I said, you get used to falling asleep beside her . . . and then, if she whispers in the dark . . ." Again he stopped. "This can be very dangerous," he said, walking on.

"Why?" asked Hatu.

"It's the whispering. At first you just fall asleep. Then after a while you tell her things before you go to sleep. At first she listens, eventually she might question or placate you . . . and after a longer while, you might listen to her views." Again he stopped, and leaned over to whisper, which, in Hatu's opinion, was unnecessary. "And then, in the dark of night, you might be tempted to ask her advice. No man of importance should ever fall into that trap."

He turned and walked again. Something in his voice told Hatu that Master Zusara didn't believe what he was saying.

"Do you know why it is forbidden for students in the same training class to have sex with one another?"

Hatu shook his head, then again realized he couldn't be seen, so said, "No, sir. We've been told about the rule since we began training, but never why it's there."

Zusara laughed. "And some of you break it anyway, I know." He fixed Hatu with a narrow gaze, then said, "We have this rule because a girl's duties are more difficult than yours, and our valuable female students do not need to be bothered by a bunch of boys whose cocks get hard every time they walk by. Besides killing men with blades, cords, or poison, they may need to make a man fall in love with them, and it is impossible for them to learn those arts if they think they are betraying some stupid boy and spreading their legs for him every night.

"Oh, we have boys who train with the Powdered Women, true, for there are powerful men and women in the world who prefer cock." He shrugged. "And some like everything. But, while the young men who leave the Powdered Women may need the same skills in seduction"—he waved his hand in the air—"they cannot become pregnant."

Hatu nodded, conceding the obvious.

"We have ten, fifteen sicari men for every woman. They must be harder than the men, more resilient, and more ruthless. They must be able to ride a man until he's spent and professing his pleasure and devotion, then kill him before he awakes the next morning. Do you understand?"

"I think so," offered Hatu.

"Then let me make it clearer, Hatu. Most of the women you see every day are not important to the nation, save as mothers. But to waste a rare girl, one who can match a man in cunning and skill, to have her grounded with child because some young lout got a stiff cock . . ." He shook his head. "One of them is the equal of any ten boys who survive training. That is how important they are. That is why the punishment is so severe. You lie with a girl student, you are beaten senseless; do it a second time, or if she gets pregnant the first time, you are killed.

"So, my advice, Hatu, is never love a woman. Thinking with your cock is stupid, and thinking with your heart has been the undoing of more than one man."

Hatu thought about Zusara and his wife but knew better than to mention it. Was the master telling him this because his marriage had succeeded, or because it had failed? He would puzzle out that mystery later if he could. Either way, he was not entirely sure he agreed with much of what he'd just heard, but was hard-pressed to say why. That could also be puzzled out later.

They came around a turn in the side of the hill, and Hatu saw the trail continue to wind its way up into a nearby mountain, but nestled against a rock face stood a building, little more than a hut, but sturdy and sheltered against the wind that would come from the other side of the peak. A light came from within, peeking through a curtained doorway that swayed gently with the night breeze.

Zusara said, "Wait here until I summon you."

Hatu watched as he mounted the three steps to the hut and spoke quietly to whoever was inside. After a moment, Zusara turned and beckoned Hatu to join him. At the entrance, Zusara spoke in low voice. "There is another valuable, important type of woman, rarer even than those who rise to be sicari. These women possess powers denied to all but a few—powers that some call magic. The woman you will now meet is such a one. Be respectful. Show regard." Zusara extinguished his torch in a bucket of sand and entered the hut, and Hatu followed the old master.

Inside there were two hanging lamps, wicks floating in oil by the look of the light they cast; their flickering glow caused shadows and objects to move out at the edge of the young man's vision. Hatu glanced around and saw many strange things: dolls of some type hanging on cords from the ceiling; an array of feathers around the stretched hide of some animal, which was painted in a design that seemed to tug at his vision. He pulled his eyes from them only to be trapped by the wall paintings. Forcing his gaze away, he turned his attention to the figure at the center of the room. As his eyes adjusted to the dim light, he saw a woman of some age, with grey hair and a fair set of wrinkles around her eyes and the corners of her mouth. She sat calmly and her straight bearing hinted at power.

Then he locked eyes with her and instantly felt the hair on his arms and neck rise. He felt a play of energies dance over him, a painful reminder of what he had experienced in the cave where he had last seen Donte and his interrogation by the Sisters of the Deep.

The woman beckoned him over and said softly, "Step here, boy, so I may see you better."

Hatu took a step forward and she said, "So, what have we here?"

Master Zusara said, "That is what I, too, would like to know. He was taken by the Sisters of the Deep and they set him free."

Her intake of breath sounded as if she had touched a hot iron, and her eyes widened as she reflexively pulled back from Hatu. After a moment, she pointed to a cushion in front of her chair and said, "Sit!"

Hatu almost jumped to sit on the cushion. Then the woman said, "I am Lorana, and I need your thoughts." Without waiting for a reply, she reached out and took his head between her hands and suddenly Hatu fell into shadow.

He swam in a murky darkness shimmering with colors that were not true colors and felt strangely familiar. The only way Hatu could describe them was that they were like the odd afterimages that lingered behind his eyelids when he stared at something bright too long, then closed his eyes, illusions of color that changed and shifted as they flashed. Making sense of the images was impossible; there were too many and they were reversed in color: blues became yellows, reds turned into greens, floating quickly away and darting from place to place. Then they started to twist and fold, to flow into one another, swell and recede like combers in a wind-tossed sea, shot through with spindrift of white and silver. It was as if every memory he had ever had was trying to rise within him; each struggled to be recognized yet all were thwarted by something else inside him, something familiar but not understood, causing his mind to race.

A voice that wasn't a voice entered Hatu's mind, asked questions, and found answers, yet as soon as the voices moved away, he could not remember their words. Feelings rose and quickly washed over him, but the moment they fled, he could put no name to them. Echoes of pain taunted him and fled when he attempted to remember their source. He had no sense of how long his interrogation lasted, for each instant slipped by.

Then suddenly he was awake.

Lorana stared into his eyes as Hatu blinked to refocus them and felt his head swimming. He shook it slightly and then glanced to where Master Zusara looked down on him.

Quietly, the master said, "Return to my home and rest. We have a long day tomorrow. You will need to repeat your tale exactly as you did today. Try to push aside those feelings I saw, for they will seem unmanly to the other masters, and be ready for one of them to vent his anger at you. Do you understand?"

Hatu hesitated for a moment and then stood up on slightly wobbly legs. He had a vague sense that something important had just happened, but he had no memory of it and he felt fatigued without understanding why. He looked at Lorana and Zusara and nodded, then departed and started down the path.

After he had left, Zusara looked at the old witch and said, "Well?"

Her voice was hoarse as she whispered, "Do you know who he is?"

"He is the last of the Firemanes."

"But do you know what that means?"

Zusara nodded. "It means he is the rightful heir to the throne of Ithrace."

She let out a long sigh, reached for his hand, and looked around the hut as if seeking some sort of inspiration. "He is so much more than that, old man."

He gripped her hand and gave it a loving squeeze. "What?"

"There is magic around us, powers that infuse our world and of which most men are ignorant. These energies manifest as . . . abilities or talents, whatever you choose to call them, and provide . . . a weight, a presence, a . . . balance.

"The experience for most people is but a moment of insignificant chance that goes this way or that, for or against them: from the breaking of a tool to the luck of a gambler, or a woman saying yes to her husband when she usually would not, and conceiving a child." She paused and looked at Zusara intensely, then took a deep breath and continued. "No matter how it appears to most of us, all of these energies are ordered and related in ways none of us can understand. Some of us, mostly women, can glimpse that order and see a bit of the pattern, and a few can even manipulate a little of that energy.

"You are blind, my love, and I have but a glimpse, but there is so much more here than we can understand . . ." She closed her eyes, gripped his hand tighter, and then let out a long, painful sigh, almost a moan of anguish.

He said nothing, letting her organize her thoughts.

Finally, Lorana said, "There is a powerful order that toys with magic so profound that anyone who trusts it is a fool. The Sisters of the Deep use the darkest blood magic known; there are others, too, but none more evil than them. They play with life, kill baby boys and raise their girls to disdain all men, save to use them to breed more daughters or to create monsters to serve them, or . . . to eat their flesh. There are others, scattered— the Order of the Spider, the Sisterhood of Storm—all hidden, most small, some more powerful than you can imagine, and all staying out of view. Those of us with gifts know of one another—not everything, but enough.

"Blood magic is powerful, a drawing upon energy that is primal, raw, and terrible. Its layers include death magic and magic wrested by pain and suffering. There are also other, lesser magics, in the life force of the forests and of wild beasts, in the energy provided by the sun, or in the power of words and music. But blood magic is among the most powerful of these arts, and when it ends in death, more powerful still."

She paused a moment, then continued. "The only

magic more significant is elemental magic. It is the foundation upon which all other magic rests. There are four: earth, air, water, and fire. And these powers reside in some men and women; there are mortals who can read history in the stones, or hear messages in the wind, and others who can travel wherever water flows. That boy, Hatu, is a living embodiment of fire. There is no magic more primal or more powerful.

"The fire magic given to the Firemanes was ancient, invested in the first Firemane, before his line became royal, even before history, and it was formidable. That magic was the reason that Ithrace became the pinnacle of creativity. Its power was spread among the children and grandchildren and became a force to shape and guide their family and then their nation." She squeezed Zusara's hand again and stared into his eyes. "Generations of Firemanes have had this gift."

"What do we need to do?" Zusara asked.

"Of the elemental magics, fire is the most creative and destructive. Occasionally the ground shakes, but earth by nature is a quiet, slow-changing thing. Water flows and alters, but if there is no flood, storm, or fall, it is not violent. It etches the rocks and shifts landscapes; it is not as slow as earth, but it is unrelenting and steady.

"Air is unpredictable, changeable, and fickle but it is

rarely violent enough to cause great havoc. Like water, it can cause storms, and given enough time, erode rock, but it is usually gentle. It is everywhere, and for those who know how to listen, air speaks.

"But fire . . ." She shook her head. "Generations of Firemanes have held that magic within them, and they have gifted the world with creativity, originality, and ingenuity. They were considered the most handsome of people, the women were exquisitely beautiful, and all had talent for singing, music, dance, and art. Their power was largely passive, giving light and warmth, but it was always there, always providing benefit to the family and the nation.

"Now all of that power has been returned to one boy, and it burns in him like an ember waiting to ignite, a sleeping anger that could burst forth at any time. It was forced into him by bloody murder and hate. It is now a thing to be feared."

"The curse?"

"You treat it as a folktale, an old story without meaning. Should the last of the Firemanes perish . . ." She smiled at him. "This is not 'cursed' like a gambler who has lost too many games, or a man who has an accident because a one-eyed dog barked at him or a hawk circled his barn, or any of the other superstitious nonsense the common folk believe. Do you know the price of ending the Firemane line?"

Zusara said, "No."

"That bad things will befall us is all that is known by most. But here is a truth: either put that child somewhere safe, let him marry and father many, many children, so that magic will again be spread among many . . ."

Zusara said, "Or?"

She stared at him for a moment, as if she couldn't believe he'd asked that question, then said, "Or you must kill him, of course. The fire magic will disperse and find another vessel. It may be generations before its power achieves this level of focus, but it will make the rest of this world safer for the time being. For if he gains control of that power, we should fear him. If he lives, he might destroy all of us."

"How?" he whispered.

"Only the gods know." She looked at Zusara, shook her head slightly and said, "Even they might not know what will happen when a foundation magic is in the control of one man."

Zusara was silent for a long time, then squeezed Lorana's hand affectionately and departed without speaking another word.

17

Unexpected Bounty and Sudden Danger

Declan twisted the blank while he watched Jusan hammer. The youngster was thriving in the new forge and might end up as a better smith than Declan and Edvalt had predicted. Declan wondered how much of that had been due to his own presence as Edvalt's journeyman, overshadowing Jusan's ability, or just Jusan's maturing and taking the craft more seriously now.

"Good, good," Declan said as Jusan knocked the blank into its first sword shape; they had worked together long enough that words were hardly necessary, and he knew just when the boy needed him to turn the iron blank. Jusan nodded and Declan held it still while his apprentice put down the hammer and picked up a bucket of water to quench the metal and prepare it for the second shaping.

"You did well," Declan said as hissing steam rose from the still-hot bar. "Your folds are better now. Your shaping is quicker than before." He set the rapidly cooling metal down on the anvil and said, "Keep this up and you'll be a journeyman soon."

Jusan returned Declan's smile. "I watched what Edvalt taught you as well as practicing what he required of me, but as your apprentice . . ." He shrugged. "I get to do more than haul coal . . . and berries." They both laughed. "Sweeping, shoveling, all the rest is the same as in Oncon, but here I'm the other pair of hands on the real work."

Declan laughed. "Should you stay after I name you journeyman, a new apprentice may have to endure the same by being behind you."

Jusan's expression turned serious, his soot-smeared face wrinkled in thought. "Do I have the makings of a master?"

Declan tilted his head a bit and shrugged slightly as he said, "Fair question. I'll know better when I name you journeyman. I'll not mislead you, Jusan. If you do have the makings of a master smith, you'll stay on; if you don't, I'll kick you out, so you can find a better teacher or start your own forge. Many smiths have a good life without reaching the rank of master. But I think it's more likely now that you're working all the time than it was back in Oncon."

Jusan let out the long breath he'd been holding in during Declan's answer. "Fair enough. It's just that you made it look easy for all those years."

"I didn't realize," said Declan. "But to be plain, you know enough for me to leave you in charge when I deliver these swords to Baron Rodrigo, or travel to buy iron . . ." Jusan smiled at that and Declan shared his pleasure. "Come, let's get cleaned up and go have an ale."

Jusan laughed. "You mean let's clean up and go see Gwen." Declan's face reddened a little, so he said, "You go and I'll finish up here. I'll join you after, so you can have some time alone with her, pretending you're just there for an ale."

Declan said, "Thank you. Now if I can just keep her father from insisting that I drink whisky . . ."

"It's grown on me," said Jusan, and he set aside the still-cooling blank and judged the need for banking the coals. "Though a little definitely goes a long way, and if you drink too much you pay a right large price the next morning, I found out soon enough."

"That's why I'll stay with ale," said Declan, crossing

to a large barrel of water that doubled as a supply for drinking and, at the end of the day, scrubbing face and hands. Jusan would empty it tonight after he washed up and refill it in the morning.

Declan quickly cleaned up as best he could and with a wave to Jusan set out to the Inn of the Three Stars. He had been in Beran's Hill a month now, his success guaranteed by the unexpected arrival of the Baron of the Copper Hills three days after Declan had agreed to buy the forge.

Baron Rodrigo was sufficiently impressed with the sword Declan had to show him that after a little haggling Declan found himself with enough gold for provisions, for a down payment on the iron they needed, and to pay others to fix the forge so he and Jusan could focus on making the weapons. With the balance paid upon receipt of the weapons, he would own the smithy at least two years sooner than planned. Life was turning out to be better than he had imagined back in Oncon.

Reaching the door to the inn, he hesitated and willed himself not to look anxious. It was in Declan's nature to keep things deep within him, as Edvalt had concluded not long ago. He knew it was becoming something of a joke among those he had come to know since his arrival in Beran's Hill that Gwen had already staked a claim on him, and some perversity within caused him to rebel against that. Declan needed to seem in charge of his life, despite the fact that he was smitten with the bright girl on the other side of that door, and had no answer as to why. He just wanted to do things in his own time.

The young master smith stepped inside and found a few familiar faces as well as a group of strangers settling at a corner table, travelers from the look of them. The Three Stars wasn't the best inn, but it was situated just off the southern entrance to the town and was often the first stop for travelers arriving from Marquenet. Location had proved to be of critical importance to Leon's success and while hardly a place of luxury accommodation, the inn was serviceable and provided better-than-average food and drink.

Reaching the bar, Declan nodded to Leon, who immediately pulled out a stoppered bottle. Declan held up his hand. "Early morning tomorrow, just an ale."

Leon fixed a narrow gaze on the young smith for a second, then shrugged. "So be it," he said, mildly amused, and drew a large jack of ale from the barrel behind him.

Declan glanced around the room and when Leon placed the ale before him, the innkeeper said, "She's in the kitchen."

Declan tried to act as if he hadn't been looking for Gwen but knew better than to say anything, as Leon would only escalate his teasing. Barely two nights passed that he wasn't at the inn, and if it was quiet he'd spend all night talking with Gwen.

Three times they had stayed up after Leon had closed, and Declan was now certain she would sleep with him willingly if he pressed her, but as much as he desired Gwen, he also knew that there was no hope of its being a casual dalliance. She wasn't the sort of woman to lie with any man; having sex would be as good as a marriage proposal, and although he was coming to see it as inevitable, Declan wasn't ready to surrender the illusion of having some say in the matter. He wanted to take the step and make her his wife, but . . . something also held him back.

After he'd drunk half the ale, the door to the kitchen swung open and Gwen emerged holding a large tray. Another girl followed her, one Declan didn't recognize, awkwardly holding a smaller tray and concentrating on not spilling it. She was very slender, even a little under-fed, and as she glanced in his direction, he saw she was pretty: fair skinned with dark hair and large blue eyes. And he realized that she was also very young, perhaps no older than fourteen or fifteen.

"Who's that?" Declan asked Leon just as Gwen caught sight of Declan. She brightened visibly and smiled.

"New girl," said Leon.

"You need a second server?"

"Will eventually," said Leon, fixing Declan with a narrow gaze. Declan had come to know this expression well since arriving in town; it was Leon's suspicious expression. "One of these days, some smart fellow is going to come along and take my girl away." He paused, his lingering stare emphasizing his point. "That is, if someone smart enough to know a rare prize when he sees it shows up." He turned, pulled out a bar rag, and began sopping up spilled ale. "I'll need someone to take her place."

"She's barely more than a child," said Declan as he watched Gwen help the girl place food on the table before the travelers.

"Her ma is having a baby soon, and without her man to provide, she can't care for the extra mouth. So, I let her stay here so she can earn her keep." Lowering his voice he said, "And I let her take the leftovers home to her ma. She has three others younger than her."

Declan shook his head. "Where's her dad?"

"Slavers took him a month or so before you got here. Bold bunch came in and out before the baron's patrol arrived. Some of our lads tried to persuade them to chase the bastards, but the baron's soldiers wouldn't cross the border. I guess he's on some slave block or serving in someone's army by now."

Declan had no words. During his short amount of traveling he had come to understand how safe and well-off he'd been in the Covenant until the slavers had shown up there. "That sort of thing happen much?" he finally asked.

"Not often enough for the baron to build a garrison up here," said Leon with a hint of bile in his tone. Seeing Declan's slightly surprised reaction, he hastily added, "Don't misunderstand me. Baron Daylon is a good ruler compared to most. Taxes aren't impossible to pay, food is plentiful, and trade is brisk. When I first opened this inn, before Gwen was born, I'd be lucky to have two, three travelers a week stop in for a meal or drink. Now I get two or three a day and my rooms are full as many nights.

"No," he said as if putting the matter to rest, "the baron's a good man, but we could really use a garrison; the town's grown big enough. It's more than half a day's ride to Esterly's garrison, and a lot can happen in an hour." He shrugged. "We have no mayor or sheriff, just a local group who settle disputes, and the like, unofficially. It doesn't do any good to call little things to the baron's attention, you see?"

Declan nodded. He knew rough justice was better than none at all. Oncon was so small a village that almost all disputes were settled by consensus, and a few by who was left standing, but most were settled peaceably. Twice in his life he'd seen someone run from the village, to avoid losing their lives, so this sort of local justice wasn't completely alien to him.

Gwen approached. "Declan," she said with a warm smile. She turned to the girl behind her and said, "This is Millie." The girl smiled shyly and nodded a greeting.

Declan gave her a cursory smile and then turned his attention to Gwen. "Busy, I see."

"Yes, very," she replied, then said, "I'll stop for a visit when things calm down. Millie, come with me."

Leon cleared his throat and Declan turned to see another ale waiting for him. "Appears you might be here for a bit."

"So it appears," echoed Declan. He felt a greater fool than ever before. Part of him knew that he was fated to be with Gwen, but he was stubborn enough to resent being told what to do, even though no one was telling him what to do, merely pointing out the obvious.

Feeling a rare moment of petulance, Declan tried to stop his gaze following Gwen around the room, but it was difficult. Their relationship was a poorly kept secret; it had become so obvious that Gwen had set her cap at the new smith that the other young men in town had stopped trying to court her. None of her previous suitors wished to find themselves facing an angry young man who looked like he could win a fight with anyone in Beran's Hill. There was no such thing as a weak smith, and Declan carried himself in a way that communicated he might not have been eager to fight for Gwen, but he was willing.

Declan nursed his ale slowly, for despite being keen to spend time with Gwen, the morning would arrive no matter how little sleep he got. He planned to finish the order of weapons in two days' time and deliver them to Baron Rodrigo's holdfast within the week. He'd sent word to Ratigan that he'd need a large wagon and a team of four the day after he finished, and he also knew Ratigan would complain bitterly if they weren't ready to depart on the day the short teamster arrived. Declan smiled to himself as he realized that despite his cross manner, Ratigan had become something of a friend and Declan actually looked forward to seeing him again.

Thinking about Ratigan took him back to their first journey, which in turn made Declan wonder about Roz. He'd had no word of her since leaving her with her husband to mend. He's asked twice if passing shippers knew of her; one didn't know her and the other only knew her by reputation. He wasn't that surprised as Beran's Hill was far off her normal shipping routes. Still, he wondered how she was doing.

Meeting Gwen had put Declan's feelings in perspective. Roz was a wonderful woman who had taught him everything he knew about sex, but about honest feelings? No: he was learning about those from Gwen.

After half an hour, the room calmed down and Gwen came over, after instructing Millie on clearing tables. "How are you?" she asked with a smile that once again made Declan feel both wonderful and nervous at the same time.

He couldn't help but smile back as he said, "Well. Tired. Getting ready to haul a shipment up to Copper Hills."

Her expression changed. "You'll be gone a while, then?" She looked worried.

"A couple of weeks," he replied. "Jusan can take care of the smithy while I'm gone."

"Travelers warn of bandits lately," she said, putting her hand on his arm. "Be cautious."

"I will be," he said, pleased by her worry. "Ratigan is a tough enough"—he was about to say *bastard,* then caught himself—"fellow, and I know my way around a blade. Besides, we're only using unpatrolled roads for a day or so between here and the frontier. There's a garrison at Middling Vale, then patrolled roads all the way through Kalar up to the border with Copper Hills." Declan had been told this by local merchants, so he hoped it reassured her. He did not want to incur the cost of hiring an additional guard, but if she pressed him on the matter, he probably would. He almost winced when he considered how much her good opinion meant to him.

Further discussion was interrupted by Jusan's arrival. Gwen greeted him and then said, "I'll fetch you an ale, and then I have to go see if that bunch in the corner needs another round."

After she departed, Jusan smiled at his master and said, "Looks like you're having an enjoyable ale."

Declan feigned a disapproving look, then smiled and nodded. "Enjoyable enough."

Gwen returned quickly and put an ale before Jusan, then hurried off to the group in the corner. Jusan glanced over his shoulder to see if Gwen was within earshot, then he said in a low voice, "I know you're my master now, but we've known each other long enough for me to tell you plainly that you're an idiot if you don't do something soon."

"Do? About what?"

"Are you really that slow? You're as much my big brother as you are my master, Declan, but when it comes to Gwen you are a fool. She will not wait forever. Have you realized that other lads are starting to spend time around her when you're not here?"

"How would I know what's going on when I'm not here?" he began, then realized that Jusan was simply keeping up with local gossip. He saw Jusan's expression change and turned to see Millie leaving the kitchen, wiping her hands on her apron. She became aware of Jusan's gaze and blushed, hurrying over to where Gwen was talking to a company of travelers at a corner table. Declan returned his attention to his apprentice, who was almost gaping.

"Who is that?" asked Jusan. Declan glanced back again to see Millie peer past Gwen, then look away. He realized that while she looked very young to him, Millie was only a year or two younger than his apprentice. He saw Leon observing it all with a wry smile and said to no one in particular, "There's something about this inn."

Jusan didn't share Declan's aversion to displaying his interest openly. After watching the boy ignore the drink Gwen had set before him for a full minute, Declan tapped him on the arm.

"What?" asked his apprentice.

"Your ale," said Declan, pointing at the large pewter jack on the table. "Her name is Millie."

"Oh," said the younger man, taking a long pull. Finally he asked, "What do you know about Millie?"

Declan told his apprentice what Leon had told him and Jusan sat staring at the girl while he listened. After he finished, Declan said, "So, now what?"

"I think she's just right," muttered Jusan.

"Right?" Declan's brow furrowed. "For what?"

Jusan looked at his master and said, "For me!"

Declan tried not to laugh. "Is that so?" asked the smith, barely containing his amusement. "Perhaps you should have a conversation with her before you marry the girl."

Jusan looked down, embarrassed, but then looked his master in the eyes. Declan allowed his apprentice a great deal more familiarity than was usual in the trade and accepted the lad's challenging expression without becoming upset.

"I'm not that stupid," said Jusan. "But back in Oncon, I never met a girl . . . I mean, I met them, but . . . you know."

Declan let out a slow sigh. He knew exactly what Jusan meant. Had things not proceeded as they had,

Roz would have no doubt seen to Jusan's instruction, but without accounting specifics, Declan understood that he was the one the girls fancied, the smith, not the boy apprentice.

"Finish your ale and get back to the forge," said Declan to Jusan. "I'm going to linger and have a word with Gwen."

Jusan's expression showed he wasn't happy with the order, but he said nothing as he nodded and took a long pull of his ale.

"I'm certain young Millie took note of your . . . attention," said Declan. "If you didn't scare her to death, I'll find out from Gwen if she's interested in meeting you."

Somewhat mollified by that, Jusan nodded and glanced around the room. Millie must have returned to the kitchen, for he finished his ale and, without a word, stood and left the inn. Declan took a sip of his own ale and wondered if at times he looked as stupid to Gwen as Jusan must have seemed to Millie, and hoped not.

As the last customers departed, Gwen approached Declan and said, "You want anything else?" She sounded tired, perhaps bordering on being cross.

"I thought we could talk?" he said as she removed the empty ale jack before him.

A series of expressions quickly crossed Gwen's face

as she put down the jack. Suddenly, she leaned over and kissed Declan hard on the mouth, then backed away slightly, looked him in the eyes, and softly said, "Declan, you're a sweet man and normally I enjoy our chats, but you are as thick as a brick sometimes. I'm tired, and I still have chores, so get out of here before I get angry."

"Angry?" he sputtered, his face a mask of confusion.

"Either you know what you want, or you don't. I've turned down lads already, and a few of them had rich fathers. I'm tired of waiting for a man too stupid to—" Now visibly close to anger, Gwen continued, "You better know what to say to me when you get back, or I'm going to stop ignoring those rich lads! I'm nineteen years old this summer and should have been married with a baby over the last year. My dad isn't going to keep me here forever. We have a new girl, which means it's time I headed out on my own." She grabbed the empty jack, turned, and left him speechless as he watched her retreating back.

Getting up slowly, Declan departed, wondering what it was he had or hadn't done this time—and, more importantly, what he was going to do. Walking the streets back to his forge, he considered that maybe he should pay more attention to what Jusan was trying to tell him.

18

A Betrayal and Plot

Hatu stood silently in the corner as the masters and preceptors arrived. He had eaten breakfast alone in his room and stayed there until summoned to the main room of the small house, where he had dined the night before.

A semicircle of cushions had been arranged around a low table, and it quickly became obvious who the masters and preceptors were as the men took their seats. The preceptors moved to the corners of the room, and the masters sat on the cushions.

The preceptors were the highest-ranking teachers in Coaltachin and worked on behalf of all the clans and families, for which they were handsomely paid and shown deference by all but the masters. Outside of families and clans, they rose to their position on skill alone and came from all backgrounds. Their one responsibility beyond teaching was to remain neutral in any conflict among the families, who presented the occasional problem, and among the clans, which was rare but not unheard of.

The seven most powerful masters formed the Council. They ruled the nation and were tasked with ensuring that when Coaltachin spoke to the outside world, it did so with one voice. Most of Coaltachin's contact with the outside world occurred through contracts and commissions, most of which involved murder, treachery, espionage, and havoc. The Council controlled trade to and from the island, either through ownership of local businesses or extortion to ensure loyalty and secrecy. The largest source of their wealth came from Coaltachin's control over much of the crime in a large region of the Northern Islands and the eastern cities of North and South Tembria.

Even rarer than the Council overtly acting in a public fashion, was anyone other than a master addressing the seven masters in person. Hatu knew he was about to experience something uncommon, perhaps unique.

A large man with a flushed face, older but powerful looking, came into the room and looked around; seeing Hatu, he took a step toward him.

"Kugal!" said Master Zusara, causing the obviously

angry man to pause. "Please, sit by me." He indicated a cushion next to the one he stood behind. Kugal paused, nodded once, and moved to stand beside his host, and the two men sat.

When the last of the five masters was seated, Master Zusara said, "Welcome. Two of the Council are too far removed to reach us this morning, so it will be for the five of us, assisted by the wisdom of the preceptors, to decide how we shall deal with what you will hear today." He looked at Hatu and with a wave of his hand indicated he should come and stand before the masters.

When he did, Zusara said, "This boy's name is Hatu. He is close to his manhood day. He is from Master Facaria's village; Facaria waits outside, in case we desire his counsel." Looking at Hatu, he said, "Now, take as much time as you need and repeat the story you told me last night."

Hatu battled nervousness, for he had never spoken in front of more than one or two men of rank before, let alone a room full of masters and preceptors, and never about a matter of such gravity. All eyes were fixed on him as he once again began his tale, starting with the assassination of the merchant and ending with being picked up from his slowly sinking boat. Several times near the end he paused to battle back tears, but no one spoke until he was finished.

Then suddenly, Master Kugal shouted, "You left my grandson to die!"

He was halfway off his cushion when Zusara gripped his arm firmly and softly said, "Kugal." There was just enough authority in his voice to cause the bull-necked master to hesitate, then sit back down.

Hatu did not know if Kugal's remark had been a question or an accusation and remained silent. From a corner behind the masters, a voice said, "I don't think he had any choice in the matter, Kugal. From what Hatu has said, Donte was near death when the boy was freed."

Suddenly Hatu realized it was Reza who spoke, transformed enough by his garb and the shadows that Hatu hadn't recognized him when he came into the room.

Zusara nodded in agreement with his youngest son.

"Then why was he alone left alive?" demanded Kugal, pointing at Hatu. "Why was he freed by those witches?" he shouted.

"A very good question," said Zusara. He inclined his head slightly toward his son and said, "We shall have to speculate on that, won't we?"

Reza came forward and motioned for Hatu to follow him outside. They left the main room and took the three steps to the courtyard. Outside, on a stone bench reading some papers, sat Master Facaria, the ruler of Morasel, the island where Hatu had lived during most of his childhood.

Hatu knew he always read every report, account, or message directed to him. He was considered a competent master when it came to running the tiny village of Otashu and his small island, and his main task was to raise the children who would go into field training.

His family was small, and it was possible that when Facaria died, his line would end and his holdings be claimed by another family. The idea another master might take over Morasel seemed odd to Hatu. While each place he visited had its own feel, Morasel felt like . . . home. Hatu couldn't imagine the small island without Master Facaria's careful oversight.

Hatu had wondered what Facaria had been like when he was young; no one rose to the rank of master by simply being a good administrator. To be a master meant that you had bloodied your hands, usually a great deal over many years, and more critically, it meant you had survived attacks from rivals within Coaltachin as well as enemies from without. You either rose to the rank or inherited it, but it took violence to hold what you had. That was the way of Coaltachin.

Facaria looked up from his papers. "Am I needed?" he asked Reza.

Reza shook his head; said, "They'll call if they need any of us"; and sat down on the stone bench next to Facaria. Hatu was left with a patch of ground beneath a shady tree.

Master Zusara said, "Well, there you have it."

There was a moment of silence before Master Kugal said, "He survived and left my grandson to die! He must be hiding something. He must be working with the witches!"

Zusara had a long personal history with Kugal; they had been boys together in the same village, so Zusara was used to his anger and his need to blame others. But despite his many flaws, Kugal was a friend, so Zusara indulged him. "Perhaps," was all he said in response.

Another voice spoke, "What is it you're not telling us, old man?"

Zusara recognized it and that it held a slight humor. "Mikial, I didn't see you arrive."

With a chuckle, the man in the corner said, "There was a time you'd have whipped me, Father, if you had noticed." A tall, powerful-looking man of middle years stepped out of the shadows. "What is it you've not shared with us yet?" Implicit in the question was the idea that the old master of masters was sharing information in such a way as to further his own goals. Zusara was not a king, by any measure, but he was very clever in ensuring he remained first among equals.

"I spoke with the seer last night. She judged the boy a grave danger to us. He is the Firemane child."

Only two of the masters, and none of the preceptors, had known. "Impossible," muttered one, "it's a myth."

"No, it's not only possible, but also true," answered Zusara. "After the Great Betrayal, a nurse at the villa where the Langene family awaited news saw the enemy soldiers coming, grabbed the baby out of his cradle, and gave it to a young girl, who fled down a pathway to the beach. She ran to a village and gave a brooch to a fisherman to take her by boat to the site of the battle."

"Why would she do that?" asked Mikial.

Another master said, "It seems the height of madness to carry the child toward the slaughter."

"I can only speculate," said Zusara. "Perhaps the servant thought the child's father still safe, that the attack on the villa was separate from the battle in the south. We can see the betrayal of the Firemanes from the vantage point of history; she endured but a moment of it." He shrugged. "Or perhaps she was urged by some property of magic the seer warned of, this elemental fire that burns within the boy."

"Burns within—?" began a question from one of the masters.

Zusara held up his hand. "Our role in the Betrayal concerned the battle, not the destruction of the villa and slaughter of the king's family. We only learned of the boy's survival after Master Facaria took Baron Daylon's charge." He shrugged as if it was of little importance. "How he was carried safely is a curiosity but has nothing to do with our charge to care for the boy. He—"

Master Kugal interrupted, almost shouting, "My grandson is dead and that boy lives because of some dark magic. He is in league with those witches! He must die!"

Zusara didn't feel the need to debate the finer points and said simply, "I agree, Kugal, but the seer warned that great destruction could be unleashed on this boy's death. That magic will flow from him . . ." The old master shrugged. "The consequences, she does not know."

"What do you propose?" demanded another master.

"The boy shall die, but far away from here." To his son he said, "Get Facaria; he waits outside with your brother and the boy." To the preceptors he said, "What needs to be discussed is for the masters only."

The preceptors departed and after a moment, Mikial returned with Facaria. He nodded in greeting and said, "I am here, Zusara."

"Tell us of the boy."

"He is angry," said Facaria without hesitation. "He has always been angry; it burned inside him even as a baby. He has learned to control it, to hide it deep within, but it is there. It is a powerful thing."

"Burned inside him," added Zusara.

"We must kill him!" shouted Kugal.

Facaria appeared surprised by the outburst but ignored the reason for it as he responded, "We cannot."

"Why the hell not?" shouted Kugal, even louder. Zusara made a "quiet down" motion with his hand and then inclined his head, as if echoing the question to Facaria.

"We have a contract and must deliver the boy to Lord Dumarch next month," Facaria said.

"*You* have a contract, you mean," said Kugal accusingly. "That battle was your last duty in the field, and you committed us all."

"You took a share of the seven weights of gold a year gladly," was Facaria's calm response.

"So the boy dies," said Kugal. "We send word to Dumarch and that's the end of it. There's no need for him to know the truth of how the boy came to die. Have him fall off a roof or drown fishing; it doesn't matter. He would never know."

"We would know," said Zusara. He sighed heavily. "Our true strength does not lie in all our wealth, nor in our mighty army, or even our noscusara. Our strength lies in our reputation. We cannot violate a contract. Our ability to live as we do rests on both equally, fear and trust. That is why—"

He interrupted himself. To Kugal he said, "How many nocusara do you count among your gangs?"

Kugal said, "You know as well as I do. I have thirty-one."

He quickly asked the same question of the other three masters, who gave similar answers, and then said, "And I have twenty-five. With those clans not in attendance our nocusara number is less than four hundred in total and we have three times as many sicari, scattered across half of Garn.

"We have less than two thousand men and women who can cow armies ten, twenty times their number. It is our reputation that protects them and makes them valuable, not magic skills or more-than-human gifts. It is the *idea* we have magic skills and superhuman gifts that protects us.

"We can *never* break a contract," he finished with quiet steel in his tone.

"I do not care where or when it happens, as long as that boy dies, so if you want to fulfill the contract, then kill him, I will accede to that." Kugal looked around the room as if daring anyone to demand more.

Facaria shrugged. "If the boy dies even a minute after our contract is fulfilled, it is of little importance." In his youth, Facaria had been one of the best of the nocusara, perhaps the best of all the men standing in this council. Even Kugal was forced to admit that it was the one area of knowledge in which Facaria was the most expert. He looked at Facaria for a moment, rage still simmering just below the surface, but finally he gave a curt nod of agreement.

Zusara also gave his agreement with a nod. "One minute would be a little too soon to avoid the look of complicity. And it might also be valuable to discover why Baron Dumarch wishes to keep him alive and a secret. So, how best to accomplish these tasks?"

Facaria said, "Let someone undertake the mission; have them pose as a traveling family, needed in Marquenet. The boy should think it a ruse and believe he is still for us. If they arrive on the appointed day, he can be turned over to the baron's man, and then after a while, when we discover Dumarch's plan, they can kill the boy."

"Who?"

Mikial spoke up. "Let Reza take the youth. They have built up a relationship. Perhaps there is some trust there."

Zusara said, "No. We need another. I want any trouble to fall as far from our families as possible."

Mikial thought for a moment, then looked at Hatu's old village master. "Who does Hatu favor?" he asked Facaria.

"Bodai," he answered without hesitation. "The students like him best of all the masters. He's . . . different."

Zusara nodded. "He is firm but can also be kind. He enjoys teaching, which is why someone hungry for knowledge, like Hatu, would be drawn to him. Where is he now?"

"Somewhere in the west of North Tembria. His village reeve will know."

"Send word we are sending him . . . a problem."

Mikial nodded once. "To reach Marquenet by the appointed time, we must send fast ships."

"Ships?"

"Until we know more about those three ships, I want to ensure the boy gets to Baron Dumarch safely." He was silent for a moment while he considered something. "Sail the Narrows," he said at last, "to the far coast of North Tembria, up to Port Colos, then on to Pashtar. Have Bodai meet Reza and the boy there. Then Reza will depart and Bodai will escort him to the baron. He will be coming from the north, and should anything befall him, that is as removed from us as we can make it."

"Shall Bodai kill the boy?"

Zusara said, "If needed, but I'd like another with them, in case something runs afoul."

Mikial looked at Facaria and said, "Is there another student, one in the nocusara, he trusts?"

"He is a boy with few friends; that temper of his . . . and his closest companion"—he glanced at Kugal, whose expression darkened at reference to Donte—"is dead." Facaria shook his head. "There is no nocusara he knows well enough to trust. He was returning from his first unsupervised mission when he was taken."

"He mentioned a girl," said Zusara.

"Hava," Facaria supplied, nodding. "They are close, and she was also friends with Donte. Separating the three of them was a problem from time to time." Facaria looked down, lost in thought for a moment. "I believe he is attracted to her. However, I'm not certain he understands his desires; his other feelings are often overwhelmed by his deep anger." He paused as if considering the girl. After a moment, he said, "She is not sicari yet, but she is very good; I have marked her to join the nocusara."

"Where is she now?" asked Zusara.

"She is on my island. She returned from training

with the Powdered Women. From reports, she's not naturally gifted and needs more instruction, or . . ." He shrugged. "Some are not suited for that type of duty."

He glanced at Kugal, who furrowed his brow. Unlike most other masters, Kugal forbade his sons and grandsons from being trained by the Powdered Women. He said it was fine for other families, but it was not the way of a warrior. The other masters found his attitude peculiar, but each master was in charge of his own family, so no one challenged him. Most thought he denied his family potentially useful agents.

Kugal attempted to salvage some dignity from the moment and said, "Facaria is right. Some are not suited for that sort of work." He fell silent, still fuming.

Zusara frowned at the digression. "Is this the girl who killed the assassin?"

Facaria nodded once.

"You think she is fit to become sicari?"

"She has the skills, but I am not yet certain she possesses the temperament. If she does, she will be very worthy."

"Could she kill the boy?"

Facaria shrugged. "I don't know. She has the skill, but again, temperament? Defending herself was impressive, but to murder a friend?" He shrugged. "At the

least she can distract him if we need to send another."
He fell silent for a moment, then said, "He would be
better than any student I've had, but his anger gets
in the way; when he keeps his wits about him, he is
faster and more dangerous than any boy I've seen at the
school. Were he one of us, I would suggest his training
for the nocusara start now. He should be able to best
her in everything, running, fighting, anything, but
sometimes she gets the best of him. As I said, I think
he desires her . . . or more."

"More?"

"He may have further romantic notions."

"Ah," said Zusara. "You may be right. He mentioned
her in passing, but . . ." He was silent as he thought,
then said, "Yes, send for her. If you leave as soon as
she arrives, you should have little trouble reaching the
baron's keep on the appointed day." Glancing at the
masters in the room, he said, "Do we have any agents
in Marquenet?"

A slightly built man, Master Rengara, nodded. "I
have a crew."

Zusara raised an eyebrow. "An entire crew? Why
did I not know that?"

Rengara shrugged off the question. "Not Council
business."

Zusara fixed the younger master with his narrow gaze for a moment. Rengara would not have been the first of them to carve out his own enterprise and deny his fellow masters their cut. "We'll discuss that later. Right now I need you to send them word. We'll wait for the girl to come down from Facaria's village and when she, Reza, and the boy arrive in Marquenet I want them alerted to Reza's arrival. We'll stage a little mummery at the appropriate time."

"Why bother with all this?" demanded Kugal, his temper getting the best of him again. "Get the boy to the city so Facaria can rest at night knowing his contract is fulfilled, then kill him!"

Looking at his old friend as if he was tired of repeating himself, Zusara used a tone that would serve a slow-witted student. "As I said before, we do not know what interest Baron Dumarch has in this boy, why he gave him over to us for protection rather than keep him in his own city. We must discover his motives, and nothing must tie us to the boy's death. Am I making myself understood?"

Kugal stiffened, unused to being addressed in such a fashion, but after a moment, he sank back into the cushion and nodded that he understood. He had lost enough debates with Zusara over the years to know he had also lost this one. Zusara was first among equals; someone might challenge his implicit authority one day, but not today.

"One more thing before we adjourn," said Zusara. "The three ships?"

A master named Tagaga, built heavily, like a worker, with dark eyes that were set in a perpetual squint, glanced around the room. "Rounders?"

The Rounders were pirates, called that because of the massive circular wind pattern that ran through the islands. They would sail from the north through the Northern Islands, head south across the Narrows, then westward through the southern islands, then turn north and up the eastern coast of South and North Tembria, and somewhere before the ice floes, turn eastward until they started their circle again. It made it very easy for pirates to intercept trade.

"I do not know of many bands who sail three ships in a squadron," said Zusara.

"And what if they are in league with those witches?" suggested Kugal.

Zusara was relieved to see Donte's grandfather inclined to spread the responsibility for his grandson's death, alleviating some blame from Hatu's shoulders; it wouldn't change his fate, but it would keep Kugal from nagging Zusara about it. "Perhaps, but let us not assume there is a relationship until it's proven. I'm more concerned about a pirate squadron that does not flee upon sighting the Coaltachin banner than I am about the remote possibility of their being in league with the Sisters of the Deep. That magic . . ." He shook his head. "We may well have to deal with those witches someday, but right now having ships that challenge us in our own waters is the immediate threat."

The other masters murmured agreement. "Send word to all our agents in the islands and along the coast of North Tembria; we need any hint of who owns those ships. Any possible sighting needs to be reported, even if it seems trivial," said Zusara. "There are a few who would attempt to take one of our ships, but they are gone and so we needn't name them."

The masters glanced around, nodding in agreement. Coaltachin had very few enemies, all well-known to the Council, but there was one enemy they feared the most, and they were all reluctant to speak of them.

Facaria said, "I disagree. We needn't name those lost to us, but we need to be cautious if it is indeed they who now prowl our waters."

Kugal seemed ready to launch another angry outburst, but his demeanor changed suddenly and instead he let out an audible sigh. "Facaria is right. Those who . . . left . . . in our grandfathers' grandfathers' time, they are like us." He looked around the room. "And I've had reports from some of my crews. Not one thing or another, just . . . hints that someone could be near."

Master Tagaga said, "Could you be any more unclear? Spit it out, Kugal."

Kugal looked ready to explode again, even come across the table at Tagaga, who looked more than ready for a physical confrontation should it come to that.

"Masters!" scolded Zusara.

Kugal looked at Zusara and said, "Fine. Those who refused to obey the Council and went south, only to be lost in the Ten Thousand Islands, may be returning."

"How would you know?" demanded Tagaga.

"Little things. Someone's nibbling around the edges of some of my crews in the south. Someone very clever. We think she is called the Spider."

"She?"

Kugal shrugged. "Some of my crew captains say it is a woman. Maybe it's misdirection, but the crews we have encountered were not the usual street thugs and bullies. They have some art; it's well hidden but there."

"Have you been openly challenged?" asked Zusara.

"No, but . . ." Kugal sat back, shaking his head. "Something is coming. I can feel it."

Zusara paused, then said, "We shall wait and discuss this when the other members of the Council have returned, and send word now to those we trust the most to stay alert and report any hint of . . . our brothers' return."

Looking at Rengara, he said, "And no more of this 'it's not the Council's business' and establishing crews where none of us knew you had any. We need to know about any hint of a threat, like this 'Spider.' It may be nothing, but it may . . ." He lowered his voice and said, "Azhante."

Just the utterance of the word caused the other masters to become still and attentive. Their expressions revealed they wished they had not heard that word.

Zusara made a gesture, closing off further discussion. "And if there is a line from those ships to the witches we will discover it soon enough. The day will come when we must put an end to those filthy cannibal women, but that day is not today.

"Now, let us return to the matter of the boy and his short future. Does anyone have anything to add to what we have decided here?" When no one spoke, he glanced from face to face, then without another word nodded, indicating that the meeting was over.

The masters arose and departed, Kugal and Tagaga exchanging dark looks as they left the room. As Facaria passed, Zusara said, "Tell the boy to be ready to travel tomorrow, if you will."

The old master nodded and inclined his head to Mikial as he left, and the young man moved to stand beside his father.

When Zusara and his eldest son were alone Mikial asked, "Why does this feel far more dangerous than it should?"

The old master nodded slightly in agreement. "I don't know, but it does reek of risk." Letting out a slow deep breath, Zusara said, "The seer has limits, and she doesn't always speak clearly of what she sees, so the scope of the danger is unknown, and that troubles me more than I can say."

Mikial reached out and gave his father's shoulder a squeeze, then said, "I'll tell Reza what he is to do with the boy." He turned and left.

Alone for a moment, Zusara looked around the largest room of his small home, at the place where he spent most of his time. He found no reassurance in the familiar surroundings because in his heart he knew that the threat they faced was far greater than he was willing to share with his son.

Facaria saw Hatu waiting alone near a tree, taking advantage of the shade in the noon heat. Reza lay nearby, on his back with his eyes closed as if he was napping. Facaria motioned for Hatu to walk with him, and a few steps down the path from Zusara's home, said, "Reza is sleeping?"

Hatu tried not to smile. "I doubt it, and he may well ask me to recount our conversation as soon as you depart."

"Departure is what I wish to speak with you about, and there is little time."

Mikial left the building and a moment later Reza was on his feet. The elder brother motioned for Hatu to approach them and Master Facaria followed.

Mikial said, "Reza, you and the boy will leave on the morning tide. Father instructed me to tell you what needs to be done."

Facaria said, "Ah, so we honor the contract."

Mikial said, "We honor the contract, yes."

Facaria handed Hatu a travel bag. "As he won't be leaving until the morning and I am leaving as soon as I reach the docks, he can carry an old man's bag one last time." He motioned for Hatu to follow him and turned away.

Hatu caught Reza begin to object, but Mikial said, "Be back as soon as you're finished, Hatushaly."

When they were beyond hearing, Facaria said, "They may be Zusara's boys, but I am still a master."

He looked at Hatu for a long moment and then said, "They will ask you what we spoke of. You will shrug and say that an old man prattled on about life."

"Sir?"

"You are part of my last class of students, Hatu." The old master let out a deep sigh of regret. "Yes, you, Donte, and the others, you are my last class. Soon, I will no longer be the master who controls Morasel. They will let me keep my house, but my family will be assimilated into another. I have no male offspring and my only remaining daughter is married to another master, so she is part of his family now."

Hatu kept pace with the old man, who walked with purpose, if slowly. He did not know what to say.

"I am the oldest master alive in Coaltachin," said Facaria. "There is an adage that age brings wisdom. If that were true, you would not be here, walking me to the boat that will take me home to wait for death's appearance."

Hatu was alarmed. He was on the verge of speaking when Facaria held up a hand, cutting him off.

"When I was your age," he said, "and I left my home to travel and learn from those older and more knowledgeable, I imagined I would either live forever or die gloriously in service to my people." He shrugged and smiled ruefully. "Little did I dream that on my retirement day, I would be the last of my class left alive. Zusara is nearly ten years younger than me and was part of a crew I once ran for a little while when he was your age."

Facaria stared off in the distance as they walked. "All my brothers, sons, nephews, all the male members of my family died before me. My wife died years ago. I do not even have a granddaughter to marry off to some promising lad able to take on the task of leading a family, even a small one such as mine."

They reached the main road down to the city and kept walking at a steady pace. Hatu knew what he was hearing was important, though he didn't know why, so he focused his attention.

Approaching the outer edge of Corbara, Facaria said, "You will be told things when you reach Marquenet, things which should make the mystery of your early life clear to you. I would tell you, but . . ." The ancient master paused and then asked, "Did Zusara call me an old woman at any time?"

Hatu simply nodded, afraid to anger a master by speaking out of turn.

Facaria laughed. "He used to call me that when we were young." He walked slowly, lost in thought for a moment, then said, "We are nearing the end, Hatushaly."

"Sir?" said Hatu, clearly showing he did not understand.

"Everything has a life span; some are very long, like those of nations. The Five-Kingdom Covenant lasted over two hundred years, longer if you consider the peaceful period that allowed the Treaty of the Covenant to be forged.

"Men often dream their creations will endure, live forever, but everything dies, eventually." He pointed into the distance, where a faint mountain peak could be seen rising through the day's haze on the north side of the island. "That mountain will be worn away someday; even the staunchest rocks succumb to rain and wind. It is the way of things." He glanced heavenward and said, "Who knows? Perhaps someday the very stars will die."

They were now entering the outskirts of the city and Facaria had to raise his voice a little but still managed to keep the conversation just between them. "So, Hatu, this is an ending, too."

"What, master? I really don't understand."

Facaria smiled. "You will someday, perhaps even soon. Now, a question: Hava? You are close?"

Hatu could not help the color that rose in his cheeks. "She and Donte . . ." He felt a stab of pain even mentioning his lost friend. "She's my best friend."

"You trust her?"

Hatu nodded.

"Don't," said Facaria. "When you reach Marquenet and learn what Baron Daylon will tell you, then make up your mind about who you will trust. I fear you will be uncertain, but trust your instincts; they are all you have. Sometimes they are all any of us have."

Hatu's confusion was obvious. Facaria stopped and gestured for Hatu to follow him into a relatively quiet doorway on the busy street. "That upsets you. Why?"

Hatu was hesitant, then said, "She's my friend."

Facaria studied Hatushaly for a moment and then shook his head. "I've watched you three grow up, you, Donte, and Hava. She is more than a friend."

Hatu shrugged, at a loss for words.

Facaria sighed theatrically. "Did Zusara give you his talk on not falling in love? Did he say that women will only weaken you?"

Hatu nodded, afraid to speak through the emotions roiling inside him, anger, confusion, and many others he could not name.

"That little hypocrite," he said with a regretful smile. "He's not only fallen in love, he's done it twice. At the same time!" Facaria chuckled. "Still, his heart was in the right place when he warned you not to get involved with any woman in the Quelli Nascosti." He studied Hatu's face for a moment, then asked, "Did he tell you why?"

"That should she become pregnant—"

Facaria cut him off with a simple wave. "That is nonsense. It can be a problem, yes, but that's not why students are forbidden to be together."

Hatu fell silent, then finally asked, "What is the reason, then, master?"

Facaria chuckled. "Sex can be a powerful glue, boy, and if you love someone truly, you're bound to that person." He looked at Hatu as they entered the market, the very last one Hatu, Donte, and Hava had watched from a nearby roof, in what seemed now like a lifetime ago. "Now, do you know why we wish you to avoid that?"

Hatu shook his head.

"Because those who rise to sicari, or even higher, to nocusara, must put their nation and their family first. In the old tongue, our female nocusara, the assassins who pose as concubines, wives, and, courtesans, are called noconochi. It was death to any man of the nocusara who took such a woman as his lover. For the fighters like your friend Hava, a female sicari, we had other names, but in the end the rule was applied in the same way.

"'You cannot be loyal to two masters' is an old

saying. And it is true of a master and a spouse, so we try to keep you from having to make that choice.

"If you are serving with someone you love and find you must leave them behind, condemn them to death or capture, to complete your mission . . ." He waved his hand around the market as they moved toward the streets leading to the docks. "Now do you see?"

Hatu said nothing. He recalled how he felt leaving Donte behind, then realized he couldn't imagine making that choice with Hava. After a moment he nodded that he understood.

He was silent until they saw the docks and the ships in the harbor beyond. "Master, if I am not born of Coaltachin, why—" Hatu struggled to find words.

"Why did we raise you as one of our own?"

"Yes, master, if I am never to be of the Quelli Nascosti, why wasn't I . . . just given an apprenticeship in a common trade?"

"I was charged with raising you as a child in my family's household. Because I am a man of my word and a master, this meant I had to treat you as if you were my son or nephew"—he smiled very slightly—"niece or daughter, as I have all of you who were once students on our island.

"It would be false to say that I have developed any special affection for you, Hatushaly. You were certainly one of the more interesting students in my school, but my affection for students began to die with my sons and the rest of my family.

"But I am certain you are to play a role in the future of Coaltachin, and while I am unsure whether your part will be for good or ill, it was my duty to give you as much knowledge as I could to perform it." He reached the edge of the docks and said, "Now, return to Zusara's home and enjoy his wife's cooking, and remember that everything he said about women was a lie, and that your task from now on is to sift lies from truth.

"Reza is clever, so share no hint of what we have talked about, and when Hava joins you—"

"Hava is coming with us?" blurted Hatu, interrupting Master Facaria. Catching his loss of manners, he added, "Apologies, master. I beg your forgiveness."

Facaria nodded. "It is a small thing. I would never have brought you back together, but perhaps it is a good thing. She will be charged with watching you, so I charge you to watch her.

"This may be my last visit here, Hatushaly. It is certainly the last time I shall see your face. May whatever gods you favor, favor you in return." He held out his hand and Hatu put the master's travel bag in it, and then watched as the old man turned and walked toward the waiting ship.

For a long time, Hatu stood motionless; then he released the long breath he hadn't realized he'd been holding in and turned to find his way back to Master Zusara's home. He tried to keep himself calm, but his heart pounded from the news that Hava was coming. He forced himself to keep a steady walk, despite his unexplained urge to run through the streets.

19

A Change in the Wind

The wagon bumped along the dusty road as the four mules slowed to go up the next incline while the afternoon sun baked the landscape.

Declan and Ratigan both wore straw hats, Ratigan's old and worn, and Declan's purchased before they left, from an old woman who made them for the workers in the vineyards, orchards, and fields around the city of Marquenet. He was grateful that Ratigan had suggested it, for the heat wave was unrelenting and a felt or leather hat would have provided little relief.

Ratigan turned to Declan. "Look at the end of the road."

Declan saw nothing at the top of the rise. "What?"

"Dust. Someone's stirring up dust just out of sight."

As soon as Ratigan said that, Declan saw it. A small

cloud of dust swirled just above the hill ahead of them, clearly indicating someone was moving around on the other side.

"Bandits?" asked Declan, shifting his sword so it could be in his hand in an instant.

"This close to Copper Hills' border? Unlikely."

Declan kept his hand on the hilt of his sword and prayed silently that if it was bandits, they had no archers. He'd face anyone with a sword, but he hadn't developed the knack of dodging arrows yet.

As they topped the rise, they saw a small contingent of soldiers dressed in the garb of a Copper Hills regiment, reddish-brown tabards with a black hammer in a fist embroidered on them. Declan had seen Baron Rodrigo wear a similar uniform. The dust was caused by a small group of wagons pulling away from their makeshift checkpoint.

Ratigan said, "Ah, that makes sense. They don't want to set up the roadblock at the crest, because folks would just spot it, and then they'd have a long chase." He flicked the reins and clicked his tongue loudly, and the horses set off briskly downhill.

They reached the checkpoint as an old soldier wearing the chevrons of a sergeant over his breast held up his hand for them to rein in. Ratigan slowed the wagon and another soldier moved to hold the reins of their lead horse, patting him reassuringly on the nose while the sergeant approached.

"Hello, Sergeant."

"What's in the wagon?" asked the bored-looking old fighter.

"Weapons," answered Ratigan.

"For the baron," added Declan quickly as the sergeant's expression first moved to concern, then relaxed.

"You the lad from Beran's Hill?"

Declan nodded.

"I was told you'd be coming soon."

"Why the early stop?" asked Declan.

The sergeant's shrug communicated that he knew but wasn't about to share that intelligence with them. He stepped aside and motioned the wagon forward.

As they headed toward the distant city of Copper Hills, Declan said, "What do you think that was about?"

"Nothing good," said Ratigan. "I've only been up here twice before, and things are usually calm once you're inside the border. Patrols and road stops are a sign something isn't as it should be. Smugglers, maybe, or perhaps they're looking for outlaws. Something is up, or we wouldn't have been stopped."

"Seems odd," said Declan. "Why so far from the city?"

"I don't know," the young teamster replied. "You get

to learn things traveling around; it's what I call 'reading the road,' getting a sense of who is going where, what goods people are shipping. If things are free and easy, and there is no trouble around, it's usually perishables like meat and fruit, but if there's a chance that trade will slow, then you see packed beans, salted pork, things that will last longer."

Ratigan reached back and patted the canvas that covered the swords Declan had made. "A hundred swords? I know the baron's arms master died and it was a while before he found a new smith, but if you want this many swords in a hurry . . ." He looked over at Declan. "Someone's making ready for a fight, and a big one at that."

After an hour they spied someone walking along the verge of the road, a slender figure in a dusty grey robe with its hood thrown back. He carried a staff in his right hand and had a small pack slung over his left shoulder. From the glistening sheen on his head, he was either bald or had shaved his pate for some reason. As they neared, he turned and regarded the two men on the wagon.

Ratigan said, "A mendicant friar."

"Mendicant?" asked Declan.

"Vow of poverty; he lives off what people give him. Tathan, I'm guessing from the shaved head."

"Mendicant?" Declan repeated as the wagon caught up with the hiker.

"You get to learn things traveling around, I told you.

"Friar!" Ratigan said loudly enough to be heard over the wagon's clatter.

The thin monk smiled and inclined his head. "Blessings, travelers." He made a gesture of benediction that Declan recognized as one common to clerics of Tathan the Pure, now called the Harbinger of the One.

"Copper Hills?" asked Ratigan.

"Yes, brother," answered the friar.

"If you don't mind sitting on some hard crates, you can ride with us," offered Ratigan. Declan's eyes narrowed, and Ratigan whispered, "Luck." He reined in the horses, and the slender hiker quickly scrambled aboard.

"It's a kindness," said the friar once he found a relatively comfortable perch in the rear of the wagon. "I'm Friar Catharian."

Declan nodded in greeting while Ratigan introduced them.

As Ratigan urged the horses forward again, Declan asked, "What takes you to Copper Hills, Friar?"

"The whims of God, I must confess. My order travels, spreading the Word, and I never know from day to day where my journey will lead. Word did reach me, however, of a new church being built in Copper Hills."

"Church?" asked Declan.

"Temple," whispered Ratigan. "The Church of the One . . ."

"I thought church is what you called your . . ." Declan found himself lost for words.

Friar Catharian smiled. "I understand the confusion. The Church is all of the faithful, one in spirit and mind, if not in body. It is also what we call our places of worship, for they are where we gather together."

Declan nodded as if he understood and decided to pursue the matter no further. Matters of religion only confused him. From Edvalt's meager teachings he had learned that when near a shire you dropped a coin in a box in the hope that it would bring you some kind of luck. Beyond that, he was completely ignorant about matters of belief, and he preferred it that way.

"Where you coming from, Friar?" asked Ratigan.

"Soladar, and before that Jebank." Both cities were inland, to the east.

"What news?" asked Ratigan in a friendly fashion.

"I pay little attention to gossip," said the friar, and instantly Declan assumed the opposite to be the case. He had learned, when living in Oncon, that travelers often bartered news and gossip for food or service. More than once Marius, the innkeeper, had traded a meal, drinks, or a sleeping mat under a table for a good story to keep the locals happy and buying more ale than usual.

Declan nodded, as if agreeing with the friar. "Who needs tales that are probably made up to cadge a meal or drink, right, Friar?"

Catharian's face showed only a flicker of annoyance, but it was enough for Declan to recognize that the dig had struck home. "Well," said the friar after a moment, "occasionally, a telling may need a little embellishment to emphasize the importance of the story." He looked away as if scanning the horizon.

Declan and Ratigan burst out laughing, and were joined by Catharian a moment later. When they'd caught their breath, Declan said, "Fairly put, Friar. When our business with Baron Rodrigo is done, I'll happily stand you a meal." He glanced at Ratigan. "Where are we staying?"

"I have no idea," said Ratigan. "Both times before it was Milrose who picked the inns, and I don't even remember their names. Once we deliver our goods, we'll find one."

Declan looked surprised. "I thought you'd been everywhere, knew everything."

"I only claim to have been everywhere, know everything," said the pugnacious teamster. "Doesn't mean it's so."

Catharian laughed. "If you have business with the baron, take the high road from his castle when you're done, go through the north gate, and turn left at the market square, and you'll find a large inn a few blocks from the western gate. You'll know it by the sign of three rams prancing above a greensward. If you get lost, ask anyone where to find the Prancing Rams."

"Fair enough," said Ratigan.

"We'll see you there?" asked Declan.

"When we arrive, I too have duties, but I'll meet you there after sundown and take up your generous offer of a meal."

Catharian and Ratigan bantered and swapped stories while Declan listened, silently amused, until they came within sight of the city of Copper Hills. "There she is," said the friar. "It's been seven years since I was last here."

"That's a fair while," said Declan.

"Enough time so memories fade," said the friar. "There were still some old believers who . . . put up a fuss, when my order first came here, and while I was not part of the Church Adamant, I was blamed the same."

"Church Adamant?" asked Declan.

Catharian said, "A martial order serving the church, but they took different vows than those of us who are ordained. You can't miss them. They carry pure white shields and wear black tabards marked with a single white circle signifying the One God, with no beginning or end."

Ratigan said nothing, but Declan nodded. "Why would they be here?"

The friar shrugged. "Why would they be anywhere? They have many men with swords, willing to do whatever the Church tells them to do in the name of God."

"Nothing terrifying in that," muttered Ratigan.

Catharian ignored the jibe. "If they're in Copper Hills it's because they expect trouble. There's a fair-sized Kes'tun population in this area, more to the north in the foothills and mountains, and they still hold fast to their beliefs." He made a circling motion with his finger, which Declan took to be some sort of new holy gesture, perhaps a warding against evil. "And Baron Rodrigo has allowed the building of a new church and a prelature to house an episkopos."

"We heard about that down in Marquenet," said Declan.

"A big city where the law is enforced and things stay under control," said Catharian. "Up here it's a little rougher. If any of the locals object to the new way of things and Baron Rodrigo can't keep order, the church will have its own means of protecting itself."

Declan nodded and looked ahead to see a faint dark

spot on the horizon that he was certain would turn out to be their destination. He kept his thoughts to himself but wondered what else that small army of faithful soldiers would do for the church if the baron didn't keep order. For no reason he could put his finger on, he felt a sudden churning discomfort in his stomach.

As they arrived, Declan said, "This is an odd city."

Ratigan shrugged. "The way I hear it," he said, "some of the ancient mining communities that were around here built roads between their towns, and all manner of byways and markets sprouted up and kind of grew around the baron's keep up ahead."

Sprawling was the only word that described the layout of the town. There was no single outer wall, as in Ilagan or Marquenet; instead they had to pass through a series of walled-off sections, four gates, to reach the outer wall of the castle. The central building was situated on a hill that gave it only a little elevation. Declan's sense of things was that this keep and the surrounding castle grounds had been built for the rulers to pull back to and dig in, not be a position from which to launch a defense of the larger city. Should an enemy reach the city of Copper Hills, it would be every man, woman, and child for themselves while the baron hunkered down for a siege.

He knew little of warfare, despite knowing a great deal about making weapons. Over the years, some of his conversations with Edvalt had touched upon a story here or there about this battle or that, but all Declan had been left with was the certainty of his own ignorance. In this case, however, he had seen enough of other cities' defenses to know should a powerful enemy turn his gaze upon Copper Hills, it would be a place quickly taken.

Twice, Declan and Catharian had to get out of the wagon and push when the mud came up halfway to the wheel hubs. Both men were filthy by the time they reached the main streets. Even then the going was difficult, as the rains had come the day before and slick cobblestones covered the oldest part of town.

As they rounded a corner that would put them on the road leading to the castle, Catharian said, "See that sign?" He pointed at a fading sign of three white rams above a greensward.

"The Prancing Rams," said Declan.

"I'll wait for you there," said the friar with a wave.

"Shouldn't be much more than an hour, two at the most," said Ratigan. As they pulled away, he said to Declan, "Odd fellow, isn't he?"

"I like him," said the blacksmith. "Not quite sure why, but he's got an easy way about him."

"So do most of the mountebanks and swindlers I've chanced across," said Ratigan with a chuckle. "Some of the most evil men I've met were likable."

They rode in relative silence; Declan gawked at the city sights as they approached the keep. Copper Hills was different from any old town he had seen. Rather than the nicer homes and shops usually located near a keep, seedier establishments were encamped beneath the walls. Taverns abounded, as did stalls of gamblers and sellers of mysterious wares. Declan caught only hints of their produce as they rode past. Prostitutes were out in the day, some servicing clients in doorways or down alleys for any passerby to see. Two men were fighting at a corner, surrounded by men who urged them on.

"Bit rough-and-tumble around here," said Ratigan. "Only been up to the castle once before, and from what I was told, the first baron who built the first keep kept drugs, drink, whores, and gambling close at hand, and the tradition stuck. The well-off built their homes over there"—he pointed westward—"so all the filth and stench stays downwind."

"I've never seen such a city," said Declan, seriously amazed and slightly embarrassed. He was hardly a prudish man—growing up on the edge of farming country meant an early introduction to sex, and the town girls had helped once he was old enough—but to see sex, drinking, and fighting in public shocked him. He was surprised by his own reaction.

Looking over at Declan, Ratigan grinned. "Wait until after dark."

"Not sure I want to," said Declan with a slight chuckle.

"That place we dropped our friar friend off seems a little more civilized," suggested the teamster.

He urged the wagon up the road until he reined in the horses before the guards at the keep entrance. The gate stood wide open, but he was halted by a sentry with an upraised hand.

"What's your business?"

"Weapons for the baron," answered Ratigan.

"Drive them up to the stabling yard and you'll see the armory right in front of you." He waved them on as he shouted to a soldier stationed at the top of the rise, "Pass word to the master-at-arms! Weapons!" He pointed at the wagon, and the other guard nodded, turned, and ran off.

The sun was sinking in the west and shadows grew longer, so the castle's grim aspect was now thrown into even deeper contrasts of dark and light. To Declan's eye, the place was a hodgepodge of buildings erected in some arbitrary order; he assumed there was a design, but it wasn't apparent.

A central tower dominated the castle, but the surrounding walls, buildings, and shorter towers seemed to have been built in haphazard fashion. Declan saw men hurrying about one task or another; most wore tabards, but he noticed a variety of dress and armor. Some servants and townsfolk also could be seen, but for the most part, the castle of Copper Hills seemed an uninspiring place.

"Ugly heap, isn't it?" said Ratigan, and Declan laughed. The teamster had a knack for cutting to the heart of the matter.

They reached the armory and saw a broad-shouldered, older man come out through the door. A fringe of bushy grey hair stretched around his head, matching his eyebrows and a mustache that looked like the end of a broom, and every other part of him looked old, tough, and tested. His manner told Declan that this was a man you wanted no dealings with; if trouble arose, you would have to kill him before he killed you.

"What have we here?" he asked. His accent was strange to Declan's ear; he used thick slurring vowels and a rolling "R" that made it sound as if he were swallowing his words as he spoke them. "I'm Collin, master-at-arms for Baron Rodrigo."

"I'm Declan Smith. I have weapons from Beran's Hill," responded Declan as he climbed down. "The baron placed the order with me four weeks ago."

Declan moved to untie the canvas covering and as he did so he realized he'd heard Collin's accent before. The master-at-arms was Kes'tun, one of the mountain people to the north. They were legendary mountain fighters, fiercely independent and bound by a code of honor that left many men dead on the ground. To find one of their soldiers in service outside their mountains was rare, but once they gave a pledge of service they would die for their lord.

Declan threw back the canvas, climbed into the wagon, and picked up a hammer nestled between the crates. He used the claw to pry open the nearest box, took out a sword, and handed it down to the master-at-arms.

The big man twirled it like an expert, and Declan could see that Collin wasn't simply showing off; he was judging the blade's balance. Common swords were quickly fashioned and often lacked balance. Too much weight at the pommel, and not enough force would be delivered; too much weight in the blade, and the arm would fatigue quickly.

"Bring me an iron spike," commanded the master-at-arms. When a soldier returned with it, he pointed to an old tree stump and said, "Put it there!"

The soldier had barely gotten his hand out of the way when the master-at-arms took a powerful over-hand swing and cut its length in half. He had to yank hard to release the blade from the old hardened wood, and when it was free he inspected its edge. He ran his thumb along the edge and nodded. Then he grinned at Declan, "Geur!" he exclaimed in his native tongue. "Now, this is a blade that'll deliver a proper insult!" To Declan he said, "How many did the baron order?"

"Forty," said Declan.

The master-at-arms made a sour expression, halfway between a frown and a wince. "Need more than that. How long for another forty?"

Declan shrugged. "Another month, perhaps a bit more, plus travel time." He looked around. "The baron had me believe I was just supplementing your supply while you found another master smith."

"Haven't found one yet. All the good ones are taken or off in the east crafting for Sandura and their bunch." He looked at the sword on Declan's hip and said, "You know how to use that or is it for show?"

"Well enough that I'm still here," said the young smith, wondering what was coming next.

"Draw your sword," said the master-at-arms. "I've a mind to see what you know."

Not feeling inclined to argue and wishing to be paid, Declan nodded, drew his sword, and said, "Let's get this over with. It's been a long trip."

"Take a position."

Declan raised the blade above his head with two hands, in what Edvalt had told him was the "perch of the falcon," a slightly more advantageous position when you were uncertain where the attack would come from, high or low. "Ready," he said.

Declan blocked high as an overhand swing descended upon him; the blow wasn't designed to injure Declan, but it could have if he hadn't been ready. The strike from the master-at-arms sent shock through his arms into his shoulders and he parried the blow, let their blades slide a bit, then disengaged and twisted his own blade to return the assault.

Steel rang out as the two men traded blows. After a few minutes, the master-at-arms stepped back, saying, "Enough." He inspected his sword, then said, "Show me that blade."

He took the sword from Declan's hand, took a quick look, then tossed it hilt-first back to the young smith. Declan put up his sword while the master-at-arms tossed his own to a nearby soldier, who caught it easily.

Stepping close to Declan, he said, "Where are you staying?"

"At an inn called the Prancing Rams."

"I know it. Go there now and when I have seen that these beauties are properly put away, I'll find the baron and get your money, and meet you there. I'm of a mind to give you a special order."

"So we don't see the baron?"

"Not usually," said the master-at-arms. "I'm supposed to tell you he's out hunting, but the truth is he's more likely to be somewhere on the edge of the city pumping some farmer's daughter. Never in my life met any man more a slave to young ass than that one. Still, it is what it is. By the time he returns, you'll have settled in, and I'll catch up to you by supper. Go now."

He turned away without another word and Declan looked over to where Ratigan waited. The men exchanged questioning looks. Declan climbed on the seat next to Ratigan as the soldiers unloaded the last of the swords. Then Ratigan slowly turned the wagon around and headed back toward the city.

Ratigan, Catharian, and Declan had finished their first round of ale and were working on the second when Collin entered the Prancing Rams. It was a pleasant enough establishment from what little Declan knew of inns, but the second the large soldier entered, the tone of the common room changed completely. Conversation fell away to a near-whisper and men seemed to hunker down a little, making themselves more inconspicuous.

Collin glanced around the room, saw Declan, and walked over to him, pushing past a knot of men standing between a table and the bar. Black looks followed but not a word was uttered.

Reaching their table, he motioned for Declan to follow him. Without looking back to see if the smith did as he was asked, the master-at-arms for Copper Hills moved to a deserted corner of the inn beneath the staircase leading up to the next floor. He turned as Declan reached him and said softly, "That sword you wear, it's noble steel?"

Declan hesitated, then nodded.

"I know of only one smith who could fashion such."

"Edvalt Tasman, once my master," said Declan.

A wide smile split the old soldier's craggy features. "It's as I thought. I saw your blade cut through an iron spike without shattering, so I knew the quality of the steel, but when I saw the nicks your blade made in the one I held . . . it was unexpected."

He looked at Declan for a long minute, then said, "I knew Edvalt, years ago, when we were campaigning with Baron Daylon Dumarch. We shared a fair bit of mud and blood in those days. Good man, who I got to know when he mended a sword for me. So what I need to know is, can you fashion blades like the one you're holding?"

Declan's eyes narrowed as if he didn't fully comprehend the question. "I made this one, master-at-arms . . . sir."

"My name is Collin. I mean, something Edvalt once said led me to believe that making these takes time, or special . . . magic. I don't know what, but it's why they're so dear and so rare. So what I should ask is how many can you make and how soon?"

Declan was wide-eyed. "I've made three in my entire life, and only this one as a master. This is my masterpiece. If I make one it—" He stopped himself.

After thinking things through for a moment, he said, "I can make one a week if I do nothing else." He factored in the time he'd need to rest and recover from the many days without sleep while the jewel steel was being fashioned.

Collin looked up as if consulting heaven for inspiration. "Is there another who can make swords like those you delivered?"

Declan weighed the question. Jusan was capable of crafting simple weapons, but he'd need another smith, a journeyman, to match the quality he'd delivered to Baron Rodrigo. Seeing an opportunity, Declan answered, "I'll find someone."

"Find two," said Collin. "Send one up here, for we are desperate for a weaponry smith in the castle. Do so and I'll toss in a bonus."

Starting to feel at ease with the master-at-arms, Declan said, "Is the baron all right with you spending his gold?" Declan had never heard of anyone but a noble making a commission like this.

The old master-at-arms chuckled with a bitter note. "As long as someone is tending to his cock, he doesn't care where the gold goes. He's like his father, though the old baron wasn't as blatant. Still, we're a prosperous enough barony; I can guarantee you'll be well paid. So, another order like this one." He lowered his voice. "And four swords like the one on your hip."

"Four?"

"For the baron, his two grown sons, and me," said the master-at-arms. "I've seen the better man die because his sword broke when facing a lesser man. I would not be a faithful servant to my baron if I didn't make this commission."

Declan nodded. Already he knew there would be a problem. Four blades would use up his supply of the special sand Edvalt had given him. Still, he'd worry about replenishing that after he'd completed this order.

"How much?" asked Collin.

"Same price for the forty blades. For the other four, double that again."

Collin winced. "Twenty to one in price?" He shook his head slightly, then nodded once. "Done. How soon?"

"As soon as possible, but I have to find that other smith. I'll send word."

"Good," said Collin, and left.

Declan returned to the table and found Catharian reading a note. "What's that?" he asked.

"A message from a prelate of the new episkopos in Marquenet. I've been summoned."

"Summoned?" asked Ratigan.

The friar shrugged. "Unusual, but not unheard of. Still, it's no pleasure to just turn around and ride back to where I came from."

"You can ride with us, if you wish," said Declan.

Ratigan looked to be on the verge of objecting, but Declan cut him off. "I have to return to Beran's Hill and then on to Marquenet."

"Back to Marquenet?" asked Ratigan. "I was planning on rounding up any load heading south. I do not like to travel empty if I can help it."

Declan nodded. "I'll make it worth your while. I have another order, and time is essential." He signaled to a passing servant for another round, then sat back against the wall. He let out a deep breath. Forty more swords and four noble blades and he would have enough gold to pay off what he owed on the smithy, make the improvements he wanted to make, and put enough by to . . . A sudden stab of cold hit him in the stomach. "Start a family," he muttered aloud.

"What?" asked Ratigan.

"Nothing," said Declan. "Just tired."

With mixed feelings, his thoughts turned to Gwen. Declan felt the start of a smile but fought it down. He'd finally run out of excuses.

20

Surprises and a Journey

Hatu stoked the forge, keeping an eye on the color of the coals as the smith had shown him. He had only worked a small forge twice before and considered the work tedious, but he had returned from the docks only to be met by Mikial, who told him to find work until they were ready to go on the journey to the barony of Marquensas. He did not say when, but simply to find a place within the city, close to the harbor, and to be ready to depart at short notice.

This was not an unusual order for a student to receive, so that didn't surprise Hatu, but the fact no mention had been made of what he had told the Council—about the Sisters of the Deep, Donte's plight, and the news of the three ships that had driven them to that terrible island—gnawed at him and made him more prone to dark introspection than normal.

He had found a small blacksmith's shop near the harbor in need of a substitute apprentice, as the one they had—a lout named Turhan—had managed to slam his left hand with a hammer a few days earlier and would be unable to work for another few days. It was an ideal situation for the smith, who had been told only that a student needed to work until he left. The smith, understanding the nature of such things, asked no more questions. So Hatu had taken his apprentice's place for a few days despite never having worked for a proper smith.

It was normal for students to be told only what they needed to know, when they needed to know it, but the practice fueled Hatu's anger more than usual. This, as well as Master Facaria's talk, which had challenged what Master Zusara had told him, coupled with his anticipation of Hava's arrival, brought him alternating flashes of aggravation and giddy anticipation. It took every shred of his self-control not to lash out at the slightest annoyance, and as the injured apprentice, Turhan, was something of a fool, Hatu found it a constant struggle.

Still, of the work he could find, Hatu considered this the best option. Reminding himself of that was the only thing that kept him from striking the obnoxious apprentice. He would suffer no official punishment for hitting the boy, but he would be given no warm place to sleep, no food, and a heavy measure of Mikial's disapproval at his failure to do what he was told and stay inconspicuous.

Working in the fields and tending livestock—stooped work for which Hatu had little liking or knack—were his only other options, so he had chosen to labor at the forge. He had only worked with tinkers before, and used the small portable forges in the back of their wagons.

Hatu was learning some new skills quickly and while the work was tedious, it gave him a warm place to rest, despite the fact that Turhan snored when he tried to sleep and took every opportunity to annoy Hatu when he was awake. It was better than being in the fields with the livestock, or in some crowded farmworkers' dormitory. He also took solace in the near certainty that before the boy learned his craft, another would replace him, as Hatu doubted Turhan was going to survive his apprenticeship.

The one other thing that diverted Hatu from the thoughts that threw him into an agitated state was the forge itself. While he found tending the fire uninspiring, he was fascinated by the smith's ability to take hot metal and form it into useful items. He didn't understand why regulating the temperature of the coals was thought of as difficult; he could do it with ease, almost without thought. He just knew where and when to add the coal, when to stir it, and when to apply the bellows. Watching the smith work was instructive and each day he noticed more about how the smith approached the tasks before him, learning things he would not forget.

When the smith wasn't working, the forge was a poor distraction from the much bigger questions Hatu wrestled with. It was worse at night as he lay in the dark, trying to sleep on the hard floor; his mind returned to his last conversation with Master Facaria and wrestled with the questions that arose from it, and he could not stop thinking of what would happen when Hava returned. The work was exhausting enough that he fell asleep once his mind stopped spinning from the worry, but it was a restless sleep.

By the traditions of Coaltachin, and most of the other nations across North and South Tembria, Hatu was soon to be counted a man, for his seventeenth birthday was approaching, or at least the day assigned to him by Master Facaria for the occasion. Hatu might have turned seventeen already and not known it.

Many of the students Hatu trained with had already

moved on to work as crew leaders or gang underbosses, or were becoming sicari. A few of the older ones were probably captains by now. Hatu was about to leave Coaltachin and everything he had ever known behind him. No matter which destination lay before the other students, all were defined. Hatu was facing the unknown. He tried not to be fearful; he had been trained to take care of himself as well as any young man his age could, yet he still felt uncertain, and that threatened to reignite his deeply buried anger.

Turhan, the injured apprentice he had replaced, entered the forge and glanced at the coals. "Good. I don't have to keep looking over your shoulder." He patted Hatu's arm in a friendly fashion and added, "Don't get too good, or my master will replace me."

Hatu shrugged and forced himself to smile. Turhan had a knack for taking even clever remarks and making them sound vacuous. His sense of humor leaned toward the obvious. "Not to worry. I am almost certain that this is not my calling," said Hatu.

Turhan smiled and said, "It's a skill that isn't obvious and is indeed hard to learn." He flexed his injured hand. "I should be fit to return in a day or two more, anyway."

"That's good," said a familiar voice from behind them.

Hatu turned and saw Hava standing in the forge doorway. She said, "Reza needs you now."

Hatu felt his stomach tighten at the way she smiled at him. He attempted to keep a stupid grin off his face and only partially succeeded as he said, "Yes." And as he tried to think of what else to say, she turned and left.

Turhan chuckled. "Well, if a master's son needs you, I guess that means I need to get back to work now. Fare you well, Hatu."

Hatu turned to look at the apprentice and nodded. "Ah . . . Yes, you as well," he said finally. He quickly gathered up his go-bag and toward the door, determined to compose himself before he reached the meeting point near the city market.

As he stepped outside, he was almost knocked over by Hava's throwing her arms around his neck and hugging him fiercely. With emotion in her voice, she whispered, "I have missed you. And I heard of what happened. Donte?"

Thinking of Donte was like having cold water thrown in his face. Hatu took a deep breath and said, "I don't know. Probably . . . gone."

She stepped back, adopted her traditionally stoic expression, and nodded once. "When we are alone, you can tell me what really happened."

She led him down a busy street where people were

getting ready to close down shops, and Hatu realized they were hurrying because Reza wanted to catch the evening tide.

As soon as Reza saw them, he shouldered his travel bag, nodded once, and said, "Follow."

As they hurried along, Hatu gave Hava a sidelong glance and saw her eyes fixed on Reza's back. She didn't know where they were going either.

Hatu knew. They were heading for the docks, and at the speed Reza was going, they didn't have much time before their ship departed. Whatever fate had in store for Hatu, it was unfolding now.

Hatu lay in a hammock, completely spent after a full day of work and a poor meal. He had been ordered into the rigging as soon as they departed, but when morning had come, he had been told to stay aloft as they were running shorthanded. He had stayed with the day watch until supper and sleep.

Reza had said little to him and Hava about their journey to Marquensas, save that on the ship, Hava was Reza's little sister and would share his portion of the officer's cabin, a large room under the stern castle divided by ropes and curtains. Hatu was his apprentice in some vague trade undertaking and would work his passage with the crew.

To say their ship, the *Odalis*, was run cost-efficiently would be a gross understatement. Hatu did not know which master owned the ship, but he speculated that it was likely to be a man named Ordan, who was notorious for his parsimonious ways. Her sails had been mended long beyond the need to replace them. Ropes and sheets were spliced in such a fashion that Hatu felt at risk every time he climbed aloft. The crew bunked in the forecastle cabin, another large common area, without the benefit of ropes and curtains. Hatu was certain that if he went belowdecks, he'd find poor caulking and stopgap plugging of leaks. If he could have bet, he would have wagered that the *Odalis* would sink before she was scrapped.

It was clear a decision had been made for Hatu and the others to travel by the most nondescript means possible, on a ship that apparently would carry little value or be a prize in and of itself. Disguise was a way of life in Coaltachin, so this decision didn't surprise Hatu, but he wished they had picked a ship in slightly better condition.

One oddity that Hatu had noticed after being aloft for a few hours was that they were being shadowed. Another ship had departed the port only minutes after they did. It lingered far enough behind to appear to be on a coincidental course but close enough to render aid quickly should the need arise. From what he had glimpsed as they had departed the home island, it was a warship, a pirate in disguise, which meant the entire crew were nocusara, every sailor a trained sicari. The sails were old tanbark, with a noticeable patch on a jib, but it rode high in the water, meaning no cargo—the pirates expected to bring loot back to Coaltachin. And it was not fully sailed: all the topsails were furled, so it had speed to spare should it be needed. Hatu didn't know if it was because he was aboard or Reza was, or both, and really didn't care. He was just glad help was close at hand should it be needed.

He had only glimpsed Reza on the deck, from above while tending sails on the old square-rigged caravel. Hava had stayed in their portion of the captain's cabin, or she had come on deck while Hatu was working the sheets and he had been too occupied with his work to notice her.

According to what the crew told him, they'd enter the Narrows. Hatu hoped they neared their destination as the food was wretched and the captain set only two watches, so he was on from first light until just before sunset. Despite his misery he felt a strange glimmer of happiness knowing Hava was with him and would continue the journey to Marquensas. He was certain that somewhere along the way they would find time to speak and catch up. He especially wanted to speak to her of Donte, for she was perhaps the only person who could understand his loss.

As he attempted to drift off to sleep, a memory came unbidden, one that jerked him back from the edge of slumber. It had been a hot and muggy day, and training with Dolcet, the fighting preceptor, had been brutal. The class had been exhausted before they were paired off for sparring, and by the time they were almost finished, some of them were at risk of heat exhaustion. Hatu knew the masters understood how far they could push the students. Still, there were times it felt as if they demanded just a little more than a student was capable of giving, but the desire for relief was always countered by the fear of failure. It was better to pass out and risk death than to ask for respite.

There had been more than a hundred children in the village when Hatu was a baby, and at the end of his time on Morasel, less than two dozen remained. It hadn't become apparent to Hatu until he got older that the children who vanished were also those who failed their training. Disappoint the teachers and you were taken away to some other village or town and given over to common labor, or if you were lucky, apprenticeship.

He lay in his hammock, half-dozing, as he continued

to remember the day everything seemed to change. He had just turned twelve, and life had suddenly become confusing. Not the obvious physical changes—gaining hair on his body, broadening shoulders, and a deepening voice. He had seen other boys begin their transformation into men, so as his own body changed, he understood it was natural.

What he hadn't been prepared for, and what no one spoke of, especially the other boys, was how these changes made him feel. He had strange dreams; his awareness was changing, and the rush of feelings was so new to him that at times he feared for his sanity.

He was always battling anger, the rage threatening to burst forth; it required more vigilance, more energy to keep in check, and was even more of a mystery to Hatu than before. There were moments he felt close to tears and had no reason to, just as there were moments of unbidden joy that had no apparent cause.

The reality of turning from a boy to a man was often overwhelming, and in that time he discovered that chaos and conflict were welcome distractions from it. He gave it no great thought; rather it was something he fled to for escape. He had watched the other boys and they seemed calm, showing none of the feelings that tormented him.

Hatu couldn't sleep. He swung his legs over the side

of the hammock, to sit for a moment, and wondered why the memories had returned. Then he realized the answer was simple: even those who failed, who were sent away, had futures that were defined. They would learn a trade or become a laborer, find a husband or wife, marry, have a family . . . or perhaps even die; there was no uncertainty.

Hatu was now aware that growing up with this sense of certainty about his future within the ordered Coaltachin society had given him constant, if not recognized, reassurance when he was younger, in ways he had not understood. Now he faced a future in which nothing was certain, little was known.

He took a deep breath and stood up, moving quietly as he left the company of snoring sailors to go up on deck. Dawn and the start of his watch were less than an hour away, so he was only missing a little rest by standing at the rail rather than lying in his hammock staring at the deck above his head.

The eastern sky was starting to lighten as the false dawn approached. Hatu saw the night watch in their positions; several were likely to be asleep as the helmsman was on a fixed course, the breeze was steady but gentle, and trimming the sails was unnecessary.

Hatu appreciated the time alone. He'd had few friends growing up, Donte being the only boy he considered close, and although he had been trained to work with others, he preferred solitude. Despite feeling lonely at times, he welcomed the freedom from worrying about other people's opinion of him; in most cases, he didn't care, but the good opinion of masters and preceptors was vital, so he took pleasure from those moments when he wasn't under scrutiny.

He was startled by a voice behind him. "Hatu?"

He turned, his heart pounding from surprise and because he recognized the voice.

Hava stood for a moment and then moved to stand beside him at the rail. "Couldn't sleep?" she asked, getting close, as if seeking warmth in the predawn cold.

"Yes, but it's almost time for my watch."

She nodded, her face in silhouette against the brightening eastern sky. "I sneaked away," she said. "Reza is playing the part of protective older brother too well. He has forbidden me to leave our sleeping quarters, as if I should fear that every man on this ship will try to rape me," she said with a slight laugh. "You and Reza are the only two I couldn't kill with my bare hands."

Hatu couldn't think of anything to say in response to that. He was still battling to keep his wits about him.

"I learned my way around rigging and decks on my last sea journey, and I needed the fresh air." She smiled. "Captain Joshua named me 'Hava the Pirate.'"

Hatu laughed. "I think that suits you!"

"I missed you," she said.

He glanced over to see her profile gazing out to sea. He said, "I've been running with a gang in Numerset for months . . ." He decided not to provide details.

She was silent a moment, then said, "I've been learning sex."

He could only nod.

She shrugged slightly. "It was . . . odd, mostly not too bad, but I don't have the talent for it some of the girls showed. Besides, I don't think I'm pretty enough to be a noconochi . . ."

He laughed quietly. "Of course you are; you just don't have the temperament to laugh at stupid jokes and pretend you don't have your own mind."

Hava tried not to laugh and Hatu continued. "First time some idiot nobleman tried to slap you . . ." He couldn't help himself and chuckled aloud. "You'd break his arm."

She nodded, sighed, and said, "Probably."

Failing to stifle his amusement, Hatu continued to laugh as he said, "No, certainly."

She joined him. "You're right, I would make a terrible noconochi." Hava rolled her eyes theatrically and fluttered her hand as if she held a large fan. "Oh, my lord, you're so clever," she said in a melodramatic fashion. "I don't know how you think of all these wonderful ideas!"

"Nessa, right?" said Hatu, unable to control his delight.

They fell into fits of laughter, causing a deckhand at the opposite rail to glance over and see what all the hilarity was about.

Hava slipped her arm through Hatu's and gave it a hug. He found himself suddenly aware of the feel of her body next to his, the press of her breast through her shirt against his arm and the faint scent of her hair near his face. He felt his mirth flee as stronger emotions took over.

She continued. "I wish we could just keep sailing."

He knew something was troubling her, and knew her well enough to know she would tell him in her own time. He remained silent.

She also was silent, and when she spoke, her tone had changed back to the more familiar bantering one he had known all his life. "Despite what you and I might think of Nessa, those women go through a lot. I didn't get to find out what the boys learn, but it can't be any easier. I didn't imagine pleasure could be such hard labor. Though the Powdered Women say it's important for students to learn how to please men and other women." Hatu's expression must have seemed questioning, for Hava said, "It's not so bad with women, and some of the girls seem to enjoy it a lot more than I do." She gazed out to sea a moment, then looked at Hatu. "I expect it's more enjoyable with someone you actually like."

She pressed hard against him again, and Hatu forced himself not to put his arms around her. He could only nod and didn't know if she saw the gesture.

He closed his eyes for a moment, then forced himself to calm. He had never in his life felt as close to anyone as he did to Hava at this moment. His mind raced as he struggled to think of something he could say without looking like a complete fool. Hatu opened his eyes and saw her looking up at him in a way that both thrilled and terrified him. He felt as if they were but moments from saying something vital. Her eyes were fixed on his face as if she expected him to speak.

Then movement in the corner of his vision, on the horizon, a speck of black against the lightening grey, caught his eye. He extended his arm and said, "Do you see that?"

Hava looked where he pointed and said, "What?"

"Keep looking." She did so and he saw the spot again, then a third time.

"I see it," she said. "What is it?"

"The lookout must be asleep." He turned and shouted, "Sails!"

The helmsman shouted back, "Where away?"

"Starboard abaft!"

Within moments, sailors erupted from below, followed by Captain Rawitch, the first mate, and Reza. If Reza had concerns about Hava's being on deck they were forgotten when he heard the alarm.

By the time the captain reached the rail and stood on Hatu's left, the first rays of dawn had struck the water, causing glimmers on it in the direction they searched. "What did you see?" he asked of Hatu.

"Sails, coming fast, and more than one ship."

The captain pulled a short brass tube from inside his tunic and stretched it out to a longer length. Hatu had heard of these spyglasses but had never seen one. A finely crafted crystal lens at each end magnified what the viewer saw, as much as five or ten times by reputation; the length of the tube was made up of a series of rings, one fitting within another, so it could be shortened for easy carrying.

"Two ships," the captain said after a moment. "Coming fast. They fly no banners." He shouted to his crew. "All sails! Come to port—" Then he glanced at the position of the sun. "Southwest by south!"

Hatu realized something as fear rose within him. "Where are we?" he asked.

"South edge of the Narrows," replied the captain as he stared through his looking glass.

Hatu's expression changed.

Reza said, "What?"

"I drifted before I was found. I don't know . . ." He looked at Master Zusara's youngest son and said, "Do you remember what I told you? About where I'd been captured?" He didn't wish to mention the Sisters of the Deep in front of the captain and crew.

It took a moment for Reza to understand what Hatu was saying, then his eyes widened and he said, "Yes, I see." To the captain, he said, "Let the boy look."

If the captain resented being spoken to in such a fashion, he masked it and handed the spyglass to Hatu. He put the small end against his eye and for a moment couldn't make sense of what he was seeing, then resolved an image of two lateen-rigged ships.

"It's them, I swear," he said. "It was a squadron of . . . three." He leapt onto the rail of the ship, grabbed a ratline, and climbed until he was halfway to the yard, then he looked around, trying to make sense of dots on the horizon where islands rested, looking for anything familiar. He scanned ahead with the spyglass.

The surrounding seas became suddenly recognizable

as two islands appeared in the direction in which they were headed. "We can't go this way!" he shouted to Reza. "They're trying to chase us into those islands!"

The captain said, "This is our only course if we're to lose them, boy! If we change course they'll overtake us."

Hatu looked behind them with the spyglass and saw the sea was empty.

"The ship that followed us from port?" he said to the captain.

Hatu tossed the glass to Reza, who took it and looked aft, and said, "It's gone!" To the captain, Reza said, "They must have fallen behind in the night."

Hatu felt fear race up his spine as he looked down. "Third ship must have attacked our escort, turning her away from our course!" For a black raider to be taken, or even held in check, while two other ships raced toward them meant this engagement was planned and the odds for their survival were slim.

Looking from Reza to the captain and back, he said, "We can't go this way!"

Annoyed about being told what to do aboard his own ship by a mere boy, the captain said, "We'll reach the Clearing within half a day."

Hatu jumped down, almost knocking against Hava as he looked at Reza. "You know why!" he insisted.

Reza was motionless for a moment, then turned to

the captain. "I can't tell you why, but we can't stay on this course."

The captain's eyes narrowed; he was clearly at the end of his patience. Reza's father might have been the most powerful master in Coaltachin, but on this ship, the captain was supreme.

Seeing the captain's hesitance, Reza stepped closer to him and said, "My father's oath bids me be silent, but you must believe me when I say this boy knows of what he speaks; if we stay on this course, we are all dead."

The captain paused, considering his options, then said, "We run, or we fight."

"Then we fight on our terms, not theirs," said Reza.

The captain nodded, then took back his spyglass from Reza and studied the two ships. After a while he said, "Yes, they're trying to keep us on our present course." The captain addressed his first mate. "How many archers?"

"We have eight," said the mate.

"I can shoot," said Hava. "And I can handle the rigging."

"So can I," Hatu added. Then he nodded at Hava and said, "And she's a better archer than I am."

The captain told his mate, "Get ready for a close pass. I want this ship turned fast and hard, so we stay to the windward side of the easternmost ship; rake her with arrows and tell our best archer to take out her helmsman and keep everyone away from the tiller." He turned to Reza. "If we cut her wind a bit and wreak confusion among her crew for long enough, the ship will turn toward her fellow, perhaps buying us enough time to escape while they move to avoid a collision. And if we can't, at least we'll face one ship at a time instead of two."

Reza nodded agreement. "We want to be gone before that third ship catches up."

Hava and Hatu headed to the locker below the forecastle, each retrieving a finely made bow and hip quiver of arrows. They were given leather belts with stout rope attached. Hatu gestured for Hava to start climbing the mainmast ratlines and followed her to the first yard. "Here," he instructed her when it became apparent that her knowledge of ships was still limited, despite her becoming "Hava the Pirate."

"Stay close to the mast," he shouted while sailors surged along footropes to obey any order from the captain to furl sails. She nodded that she understood as he took up position on the other side of the mast.

The captain shouted and sailors began to furl, while those below on the sheets changed the angle of the yards just enough for the two ships bearing down on them to think they were gaining. Hatu heard the captain tell Reza, "Now comes the tricky part." He shouted, "Ready to come about!

"On my command, hard to starboard." He waited, then shouted, "Come about!"

The ship heeled over as Hatu and Hava hung on tightly to the mast while the yard below their feet moved in response to sailors hauling sheets. Hatu touched Hava lightly on the shoulder and motioned that she should watch him. He stepped down on the footrope and quickly tied the line attached to his belt onto the yard. He shouted, "It's better if you don't fall off!"

"I don't plan to," she replied, and made a face while she duplicated his actions, securing her belt rope to the yard. "You don't fall off, either!"

He laughed, but it was as much nervous laughter as bravado. There was just enough room between them to aim his bow and move his shooting field from left to right. Hatu checked to make sure Hava had enough clearance and saw she needed more room. Once she was seated, feet firmly on the ropes, one hand gripping the yard, he adjusted his position, moving slightly further down the yard, so as not to interfere with her field of fire.

Hatu could see the crew of the easternmost ship

scramble to respond to their captain's commands. Their move was completely unexpected and the pursuing ship had to give way or risk a full collision.

As soon as they came in range, he nodded to Hava and picked a target in the rigging, a sailor frantically trying to reef a sail. The arrow missed but passed close enough to startle the man; he lost his grip and fell from the yard into the sea. The sail he had been trying to gather flapped in the wind between the other two men on the yard.

Hava let fly her arrow and it struck true, taking the outermost sailor from the yard. Hatu saw other archers were equally effective and that the order to kill the helmsman had been met with success as the following ship was now wallowing. Hatu realized the pursuing ship's captain had expected a longer chase and had positioned no archers in the rigging or armed men on deck.

They would pass the first ship in less than a minute and then be on their way, beating a long tack, but one that would quickly take them back into home waters. If the three ships followed, others from Coaltachin would likely come to the *Odalis*'s aid as soon as they saw its banner and other ships in pursuit.

Suddenly they were past, and there were no more targets. Hatu turned to see Hava smiling, pleased with her performance. He nodded once, then indicated the rope still tied to the yard. "Carefully," he shouted over the wind. "It wouldn't do for you to take a tumble now."

She nodded, unfastened herself, and climbed safely to the mast, then shimmied down to the top of the ratlines and began her descent. Hatu was only a few moments behind her reaching the deck.

The captain had moved to the poop deck, and Hatu and Hava climbed the short ladder to join him and Reza. They were looking back at the two ships and said, "They're in a fine tangle." He put away his spyglass and said, "Now we get to see who the better sailors are, me or those three captains . It'll be midday at best, later perhaps, before we reach friendlier waters. Let's hope we can stay on this course. The winds are not kind on this tack. We're slowed, but so are they. Once we clear the last island, we can turn and put more distance between us."

Reza nodded to both Hava and Hatu and said, "Follow me."

He led them down into the poop cabin, which was now empty, and said, "I did not plan on this." He fell silent, then looked at Hatu. "Twice now, the ship you sail upon has come under attack by these . . ." He let his thoughts fall away.

Hatu had questions, the number increasing by the

moment, but the expression on Reza's face kept him silent. He glanced at Hava but her face was unreadable.

"Much of this mission must remain hidden," began Reza again, his gaze shifting from Hatu to Hava and back. "This much you should know in case ill fortune visits us again and you find yourself alone. Hava, you will assist Hatu in reaching Port Colos before the first day of the Month of the Turning Moon. That gives you two and a half months to reach the barony of Marquensas on the other side of the world.

"Seek out Master Bodai. He will be either in Port Colos or somewhere nearby. Find our people there and they'll know how to contact him. Bodai will have received word on what to do next. Find him as soon as you can."

Looking at Hatu, he said, "He will take you to meet a man named Balven in the city of Marquenet. He is in the baron's service and will take you to see him. You will do whatever they tell you to do until further word reaches you. Do you understand?"

Hatu nodded, and Reza said, "You will serve at the baron's pleasure. If he swears you to his service, you must feign allegiance. Again, do you understand?" Hatu nodded. "Go back up on deck. The rest of this is for Hava alone."

After Hatu had departed, Reza said to Hava, "Master

Rengara has a crew in Marquenet. Should you fail to find Bodai, whatever the cause, then locate someone in Rengara's crew and tell them who you are. Say, 'I carry a message from our grandfather for your leader.' Once you are alone with whoever runs Rengara's crew, simply say, 'Grandfather sent me.' If you are questioned after that, repeat the phrase twice. Say it less than three times and you will be killed where you stand as a spy. Understand?"

She nodded and then asked, "What then?"

"If you can stay with Hatushaly, do so. If you can't, stay out of sight and find where the man Balven takes Hatushaly. Ask Rengara's crew for whatever help you need. Keep an eye on Hatu and follow him as closely as you can without being discovered. Find out what the baron wants from the boy, and if you can, keep in touch with Hatu somehow."

Reza considered what he was saying, then nodded once. "Yes, make him want to stay close to you; he likes you already, I know."

Her training stood Hava in good stead as she listened without betraying any reaction. She knew Reza understated Hatu's feelings for her, and her feelings for him.

Again the master was silent for a moment, then said, "Gather whatever information from Hatu you think might be of interest, whatever the baron is doing, anything of potential importance. If you think something vital, find Rengara's crew boss and pass the message through him."

Reza then stared hard at her as if appraising her; she had demonstrated toughness and talent but she was still very inexperienced and normally would not have been given any unsupervised missions for a few more years. He studied her closely as he spoke, "Eventually you will receive new orders: either you or a member of Rengara's crew will have to kill Hatushaly."

Her eyes widened slightly at his words and she felt shock run through her body, but Hava's training still masked her feelings. She knew Reza would notice something, so she turned her head slightly, as if absorbing her instructions, and after a second she nodded once, showing she understood.

"Good," said Reza. "Now, stay here while I speak to the captain about a new course."

He departed and Hava, her mind in a whirl, just sat on her bed mat as she had absolutely no idea what she should do next.

21

A Quiet Journey Interrupted

Catharian finished one of his tales and even Ratigan was forced to laugh. On the trip south the friar had proven his worth in entertainment, with both storytelling and wry observations on life. His travels had exposed him to a wealth of anecdotes and insights on the human condition, and he was not shy about sharing them.

Declan quickly decided that he liked the friar, disagreements over faith notwithstanding. While not as insistent on the adherence to belief in the One as were other members of the "Church of God," as it was becoming known, Catharian was still firm in his belief. Declan was, on the other hand, if not disinterested, then disinclined to give religion much thought. Like his old master, he saw tossing a coin in a prayer dish as more of a duty than an impulse driven by strong belief in the possible intercession of any god on his behalf. As Edvalt had once said, "If any god helps me, I'll welcome it, but I'd also be surprised."

For some reason Declan found the concept behind the One God even more abstract and distant than Edvalt's faint sense of faith. This god, it was claimed, was in charge of everything. The old gods had once maintained order. Each had a domain and responsibility, for the sea, the weather, luck, anything you could imagine, but this One . . . Declan wondered how, if he was in charge of everything, he'd get anything done.

Ratigan was an outright atheist, almost contemptuous of religion when the topic arose. With someone like Catharian, Declan felt Ratigan would most likely be safe from any sort of reprisals, but should others hear him, like those soldiers with the white shields in Copper Hills, it would be another story. Word from the east spoke of more heretic burnings as Sandura expanded its influence. If trouble was coming from the east, as many now surmised, a far less tolerant attitude toward nonbelievers would almost certainly come with it.

Declan decided that when the right moment came, he'd have a word with Ratigan. The young teamster didn't seem to understand that the day was fast approaching when words could get you burned at the stake here in the west. At times he was one of the most annoying people Declan had ever encountered, but somewhere along the way Ratigan had become a good friend, reliable and trustworthy, despite his constant complaining and general sour attitude on life. Declan didn't wish to see him dead for not watching what he said.

The journey going south seemed to take longer than it had coming north, or so it felt to Declan. He wagered that was as much due to his anticipation of seeing Gwen as it was about any real delay. One monstrous thunderstorm had forced them to tarry in a village for a day, then slog through deep mud until the returning sun dried the road. Otherwise the journey had been quiet and moved along at a good pace.

Declan reflected on his decision. He realized that he had been torn three ways: First, by a need to be financially stable before he took on the responsibility of a family, and that issue would be resolved once he finished the order given to him by the master-at-arms of Copper Hill. Second, by a desire to find someone who excited him as much as Roz. He'd finally decided that wasn't possible; Roz was who she was because of the life she'd lived, her travel and experience, and her adventurous abandon with men. Declan decided he'd been gulling himself by thinking he was somehow unique in Roz's life. Lastly, by the fact that he had simply been unsure, and now he realized that he cared deeply for Gwen, and that she wouldn't wait forever. He finally had decided that different wasn't better or worse; it was just different. Gwen was different from Roz and that was just fine.

"What's that?" asked Catharian.

He pointed to the east, where a dust cloud was rising.

"Riders," answered Ratigan. "If they're bandits, the fact we're empty might keep them from killing us, unless they're peeved." Without taking his eyes from the approaching dust, he asked Declan, "Your gold well hidden?"

"In that box you've got bolted underneath the seat, hidden between the boards. I put mine in there with yours."

"How did you know there was a hidey box there?" asked Ratigan, glancing at the young smith.

"Just how many wagons like this do you think I've repaired in my day?"

Ratigan gave a slight shrug in response.

The riders appeared, and after a few minutes resolved into a company of about a dozen men, moving quickly at an efficient canter.

As they got closer Declan could see they were clearly mercenaries, for they wore neither tabards nor badges, and their armor and weapons were plentiful and varied. By the time they reached the intersection of the two roads, Ratigan's wagon was across it, and the riders passed, ignoring the wagon.

"They're not turning to Copper Hills," said Declan after a moment.

"Heading west," said Ratigan.

"Must be making for a port," suggested Catharian.

"What's that about?" wondered Ratigan.

Declan shook his head slightly, indicating he had no idea.

Catharian said, "If they're in a rush to go east, a ship would be faster, even from up here. Northern coast will be ice covered in a few weeks, so it's through the Narrows."

"Through the Narrows," echoed Declan, thinking of Oncon, and for the first time in weeks wondering what had happened to all the people he knew.

"War must be heating up," suggested Catharian.

Ratigan nodded. "Still east of here, but if local mercenaries are rushing off to fight for gold, it's heading this way."

Declan considered the order he'd just accepted for the swords. "Must be," he echoed.

Gwen shook her head to stop Declan from talking. He had arrived home early enough the previous afternoon to seek her out and ask her to marry him. She had said yes before he could finish and insisted that he find her father before the inn got busy.

So, Declan sputtered out an almost incoherent request for permission to marry Gwen, waited nervously for Leon's answer. The innkeeper leaned back against the bar, arms crossed, a dubious expression on his face. He let out a long, dramatic sigh, then turned to his daughter. "You're certain you can't do better than this lout?"

Gwen's expression darkened and her tone was sharp. "Da, don't be mean to him! You know he's the only boy who's courted me that you've liked."

Leon's dark look was betrayed by a faint smile, and then a grin. "Then you have my blessing," he said, gripping Declan's hand. Then he jerked the young smith forward and whispered in his ear loudly enough for Gwen to hear, "Took you long enough. You were doomed the day you met."

Declan tried not to laugh as Gwen's expression darkened further and she said, "Doomed, was it?"

He avoided eye contact with his betrothed, caught halfway between being amused and realizing Gwen could easily turn this celebratory moment into a family argument; she was a young woman of easy temper but strong mind, and her father had the habit of saying just the thing to set her off.

Instead he glanced at the old man who sat quietly in the corner, the only customer this early in the afternoon. His age was hard to determine; he could have been in his late forties or early sixties. His grey hair fell from a receding hairline, predicting eventual baldness, and his face was heavily wrinkled, but whether they were lines of age or harsh weather was unclear. He wore an odd tunic and the short-legged pantaloons favored in nations far to the east, and his skin was an unusual bronze color that Declan had only seen on traders from the Far Islands.

The old man appeared not to be listening, which would be impossible, Declan decided, but he was pleased by his courtesy. Most people would have been laughing aloud.

"Ah, I think it's time for a drink!" said Leon brightly. He scurried behind the bar, reached under it, and pulled out a porcelain bottle of whisky. He poured two stiff drinks into two matching cups and handed one to Declan.

Gwen stood watching, her expression halfway between delight over her father's giving his blessing to her and Declan's marriage, and annoyance that Leon seemed incapable of even the simplest act without a weak attempt at humor, often turning into embarrassment. She knew her father wouldn't offer her a celebratory drink as it was "a man's thing," and besides, he knew she rarely drank, and would be needing a clear head for the day's business while the men stood there drinking.

Declan looked at her for a long moment, smiling, and she gave him a quick nod, saying he should go ahead, and he indulged himself in an almost audible sigh of relief that the asking and getting permission were over. He smiled quickly at her, turned to face Leon, and lifted his little glass of the amber fluid.

The young smith still hadn't developed a taste for whisky, preferring beer and ale, but each time Leon offered him a drink, it was this strong spirit. Declan was getting used to the taste and burning in his mouth, and he was even becoming able to judge the quality, but he wasn't sure he was ever going to truly enjoy it.

Leon returned Declan's salute with his own lifted glass. Declan threw back the drink and swallowed it. He noticed a nutty aftertaste and said, "That's different."

Leon smiled and said, "You noticed! It's a new distiller over on the Namoor frontier who set up shop a few years ago and this is his first shipment, and not only is he good, his prices are reasonable."

Declan nodded as he let the flavor diminish. "I think this is the best one you've given me, Leon."

"Well, it's still mostly ale, wine, and seasonal beers, and we do get a few that do with just water, but if I'm going to have whisky behind this bar, I'd rather it be the good ones . . ." He lowered his voice. "Especially if they cost less." He laughed.

Gwen moved to stand close to Declan and said, "The dowry?"

Leon feigned surprise. "Dowry?" Looking at Declan, he said, "Are you asking for a dowry, lad?"

Declan's eyes widened and he was for a moment speechless.

Gwen's expression instantly flashed anger and she took a step closer to her father, foreclosing any need for Declan to speak. "You'll not be playing that with me, Da!" She poked him hard in the chest with her right index finger. "Ma explained how it was when I was little, and I've never forgotten, and you'll not be robbing me of my due and proper!"

Leon put up his hands in surrender, taking half a step back. "Wouldn't think of it." He grinned. "Just having a bit of a tease with Declan."

Further discussion was cut short by the sound of horsemen arriving outside, at least half a dozen from the sound.

"Millie!" shouted Leon, and the girl appeared through the kitchen door.

"Yes?"

"Horses," Leon said, indicating outside with a tilt of his head. "Tell Peter to be ready to stable them should we need to."

"Yes, Leon," she said, moving back into the kitchen.

Turning back to Gwen, Leon said, "We'll have a lovely wedding. But you're not yet married to this young lout, and we will soon have customers—"

Six armed men, dusty and tired from their appearance, entered the common room. "See what's ready in the kitchen," finished Leon. Gwen was through the kitchen door before he'd even completed the sentence.

Declan was left to stand alone as Leon hurried back to the storeroom to replenish the bottle he'd just emptied. Declan recognized the men as what the locals called lejats—swords for hire—as they moved past him to the bar. They were dressed in a variety of armor, none of it of high quality. Four of them wore cured leather over thick shirts, three sleeveless and the fourth sporting rivets on his shoulders and spaulders of darkly tarnished brass. The other two wore chain mail shirts.

Leon appeared from the storeroom, holding two bottles in each hand. Holding them down behind the bar, he asked, "Stabling your horses?"

An older fighter shook his head and said, "We'll ride on after we rest." One bumped into Declan, intentionally, and gave him a challenging stare. He was a young man with a thick dark thatch of unruly hair and dark eyes with a strange look to them, one that had Declan's hand moving toward his sword hilt.

Before any words could be exchanged, another rider, an older fighter with grey in his hair and beard, grabbed the younger man and shoved him toward the bar. "Get your ass over there, Tyree. Trying to start trouble and you're not even drunk yet? What is the matter with you?"

Declan felt a sense of danger he hadn't experienced since the raid on Oncon. The manner of these men was different from that of most of the hired swords who rode through Beran's Hill. These men were even harder looking than usual, faces worn by life outdoors for the most part, sleeping on the ground without even a tent to shelter in. They looked to be one step away from banditry, the sort that a sheriff or marshal would watch closely, or encourage to ride on.

Of all the larger towns within the borders of Marquensas, Beran's Hill was absent of any military or civil law. It was a place of rough justice, and the residents of Beran's Hill had to protect themselves from predation. Esterly, half a day's ride into Lord Dumarch's territory, was the closest town with a garrison. Given these conditions, Declan knew that should trouble come, he and Leon would be among the first to answer. If all of the able men of Beran's Hill responded, these six mercenaries could be dealt with, but a lot of blood would likely be shed.

Declan glanced at his future father-in-law, and after a moment Leon returned his look, his expression conveying his gratitude that Declan remained. The young smith glanced around and noticed that the old man also watched the newcomers. He and Declan locked eyes for a brief moment, then the old man nodded slightly and returned to his meal.

Declan's decision to stay a while longer had not been difficult; the forge was in good hands with Jusan, and should the need arise, his apprentice would fetch him. Otherwise Jusan would assume that an impromptu party was under way, celebrating the betrothal.

The old man motioned for Declan to come over to his table, and curious, Declan went over and sat opposite him. "You expecting trouble?" asked the stranger.

Declan nodded without speaking, not taking his eyes off the six men clustered around the bar. "It's just a question of what kind of trouble, and when."

The old man inclined his head slightly and said,

"The old rooster barely keeps his young bird in check. Soon there will be a challenge and one of them will die. Hopefully, not today."

"As long as it happens after they've left Beran's Hill," Declan agreed softly.

"A man feels protective of his home," said the old man.

Declan nodded. "Especially now," he said, not taking his eyes off the six men at the bar drinking their first round of ale. "I care about these people. It is my home now."

"Not born here?" asked the old man.

Declan turned to him and said, "No. I'm from the Covenant. A village called Oncon."

The man inclined his head. "Ah, the Covenant. A wonderful notion, no longer, I'm afraid." He looked Declan in the eye and said, "Oncon? You survived the sacking?"

Declan felt the hair on his arms rise and felt a sinking in the pit of his stomach. "Sacking?"

"Ah, you left before it happened." He carefully lifted a bit of bread and cheese to his mouth and began to chew. Declan said nothing. The old man swallowed, then said, "Slavers, so the story goes. Some time ago, they attempted to take some boys and girls and were repulsed. They returned a day or two later and burned the entire village to cinders and ash."

"The people?"

"The tale is they had already fled, which is why the slavers acted with rage and destroyed everything."

Declan let out a slow sigh. He hadn't realized until this moment how deeply he had buried his concern for those he'd left behind. "So the villagers survived?"

"One can assume so," said the old man. "Still, it marked the beginning of the end of the Covenant."

"How do you mean?"

The old man said, "I am called Bodai; I trade in horses."

"You're the one who brought in the six horses for Tenda yesterday."

"This is true. We've done business before. He's an honest trader."

"I'm Declan Smith. I reshod a pair of them this morning."

Bodai fell silent, studying the younger man's face.

"The Covenant?" asked Declan.

Bodai nodded slightly and returned to his narrative. "I travel. I hear many things. When the Five Kingdoms were at peace, the Covenant was as you remember. But since the fall of Ithrace, things have changed slowly, but changed . . ." He paused and studied Declan's face a moment, then continued ". . . and now with the sacking of Oncon, it is clear the agreement that created the Covenant is over."

"Sandura," said Declan. "The men who raided the village wore badges of Sandura."

Bodai shrugged. "That I did not know. You were there, then?"

"I was there when the slavers arrived. I fought. I departed with my apprentice before they returned."

Bodai nodded. "Change is the nature of existence. There were warlords and kings before the Covenant, and will continue to be even as the Covenant fails, and long after. It is the way of things."

Declan was silent, watching as Gwen emerged from the kitchen with a platter of hot bread and heavily salted butter for the newly arrived mercenaries. It was a "gift" from Leon, who had learned that providing customers with something to nibble on tended to make them linger, and if there was extra salt in the butter, they purchased more drinks, and many stayed to eat a full meal.

Still, something about this band put Declan on edge, and it wasn't just the aggressive Tyree who caused him concern. They might have acted like common caravan guards or roving mercenaries, but there was something different about them, and Declan couldn't quite put his finger on what that was. He did know he wasn't leaving Gwen and her father here alone with them.

The armed men at the bar made happy sounds and a few leered at Gwen, but they fell on the bread eagerly. Declan saw Tyree's eyes following Gwen as she returned to the kitchen. The young smith felt the hair on his neck bristle and he tensed to act should the need arise. Tyree whispered something to one of his companions, who laughed, and the two men returned to the bread and ale.

Declan let out his breath slowly. Without a local garrison, sheriff, or even constabulary in Beran's Hill, he had taken to wearing his sword when away from the forge, like many men in the town. Those who had no sword carried a dagger, a sap, or a cudgel. Most of the time it wasn't necessary, but occasionally there came a need. Declan slowly shifted his weight to make his sword hilt more accessible if he had to rise from the table in a hurry. He settled in to watch.

A couple of hours later Jusan showed up at the inn to find Declan still sitting at the table with Bodai. The young apprentice came over and was introduced, then sat with his master and the horse merchant.

Millie came out of the kitchen and, seeing Jusan, hurried over. From their smiles, Declan assumed they had taken some time to get to know one another while he was up in Copper Hills. "Jusan," she said shyly in a soft tone.

"Work's finished; your friar friend went off on some errand with Ratigan," said Jusan, "so I thought I'd come down and join the party, but apparently there isn't one."

"We'll have a proper party when it's time," said Declan, keeping his eyes on the men at the bar.

Sensing something amiss, Jusan glanced over his shoulder and saw two of the mercenaries looking at Millie and whispering. One laughed, and something about their tone caused Jusan to stand. Declan grabbed his arm and forced him down. "Coarse insults are not worth shedding blood over," he said just loud enough to be heard at the table but not at the bar.

Bodai said, "You're wiser than your years, young man."

Millie said, "They're no worse than others who've come by. It'll be fine. They told Leon they're not staying in town, but camping along the road somewhere. They'll be gone soon."

Jusan's expression showed that he was not reassured. "I'll stay for a bit," he offered.

Declan understood. Try as he might, his outward

calm was only a facade. He was on edge, and it wasn't just the usual annoyance he felt with other men paying too much attention to Gwen; this was something else.

The old man named Bodai said, "I'm bound for Pashtar. Any word of trouble between here and there?"

Declan kept his eyes on the men at the bar as he answered, "I just returned from Copper Hills. Jusan?"

"There's gossip that men and weapons are heading to Port Colos, on the other side of Pashtar. I've heard of no trouble, but it feels like it's coming." He turned to look at Bodai. "What's in Pashtar?"

"A nephew. I am to care for him until he reaches Marquenet. He hasn't quite reached manhood yet, and . . ." The old man shrugged. "It's a family thing."

Jusan inclined his head, acknowledging Bodai's words, but he also had his eyes on the men at the bar.

Suddenly the young fighter named Tyree said, "They're looking at me!"

He took a full step toward the table where Declan and the others sat, and Declan reached for his sword, but before he had lifted the blade from its scabbard, the older fighter, the leader of the band, stepped in front of Tyree and pushed him back hard enough that he would have hit the floor if two men behind hadn't caught him. "Now you're drunk!" he shouted at the troublemaker. "It's time to leave!" he commanded the others. With a nod and a look, he indicated that the two men who had caught the young drunk should hang on to him as they left the inn.

Tyree was intoxicated enough that his attention wandered as he attempted to salvage his pride; he glanced at Declan as they left the inn and continued his loud complaining outside: "But they were looking at me!"

His whining drew some response as the riders mounted, but Declan couldn't make out what was said.

The old man said, "Well, that was . . . interesting."

Declan watched the door as he said, "Our master, Edvalt, told us a story once . . ."

Jusan nodded as if he knew which story Declan referred to.

"It's a long one, but the point of it was that there is such a thing as a man who needs killing."

Jusan said, "It's like putting down a mad dog, Edvalt said."

"You think that man, Tyree, is such a man? One who needs killing?"

"I'm not saying so," said Declan, "but let's just say I wouldn't be surprised to find out he was."

Gwen came over and motioned to speak with Declan privately in the corner. When they were away, she kissed him lightly and said, "Thank you for staying, and thank Jusan, too. I've not seen many like those, but the few I have . . ." She looked down and said, "Father isn't as young or as bold as he thinks he is, and . . . I'm glad you were here."

"I wasn't going to leave you with that crew here," he said, trying to sound matter-of-fact.

"Now go away so I can get ready for the evening business." She pulled away with mock disapproval. "Don't you have any work to do, you layabout?"

He laughed. "More than I think I can handle, truth to tell. After I get Jusan started on some things, I need to take a trip down to Marquenet, and I think I'm going to need another apprentice."

"Another one?" she said. "That forge is going to get crowded."

Declan laughed. He hadn't thought of it until this moment, but Gwen would be moving in after the wedding, which meant Jusan would be moving out. It would be back to sleeping in the forge for him.

"I'll stop by—"

"No, get to sleep. You've been on the road and you're about to travel again, so rest and I'll see you tomorrow."

He nodded and smiled. He motioned to Jusan to come with him and waved a friendly goodbye to the old man. As he walked back toward his smithy, he considered that this wouldn't be the last time Gwen told him what to do.

22

Different Ideas and Hasty Decisions

The passage had been slow, as Captain Rawitch kept the *Odalis* on a course as far north as he could manage and still make westward progress. The majority of the ships they had sighted had been heading in the other direction, so unless their pursuers had some magic means by which to conjure an ambush in front of them, all those on the *Odalis* had to worry about was being overtaken from behind.

For the first three days after the attack, they had kept every weapon close at hand, and every man, and woman, had stood a watch on top of their usual duties. Even Reza spent hours aloft scanning the horizon for signs the attackers had found them again.

They slowed even more as they were approaching the Narrows, mindful of the sub-surface rocks which waited too close to either shore. Lookouts were posted watching for signs in the water, shifts in current eddies and changes in color indicating shallower waters close to the ship.

Hatu watched from the railing as they sailed the north side of the straits, under bluffs from which it would be easy to attack passing ships, raining arrows and boulders down upon them. Glancing to the south, he saw that even trying to sail dead center through the Narrows would still keep a ship within range of catapults and ballistas from both sides. Anyone holding both sides of the Narrows would be in complete control of the passage.

The captain was taking a careful course, as while the straits were surprisingly free of rocks, nasty ones hid just below the surface close to the cliff faces. They were granite interspersed with hard chalk and flint, which gave them a mottled look. There was no beach to speak of, so Hatu expected that the strong currents swept away any silt that fell from the cliffs above. He wondered how this gap between the continents came to be, as it looked as if giant hands had pulled Tembria asunder to form the two continents and flood the path between them.

The prevailing winds and currents ran west to east, so on the south side of the Narrows ships moved briskly in roughly a straight line, while the *Odalis* and the other westbound ships tacked in closely, seeming to swing first left and then right, an odd dance of sails fore and aft. The constant need to shift yards and shorten or lengthen sheets had the crew close to exhaustion by sunset, but the need for control also forced those ships to heave to for the night. They had taken rests each night for a week, which was welcomed by the entire crew, and this would be the second-to-last night they would have to slow their progress, as once past the Narrows the channel quickly broadened so that ships heading westward could sail through the night.

Hava came up on deck and stood at the rail next to him. Hatu assumed she had been talking to Reza. He was suddenly painfully aware of her being very close as she rested her elbows on the railing and he could feel her arm touch his; it took all his control to remain still. He wanted to put his arm around her but still couldn't risk the crew's seeing and saying something to Reza.

"It's spectacular," said Hava softly as she gazed up at the massive bluffs rising to the north of them. The sun had sunk below the horizon, lighting the west with a peach and orange glow, while a thick canopy of stars was emerging above. Even on their home island, evening mist and the village lights dimmed the heavens. Hatu felt her lean against him ever so slightly. His skin felt electric and he began to harden at her touch. He feigned a stumble with the ship's gently rocking motion and quickly slammed his knee into the plank reinforcing the boards below the bulwark, a sharp pain that instantly drove away every sexual thought.

"Are you all right?" asked Hava with barely hidden amusement.

Tears of pain welled in his eyes, but Hatu's voice was steady as he said, "I just slipped. Stupid thing to do. Been on ships since I was a boy and I'm standing here doing nothing . . ."

She stood just inches away looking into his eyes, trying hard not to laugh. "It's fine. Everyone is clumsy once in a while."

Wishing he had come up with a better way to stem his arousal, he nodded as he rubbed his knee. "Yes, everyone . . ."

He had to remember to keep some distance between them. He wanted to be inside of her more than any girl he knew, but to do so would be to risk punishment and death. She was driving him mad now that it was clear she returned his feelings. He knew they would eventually be together, despite it being forbidden. But knowing it was going to happen made being near her even worse. "I've got to stretch this out," he said, climbing into the rigging.

Again trying not to laugh, she said, "I understand."

Hatu made a show of stretching his knee as he moved through the ratlines to the top of the mast and took a seat on a small platform that circled the top yard. It was designed to stand upon; for generations lookouts had sat on it, legs around the mast as they watched the horizon. Not the most comfortable of places, but at least it offered relief for fatigued legs from standing in one position too long.

After a while, the novelty of the horizon began to wear off and he glanced down at the deck to see Hava lost in her own thoughts as she gazed at the cliffs. Glancing skyward, Hatu judged it would be a full hour more before the sunset, and knew that the captain would soon lower sails and anchor. It was what everyone did in the Narrows.

As the Narrows were at the heart of the Covenant, ships were used to a guarantee of safe passage, and Hatu could see that unless someone seized the bluff above, there was little threat. Each ship would light their lanterns and wait until dawn, and not lift anchor until the ship ahead of them began to move.

Once the sun had set, he would eat, and then he was on the night watch. Looking at where they were, he anticipated that his most daunting task would be to remain awake.

As they entered the narrowest part of the passage, Hatu noticed there were more uneven breaks, crevices, and eroded cuts in the rock face. To amuse himself he began planning his ascent in his mind, tracing routes to the plateau above. He lacked any serious climbing experience, though like most boys his age he had been given some instruction. He was nimble and had a knack for it, and found himself wondering if he could actually climb from the rocky shore up to the top of the bluff. It was four times the height of the tallest building he'd ever seen, making those cliffs at least forty stories high—even the cathedral in Sandura stood less than half that height.

Time passed and the sky darkened, and Hatu knew the evening meal would be served soon, so he shimmied down a sheet and landed on the deck where Hava still waited. She smiled at him, the first time in recent memory she seemed genuinely glad to see him. "Food?" she asked.

Hatu nodded, and suddenly she was at his side, their hips touching. He faltered but saved his dignity by indicating that she should go down the companionway before him.

It was relatively quiet at Hatu's end of the table during

the late meal. Hava sat opposite him, and Reza to his left. They spoke little while others in the crew quarters went on about this and that, often loudly, removing any need for Hatu to speak. He was grateful for that.

As the meal wound down, he said to Reza, "How soon do we reach Port Colos?"

Reza said, "If the weather holds, we should be there in a week or so. We'll clear the Narrows tomorrow before sundown, so we have no need to heave to, and from there the currents and wind will be in our favor."

The night watch quickly consumed their meal as the day watch waited above for their food. Hatu nodded once to Reza and Hava and left the table before anyone else, thankful for the time away from the young woman.

He climbed the rigging, seeking his perch aloft. As they were stationary, only a third of the watch was on duty; the rest of the night watch was enjoying a rare night off. The mate hadn't asked why Hatu had volunteered, as he was prepared for grumbling from those he selected for duty.

Once he was settled, Hatu did a quick survey of his surroundings and, seeing nothing out of the ordinary, turned his mind back to his immediate concern: Hava.

Hatu was not introspective by nature; that type of thinking was discouraged among the students of Coaltachin. He had a tendency to brood and gave in to his dark anger if he didn't keep his mind on other things. So, over the years he had learned to obey and act without thought; the only original thought that had ever been encouraged during his training was being clever when executing orders, not questioning them. He had been in tumult so long that avoiding introspection was a habit. Now that he had learned to master his rage, to keep it under control, an original thought formed in a corner of his mind.

All of this turbulence was far more extreme than was warranted by the situation, and for the first time in his young life, Hatu looked inside and asked, *Why am I the way I am?*

Hava had gone back to the quarters she shared with Reza. Keeping watch above, Hatu now sat alone again in the still darkness, which was punctuated by the distant creaking of hulls and the slight groan of anchor chains shifting and rubbing against the wooden eye through which they were fitted.

These faint sounds accompanied the distant splashing of the waves against the rocks below the cliffs, and all conspired to lull Hatu into a near-meditative state. He recognized the feeling because of the calming exercises taught to him as a student, but rather than becoming more focused and ready for action, he instead allowed his mind to drift as never before.

Images rushed past his mind's eye as he focused on how he felt deep inside. There, he found the ever-burning ember the source of his constant anger. Keeping that rage in check had been vital to Hatu's survival, and to harbor it against future need. He'd endured many beatings, countless fights, and long instruction from several masters to bring it under his control. He remembered the witches, and as the first sharp echo of pain surfaced he pushed it aside and let the burning desire to punish them illuminate the memory; for the first time since his escape, Hatu could recall every detail of his captivity dispassionately, his rage set at perfect balance against his fear.

Echoes of his younger days spun past him, images flickered, came and went, and behind them was the rage, trying to burst into flame. A voice from weeks before returned to his memory: *Thinking with your heart has been the undoing of more than one man.*

Zusara's words lingered in his mind, and the feelings he had when Hava pressed up against him came to him unbidden. The echo of desire stirred him and he pushed his arousal aside without having to injure his knee; instead he found a new strength within him that ordered his thinking.

He desired Hava more than any girl or woman he had ever known, yet until he had seen her in Corbara he could not say why. In that instant Hatu knew. He loved her. All the tales and songs he had learned as a student, about love's being a sign of weakness and stupidity, were to be ignored. The burning energy he felt seemed at odds with it, as if it fed mindless passion, not considered thought, but he knew that with contemplation he could reconcile the apparent contradiction.

He suddenly broke out of his reverie and stretched, allowing himself a big yawn. Hatu realized that a deeper trance might uncover something important, but only as he tumbled to the deck below. Still, he had maintained his balance on the small lookout's platform without thought.

That was another thing he needed to explore, he realized, the ability to set his mind to one task while his body completed another. He'd been told only the great adepts and holy men could achieve that state at will.

He realized that because his tenure as a student was almost finished, his need to learn was just beginning. As if it were a cold wave crashing over him, he became aware that his ambitions were outstripping his ability. He was hardly a master of anything. So, then, he asked himself, what were his strengths?

Hatu fell into a near-reverie as he dwelled on what

he was good at, and time passed without his keeping account of it. Suddenly he felt a strange tug he could only interpret as a pull against his mind.

He looked around and up and saw what appeared to be torches at the edge of the bluffs above. From this distance the pinpricks of light were barely perceptible, almost invisible to the human eye, yet he knew they were there, could identify their number and movement, and even somehow feel their presence.

He felt as if his spirit or mind, some essential element of his being, detached from his body, spread out, and sought out something in the lights. He looked around and abruptly knew where every flame, candle, lantern, burned on the ship, even a tiny flame at the end of a taper set to a clay pipe in the captain's quarters.

He didn't find this disassociation with his body alarming; in fact, it felt oddly reassuring and filled him with warmth, a calm glow he had never known before. He could still feel his body, at rest and in balance on the yard with his back to the mast, and he was aware of the night breeze gently ruffling the sail and the slight sway of the ship. Yet he was apart from it, and felt something within him welcoming and drawing the glow to him.

Things that he couldn't put words to were happening to Hatu, things that were as fundamental as the beating of his heart, or breathing without thought, yet as he was aware, from time to time, of his heartbeat and his breathing, he was now aware of this new thing.

He could not name it. Yet he knew it was as much a part of him as his physical body. He knew it was an awakening, something that had always been within him now able to function.

He let his mind follow a flow of energy and felt as if he could ride it to the lights on the ridge above the ship. He let his consciousness be drawn to that warmth.

Time ceased and his senses became attuned to new things, sensations without name, flows and flickers, pulses and slow-moving waves. For the first time in his life he felt an absence of frustration and anger at this lack of understanding. It was a unique experience in Hatu's life.

He looked down at his hand clasped around a rope, and it was awash with a faint glow, like the glimmering of moonlight reflected from rippling water. For the briefest instant he felt on the verge of something wonderful, then it abruptly vanished.

Hatu was jerked into a state of wakefulness that felt almost painful, as if a cold bowl of water had been poured over his face while he had been in the deepest part of sleep. He felt the cool breeze on his damp skin, felt the slow rolling of the ship beneath his feet, and for an instant, the echo of an ache passed through him.

He let out a slow breath. Suddenly he was aware of someone next to him. He turned his head and saw Hava just inches away, her eyes wide and her face pale in the lantern light.

Softly she said, "You were glowing."

He smiled, a feeling of calm pulsing through him. "I know," he answered quietly.

She slowly reached over to touch his arm. "What was that?"

Again he spoke softly, his consciousness spreading outward from the tiny focus he had enjoyed moments before. He was mindful that they were alone on this yard, and that there was a lookout in the bow gazing ahead, and the steersman stood at the helm. The man obviously hadn't been looking up when Hatu's transformation had commenced. For that was how he felt: transformed.

"What did I see?" Hava asked in a low voice, so no one below could overhear her. "You seemed to be bathed in moonlight, but the moon is not risen, and the light came from within you!"

Hatu's mind slowly retreated from the bliss of the experience to a more prosaic awareness. He could feel the nameless sense that had visited him drain away, and the usual concerns of his life return. He was suddenly aware of Hava's hand gripping his forearm, and how close she was.

Without thought, before all sense of what he had experienced was gone, he leaned forward and kissed her, held her close for a long moment, then pulled away.

Her eyes widened even more. "Why did you kiss me?" she whispered.

"Because I wanted to," he answered with a note of humor in his voice.

"You picked the damnedest moment." She looked him in the eyes. "You always were the strangest boy I knew," she said, then leaned forward and kissed him back, briefly, not as an invitation to passion, but as a reassurance and acknowledgment. Hatu understood intuitively without being told.

He whispered, "If anyone noticed, just tell them you saw Erasmus's Fire."

"That only happens when there's a storm coming," Hava replied, though she seemed relieved to have something to discuss besides what had just happened between them.

"So, you were mistaken, but if someone did see, it will throw doubt on what they saw." His gaze narrowed. "So, why were you on deck looking up at me?"

She sighed. "I couldn't sleep, something woke me."

She shrugged. "I knew you were on watch and thought I'd find you so we . . . To have someone to talk with, I guess."

He looked deep into her eyes and then smiled.

"You've changed," she whispered. "What was it that I saw?"

He chuckled. "I have no name for it, but it was perfect."

She whispered again, "You are the strangest boy." She glanced down to see if anyone was watching, then quickly kissed him again. "Very strange."

He touched her cheek gently and said, "You'll help me understand." It wasn't a question or request.

She shivered and without another word moved off the yard and quickly descended the halyard, landing lightly on the deck next to the pin rail. He saw her glance up at him and hurry off to her quarters.

Hatu looked to the east and knew that within minutes the first hints of dawn would announce the coming of the sun; his watch would be over in less than two hours. He scanned all quarters and saw nothing amiss. In his heart he knew there wouldn't be, for he was at this moment at peace for the first time in his anger-filled life, and everything was perfect.

23

An Awakening and Alarm

The young woman's eyes snapped open, as if she had been suddenly yanked from sleep. She stared at the flickering flame in the stone circle before her for a long moment, and then whispered, "I've found him."

Three other acolytes sat, eyes closed, cross-legged and motionless, their hands resting on their knees, on small cushions on the stone floor at the three other compass points,. All wore light brown robes with a crimson trim at the collars and sleeves.

The woman, Sabella, was the youngest, and still possessed a gawkiness many might call "coltish." The description was reinforced for a moment as she stood, her legs uncertain from the long hours sitting in her altered state. She had little idea of how much time she had spent on the search, but from the slowly returning feeling in her legs, it must have been most of the night. She had a round face dominated by large brown eyes made more dramatic by her dark skin and almost featherlike fine dark brown hair.

Sister Sabella hurried from the Room of the Seeking Circle to the stairs leading up to the library, then rushed between the rows of scrolls, tomes, and books, and quickly climbed the stairs to the ground floor of the Sanctuary. The stairway exited under an old but durable oiled canopy arch, keeping all but the worst storms from threatening the already damp lower floors with more water. A lip of raised stone surrounded the entrance, a feature Sabella had stumbled over more times than she cared to remember.

Stepping lightly over that six-inch-high barrier, Sabella took a deep breath of the brisk mountain air. The darkness, illuminated only by distant torches, caused her to pause for a moment as her eyes adjusted. The sight of the Sanctuary before her always provoked awe in her, no matter how many times she'd seen it reflecting brilliant sunlight that caused colors seemingly to dance across the stone faces, or at night when dozens of huge torches and light from behind tall windows gave it an almost otherworldly aspect.

She stood for a moment, calming herself with a deep breath, fighting back the urge to run with abandon toward the massive facade carved into the rock face of the mountain. She knew behind her rose a short stone wall, a few feet beyond that a precipice falling away several hundred feet to another plateau below.

The half-covered yard of the sprawling ancient building shimmered with reflected starlight, as a sudden thundershower had flooded the stone floor. Lifting the hem of her robe, Sabella splashed through shallow puddles to reach the staircase to the upper floor. She climbed until she reached the entrance to the floor where the quarters she shared with the other sisters lay, and the kitchen, work areas, and a door to the outside. The Sanctuary was partially embedded in a mountainside, so the eastern exit was a full story above the western one.

She hurried up the tower steps until she reached the second-to-last landing, which had only two accessible doors. The one on the right was her destination. She knocked loudly.

A sleepy voice from within asked, "Who is it?"

"Sabella. I've found him!"

Within moments, the door was flung open and a middle-aged man in a long nightshirt stood regarding the young woman. His hair, black and tightly curled, was scattered with iron grey, and his skin was darker even than hers, but his eyes were sunken from years of reading tomes in dark towers or deep basements, in poor light. He still had broad shoulders, all that was left of his youthful power. He was a man with more days behind him than ahead. "You're certain?"

Eyes shining and almost in tears, she said, "Yes, only for a moment, but . . . I'm certain."

"Where?" said the man, now wide awake.

"The Narrows."

A thoughtful expression crossed the man's face and he said, "Wait."

He closed the door and in a few moments it reopened, revealing him in a serviceable pair of trousers, a well-worn tunic, and boots and a belt of black leather. "He should be told," said the man.

They hurried up the last flight of stairs to the top-most quarters in the ancient tower. The man knocked on the door and almost at once heard a voice say, "Come in, Denbe."

Pushing the door open, Denbe said, "We—"

"You found him," said the old man.

The room was small, as the tower sloped inward from a large foundation. It was cluttered with scrolls, books, and other items borrowed from the library below. The old man sitting at its desk was dressed in a robe of similar design to the one Sabella wore: light tan in color, but with a broader red trim. Elmish the prior, first of the order, had kept this fading confraternity alive for the last twenty years, by the force of his personality, experience, and unmatched intellect. He was an old man with a fair complexion, his skin almost parchmentlike with red blossoms across his cheeks, and age spots on his forearms and hands. Despite his many years he was still nimble, rising from his seat and moving quickly to the door.

As he hurried onto the landing, he turned to Sabella and said, "Show me," then followed her down the stairs, through the Sanctuary, across the courtyard, and down more stairs to the lower halls and the Seeking Circle. The three women who had searched with Sabella still sat motionless and ignored their arrival.

Motioning for Sabella to retake her seat, Elmish stood behind her and put his hands on her shoulders. Again he said, "Show me."

Sabella closed her eyes. The young woman had almost perfect recall, which was one of the reasons she had risen so quickly among the acolytes, despite her youth. Theirs was an ancient society, secretive and small, known as the Flame Guard to a few, but those who answered its call were always gifted, some even prodigious in their potential.

She felt Prior Elmish in her mind, observing as she recalled the moment she sensed the aura of the one they sought, and lost no detail in the retelling. The first time he had entered her mind, it had been unnerving to the point of causing Sabella to flee the order, but now it was as familiar to her as having a conversation. He possessed unusual abilities that he shared with very few of the order.

When she was finished, Elmish stood behind her silently. While he thought, he held his left arm across his chest and rested his right elbow on it to cup his chin. It was an odd habit, but one she had observed for more than three years now.

Finally he said, "Can you find him again?"

"Perhaps," answered Sabella. "I only found him because . . . something changed. If that happens again . . ."

Elmish shook his head. "It won't. Not in that fashion."

Denbe looked at the other three Seekers, who were still in their trances, and said, "They sensed nothing?"

Elmish gave out a long sigh, due only in part to going without sleep for many hours. "We are not as blessed with adepts as we once were. The destruction of Ithrace . . ." He shrugged. "Still, enough of us have survived."

"As did the child, apparently," said Denbe. He scratched his cheek absently as he observed. "How did we not find him for so many years, when now . . . it appears easy?"

Elmish said, "He's changing."

"How?" asked Denbe.

Elmish moved his hand and the other three acolytes started to blink as they came out of their trances. He said, "We have accomplished much. Thank you. We may need you again soon, but for now, get some food and rest."

Unsteady at first, the three young women stood up without comment and then moved quickly up the stairs. When they were gone, Elmish said, "As a child . . . the fire that burned within him must have been buried very deeply."

"But without our training, how did it not consume him?" asked Denbe.

Elmish shook his head slowly. "I don't know," he admitted. "He must have been an angry child, but by some stroke of fortune he has learned to keep that anger contained." The old man shrugged, then said, "We must find him. Then we'll get the answer to that question and others."

"What next?" asked Denbe.

"He was heading west?" Elmish asked Sabella, to ensure his interpretation of the vision matched hers.

"I think so," she answered. "Yes, I'm almost certain it was west."

The old man thought on this, then said, "If he travels from the east side of the continents, or the islands, through the Narrows, he will seek a port somewhere between the Covenant and . . . Copper Hills."

Denbe gave him a questioning look.

"Any further up the western coast than Copper Hills or along the north shore and it would be easier to sail up the eastern coast and then westward past the ice floes, before winter closes them."

Denbe nodded once, accepting his logic.

Elmish pointed to Sabella and said, "Pack for travel. Be ready to leave—" He paused. "What time is it?"

"Two hours until dawn," answered Denbe.

"Then you shall leave at dawn," said Elmish to the young woman.

Sabella rose from her kneeling position, bowed slightly to the leader of the order, and then hurried up the stairs.

Elmish said, "She has had little training in the ways of the world, so I need you to care for her."

"Me?" asked the old soldier.

"There is no other candidate with the skill I trust," answered the prior. "Too many of us perished at the Betrayal. Few outside of our order and the king's family knew we were not a normal detachment of soldiers in Ithrace's army. Replacing them has taken a while and we are still but an echo of what we once were, but the boy hiding his gifts gave us time." He reached out and gripped Denbe's arm. "She has the greatest chance of finding the boy . . . young man by now, I expect." He sighed. "If he revealed himself to her by accident, he may have also alerted others. We are not the only ones who know the Firemane child survived." He looked Denbe in the eyes. "Take the girl, follow her, protect her, and find the boy. Then bring him back here."

"Then what?"

"Then we begin to right a terrible wrong."

24

An Arrival and a Sudden Change of Plans

Jumping from the side of the ship, Hatu landed on the dock; tossing aside his travel bag, so it was in reach but out of the way, he helped two other men quickly tie the hawser down to a dock cleat.

Once the bowline was secured he looked aft to see another trio of men tying off the stern line. The spring lines he'd leave to the permanent crew, as he was certain that as soon as the gangplank was put out, Reza would be the first ashore, with Hava a step behind.

Hatu thought of what had occurred a few nights earlier on the ship as an awakening. He was uncertain what it truly was, but he knew that it was something he needed no longer to fight, but rather to understand, harness, and make work for him.

Since it had happened, Hatu had experienced strange dreams that left him with fleeting images, seemingly unconnected and sometimes alien to him, yet they tickled something deep inside, some faint recognition.

At times, images surfaced from when he was apparently very tiny, for the people around him loomed over him, and he was lifted and carried. He grabbed glimpses of skies filled with clouds, a flock of birds flying above, a dog barking as someone carried him past a distant farmhouse. The images were vivid in color but faint in sound.

Other dreams made him feel as if he were someone else, in other places, even other times. He had glanced in a mirror to see an elderly man looking back at him, almost defeated by age yet satisfied in some way Hatushaly couldn't grasp. Another image was of a young woman he yearned for, but not in a sexual way; it was a deep need for closeness and comfort.

Instead of the usual frustration he experienced, this time Hatu felt certain that he would come to understand those dreams and images at some point. For the first time in his life, he was close to being at peace, rather than feeling frustration and rage. He considered the images a promise of knowledge to come, answering not only questions he had now, but also those he'd carried with him since childhood. He was almost happy at the prospect. He simply knew better things were in store for him—knew it, not hoped—and Hava was a huge part of that certainty.

She seemed to have noticed the changes in him, though she said nothing to Hatu about them, or the mysterious glow that had engulfed him. She just smiled at him more often. Neither Reza nor the crew seemed aware of any change.

As Hatu had anticipated, the master was the first down the gangplank, followed closely by Hava. Reza motioned for Hatu to follow, so he grabbed his travel bag and hurried a few paces until he caught up.

Hatu followed along. One part of him, what he thought of as his "old mind," kept alert for trouble as he had been trained, marking locations so he could find his way back to the docks. He also evaluated possible escape routes should misfortune befall them, forcing them to flee.

His new perception probed, scanned, and assigned importance to what he witnessed, the trivial but entertaining, the seemingly prosaic but significant. The sense was still forming, and Hatu wasn't sure why it attempted to take in everything around him at once, creating confusion, but that's how his mind insisted on working. He found the new perception odd but not troubling.

A few blocks from the docks, Reza glanced back and saw him staring. "What?" he asked.

Swinging his gaze around as if he were merely sightseeing, Hatu smiled broadly, nodding as if Reza had just said something humorous. Reza and Hava both looked at him sharply. Hatu laughed aloud, then whispered, "We're being watched."

"I know," said Reza. "Port Colos is one of the deepest hives of thieves and murderers on the western shores."

Hatu nodded and chuckled, but said, "No. This is no street watch; I know them very well. This is . . . something else."

"Where?" asked Reza. Without breaking his stride, he leaned down slightly and behaved as if the two of them were sharing a jest.

Hatu said, "Balcony, two buildings ahead on the left. A man in a blue shirt, broad-brimmed black hat."

Reza made a show of laughing and glanced up at the area Hatu indicated. "Gods, how can you know? I can't see his eyes, let alone tell where he's looking."

"I just know," said Hatu calmly. "He's the third. They've been watching us since we left the docks."

Reza looked unconvinced but said to Hava, "Watch the right. Hatu, the left." He laughed one more time and patted Hatu on the shoulder, and they resumed walking.

As they made their way through the crowded streets, Hatu absorbed every detail he could. While part of his mind considered the fastest exit from conflict, another part explored the exotic spice aromas carried from an open stove in a set-back food stall, or wondered why the locals seemed to favor indigo as the dominant color in their clothing, despite the wide variety in their heritage. Their races varied: dark skin, blond hair, short, tall, descendants of mountain people, those whose ancestors rode the planes or trekked the barrens. Yet, those who now lived here dressed in a surprisingly similar fashion: loose shirts, trim trousers, heavy low-cut boots for the men, lighter shoes for the women—no sandals, he noticed. The only variety was in head covers: hats, scarves, or none. Yet most of the fabric used was indigo in color.

As he kept track of Reza and the route he chose toward their destination, Hatu also kept his attention on his surroundings. He knew he could find his way back to any point, despite Reza's circuitous course. He was feeling comfortable with having such heightened senses, this ability to perform multiple tasks while still being able to reflect and evaluate, but he was nowhere near to understanding. It was a new ability, yet familiar somehow, as if it had been part of his nature his entire life.

A new bloom of movement alerted him that something had changed, a warning. "They're moving to cut us off," he said.

Reza glanced at him, a question in his expression. He nodded, then said, "Second door on the right. When I turn, follow me; we move straight through the shop, out the back, and over the wall. Then we run. Do not fall behind. If you get lost, you die."

Suddenly, Reza moved, Hatu and Hava half a step behind him. The shop they dashed into belonged to a fabric seller, its shelves loaded with bolts of cloth and long samples that hung from the ceiling. Reza was already through the rear door when Hava and Hatu entered, and they picked up their pace to keep sight of him. He was clearing the wall as they rushed through the back door, past a surprised-looking shop owner, a woman of advancing years who was too startled to voice any complaint.

Once over the wall, Hatu saw that Reza was heading in the same direction but taking them on a course parallel to the original one. It would take a few minutes for their pursuers to communicate the change in route to those who waited ahead, and Reza was determined to get ahead of all of them.

Having no idea of the layout of this city, Hatu could only guess their destination. He could easily backtrack to any point along the route, but if he left the path, he would be just as lost as he would have been before his newfound abilities manifested.

He had traveled enough to understand how most cities grew, the factors that led to their layout. Businesses that stank—butchers, tanners, dyers, and waste haulers—were always found downwind of the wealthy residential areas. Markets were situated at the intersections of major roads, and citadels and keeps always occupied the high ground. By speculating on what he had seen so far and the type of destination usually used by the gangs of Coaltachin, Hatu anticipated that they were heading toward the merchant sector of the city, to the warehouses. It wasn't a particularly brilliant guess, but he had never thought to extrapolate things before, and that newfound awareness was unique.

As hungry as Hatu was for understanding, prior to the events on the ship, he had never been able to speculate or calculate without emotion. He usually brooded and wallowed in anger, and so cold reason was new to him, but he was enjoying it despite the odd novelty of it.

Hatu was awash with sensations he couldn't name, but sensing little danger, despite the overshadowing threat. He glanced at Hava and saw she was frightened, and for a moment he wondered about that. He considered her fearless and had trouble reconciling it with her visible fear. Then it came to him; she wasn't afraid for her life, she was afraid of failing. She had undertaken a task, and she would rather have died than fallen short of accomplishing it.

He took a moment to catch her eye and when she looked back, he simply nodded, trying to communicate that he thought they'd be all right. She smiled slightly and then returned her attention to Reza's back.

Hatu then understood that there had been truth in Donte's chiding. When he faced Hava in practice, he always wanted to please her, and she desperately wanted to please the masters. It was why he always fell to her. He had always been in love with her, even before he knew what it meant to feel that way, and Donte had known it even if he said nothing directly. Thinking of Donte brought forth a strong echo of regret.

The sound of their feet striking the cobbles and the shouts of angry bystanders marked their hasty course, but Hatu knew that whatever advantage Reza had gained them would be lost in another few minutes.

Suddenly, the master darted right into an alley and made a short dash between two buildings, and they faced a large warehouse. Reza halted and motioned for silence, pointing to his right. They started moving back the way they had come, almost running the short distance and turning left to stand before an unmarked door.

Hatu looked for any sign of pursuit and saw none, but he knew it would only be minutes before those who followed discerned their true path. He saw Reza knock a code on the door, and a moment later it opened. A large man stood in front of them, filling the entrance. "Yes?"

Reza said, "I carry a message from our grandfather for your leader."

The big man stroked his black-bearded chin, his eyes narrowing. "Is that so? And who might you be?"

"I have a message from our grandfather for your leader," repeated Reza.

"I heard you the first time," said the big man. "And I asked who you were." His hand fell to the hilt of a large knife at his belt.

"I have a message from our grandfather for your leader," Reza said a third time.

The man stood aside. "Enter, friend. Can't be too careful."

"I'm Reza."

The big man said, "A name well-known. I'm Lachlan. Let me get Killebrew."

Hatu glanced around and saw familiar surroundings.

The warehouse served a double duty as a trans-shipping location for goods both legitimate and purloined. Contraband combined with legal merchandise would pass more easily through customs. He assumed that Port Colos had no duty inspectors, as the captain had ordered the men to start unloading the cargo before Hatu, Hava, and Reza left the *Odalis*. But goods shipped to more regulated ports, like those in the barony of Marquensas and Kingdom of Ilcomen, would have to go through some sort of examination.

The rest of the building belonged to the crew, and from what Hatu could see, it was a fairly large base. He assumed that its size meant that the masters of Coaltachin controlled most crime in the city, which led him to wonder who served them here. Hidden from casual sight would be a kitchen, a rude dormitory, secret entrances, and an emergency exit.

Lachlan returned accompanied by an older man, and as soon as he saw him, Hatu understood that Port Colos was indeed a critical port, because unless he was completely mistaken, this man they called Killebrew, which was almost certainly not his real name, was a master himself, or at least a first captain.

The older man stood slightly shorter than Lachlan but was still broad, and his grey hair and beard didn't diminish his look of authority and strength. He smiled broadly when he caught sight of Reza and they embraced like old friends. Then Killebrew pulled away and said, "How's your father?"

"Well enough, thank you. Not wishing to cut short the pleasantries, but we were almost intercepted on our way here."

With a single gesture, Killebrew indicated that Lachlan should investigate that claim. Hatu knew that members of this crew would be on the streets within minutes, trying to identify whoever chased them.

"Come along and rest," said Killebrew. He took one step toward the back of the building and the door behind Hatu was crashed off its hinges and flew inward, slamming against the stone floor.

Weapons were drawn immediately, and Hatu, Hava, and the others turned to see armed men pour through the door. They wore a variety of dress, but from the way they moved, Hatu instantly recognized they were not common thugs, but soldiers or assassins. They came through the door in an organized fashion, ready for a fight the instant they entered the warehouse. A voice from outside shouted, "Take him alive!"

The man nearest Hatu hesitated for the briefest moment, uncertain how to proceed after hearing that command. Hatu stepped forward and cut the man's neck before he could respond.

It was clear that the attackers had no regard for anyone else. An arrow shot past Hatu, close enough for him to feel the air move against his cheek, and a scream erupted behind him, followed by the sound of someone thrashing on the floor.

Hatu slashed a man who came at him unarmed, trying to wrestle him down. As the man fell back, Hatu saw two more a step behind him. For a moment time froze and Hatu considered his choices; bracing to engage their attackers or turning to flee, but the decision was taken from him as a strong hand grabbed him by the collar and yanked him backward.

The big man, Killebrew, jerked him around and pushed him toward Reza. Hava had found a bow in a nearby weapons locker and started firing at the men in the doorway, who made easy targets outlined by the light.

"Behind me, the door!" shouted Reza.

Hatu was one step past him when he heard an arrow strike home and Hava gasp. He looked back and saw Reza slowly turning to face him, an arrow in his neck and blood fountaining from the wound in an arc as he fell sideways, his eyes already vacant. Hava's eyes were wide, but she turned back and quickly loosed another arrow.

Hatu hesitated for only an instant after witnessing Reza's death. He shouted, "This way!" and Hava glanced around to see if there was an immediate threat. Killebrew's men were holding the attackers at bay for a moment, so she hurried after Hatu. They rushed through a door into a narrow alley between the warehouses, facing a solid wall with no doors or windows, and without hesitation Hatu turned right and ran.

He only had a vague idea of where they were in the city, but Hatu felt a calm sense of certainty that he couldn't explain as he ran as fast as he could, wending his way between buildings and making turns using only his instincts. He knew they were moving away from the harbor and then realized that the pattern of streets he had previously observed gave him confidence in his route. His newfound ability to map where he had been, the strange intuition he now possessed, and his understanding of how the city should have been organized combined to erase any uncertainty.

Hava trusted his lead, following with as much speed as she could muster. Hatu might have been the fastest boy in their class, but she had been the fastest girl and she could keep pace with him.

While he ran, keenly aware of his surroundings and using his newly discovered abilities to keep them from running into a dead end, or up a blind alley, Hatu considered what had just occurred. He'd warned Reza of the ambush and they'd wrongly thought they'd eluded those men. Obviously whoever had waited in ambush had caught up with them and entered the warehouse with murderous efficiency and overwhelming numbers. It was a certainty that those who'd invaded the gang's hideout would eventually kill Killebrew and his crew—some of whom might have fled in time— but despite their sacrifice, those who'd attacked would soon be on Hatu and Hava's trail. For all his abilities and speed, he had no doubt those chasing them would include a few good trackers, and two youths running frantically through the city would hardly escape notice. He knew little beyond that, except evasion and finding shelter were his only goals.

Both Hatu and Hava were the products of rigorous training and were able to run faster and further than most, but those in pursuit were clearly not most people. They needed to go to ground quickly, in a sheltered, defensible location, or find a way to disappear.

Hatu halted in the alley just before they reached the open street, and Hava, half a step behind him, stopped. He scanned the area but saw nothing that offered them a defensible position. He glanced back and saw no signs of pursuit. Hava watched him intensely as she waited for him to act.

Hatu couldn't explain why, but he felt a need to turn

left down this new street. He nodded at her once and walked on, moving slightly faster than those around him, but not so quickly as to attract attention. At the next intersection he turned right and instantly understood why he was taking this route.

Straight ahead lay a busy market, and past that a substantial gate. Hatu knew there would be a caravanserai outside, as they were in the southeast corner of the city, and the road from the gate was the major southern trading artery for the baronies of the Copper Hills, Marquensas, and others on the western frontier of the kingdom of Ilcomen. And it would lead them to the town of Pashtar and Master Bodai.

A glance over his shoulder reassured Hatu that he was still not being followed, but he knew it would not be the case for long. To Hava he said, "How much coin do you have?"

"A few gold coins and small gems sewn in the hem of my shirt," she answered quietly between heavy breaths. He nodded once, and she took it to mean he wanted the coins.

She ripped the bottom of her shirt, deftly caught the coins and gems as they fell out, and handed them to Hatu. He handed back one gold coin and said, "Find us new shirts of a different color, and get yourself a man's hat. When we ride out we will look like two men. I'll find us some horses and meet you just beyond the gate. Find a sack of travel food and a water skin each, as well. All right?"

She nodded once and scurried off. He paused for just a moment, recognizing he had taken command without hesitation and Hava did not dispute his being in charge. With Reza dead someone had to decide what to do, and he possessed a certainty that was new but somehow surprised neither of them. He took one more deep breath, then moved through the crowded square, and beyond the gate he saw a horse merchant with a string of mounts. Wagons, carts, and pack mules were also being loaded. Glancing skyward he realized it was just after midday and most of those departing soon would do so the next morning.

Hatu paid too much for the two horses with tack, but he haggled just enough that the trader wouldn't take notice of his expertise. Leaving a satisfied merchant behind would ensure more anonymity than leaving one who felt abused by a bargain.

Hatu almost didn't recognize Hava until she was a few feet away. She wore a large-brimmed floppy hat and had smeared a fair bit of dirt on her face. Her walk was now a more masculine rolling gait, she had a fair-sized sack slung over one shoulder, and she spoke in a lower tone. "We ready?" she asked.

He nodded, saying, "Yes, brother."

The merchant glanced at Hava and then promptly ignored her. Hatu and Hava quickly mounted and started down the road.

Hatu gave one last glance behind them and again saw no pursuit. He surmised that the crew in the warehouse had slowed the attackers down enough to give Hatu and Hava a decent head start, and it would take some time for their unknown enemy to pick up their trail again, if they somehow could. Hatu was not presuming they were away free but counted it possible. They rode away at a canter and put Port Colos behind them.

As the sun lowered in the west, Hatu took for granted that they would not be overtaken before nightfall. He started looking for a secure place to camp and spied a large rock formation halfway up a tree-covered hillside.

"That looks like a good spot," he said to Hava, who nodded agreement.

"If we can tie the horses up a bit beyond, and they stay silent, no one is likely to notice us," she responded.

He looked around and saw a rocky patch of ground near the verge of the road and pointed to it. She fell in behind him, leading her mount as Hatu led his horse there. To any tracker it would look as if they had chosen to leave the road here. He knew that by dismounting their tracks would be shallower—though only an experienced tracker would notice the difference, and while Hatu was almost certain they had one with them, he wouldn't speculate on his skill. It was better to assume he knew his trade.

He picked his way between trees and over the rocky ground, attempting to leave a false trail to the crest of the rise. A long barren ridge of rock lay along the spine of these hills, and when he reached it, Hatu saw the patches of rock and scrubby trees continued down the slope and into the distance. He quickly calculated a route down but led their horses north, doubling back parallel to the road until they met a long patch of hard-packed earth that led uphill to a sheltered outcrop above the rock formation he had spied from the road. It was broad and deep enough for them to take cover for the night. They tied off the horses downhill, keeping them tacked up in case they needed to make a swift departure.

Hava said, "That's a good false trail, Hatu. Even if they follow it and double back, we'll hear them go past and be gone by the time they return."

He smiled at her approval and took a deep breath, as close to relaxing as he could get. "No fire, I think."

Hava nodded. She opened her backpack, pulled out

a tightly wrapped oilskin package, and unrolled it. Hatu recognized the travel food: dried rolls of crushed peas, a specific type of white fish, and a few other ingredients that had been selected for their scentless quality. An agent might easily be betrayed by body odor, so producing any distinctive scent, by consuming spicy, perfumed, or pungent foods like garlic, onion, and peppers, was avoided when traveling. Their meal was slightly bitter but nourishing.

Hava handed Hatu a roll. He nodded his thanks and softly asked, "Where did you find travel rolls?"

She smiled. "In my backpack. I didn't buy us food because I already had some. We can buy more along the way if we need to."

He nodded. "Always one step ahead of me, aren't you?"

Her smile broadened. "Usually."

As night fell, they huddled together for warmth and Hatu found himself comforted by her closeness and fascinated by his feelings. Hava had been a mystery to him his entire life, even though he felt he knew her better than anyone but Donte. There were things he wanted to talk to her about, his feelings and his new-found abilities, but this hardly seemed like the time or the place. He also knew that neither of them would be quick to sleep, though resting this way would keep them more alert and able to defend themselves should the need arise.

After a while he could feel her tension and he whispered, "Reza?"

He could feel her start to nod in the darkness, then she whispered, "Yes. It was a lucky shot for the archer, unfortunate for Reza."

"His father will understand; he will not be pleased, but he will understand," whispered Hatu. "No blame will come to us." He thought of Master Kugal's rage at Donte's fate and hoped he spoke the truth.

She shrugged in the dark and he felt her relax a little.

After a few minutes of silence, he whispered, "Noconochi training, what's that like?"

"Why?" she responded. She reached back and put her hand to his groin. "Do you wish to have sex with me?" she asked, trying to be playful despite the circumstances.

"Yes," he replied, "just not now." He gently moved her hand so as not to become even more distracted. "I am just curious; I know little of the Powdered Women."

"I understand. You're not pretty enough to be sent there . . ."

He made a shushing sound and then chuckled. "I try not to dwell on my hideous appearance."

She laughed, then said, "The act itself is simple, just

like when the farm animals do it, but it's other things, like learning how to behave as if a man is pleasing you. A lot of it is acting. Some roles are difficult at first, but once you master them, they are just something you do. The men they pick to train with us are . . . eager, but most of them are very uninteresting to be around, though they only let them linger when we practiced in the way of little talk."

"Little talk?"

"After a man spends himself, most wish to leave or simply roll over and sleep. So keeping him in the bed requires some talent. Holding his cock as if getting him ready for more sex works sometimes; asking questions to make him feel important can work, too. Many men get stupid or let their guard down after sex. So that 'little talk' while in the fading glow of sex is when some men reveal the things they should keep secret. It's easy to take advantage of them because they want to show you how clever they are, how much power they have, or how important their influence is to others. Small talk is very important to a Powdered Woman. It is a little-recognized art of spy craft.

"I didn't care that much for being with other girls, and thank the gods I was never paired with Nessa."

Hatu couldn't help but laugh at that and forced himself to keep his laughter as quiet as possible. "Well, that might have been . . . interesting." He snuggled closer to her as the night began to grow colder. "And maybe fun to watch."

She elbowed him hard in the ribs and he winced. "Sorry."

"They were going to teach us how to sing, though I'm not very good, and dance, play instruments, cook special dishes . . . Had I not been sent home . . ."

"You never said why," he observed.

She shrugged. "I had a talk with the mistress who is in charge of the school. She suggested my talents would better serve elsewhere.

"They teach anything and everything to lure a man into betrayal." She let out a small sigh. "I don't think I was going to be very good as a Powdered Woman." She wished she could tell Hatu about her fight with the spy, but she obeyed her orders to remain silent.

Hatu said nothing. He realized that he had been thrown so off balance by Hava's appearance, he had never asked why she might be on this journey with him. Master Facaria had told him only that she was coming with him, but not why. Why the journey in the first place? He felt a chill wash over him. There was a reason that wasn't apparent, but should be.

She continued to chat about the skills she'd been taught, and as he heard every word, his mind also raced through the possible reasons why she of all people would be called out of training to accompany Reza and himself on this mission. Reza would have sufficed, or Hatu could even have traveled alone at his age. Or any student or young sicari on the island could have served, but instead Zusara had sent for Hava.

His mind quickly discarded probable reasons and finally he realized why Master Facaria had been summoned to the meeting of the masters. He had told Zusara to pick Hava for this journey.

But why her? One reason kept presenting itself to Hatu, but he kept pushing it aside as he explored other choices. He narrowed down every possible motive until he remembered his conversations with both Masters Facaria and Zusara and how they had both focused on his feelings for Hava.

Hava fell silent and Hatu realized she had dozed off. He decided to let her sleep while he kept alert and concentrated on this new conundrum. After a while he realized that only one thing was certain: Facaria had told Zusara of his infatuation with Hava, and Zusara had probably concluded that she was now the only person on Garn who could get inside Hatu's defenses. Both masters considered her to be the most important person in Hatu's life: she could be a powerful weapon to use for him or against him. The yet-unanswered question was, why would the masters feel the need to have someone able to get this close to him?

A distant sound interrupted his reverie and he roused Hava with a gentle squeeze of her shoulder. She came alert, heard the sound of approaching horses, and was on her feet at the same moment as Hatu.

They scampered out from beneath the overhang and down to where the horses were tied. They calmed the horses, stroking their muzzles and holding their bridles gently. There was a risk that they would catch the scent of the approaching horses and nicker in greeting. Even the slightest chance of being heard had to be avoided.

Hava and Hatu were near motionless as the sound of riders became louder, reached a crescendo, and then faded away. Hatu was almost certain they were from the group that had attacked the warehouse. Once they reached the next town and asked about riders passing through, they would double back to check the road again.

Neither Hatu nor Hava had any knowledge of the terrain or the region, other than knowing where the road led. Hatu said, "They'll return."

"How soon?"

He considered for a minute. "They fought Killebrew's men and will ride through the night. They can trade horses in the next village, but they will be tired . . . They will probably rest and wait for us to overtake them. When we fail to show tomorrow, they will come back. Noon at the latest, I think."

Hava remained silent, watching him in the faint light of the rising moon.

After a while he said, "If we can catch up with them, arrive at the town without being seen, while they ask about us, find new mounts and the rest . . ."

Hava said, "We could circle around the town perhaps?"

"If it's not surrounded by bloody farms, yes, we could. Even a small wood could conceal our passing." Passing through any farm would prove risky; one barking dog would bring a farmer outside to care for his animals or crops and short of killing that farmer, there was no guarantee their presence would be kept secret, especially if those following Hatu and Hava offered a reward for information on their whereabouts. They would still have a head start, but Hatu would rather have lost them altogether.

"What if it is all farms?"

"We go to ground and wait for them to come back this way." He thought. "They might have to travel all the way to Port Colos to be certain we didn't double back and pass them in the night. They might think we've decided to look for a ship." Almost whispering to himself, he added, "We only have a problem if they fan out and search all around the town." Seeing her brow furrow he quickly added, "We should be able to best one or two of them."

Hatu decided it was not a good idea to mention to Hava that he didn't know what they would do if they were being tracked using magic, or whatever it was that had given him his unusual awareness.

She nodded.

"If we can reach the other side of the next town without being seen, we should be well free of them."

"Who are they?" she asked.

"I don't know," Hatu replied. "But they may be related to the ships that tried to attack us." He took a deep breath and let it out slowly. "Speculation is futile."

She looked at him, then said, "I don't have any better ideas."

"Let's go, then," he said finally.

As he mounted, Hatu again thought about why Hava had been summoned, and as they rode quietly through the trees to the road, he speculated about why she might attempt to kill him and how to stop her feeling the need to do so.

25

Upheaval and Changes

Declan awoke to the sound of voices. His room at the top of the house was usually quiet, but the noise was loud enough to carry from the street. He pulled on his trousers, boots, and tunic and by the time he was downstairs, he saw Jusan opening the front door.

"What is it?" Declan asked.

"Don't know," said his apprentice, "but it's getting louder."

They hurried outside to see an orange-yellow glow in the sky, and Jusan said, "Fire!"

Both men hurried toward the glow and joined the growing crowd making their way toward the blaze. The closer they got to the fire, the louder the clamor and the more anxious both Declan and Jusan became. Before they turned the last corner they knew the fire was at the Inn of the Three Stars, and the young men sprinted the last half block until they encountered a wall of onlookers.

Nothing had been organized to combat the fire, and Declan had to push his way through the press of people who were merely watching the inn's destruction. "Gwen!" he shouted as loud as he could.

People gave way as he continued shouting Gwen's name and pushing past gawkers. Jusan followed closely. They reached a small clearing in the crowd just a short distance from where the heat became too intense. A pair of men knelt over a figure on the ground. Leon lay motionless, his face covered in blood, and Declan didn't need a second look to see he was dead.

"Gwen!" he shouted.

"Millie!" Jusan called a moment after.

A woman nearby said, "They only pulled Leon out."

A man near her said, "Those men, they took the girls, I think."

"What men?" demanded Declan.

"Half a dozen mean-looking bastards," said a third. "I saw them ride up as Leon was about to close. I think he tried to argue but they pushed and he let them in." Glancing at the dead man on the ground he added, "He'd pick a profit over a fight any day, though he was no coward, that I know."

Grabbing Jusan by the arm, Declan said, "Go saddle two horses."

"What horses?" said the young man, visibly shaken.

"Any horses. Steal them if you have to!"

As Jusan ran off, Declan shouted, "They've taken Gwen and Millie! Jusan and I are going after them. Will anyone ride with us?" Declan turned to a youth standing next to him and said, "You, Mick."

The boy turned his attention from the fire and said, "Yes?"

"Tomas Bowman, do you know him?"

The boy nodded. "Everyone does." Bowman was a near-legendary tracker in the region and reputed to have once been the best archer in Marquensas.

"Carry word that we need him, now go."

The boy hesitated as if he wished to stay and watch the fire, but then realized he was being asked to do something important, nodded, and ran off.

Several people muttered about what they considered good reasons not to pursue the riders—how they looked like mercenaries or bandits, or the fact that they themselves were not fighters—but one man pushed through the crowd. Declan recognized Bergun, a large fellow who'd often frequented the Three Stars.

He regarded the crowd darkly and with a contemptuous tone said, "I'll ride with you. Leon was my friend. I'll help you fetch his girls back."

After a moment, two other men held up their hands, and slowly, four others stepped forward. They were all hard men, used to defending the village, but chasing after trained warriors was something to make any farmer or merchant take pause.

When it was clear no more men would volunteer, Declan shouted, "Get horses! We ride as soon as everyone reaches the south-bend road!"

He pushed his way past onlookers and ran to his smithy. He found Jusan leading a pair of horses toward him. "Whose are they?" asked Declan.

"Donald Dumple's," replied his apprentice as he handed him the reins to a stocky bay gelding.

"You ask him?" said Declan as he mounted.

"He wasn't home," answered Jusan. "I expect he's down there watching the fire."

Declan saw the boy Mick running toward him. Almost out of breath, the lad said, "Tomas Bowman is passed out drunk, said his daughter." The boy took a deep breath. "She said she'd try to rouse him and get him to follow."

Declan nodded once and said, "You did well, Mick. Now go and see if anyone else down by the inn needs help." The boy turned and scurried off toward the burning inn.

Declan led Jusan to the south end of town and waited until the four other men rode up. He surveyed the men who had decided to help rescue Gwen and Millie and said, "The men we're chasing are brutal, do not forget that. I thank you for being here." Without waiting for anyone to respond, he turned his mount southward, put heels to flanks, and set the horse off at a fast canter.

Declan's party rode as fast as possible without punishing the horses. He hoped whoever kidnapped the girls assumed they were clear of pursuit and had slowed their pace. He also prayed silently to any god who would listen that they wouldn't stop, because he knew what that would mean.

After ten minutes of hard riding, Declan held up his hand to slow his company down, to save the horses. It could be a long chase. As he looked over his shoulder, he noticed they had picked up another rider, one he'd not seen at the south-bend road out of town.

He waved the company to a halt and rode back to confront the new horseman. Declan rode closer and saw a familiar face, half-hidden by a deep hood. He leaned forward and said, "Molly Bowman, what do you think you're doing?"

The young woman threw back her hood and tossed her cloak over one shoulder, revealing a horse bow and back quiver full of arrows. "Gwen's my friend, Declan. I've known her a damn sight longer than you have. Besides, you don't have one archer in this company of fools; you're chasing after experienced mercenaries, not stupid town bullies. And I'm as good a tracker as my da."

Declan glanced over his shoulder at the men, who had turned to watch the encounter, men who knew Molly well. Several nodded slightly. Declan said, "Does your father know? I sent a lad to fetch him."

"Hell no," she almost spat. "He's home, asleep drunk as usual. Didn't even stir with all the fuss just down the street. When Mick showed up, I couldn't rouse him, so I decided to take his place."

Tomas Bowman had been an almost legendary hunter, but it was common knowledge that since the death of his wife, Molly's mother, he had taken to heavy drinking. It was also common knowledge that Molly now did most of the hunting and provided for her family. She was of modest height, slightly stocky, but stronger than a lot of men her size. Declan had seen her carry a deer into town on her shoulders.

Declan said nothing for a moment, then nodded, having no good argument against her joining them, and by the time he'd returned to the front of his makeshift company, he was glad to have her bow. He'd never seen a better archer than Molly, in Oncon or Beran's Hill.

They moved out quickly and rode through the night. As the sun began to rise, Declan saw fresh horse droppings, steaming a little in the morning chill. He signaled a stop and dismounted. He whispered, "They're close."

He held up a hand, indicating the others should wait while he scouted ahead on foot. He heard low voices before he saw the dim light of a smoldering campfire.

Creeping between trees, treading cautiously to avoid stepping on twigs or anything else likely to make a noise, Declan knelt and peered at the backs of two men talking quietly. He moved slowly in a crawl, so he could hear.

". . . soon and sell them," one of the two men was saying.

"Tyree has a fancy for the plump one and if he thinks we're clear, he'll take her right in the road, the rest of us be damned. Hell, he might enjoy an audience."

"No procurer in any city is going to give us a copper for her after Tyree is done."

"You saw what he did to Misener. You going to call him out over a few coins? Choy looked like he was rooting for Misener, and Tyree opened him up from throat to groin, let him stand there for a second and watch his own guts fall out! You want to face that madman?"

The other man shook his head. "We came this way to find a ship. Sandura's paying top price for fighters; everyone says so. Now we're not even heading in the right direction. We're supposed to ship out at Port Colos, but here we are riding right back into Marquensas, halfway to Marquenet. All because Tyree has a bloody temper and a stiff prick."

"Like I said, you going to tell him no?"

Declan couldn't see everyone around the fading campfire. He thought he caught a glimpse of two shadowy figures huddled on the other side of the glowing pit, but he couldn't be certain it was the two girls.

Declan quietly crept away until he felt confident he was far enough to stand and hurry back. He motioned for his companions to dismount. He whispered, "The sun will be up soon, and they'll stir. I think the girls are safe, but I can't be certain. If we approach too quickly, we'll give them warning . . ." He hesitated, uncertain what to do next. In the gloom outside the campfire he could see where Tyree might be. If Declan could find the means to quickly kill him, perhaps the others might be less willing to fight.

Molly stepped forward and said, "Where's the campfire?"

Declan pointed, and she nodded. "Give me two minutes to get behind them, then come rushing in. I'll kill anyone who goes near the girls. If you hear any noise, don't wait."

As Molly hurried off silently, like the practiced hunter she was, Declan looked at his companions. Jusan was near frantic with worry about Millie, so he put a hand on his apprentice's shoulder and said, "Calm. Remember how you were injured in Oncon? This is worse; rashness will get both you and her killed."

The others were tough, resolute men, several of them experienced brawlers, Declan was certain, but none of them were trained soldiers. Declan had the numbers and the element of surprise, but if they didn't disable at least two of the mercenaries before the others discovered that they were under attack, it would be a close fight, and more, the girls would be at risk.

Declan waited and after what he judged to be enough time for Molly to reach the other side of the clearing, he pulled his sword and nodded to the others. They produced various weapons, swords, axes, and long knives, and looked resolute. Declan gave Jusan one last glance, trying to communicate that the apprentice needed to keep his focus and not do anything stupid, then he turned and walked quickly toward the campfire.

A steady stride coupled with purpose seemed to have a calming effect on Declan. He felt the anxiety over Gwen's safety, anger, and nervousness drain away, and again became aware of the odd sense of calm that had enveloped him when the slavers struck Oncon. He welcomed it. Clarity settled over him and his feelings for Gwen faded into the background as his need to emerge victorious came to the fore.

Declan was the first to run into the faint light of the campfire, and by the time the first mercenary stood and turned, blood was fountaining from a deep gash on his neck. The second man had his sword and shouted a warning, and the others in the camp sprang to their feet.

The woods echoed with the ringing of steel on steel, and the battle was joined. For the second time in his life, Declan felt time slow and gained a clear vision of his surroundings. He was aware of the man he faced, but he could also see what occurred beyond his own struggle. He sensed as much as saw the men of Beran's Hill driving back the mercenaries, two against one in most cases.

As he parried a blow from the man in front of him,

Declan saw a figure racing toward the two bound women on the ground. "Molly!" he shouted as an arrow sped through the air. The figure ducked, rolled, and came up in a crouch over the two recumbent forms, a large knife in his hand. Declan's hesitation at the sight of the blade almost cost him his life, for it allowed his current foe to get his blade inside his guard and Declan felt the man's sword cut through his leather vest and shirt, almost grazing his ribs.

He slipped his blade inside the other man's hold and jerked upward, slicing into his armpit and almost taking his arm off at the shoulder. The swordsman screamed, but then quickly fell silent as he passed out from pain and blood loss. Declan kicked him aside as he sought out the figure menacing the girls.

A mercenary hurried to where the girls were trussed like poultry waiting to be cooked, with a knife-wielding figure hunched over them. Suddenly the running mercenary fell back, an arrow in his chest. Another arrow missed the crouching man by mere inches, and Declan recognized him as the one called Tyree.

Tyree fell on top of the two bound girls, eliciting muffled cries, and Declan realized they had been gagged as well as bound. Throwing an elbow at Millie, Tyree grabbed Gwen and crawled backward as another arrow sped past, just missing him. He pulled himself up against a sheltering tree and yanked the bound girl up by her hair, causing her to cry out despite the gag.

Arrows flew through the air, as Molly Bowman seemed able to pick off targets despite their swift changes of position. Not every shot was a kill shot, but enough damage was being done that it seemed like several archers lingered in the woods.

Declan's heartbeat skipped as he realized the crazy young mercenary was using Gwen as a human shield. As his companions were overcome, several of them throwing down their swords in surrender, the young mercenary raised the belt knife he held to her throat a little, twisting it so the fire threw a flashing reflection, emphasizing the danger she was in.

"Molly, don't shoot!" Declan shouted as Tyree huddled against the tree, clutching a whimpering Gwen. His awkward efforts to rise were foiled by the struggling girl and the tree bark catching his armor.

"Let her go!" Declan demanded.

The young fighter laughed, and the sound of it chilled Declan, for there was a ring of unmistakable madness in it. "Let her go? So your archer can use me for target practice?" Resting his chin on Gwen's shoulder, Tyree said, "Here's how this is going to play . . ." He pressed his dagger against the side of Gwen's neck, which brought a muffled sound of pain and fear from her.

Declan's anger rose, and he heard Jusan say, "Remember what you told me!" His eyes traveled to the still-motionless form of Millie on the ground and he knew Jusan was fighting each second to keep from rushing to her. Without taking his eyes off Tyree, Declan nodded that he understood his apprentice's admonishment to keep his wits about him.

For a tense moment Tyree remained silent, then he continued. "I'm going to stand and if any of you fools decide to do something stupid, this girl dies before I do." He pushed her away, causing the blade to slice into her neck a little, a trickle of blood punctuating his warning.

Tyree gathered his feet under him in a crouch and then stood, yanking Gwen upward by her hair. She cried in pain, again muffled by her gag, but she fell silent once she had her feet under her.

Her eyes were wide, and Declan could see Gwen was terrified. For a moment he was motionless, riveted by indecision. One wrong move and the woman he loved would be dead, yet part of him was equally intent on killing the man who held her captive. Then he saw movement off to the left.

Circling the edge of the clearing, Molly Bowman appeared to be looking for a clear shot at Tyree. Declan found himself even more rooted, fearful that any gesture or expression might inform the mercenary that

Molly was moving behind him, yet he was also fighting to keep himself from charging the murderer, as if he could rescue Gwen by force of will alone.

Apparently at an impasse, the two men stared at one another for a few seconds, until finally Declan said, "What do you want?"

"I'm leaving," said Tyree. "Should any of you fucking fools try to stop me, she dies."

"You're not getting on your horse," said Declan calmly. "You try to get on a horse with her, you're dead before you're in the saddle."

"Well, then, maybe I should just kill the bitch and get it over with."

Declan slowly lowered his sword and held up his left hand, palm outward. "If I let you ride out unharmed, you'll let her go?"

Tyree laughed. "And I'm supposed to believe you'd let me ride away? After I killed her da?"

Declan glanced around, seeing the rest of Tyree's company either dead or captive. He saw the fear in Gwen's eyes, the pleading, and finally he said, "Here's my bargain. You let her go and fight me. You win, you and your men ride out of here. You lose . . ." Declan shrugged. "You won't care what happens to them." He inclined his head toward the remaining mercenaries.

Tyree tilted his head slightly to one side while he

thought for a moment. "Have those archers come around where I can see them."

Declan motioned for Molly to come to his side.

When she reached a spot near Declan, Tyree said, "One? One girl?" He grinned and said, "Damn, girl, you're a wonder. After I kill this boy, come ride with me. I'll show you how to hunt gold instead of rabbits."

He laughed and threw Gwen aside. Taking a stride and making half a leap, he brought his sword down toward Declan's head almost before Declan could get his sword up to block. One of the onlookers swore, and another complained, "Nothing fair about this fight."

Declan threw his weight behind the block, causing Tyree's blade to slide along his, and then put his shoulder to the mercenary, forcing the man off balance. Declan then spun, bringing his blade around in a circular blow that should have taken Tyree's head from his shoulders if it connected, but the experienced fighter had his sword up high to block as he slipped to his left and avoided being decapitated.

Moving back half a step in a crouch, Tyree's eyes seemed to glow with madness. "Boy can fight a bit? That's nice. Slaughter is fun but no accomplishment. The girl's da, he was easy enough. Wept like a child as I drove my sword point into his gut." Declan realized Tyree was attempting to goad him into acting rashly.

Declan also recognized that this fighter was no less deadly for his madness. If anything, his demented thinking might cause him to act in a way that could not be anticipated, ending Declan's life and perhaps others', including Gwen's. There was no guarantee she'd be safe if he died. Molly might start shooting and the captives might try to attack.

Declan turned his mind away from speculation a second before Tyree took a step forward with a high arching blow that Declan turned to his right. The smith then made a simple extended counterthrust, his sword's point almost reaching the mercenary's chest. Only a rapid disengagement and step back kept Tyree from a serious wound.

Declan let his surface thoughts fade, and again felt time slow and the image of his opponent take on a more detailed aspect, as if light and dark were intensified, and details came alive. He felt as he had when fighting in Oncon; his awareness expanded.

He could see the muscles tense beneath the man's skin, flexing and getting ready, see the tiniest shift in weight from one foot to another. Tyree's eyes darted, seeking an obvious opening, and Declan decided to show him one.

Declan lifted his right elbow and flexed his arm as if he was going to take a round swing at Tyree's more vulnerable left side. Tyree leapt inside the blow, holding his blade back for a forward thrust , as he anticipated that Declan's front would become exposed.

Declan turned his blade point down, pushing Tyree's sword to his left and skimming his side, then he lifted the hilt of his sword and slammed it into Tyree's exposed neck with the forte of the blade—the heavy base just below the crossguard—which was rarely used except in situations like this, extremely close combat. Which was why Edvalt had taught him to put an edge there, up to the quillon block, where the crossguard was seated. He snapped the hilt of the sword forward, and Tyree staggered back, blood fountaining from a severed artery in his neck.

He looked at Declan, eyes wide, then put his hand to his neck and saw it come away red. He staggered again, then fell to the ground, next to the tree, his eyes staring blankly up at the early morning sky as he went limp.

Declan felt an icy detachment. He looked at Gwen, still bound and gagged, and for a long moment it was as if he looked at a complete stranger. Then a wave of heat passed through him, and suddenly relief surged within, bringing him to the point of tears. He rushed over to Gwen and untied her, and she fell into his arms sobbing. He held her, saying nothing, letting her release her terror. After a while, she whispered, "I knew you'd come for me."

"I'll always come for you."

He saw that Jusan had freed Millie; her eyes were round with terror and her features were drained of blood. She looked on the verge of madness, and Declan realized he now had additional responsibilities. With the inn burned, Gwen and Millie had nothing, no roof over their heads and no way to make a living, only the clothes on their backs. He spoke loud enough for Jusan and Millie to hear, "We'll get you home to rest, and we'll decide what to do about the inn tomorrow."

"The inn is gone," said Gwen. She sobbed, "I saw Da die . . ." Her voice dwindled as tears, of both relief and sorrow, overwhelmed her.

"It can be rebuilt," said Declan. "If you want; I'll rebuild it."

"Tomorrow," she said with a burst of anger. Declan helped her rise. She could barely keep steady on her feet, so long had she been tied. He could see bruises on her face, neck, and lower arms, and he assumed there would be more on the rest of her body. Two of her nails were badly broken, probably torn as she struggled against her captors. Her clothing was ripped and filthy and Declan felt anger start to rise now that his battle calm had fled.

He turned to see the results of the struggle and was pleased to find that his plan had caused no great harm to the townsmen, save for bloody knuckles, a few minor cuts and scrapes, and some black eyes. Four mercenaries remained of the six who had been with Tyree, the other three lying lifeless on the ground.

Gwen took Molly's arm for support as Declan came to stand before the four captives. He scanned their faces and settled on the youngest-looking fighter. "Stand up," he said.

The young fighter stood and Declan said, "How long have you ridden with this company?"

"Less than a year," answered the young man. His hair was a sandy blond, and he had badly sunburned cheeks and the promise of a beard, but still looked more boy than man.

"So, done less murdering and raping than the others?" asked Declan.

"Until now only straight-up fights. Misener never allowed for banditry. This was all Tyree's doing." He glanced at the corpse of the mad fighter. "He killed Misener and came back for the girls. Had some mad idea to sell them. I don't know . . ." His voice fell away.

Looking at the bound men, Declan said, "And you went along with him?"

One of the men on his knees said, "He killed

Misener. No one was going to argue with the man who killed Misener. Ask any hired sword between here and Sandura."

Declan realized that Misener must have been the old fighter in charge of the band, the one who had stopped Tyree from fighting before they left the inn. He assumed the old man had lived on reputation, and that had come to an end.

Declan said, "But you let him kill Leon, and burn his inn, take the girls." He grabbed the youngest mercenary by the arm and pulled him aside. "What's your name?"

"Will," said the youthful fighter, looking frightened. "My name is Will."

"Will," said Declan. "I want you to watch this."

Declan nodded to the men standing behind the three remaining mercenaries. The townsmen bent over the kneeling men and cut their throats.

Declan felt Will stiffen and try to pull away, but the young smith kept a strong grip on him. "You will be spared," said Declan. "Take a horse and ride wherever you wish, but never return to Beran's Hill. Tell anyone and everyone you meet that this is what happens to brigands, outlaws, rapists, and murderers who come to Beran's Hill. They will receive swift and rough justice. Go!"

The young fighter didn't hesitate; he ran to the waiting horses, mounted quickly, and rode off back toward the road. Declan said, "Let's bury the rest of these bastards, and take their weapons and horses back home. We can find use for the arms, and we'll sell the horses to . . ." He looked over to where Gwen still clung to Molly's arm. "Pay what costs need paying."

Declan looked at the faces of the strong townsmen who had risked their lives to do what was right. He finally said, "You are all good men, and I owe you my thanks."

One of them, a heavyset fellow named Becker, shrugged. "Nasty business, but it needed doing."

For a brief moment Declan understood that every man here, and Molly, who had fought knew the necessity of the cold killing after the heat of the fight. Nasty business, indeed, but as Becker said, it needed doing.

The others nodded their agreement. "Let's be about this, then," said another man, and he said, "Anyone bring a shovel?"

A third man said, "Tied to my saddle back."

As they set about finishing the morning's business, Declan looked at Jusan hovering over Millie, who was still mute from terror, and then at Gwen. He knew nothing would ever be the same again.

26

A Meeting and Revelations

Hatu crept along a hedgerow, stopping occasionally to peek over the top, into the town already busy with early risers. As the sun crested the eastern horizon, the residents were stirring to wakefulness. The outlying farmers had been about their morning chores since the false dawn, and the shopkeepers and market merchants would soon be opening doors or erecting their stalls.

Hatu turned and beckoned Hava to join him from her hiding place in a small copse. When she crouched beside him, he said, "We need a change of clothing. Just in case someone caught sight of us after we left Port Colos." He smiled. "Besides, no matter how hard you try, you can't look like a man."

She frowned as she brushed off his weak compliment.

As they had traveled, his quips had been rewarded with the occasional slight chuckle, but it was clear Hava endured most of his humor more than she appreciated it.

She took off her travel bag, opened it, and pulled out a long dark blue dress. Hava tossed it aside in favor of a deep-green long-sleeved shirt and black trousers, cut off at the knees. She stripped off her grey tunic and blue trousers and tossed them on top of the dress.

Hatu had seen Hava naked many times since they were children but appreciated her unique beauty now more than ever. Long of frame, graceful, and firmly muscled, her athletic form was lovely; he smiled.

"Don't enjoy yourself too much," she said dryly. "People are trying to kill us."

"As fine a reason as any to grab a small moment of pleasure when it happens," he said.

"You enjoy seeing me naked?" she said with a slight smile.

"Yes," he said as pulled his attention from her and peered over the hedge. "And I hope to again, soon, and many times after, but at this moment, I need to seek out a change of clothing. My travel bag was lost in the warehouse."

"What about the horses?"

He looked at her and said, "We have three choices:

Leave them to be found. Sell them and arrange transport to Pashtar by wagon. Or let them rest and then ride south."

"That is the most logical choice, it seems to me," Hava said. She put her old clothing and the dress back into her bag and waited for his next comment.

"Agreed." Hatu scanned the area again and said, "Let us do this. You return to the horses and guard them, while I steal into the town and find a change of clothes, and see if those who chased us are holed up here. If they are looking for the pair of us, a boy alone may not be noticed."

She took off her floppy hat and stuck it on his head. "You will if anyone sees that ridiculous red hair of yours. I assume your darkening oil was in your travel bag?"

He smiled ruefully and nodded. "I've made do with other things before. Some charcoal dust or even a little axle grease makes it look brown."

"We need to reach a city where the highborn ladies color their hair," said Hava.

"Marquenet," said Hatu. "Where we are to go once we meet with Master Bodai in Pashtar." He glanced over the hedge again. "Until then, I'll find something else."

"Wear my hat until you do," she cautioned.

Hatu squashed it on his head, making sure the brim shaded his features. As they readied themselves for their tasks, he reached out and touched her arm. "Someday you must make a choice."

"What do you mean?" Without thought she drew away from him slightly.

"You will know when the time comes and what the choice is, but you *must* choose. Your decision will change both our lives."

Without waiting for any response, he stood and pushed through the hedge, ignoring the scrape of its small branches on his clothing and exposed skin.

Hava sat for a long moment, then pushed her confusion aside and turned toward the path that would take her back to the horses.

Hatushaly kept to the shadows cast by the early morning sun but did so casually, walking calmly but with purpose.

At every inn he passed he looked for signs that those who were chasing them might be nearby, but Hatu had only the vaguest idea what to look for, as the chaos of the attack on the warehouse where Reza died and his brief glimpse of distant riders were not much to go on. He just hoped that by some unlikely chance, luck, or unearned miracle he'd recognize them before they saw him. He had confidence in his newfound abilities, but discerning enemies he had never set eyes on wasn't one he counted on.

Absently he fingered the small belt pouch containing the coins left from Hava's stash, tucked inside his waistband. He thought better of entering a shop and calling attention to himself, deciding that he would stand out less in the morning market.

By the time Hatu reached the center of the town, all of the market stalls had been erected and the sellers were setting out their wares. He kept to the shaded side of the square as he scanned the area for a clothes vendor. A cord strung between two poles holding an array of shirts caught his eye and he crossed over to it, careful not to look anxious.

As he reached the booth, the merchant looked up and said, "You want to buy?"

Hatu shrugged. "I could use another tunic, heavy work shirt, maybe."

"Shirts and tunics, I have." His accent betrayed his foreign roots, but Hatu was too hard-pressed to dwell on its origin. Something about it sounded vaguely familiar but he couldn't quite identify what it was.

He stepped into the booth and made a show of examining various garments, though he had already decided on a pale yellow shirt. It was bright enough to convince a casual onlooker that he wasn't someone trying to hide, yet not so bright as to call undue attention.

After a little more browsing, and ignoring the merchant's constant babble, which guaranteed that each shirtwas somehow superior to the previous one, Hatu walked over to the yellow shirt. It had long sleeves, a lace-up front, and an attached collar, marking it as a finer shirt than most commoners wore. He pointed to the collar and gave the merchant an inquiring expression.

"The tailor who fashioned it claims that by turning it up, you prevent the back of the neck from becoming sunburned, and that it can cut the lash of a cold wind; or so she says." He shrugged as if to say he was neutral on the efficacy of the design.

The vendor said, "She also made that coat." He pointed to a long dark-grey coat and led Hatu over to look at it. "It's felted wool, a very tight weave."

Hatu examined the coat. He took it off the hook and slipped it on. It fell to his knees and was slightly loose in the shoulders, but not enough to be uncomfortable. The vendor turned up the collar. "Like the shirt, see? The wind and sun do not trouble the neck. She treats the wool with grease so it resists the rain, too, and keeps one dry."

Hatu sniffed at the sleeve and said, "I smell no hint of grease."

"Not black grease: wool grease. She said it is the natural way sheep keep dry. It is very clever, is it not?"

Far better at changing his appearance than a yellow shirt, thought Hatu, no matter how quirky the design. "How much?"

The haggling went on for a few minutes longer than was normal, but Hatu wanted to give Hava time to reach the horses. They finally settled on a price when Hatu offered slightly more, insisting the yellow shirt be thrown in, too. When the merchant agreed, protesting that he would starve, Hatu realized he was getting a fair bargain.

Behind the stall, Hatu removed his old coat and quickly changed into the yellow shirt. He tossed his dirty old coat into a corner, almost certain the merchant would find it, wash it, and try to sell it tomorrow, and put the new coat on, leaving the buttons undone to show the yellow shirt underneath. He was convinced he appeared different enough not to be recognized.

He set off with a slow but measured stride, looking in every open door and both ways at street intersections, trying to gain any intelligence about those who had pursued them the night before. Hatu was young and healthy but tired to his bones, for he'd had little true rest over the last few days. Still, the sooner he and Hava got back on the road, the sooner they would reach Pashtar and Master Bodai.

He neared the north side of the town and turned east onto a street that would lead to a small bridge over a creek, and on to a road leading up into the farmlands. He had spied the road and bridge as they'd skirted the east side of the town and he knew it was his fastest route to where Hava waited with the horses. He wished he could have secured some food for the mounts, but a man carrying a bag of grain out of town would appear too conspicuous. The horses would have to make do with another day of foraging and whatever else his inspection of the town afforded them.

As he reached the edge of the town, he saw a figure standing in the shadows. He lowered his chin slightly, shielding more of his face from view under the broad-brimmed hat. As he passed, he felt more than heard the rush from behind.

He took a sidestep and the attacker flew through the space where Hatu had stood a moment before. Hatu spun, crouching, as his hand went under his coat and came out with a long dagger.

A swift rap on the knuckles from a short slender club almost caused Hatu to loosen his grip. He was thrown off balance by the unexpected blow to the hand and, as he attempted to shift his weight to compensate, abruptly found himself forced to the wall with the espontoon held across his throat; a powerful hand gripped his wrist to keep him from striking with his dagger. The truncheon at his throat could have crushed his windpipe, but no extra pressure was being applied.

A familiar voice said, "If you weren't wearing that ridiculous coat, boy, you damn well might have killed me. It slows you down!"

At that, Hatu realized his attacker was Master Bodai. Hesitating for a moment, he said, "I wasn't looking for combat, only trying to stay disguised."

The older man let go of Hatu and said, "Well, you probably would have done well against most men. So, why hide when I was supposed to find you easily?"

Suddenly Hatu said, "Weren't we supposed to meet you in Pashtar?"

The old man rolled his eyes heavenward. "This is Pashtar, you fool. Where did you think you were?"

"We fled through the woods and were uncertain how far we traveled."

"Where's Reza and the girl?"

"Reza's dead," said Hatu.

Bodai closed his eyes for a second, as if in pain. "Zusara will not be pleased," he said softly. "The girl?"

"She's with the horses, a short distance from here."

Bodai was silent, then he said, "Go fetch her here. Double back north until just out of sight, then ride the main road into town. Those who are looking for you are still around, though they may have doubled back to Port Colos. Once you get back here, find me at the horse market."

"Yes, sir."

Hatu hurried to where Hava waited and explained the situation, and they both rode into Pashtar. Given that he hadn't passed any horse market on his way into the town, Hatu deduced that it must lie to the south, and they quickly found it.

Bodai made a show of hugging both Hatu and Hava, whispering to them both, "We are horse traders. It's the cover I've been using since reaching this part of the world. You are my children."

Hava threw Hatu a warning look, shaking her head slightly, and for a moment he was confused; then he realized that while she might have been willing to argue with other lads her age, she was concerned about something and unwilling to question the master.

Bodai noticed something pass between them and said, "What?"

Hava almost whispered as she said, "How we look."

Both Bodai and Hava had similar skin coloring, a

slightly olive complexion, and shared a vague resemblance around their forehead and eyes, but Hatu looked nothing like them; his skin tone was pale and prone to freckles if he got sun.

Bodai was unsure of her meaning, but Hatu instantly grasped it. Bodai said, "Any suggestions?"

"Yes," said Hatu. "Hava could pass for your daughter, but I look nothing like either one of you, so I should be your daughter's husband."

Bodai was motionless for a second, then nodded. "Your wife! Zusara wanted her to stay close to you, so why not? Our arrangement with the baron said nothing about you having to be alone. Yes, this will do. With luck we will never have to explain it to anyone, but should the question arise, that is a good answer.

"I will go purchase a small string of mounts, and we shall be horse traders, then we can be off. There's a town at the north edge of Marquensas called Beran's Hill where we can sell them, then travel quickly on to Marquenet. Once we have discharged our duty to the baron, I will linger a few days, and we can get Hava established."

Hatu followed Bodai as he returned to the market to select their horses, and as he glanced at Hava, he realized that if it was indeed her mission to kill him eventually, it would be Bodai who would tell her when to do it.

Days later, the trio of riders reached the northwestern edge of Beran's Hill, each leading two additional horses. Bodai led them through the first street heading east, and then down another road, until they again turned east and found the entrance to a yard belonging to Tenda, the horse trader.

A stocky man with a slight limp in his left leg turned to greet the trio and said loudly, "Bodai! Back so soon?"

"I found a man desperate to trade up in Pashtar. So I thought, why travel back this way without something to sell?" He nodded at Hava as he dismounted. "This is my daughter and her worthless husband." The last was said with a laugh, to indicate he jested.

Tenda ran his hand over his balding pate and said, "Well, there seems to be an unusual demand for mounts at the moment, so I'll take them off your hands if the price is right."

They had struck a deal before Hava and Hatu could dismount. Bodai actually lost any profit on the trade, but since it was only a cover, the sum wasn't important. He needed to unload the horses so they could pick up speed and reach Marquenet the day after tomorrow, which was the appointed day of their meeting with a man called Balven.

They rode out of the horse trader's yard and southward through the town. Reaching the Inn of the Three Stars, they found workers restoring a building recently gutted by fire. Bodai spied a familiar figure on the roof, using a pry bar to rip away scorched wood from barely intact beams, while other workers were replacing charred framing. "Declan!" he shouted.

It seemed to take a moment for Declan to recognize the speaker, as they had only met once, but eventually he did. "Bodai!"

"What happened?"

"Remember that young rooster you warned me about?" said Declan as he moved to the edge of the roof and leapt nimbly to the ground.

"I do," answered the counterfeit horse trader.

"He killed the old rooster, a man named Misener."

"Misener!" Bodai exclaimed, dismounting. "I didn't realize that's who he was. He was a legendary captain in the east. I don't know why he was here, but if the man killed Misener, he was a fighter of great skill."

"He came back here, killed my friend Leon, and kidnapped his daughter and another girl."

"That is tragic," said Bodai. "A terrible loss."

"It was," agreed Declan.

A nearby worker said, "He's not telling all, stranger.

Declan led some of the boys after them; they found this man Tyree, killed him, and freed the girls."

Bodai regarded the young smith for a long moment, then said, "If you've slain Misener's killer, then you have made a name for yourself, my young friend. Though perhaps not a name you wish to have earned."

"I'm no warrior," said Declan, clapping his hands to remove the soot. "I have no plans to capitalize on that reputation, unless it sells more swords."

"From what I see on my travels," Bodai replied, "selling more swords will not be a problem. Making them fast enough, perhaps."

Declan nodded. "I see that as well. As soon as we get this inn back under control, I am to travel to Marquenet to hire another smith." He looked at Bodai. "And to speak to the baron if he'll hear me out."

Bodai's expression was more or less neutral but indicated that it might prove a difficult task. "Might you know a place where I, my daughter, and her husband might spend the night?"

"Turn around and go left at the next street. The Inn of the Green Oak is a fair place for travelers. You'll have your choice of the barn, under the tables in the commons, or a room if no one else has taken it. You leave for Marquenet tomorrow?"

"We do," said Bodai.

Declan said, "If you don't mind, I'll ride with you. I have business with the baron. In these times, a group on the road is far safer."

Bodai didn't hesitate. Four riders looked even less conspicuous than three. "We leave at first light."

"I'll meet you here," said Declan.

Bodai remounted and led Hava and Hatu away, leaving Declan to climb the roof of the inn and return to repairing the damage.

Late in the day the next afternoon, the four riders topped a rise and looked down into a large valley that ran from that point down toward the coast, reaching the edge of the rich groves and farmlands Declan had observed on his first trip to Beran's Hill.

Declan looked at Bodai. "I've only traveled this way once before. We found a natural well with grass around it down there, on the left side of the road." He motioned in that general direction. "It was a good place to spend the night, but we kept on as we had ample daylight when we passed. Do you know the spot?"

Bodai said, "I've traveled this road several times. That is indeed where I would suggest we make camp. We will be in the city before midday, which is when I'm expected. That's a good place to rest."

They had traveled from Beran's Hill in relative silence. Declan was by nature far from verbose, and his three companions seemed equally inclined to keep their own counsel. Whatever conversation occurred tended to focus on their journey, or trivial observations about the countryside through which they passed.

By the time they reached the campsite, the sun was lowering in the west. Hatu climbed off his horse and said, "I'll start a fire." He handed the reins of his horse to Hava as Bodai handed his mount's reins to Declan, who took them. The horses could smell the water from the spring close by and needed little urging to go drink.

By the time the animals had been cared for and staked out for the night, Hava and Declan returned to discover that Hatu and Bodai had made a full camp. There was abundant wood in a thick copse of trees a short distance away, and a lively fire was burning. He'd taken the liberty of unpacking Hava's travel packs and had placed ground cloths near the fires. "I didn't know if you'd appreciate me unpacking for you," he said to Declan quietly.

Declan waved away the comment, appreciating the courtesy. "No, it's fine."

As he unloaded his own gear, Declan considered that most people would have left him to unpack without comment. Something about this fellow, who was only a few years younger than him, struck Declan as a little odd—not in a way to cause discomfort; he just seemed different. The older man and the girl were ordinary enough, though Declan would never have marked them as father and daughter. The way they behaved was a little strange . . . from another land, Declan reminded himself.

He put aside such thoughts and decided that he was simply feeling uneasy about strangers after what happened to Gwen's father. Declan reminded himself that he had been a stranger, too, until recently. He pulled out a bundle wrapped in oiled cloth. "I've got jerked meat but fresh fruit," said the smith. "I knew it was a short trip, so I didn't think we needed a lot of food."

Bodai accepted an apple. "I appreciate it. Trail fare is often nourishing but lacking flavor. I've plenty of dried food, so this is very welcome."

They settled in, and Declan said, "You got that fire going quickly. I see ample wood, but not much dry kindling around."

Hatu shrugged. "I have a knack for fires."

"My son-in-law had many trades before joining my family," said Bodai. "I'm sure he has a story about fire making." He fixed Hatu with an expression that both half-warned the young man and demanded a story to satisfy Declan's curiosity.

Hatu was silent as he returned Bodai's stare, then he

glanced at Hava, whose expression remained neutral. Finally he said, "Before I met my beloved, I struggled to find a craft. I was born an orphan—"

"So was I!" Declan interrupted. "I wouldn't be a master smith today save for the generosity of my teacher and his wife."

Hatu smiled and continued. "Tinkering and smithing were among the many trades at which I tried my hand. I know little of serious craft in a proper forge, but I learned how to start a fire from whatever is lying around; you know how those traveling forges are."

Declan nodded. "Most tinker work doesn't require the heat that forging steel does. Start with any fire and just add a few small pieces of coal . . ." After a moment he said, "Well, you've found your true trade, apparently." He nodded at Hava and Bodai. "Truth is, I'd try to find out if you have the knack, had you no employment. There's a shortage of decent smiths and apprentices these days. When I reach Marquenet, I've been asked to inquire if there's a good smith willing to move up to Copper Hills."

Bodai tilted his head slightly, as if he found that information interesting.

With a smile, Hatu said, "I'll bear that in mind should my beloved's father grow tired of my poor skill with horses."

Bodai tried to turn it into a jest. "It's not your poor skill with horses," he said in a light tone. "The boy does well enough with showing and keeping them fit; he is a fair judge of horseflesh." He nodded approval. "He's even become gifted at spotting any injuries that the seller has disguised with tricks, drugs, and unguents.

"It's simply that he does not understand how to bargain. Haggling is not a skill that comes naturally to him. If I left our business to him, I would die an impoverished old man."

Declan chuckled.

After a moment, Bodai looked at Declan. "What became of the girls at that inn?"

"One of them was Leon's daughter. She's to be my wife. We shall say our vows as soon as we find time; perhaps at midsummer. It's a common time here, as there's a celebration anyway. The other girl, Millie, I fear isn't doing well. My apprentice is smitten with her, and tries to care for her, but she spends her days huddled in his room, only coming out to eat. He's taken to sleeping in the barn again, for she will have no one close to her. My Gwen has to force her to bathe. I don't know what to expect."

Bodai gave out a long sigh of sympathy and said, "Like any part of a human body, the mind can be strong or fragile. Some people face adversity and withstand it, even thrive in rare cases, but some are shattered like pottery on rock."

Declan nodded. He recalled with vivid clarity his realization that once he had killed Tyree, nothing in his life would ever be the same. Gwen tried to put it in the past, but he had seen her cry quietly when she thought he wasn't looking, or staring out the window in the kitchen of the house behind the smithy.

He tried to get her to shop for things to replace what she and Millie had lost, and she had purchased a few bits and pieces, mostly for Millie. He thought she was recovering but also realized it might simply be his hope urging him to feel that way.

Declan sighed. "And I now have an inn to rebuild."

"Why bother?" asked Hatu.

"Because my soon-to-be wife insisted that her father provide a dowry. She lost everything in the fire. Some coins were melted, so the metal's there, but . . . it's not the same. So, I will rebuild the inn, and Gwen will pretend that I'm not spending my money to do it. Then we will sell it, and she can give me the gold as if it's her dowry."

Hatu shrugged as he looked at Hava. "Would—" He stopped himself, for he was about to ask her if she wanted a dowry when they were pretending to be already wed. "Would you have wanted such, had we been in that situation?"

Hava shrugged, then softly said, "He's trying to make her whole again, even happy. He is a good man."

Declan inclined his head in thanks, then said, "Sleep now. We should need no watch this close to the baron's home."

Bodai nodded. "Still, I'll stay awake for a bit. Old habits."

Declan lay on his mat and pulled a travel blanket over him. He kept his boots on out of prudence. In one more day they would reach the city of Marquenet, and after he had spoken with the baron and talked to a few of the smiths in the city, he would find a good room in a decent inn, a hot bath, and a meal. As much as Declan was concerned about being away from Gwen, he also welcomed this short respite from the worry and doubt.

27

Fate Wheels
and Lives Change

The three younger riders followed Bodai into the city at noon. When they were within sight of the northern entrance to the old citadel, Bodai reined in and said to Declan, "Here we must part company, my young friend. Our business with the baron's agent is not to be shared, and besides, if you seek an audience, you will need to approach his agent at this gate, correct?"

Declan nodded. "True. I thank you for your company. Should you ever return to Beran's Hill, come find me and I will happily stand you a round of drinks."

"My thanks," said Bodai. Hava and Hatu also bid Declan goodbye, then followed Bodai as he rode off to the southwest.

Riding a short distance behind Bodai, Hava turned to Hatu and said, "I liked him."

Hatu nodded. "Seemed like a solid fellow. I don't envy him the nursing of Gwen's wounds."

Hava looked at him as if about to ask, then understood. "Those kind are hard to heal." She then looked at him with a questioning expression.

He nodded and said, "Of course I would do as much for you."

Hava smiled, then looked to see if Master Bodai was listening. They skirted the citadel, taking their time to wend their way through the crowded streets.

Hatu had visited many cities since leaving the home island, but none like this. Everything he saw revealed its wealth. The splendor of Marquenet wasn't simply a reflection of the baron's treasury; its people were rich in peace and safety as well as material prosperity. Few beggars could be seen, and the urchins who roamed the streets looked nothing like the street gangs Hatu and Hava had run with in the east. The children playing at their mothers' feet were well fed and properly clothed.

City guards walked through the markets, keeping an eye out for thievery or conflict, but they lacked the wary, tense appearance that guardsmen possessed in other cities; these men seemed at ease. Hatu widened his eyes in wonder as merchants greeted the guards by name, and the guards returned their smiles and exchanged pleasantries. Bodai glanced back at the two youngsters and noticed Hatu's expression, and said, "Marvelous city, isn't it?"

"Yes," said Hatu, looking at Hava.

She nodded her agreement. "I've never seen its like."

"Like Ithrace," said Bodai. "Destroyed when you both were babies." He glanced back again and then added, "Marquenet is the richest and most prosperous city as exists on all of Garn, since the destruction of Ithrace.

"The baron and the last king of Ithrace were close, by all accounts, and it seems they shared the idea of maintaining a common good; most rulers simply take from their people. Better ones give as well, and their prosperity is shared with everyone. Baron Daylon is generous in his protection and lenient with taxes; he possesses the richest farmlands and groves on the west coast of North Tembria, and trades fairly and dispenses justice with an even hand. What is there not to love?"

Hatu realized it was perhaps more than a rhetorical question. "Little that is apparent," he replied.

Bodai chuckled. "Hava?" he asked.

She looked around for a while, then said, "As Hatu said, nothing is immediately apparent."

Bodai grunted. "You are both young. You will learn. Cities are like creatures in and of themselves. They live, they try to grow, and sometimes that growth is beyond their ability to sustain, so they collapse in on themselves and wither. This is a city at its peak. It has two choices: to continue to expand until it can no longer sustain itself, or to find a comfortable limit."

Hatu finished, "And finding that limit without harming itself is the trick."

"Very good. Some cities, states, and nations are in a near-constant state of flux: disorder, calm, peace, and warfare. Others are limited by their natural resources, bad trade links, disease, or other factors. But here . . ." Bodai made a sweeping gesture with his hand. "None of that is apparent.

"And this you must know, Hatushaly, for it is not anything you were trained in; I don't speak of smugglers, criminals, bribed customs agents, or all the unseen things you know too well. It is other things that are not apparent, hidden, unseen, that are often the most important.

"Baron Dumarch is a very clever man; some might say he is the next Firemane, and Marquensas the next Ithrace. Here, theaters are built, music composed, and wealth spreads from the most powerful to the poorest citizen. This is paradise."

Hava said, "So, someone will come and try to take it from him."

Bodai laughed. He shook his head. "That is a very uncomplicated conclusion. It's not quite that simple, but that doesn't mean you're wrong; there's a cleverness in you, not appreciated by most." He glanced back and forth between the youths. "You two are well matched." Pointing at Hatu, he said, "You spend a little too much time thinking." Then Bodai pointed at Hava. "And you, sometimes, not enough." He laughed. Then he turned back to Hatu. "But you, boy, prepare well before you act." He pointed again at Hava. "And you could learn from that, Hava," he said, grinning, "as you're a little impulsive." He studied Hatu for a moment and said, "From her you can learn to hesitate less." Then he lost his smile. "Together you may prove to be very dangerous."

Hava and Hatu regarded the master with dubious expressions as he continued. "I do not limit the study of my students to the times I work with them directly; I know Facaria, and the other village masters, and I ask about my charges." He pointed at Hatu and spoke to Hava. "He and I have traveled together, so I believe I know him quite well. You"—he pointed at her—"I know less about." He shrugged and turned forward again, motioning for them to continue.

They followed him until they reached a major road stretching from the south and leading up to the main gate. Standing at the side of the entrance was a man of advancing years.

"We are almost done," said Bodai. "But first, I will speak to each of you privately."

He motioned for Hatu to dismount and follow him a short distance away. When they were out of Hava's earshot, Bodai said, "Now that this Declan and others in Beran's Hill have met you, you will continue with the ruse that Hava is your wife. She will support you in this mission. You must maintain this facade for a while, perhaps months, or years even, but until you are told otherwise, do as that man over there tells you." He pointed to the man standing by the gate. "He is the baron's body man, but he is also his bastard brother, and no one is more trusted by the baron than he is. Wait here."

Bodai walked over to where Hava stood with the horses and placed his hand on her shoulder. "You are Hatu's wife now. You will need to keep to that ploy for as long as necessary. Go wherever he goes. Give him every reason to trust you. Make babies if you must. This is a long game." Hava understood. Some agents of the home island lived years in disguise, establishing themselves deep within a community before being called upon to act.

Bodai continued, his expression even more serious, as he looked into her eyes as if studying her. "The moment word arrives, do as you are told, even if it means you must kill him and return to the home island immediately. Even if you are the mother of his children. Can you do that?"

She hesitated only briefly, and then nodded.

Bodai waved at Hatu to join them and when he had, the master said, "These are your last orders: wait, watch, and learn. If you discover something vital to our interests, find one of our agents at an inn called the Sign of the Gulls." He pointed to the southeast. "You should have no trouble finding it. It lies across the street from a small curio shop, which sells goods from all over the world. A man named Petyr is master there. Find him and repeat this greeting three times: 'I bring a message for grandfather.' And then give him whatever message you have. He will send it to us as quickly as possible and get word back to you if there is a reply.

"This is the end of my part in this." He turned toward the gate of the keep and saw Balven approaching. Pointing, he said, "That man will tell you everything else you need to know. Come with me."

He motioned for them to follow him. They led their mounts to the gate and stopped before Balven. Bodai introduced him to Hatu and Hava and said again, "You will do whatever he tells you to do." He then turned to look at Balven. "This is the boy," Bodai said without preamble. "Our task is discharged. Our arrangement is over."

As Bodai started to turn away, Balven asked, "Who is this girl?"

"His wife," said Bodai as he mounted. "By the name of Hava."

"Wife? There was no—"

Bodai interrupted. "There was no instruction to keep him from marrying." With a wry smile he said, "So, you get two for the price of one!" Without waiting for another reply, Bodai turned his mount and rode off.

Balven looked at Hatu and said, "Take off your hat."

He did as instructed and Balven took a quick glance at the dirty but still recognizable copper and gold and said, "Put it back on. Come with me."

He turned and Hatu and Hava followed. Hava glanced at Hatu, tilting her head and raising her eyebrow slightly, a hardly noticeable expression that he recognized immediately: did he know what was going on? He answered with a tiny shake of his head, but added a reassuring smile, trying to communicate that he thought everything would be all right.

As they entered the sprawling forecourt, Hatu could see a stable on the right side of the castle in the distance.

He suspected a large marshaling yard was behind the massive central keep. Two men hurried forward and took their horses. Balven said, "Water and rest them, groom them quickly, but tack them back up; our guests will be leaving soon." The lackeys nodded and led the mounts away toward the stable.

Hatu and Hava followed Balven through the entrance to the baron's castle. The ancient keep walls had been repaired and renovated many times, so that it looked less like a fortress and more like a grand monument to peace and wealth. Generations of Baron Daylon's ancestors had added facades and refinements, such as carved and polished wooden doors in the main archway where heavy timbers reinforced with iron had been used decades ago.

The floors of the entry hall were made of polished marble and covered in thick woven carpets, instead of rough granite and furs, and the iron banisters had been replaced with polished wood. A massive chandelier hung over their heads, raised and lowered by brightly polished chains, so that a hundred candles could be easily lit or extinguished.

It took all of Hatu and Hava's self-discipline not to gawk at the fine tapestries on the wall to the left of the huge staircase, as the tall, arched windows illuminated the grand entrance in brilliant sunlight.

The newcomers were led to a massive hall dominated by a long table. A large double door on the far left
side of the room led them into another hallway, which
ended in a good-sized room with chairs set around a
circular table.

"Wait over there," said Balven, pointing to a corner.

Not being invited to sit didn't surprise Hatu, as his
previous encounters with nobility, albeit of the minor
variety, had taught him that commoners were not
granted seats. A few minutes later, Balven entered with
another man who wore finely tailored clothing, a silk
shirt, linen trousers, leather ankle boots, and a matching belt. "I am Baron Daylon Dumarch," said the finely
dressed man. He motioned for Hatu to approach, while
Balven came to stand next to Hava, making it clear she
was to remain where she was.

The baron pulled out his own chair and then indicated that Hatu should also sit.

Hatu was surprised but did as he was asked. When
Hatu was seated, Daylon leaned forward. "Do you
know who you are?"

Hatu remained silent for a moment, then said, "I am
Hatushaly. I am from the east."

Daylon laughed. "From the east . . . And you have
some interesting tales to tell about that upbringing,
I'll wager . . . But, for some other time."

He paused as if considering what to say. Finally he spoke, "I knew your father, Hatu; he was a dear friend. Your real name is Sefan Langene. And you are the son of Steveren Langene, king of Ithrace, known as Firemane. By right, you became ruler of the Kingdom of Fire upon his death, and the death of all your siblings. You are a king."

Hatu sat motionless. "King?"

"A king of ashes, perhaps, but a king nevertheless." He let out a sigh, as if he was dealing with a task long in coming and not welcome. "I hid you away from the many people who wished to see an end to your father's line. But while you have a claim to this dead kingdom, you have no means to take it." He paused, then spoke almost as if to himself, not to Hatu. "And what is left to reclaim? Scattered villages? A once-proud city reduced to blackened stones, poisoned wells, and charred timbers?" He seemed to come out of this momentary reverie and addressed Hatu. "So, now the question is, what are we to do with you?" He glanced at Hava. "And your wife?"

Hatu said, "My lord, I have no knowledge of the things you speak of, nor any sense of their importance. I have spent my life as a common man. I have modest skills in a few crafts, but until this morning I was but a horse trader, working for Bodai. My wife's father," he quickly added.

Hatu paused as he studied the baron for a moment, then said, "I was apprenticed in Coaltachin, but I am not one of them. I am not of their army. I never understood why . . . But now I do." He fell silent, but his mind raced. Everything fell into place: why he had been trained as if he were the son of a master, and why he would never become a master himself.

Hatu paused and took a deep breath, then continued. "I was kept safe; they allowed me to become adept at the skills that keep their own children alive." He glanced at Hava. "My wife is equally able to care for herself, so I now suspect our marriage was planned." That last was a lie, but close enough to the truth to withstand scrutiny, should it ever come into question. His main reason for telling that falsehood was to let the baron know he was able to care for himself.

"Very well," said Daylon. "If you wish to remain in my barony, you are welcome. But I would rather you did not remain in the city. It has been seventeen years since your kingdom fell, but too many who visit here remember the glory of Ithrace and the legacy of the Firemanes." He pointed at Hatu's head. "That hair of yours is hard not to notice."

Hatu smiled. "I've been hiding my hair since child-hood. I can continue to do so."

The baron fell silent for a moment, then said, "I must be truthful: I betrayed your father." He studied Hatu's face, waiting for a reaction, and seeing none, he continued. "If you wish, at some point in the future, I will explain in detail how it came to pass, but for now all I will say is I faced the choice of aiding your father's enemies or enduring destruction at his side."

Hatu shrugged slightly, then said, "I can make no judgment; I have no understanding of this, no clear sense of right or wrong." He shrugged for a second time. "It must have been a difficult choice."

Daylon looked regretful as he said, "It's been a long time—your entire life—but at times I can still . . ." He closed his eyes for only a few seconds, but Hatu sensed that the baron witnessed a flood of memories in that time.

Daylon leaned forward even further, as if he wished to prevent any chance of Balven or Hava's overhearing. "I loved your father like a brother, Hatu, but I had to choose between him and my people."

Hatu nodded. "I've seen your people, my lord. They are happy." He spoke in a tone that conveyed his approval of the choice. "I—" he began, then stopped. "This king . . ."

"Steveren," supplied Daylon. "Your father's name was Steveren."

"He was unknown to me until this moment. I have no sense of being his kin or . . ." Hatu fought for the concepts and suddenly they came, as if the words and knowledge he needed simply appeared without his prior understanding. He pushed aside surprise, deciding that he would deal with it later, and continued his thought. "He was my father, yet I feel nothing. From what you say, he was a great ruler, so his people must have felt more aggrieved by his loss than I ever could."

He took a moment and then continued. "I thank you for telling me this, my lord, and for keeping me safe all these years. But I am still a common man looking to make a life for myself and my wife." He nodded toward Hava, who was watching him intently. He knew that she understood something important was being discussed and trusted Hatu to let her know all that was said later.

Daylon sat back. "There's a town to the north called Beran's Hill. It lies on the far edge of my lands but is still within the borders of Marquensas. I recommend you consider it. Trade is brisk, the surrounding lands rich, and an enterprising couple could make a fine life, even prosper there. It's growing, so newcomers are far less noticeable than in other towns within my demesne.

You can live there peacefully for the rest of your days if you keep your identity hidden."

The baron had no idea that Hatu already knew the town. Hatu said, "I will look into it, my lord. You are very generous."

Daylon produced a small pouch and pushed it toward the young man. "A token of my affection for your father. He was a truly great man, perhaps the finest I've ever known. Even though his kingdom is gone, it is good that his line is not. I'm guilty of betraying a man I loved, but I can save his son. I hope you'll consider all our debts balanced."

Hatu again shrugged slightly. "As I said, I never knew the man, so your loss is greater than my own. For my life, I thank you and consider there to be a debt on my part. I do not know what a simple fellow such as myself could do for you, my lord, but you only need ask."

"Again, I suggest you go to Beran's Hill. If you settle there, send me a message from time to time. I'd like to hear how my old friend's son is doing." He stood and Hatu rose a moment after him.

Hatu bowed slightly, uncertain how his unexpected elevation into the ranks of royalty changed anything. Lacking a castle and army, Hatu judged it changed very little. He glanced at Balven, who then indicated that it was time for Hatu and Hava to depart.

Hava said nothing as they were escorted to the stables, where their freshly groomed and saddled mounts waited. Hatu thanked Balven and the two young people then rode slowly out the gate and back into the city. When they had reached a relatively quiet spot in the square in front of the gate, away from the busy markets below, Hava reined in and asked, "So, you're a king?"

"In name only, it appears. From what little I know of Ithrace's history it is now a wild land of scorched cities and abandoned towns. Whatever there was of worth was carried off when it fell." He smiled. "Still, if you like, I can call you my queen."

Hava's expression revealed that it wasn't what she wanted. "What now?"

Hatu took a quick look inside the pouch given him by Baron Daylon and said, "Apparently we are to return to Beran's Hill."

"Do we?"

"I think so. The baron seems to want us there, and I doubt we'll be invited back here soon, so finding out anything useful in the city is unlikely." He glanced around. "Besides, as he told me, there are too many people here likely to spread word of my existence, word that will easily find the ear of those who wish me dead."

He pointed to his hat. "We need dye, good-quality dye, the type that doesn't wash out easily. Just enough to turn my hair reddish brown." He patted his stomach. "And I am hungry, so we also need a good inn with a good room." He smiled at her. "And once we are alone, the pleasures of a man and his wife."

"We are not truly married," she reminded him with mock disapproval.

"An oversight we must rectify as soon as we can. Declan spoke of the many weddings held at midsummer. We shall make up a story about wanting a more serious ceremony than . . . whatever we had before." He started laughing. "Tonight, we shall sleep in a soft bed after eating a grand meal"—he jingled the purse given to him by the baron—"and we shall concoct a believable story. We shall be man and wife and we shall stay in Beran's Hill until we need to depart."

Hatu knew he would never again answer to the demands of Coaltachin, for it was clear to him that Bodai's words to Balven had freed him from any obligation to the Invisible Nation. But Hava didn't need to know that yet.

He put away the possibility that he might one day need a way to prevent his wife from killing him in the corner of his mind.

"Where to?" she asked.

"A fine inn, and then tomorrow Beran's Hill."

"What then?" she asked as they both mounted.

"Let us consider that when we get there, but Declan mentioned selling an inn. If there is any better place to hear rumors and stories from drunken travelers, I do not know of it. Perhaps we shall become innkeepers?"

Hava smiled. "A warm bed every night, and playing a wife instead of a whore? That sounds very agreeable." She paused, then said, "Speaking of Declan, am I bereft of my senses, or does he look a great deal like the baron?"

Hatu's eyes widened. "That's why I thought I'd seen him before! Yes, there is a resemblance." From their history lessons, both of them knew that many nobles had bastards, and if there was any kinship between Declan and Baron Daylon, then it was hardly remarkable.

Hava said, "Well, let us find an inn, eat, and make some plans . . ." She smiled, and then added, "Husband."

He reached over and almost pulled her out of her saddle. She laughed and said, "What?"

He hugged her close and whispered into her ear. "I have always loved you, Hava, ever since we were children. I just didn't realize it until we came on this journey together."

She pulled away a little. Her eyes glistened as tears welled within them. She blinked them away and said, "And I you. You are my heart."

He grinned and wiped his own tears away with the back of his hand. "It seems we have a great deal to share. And . . . ," he laughed, "I'm still very hungry."

She couldn't help but laugh in return. "I am as well."

"And perhaps, wife, we can . . . discuss what you've learned from the Powdered Women after we eat?"

She regarded him for a moment and then gave him one of her teasing smiles. "Perhaps."

Declan stood motionless, holding the reins of his restless horse. He'd been waiting at the gate for the better part of an hour after dealing with a reluctant guard, who finally agreed to send word to the castle that the smith from Beran's Hill sought an audience with the baron.

Finally the familiar figure of Balven appeared and walked toward him. When close enough to be heard, he said, "You need to speak with my lord?"

Declan said, "Beran's Hill was attacked."

"Was word sent to the garrison at Esterly?"

"That's what I wanted to speak to his lordship about,

sir. It was over and done with before a rider could be sent to the garrison."

Balven looked at Declan and said, "Come with me." He signaled for a servant, a young boy, to come take Declan's horse. "Just wait. We won't be long."

Balven led Declan into a small room where Baron Daylon was reading a report of some kind. He looked up and smiled. "The smith from the Covenant."

"From Beran's Hill now, my lord."

"How fare things in Beran's Hill, then . . . Declan, isn't it?"

"Yes, my lord. Things are not going well. We were attacked by a group of mercenaries who killed the owner of an inn, the father of my betrothed. They carried her off with another girl, and also fired the building."

"That is dire news," said Daylon. "But why come here? You should have gone to Esterly so the garrison could have been turned out and the girls rescued."

"We had no time. We chased them down and put them all but one to the sword. The girls were saved." He decided it was pointless to mention the damage done to Millie or his worry about Gwen.

"Oh," said Baron Daylon. He looked at Declan and said, "You said but one."

"I chose the youngest of the bandits and told him to spread the word wherever he goes that only harsh and swift justice awaits brigands in Beran's Hill."

Daylon smiled. "That was very clever."

"We need a garrison now, my lord. The town is so large that even the lack of a constable is a problem. Most people are neighborly, but we get so many travelers it is . . . difficult to maintain order at times. We are part of your barony, but . . ." Declan struggled to put his thoughts into words, even though he had rehearsed this speech a dozen times while waiting.

"You feel neglected," supplied Balven.

Declan said, "Yes. We keep to the law, we pay our taxes, and we ask for little, but now we need your protection."

Daylon said, "It is difficult. I cannot simply build a new garrison, and yet . . ." He paused to think, then said, "I can do this much. As it was clearly you who rescued the girls and led the men who took care of those bandits, I'm naming you as my constable in Beran's Hill." He motioned to Balven. "Get me a purse of thirty gold pieces."

As Balven hurried off, Daylon said to Declan, "I'll give you a stipend to raise a militia. Arm the men who lack weapons and see if you can convince them to train. Soldiers who sit around waiting for trouble are costly, but a group of willing townsmen who can be reinforced from Esterly should suffice until such time as I can afford to add another garrison. Are you willing?"

As Balven returned with a purse of gold, Declan hesitated, then said, "I'll see what I can do, my lord."

"Good," said Daylon. He motioned for Balven to give Declan the purse and then motioned that the interview was over.

As they reached the door to the courtyard where Declan's horse waited, Balven said, "Send word in a week's time, and every month thereafter, to let me know how your militia progresses." In a friendly fashion he said, "The baron is a cautious man when it comes to expense—he'd rather make sure commerce flourishes and the people are fed than pay for soldiers to sit around—but I think you're right. We will need a garrison in Beran's Hill soon. I'll keep that thought fresh in his mind. Now, thank you for bringing this to our attention. A report from Esterly on the matter should get here in a week or two. Good day to you."

He turned and walked away. Declan sighed. It was not the outcome he desired—he didn't relish more responsibility—but it was better than simply being turned away. He glanced at the sun and realized he would have to spend the night in the city before starting north. He'd look for an inn, but first he'd seek out Gildy and discuss the need for a couple of good smiths, one for his forge and one for Baron Rodrigo. Then he had to hurry home, see to the inn's repair, and start making swords for Copper Hills' master-at-arms.

Declan mounted and rode away from the castle.

Daylon looked up as Balven entered the room. "That was unexpected," observed his body man.

Balven sat down at the table and his brother poured him a flagon of wine. Sliding it across the table, Daylon said, "It might prove useful."

Balven took a long drink, then said, "This is a long first act, brother."

"Seventeen years. But I've had ample time to plan since finding that baby in my tent."

Balven said, "You're playing a very dangerous game."

Daylon took a long pull of wine, then said, "I have . . . *We* have no choice. Centuries of tradition and order were overturned on the day we stood with those who betrayed Steveren Langene. Many would have joined me had I turned the next morning and launched an attack on Lodavico, but even had we won, every kingdom, every barony, would have been reduced to complete chaos. We would have entered an age of darkness and savagery. At least now we are almost ready. I have firm allies, all preparing for the coming confrontation. And I am preparing the field of battle, luring Lodavico to where I want him."

"Beran's Hill?"

Daylon nodded. "It's too tempting a target. He will think he has gained the most important commercial junction in the northwest, not realizing until too late that he's trapped between three armies, with his only escape back the way he came through pillaged and barren lands." He sighed. "We are almost ready."

"Almost?"

"Lodavico is sparring with some minor warlords and so-called barons across the straits in South Tembria. He thinks he's going to win resources and perhaps loyal retainers, possibly enough to seize the Narrows, but we both know he's simply wasting time."

Balven asked, "So when?"

"Soon, compared to how long we've waited. A year or two, three at most. If Lodavico is not ready by then, we'll lure him in."

Balven read every report that reached his half brother, so he knew the plan as well as Daylon, but he didn't know what their next move was. After a minute of silence, he said, "And the boy?"

Daylon laughed. "For years I've wondered how to

lure Lodavico to Beran's Hill at the right time. As the boy grew, I realized my best use for him was as bait. I loved his father and regret my part in his murder; I wish to protect his son, but I need to avenge Steveren."

"Ah," said Balven with a rueful expression. "You've made Beran's Hill the most tempting target in your barony. Even if it is dangled in front of him, Lodavico might still linger elsewhere, but let word out that the Firemane child has been found there, and . . ."

"Nothing could keep him away."

Balven hesitated.

"What?" asked Daylon.

"You just sent our brother into that trap."

Daylon frowned. "A young man you've met twice is now our 'brother'?"

"You can't deny his resemblance to our father."

"Of course I can, but I won't. Still, knowing Father, you and I probably have another half a dozen brothers or sisters in cities across the two continents, maybe more. I don't see your concern for them."

"I haven't met them," answered Balven. "You must admit, that business with the mercenary band and how he dealt with them, that was very Father."

Daylon was silent for a moment, then nodded. "Yes, that is exactly how Father would have dealt with the situation. He was never one to wait around for others to help him." Daylon again fell silent, then said, "Perhaps we can turn that knowledge to our advantage. If he is like our father then our brother may prove to be a useful agent in Beran's Hill."

Balven said, "I've already instructed him to send us word of his progress. An occasional pat on the back and a bit of gold now and again for his expenses would go a long way to keeping up the appearance that Beran's Hill is not a honey trap."

"Cultivate him," instructed Daylon.

Balven nodded. "I'll go see to household matters and then after supper I'll instruct an agent to visit the smith in a week."

Daylon nodded his dismissal of his brother and sat back in his chair.

There were still many unsettled matters to consider, not the least of which was the growing alliance between Lodavico and the Church of the One. That was a problem he had not anticipated when he sent the baby away for safekeeping. In less than twenty years the Church had gone from being a just cause for concern to a major threat.

Daylon was moving the pieces into place as well as he could manage, and there was never a moment he thought his actions were without risk. Still, the prize was something his father could never have envisioned:

Marquensas as the new Ithrace, the new center of knowledge and beauty on Garn, and himself no longer a baron, but a king.

And not for the first time in his life, Baron Daylon Dumarch wondered about that man he saw in the mirror.

28

Watching and Waiting

Three figures huddled around a small table at the inn of a village on the south coast of Marquensas. Catharian, the false friar of the Order of Tathan, said, "No rumors, and no sighting of one with copper and gold hair, yet."

Denbe sat forward, interlacing the fingers of his large hands. To the slight figure next to him he said, "Anything?"

Sabella said, "Only occasional flickers, but they come from the north. I fear he has somehow come to master his power, hiding it at will."

Catharian shook his head. "How is that possible? He has all of the Firemane power and no training."

Denbe sighed as if exhausted. "We wrestled with that question the night before we left. We can only speculate; perhaps his training under the Coaltachin gave him some means to keep the fires within under control. Or perhaps he is simply gifted, as the last of his line."

Denbe and Sabella had departed from the Hall of the Guardians the day after she detected the presence of the Firemane child. The Guardians had agents in key locations around the world, as did those of the other elemental orders. Elmish, as leader of the Fire Guard, and Denbe, as master of the Art, had debated how best to approach the problem of the rediscovered heir to the throne of Ithrace. Elmish had warned Denbe that if they had noticed the child's existence, so might others.

Catharian said, "Then tomorrow we start north and continue our search." He stood. "Now, I'm for bed. We need our rest. We must find the boy—*young man,* soon. We may be the only people in this world who seek him and do not want him dead."

Epilogue: Return

The old man sat on a tiny wooden stool before his small campfire as the sun vanished below the horizon. His pole was stuck in the sand a few yards away, and he waited for it to move, signaling a catch. Sunrise and sunset were traditionally his best chances to catch more than trash fish or sharks. He considered calling it a day and gathering up his pole and creel, returning home to his wife with his catch. Since his sons had taken over his boat years before, he'd spent most of his day doing as his wife bid him, or fishing beyond the surf.

Just as he decided to pack up, Macomb the Fisher saw something rise up out of the ocean. He stood, his hand on his cleaning knife, the only thing he had that was remotely like a weapon.

He stepped forward as the hunched form of a man

arose out of the surf, his features hidden in the twilight as the western sunset lit him from behind. The man staggered in the water, and after a moment Macomb judged he wasn't a threat. The old fisherman put his knife in his belt and waded out into the knee-deep water to help him.

"Come, warm yourself by the fire," he said, and led the man to where he could warm himself a little. The evening was still pleasant, but the fellow was dripping wet and it would turn cooler quickly now that the sun was down.

In the light Macomb could see he was a large young man and he was shivering. "If I had a blanket I'd give it to you," he said. "Get in close to the fire and I'll stoke it up a bit." The stranger shuffled closer and almost fell to his knees.

Macomb only had a few bits of kindling left, but he tossed them on, and as the flames quickly rose he could see that the youngster was regaining a bit of color. He had brown hair and eyes which now seemed to be coming back into focus, and he was perhaps not quite twenty years old. His cheeks were smooth and his body was clothed in a simple linen shirt and trousers, and otherwise he had no other belongings, no boots, jacket, hat, or pack. "How'd you end up in the sea, young man?"

The man stared into the flames for a moment. Finally he spoke. "I was on a ship . . . ," he said, barely above a whisper.

"Fell overboard?" supplied the old fisherman.

"I don't know . . . I think so . . ." He wiped water from his face and then brushed back his dripping hair. Looking toward the sea, he said, "I must have . . . I remember something about a ship . . ." He closed his eyes tightly, as if his head hurt. "Where am I?"

"Marquensas, near a village known as Calimar. My home is over there," Macomb said, pointing off to the east. "If you're up to it, we can walk over and my missus will probably have some proper food you can share."

"Thank you," said the stranger. He closed his eyes. "I must have hit my head. It hurts."

"Did you fall off a ship?" Macomb repeated the question.

"I don't remember . . ." He took a deep breath. "Marquensas?"

"Where were you bound?"

Again silence, then, "I don't remember."

"Ah, a blow to the head can muddle your skull, that's a fact." He offered his arm and said, "Let me help you."

The youngster took the old man's arm as he stood up on unsteady legs.

"What is your name, if you remember?"

Accepting the old fisherman's help, the stranger said, "My name is Donte."